The WEDDING FAVOR

She checked her dress in the mirror. Wrinkled, of course. But how could it not be, after Ty's long, hot body crushed her to the door . . . ?

She slapped her own cheek. Enough, already! Enough of behaving like one of his brainless bimbos, another helpless victim of his sexual mojo. For God's sake, he'd barely touched her breast and she'd kicked her vaunted ethics to the curb. How humiliating.

Well, she wasn't going *there* again. She was smart, she was savvy, and if she could just remember that and steer clear of him for the next thirty-six hours, she could still get out of France with her dignity—and her professional integrity—intact.

By Cara Connelly

The Wedding Favor

Available from Avon Impulse
The Wedding Date

CARA
CONNELLY

The WEDDING FAVOR

A SAVE THE DATE NOVEL

AVON

An Imprint of HarperCollinsPublishers

AVON BOOKS
An Imprint of HarperCollins*Publishers*
10 East 53rd Street
New York, New York 10022-5299

Copyright © 2013 by Lisa Connelly
Excerpt from *The Wedding Date* copyright © 2013 by Lisa Connelly
Excerpt from *The Wedding Vow* copyright © 2014 by Lisa Connelly
ISBN 978-0-06-228226-2
www.avonromance.com

First Avon Books mass market printing: January 2014

Avon Trademark Reg. U.S. Pat. Off. and in Other Countries, Marca Registrada, Hecho en U.S.A.
HarperCollins® is a registered trademark of HarperCollins Publishers.

Printed in the U.S.A.

10 9 8 7 6 5 4 3 2 1

For Billy, my love, my center.

ACKNOWLEDGMENTS

I OWE THIS book and my sanity to my two best writing buddies: Anne Barton—cousin, friend, and crit partner extraordinaire; and Karla Doyle, who kindly holds my hand while firmly kicking my ass.

My sister Roberta Peppin had a hand in it too. So did Katie Rotello, though she'll try to deny it. And my parents, who told me the world is my oyster. A whole host of others cheered me on too—it means more to me than you know.

But even with all that love and support, this book would still be a file on my computer without Jill Marsal. She doesn't gush, or give an inch. And she never gives less than her all.

The WEDDING FAVOR

CHAPTER ONE

"THAT WOMAN"—TYRELL AIMED his finger like a gun at the blonde across the hall—"is a bitch on wheels."

Angela set a calming hand on his arm. "That's why she's here, Ty. That's why they sent her."

He paced away from Angela, then back again, eyes locked on the object of his fury. She was talking on a cell phone, angled away from him so all he could see was her smooth French twist and the simple gold hoop in her right earlobe.

"She's got ice water in her veins," he muttered. "Or arsenic. Or whatever the hell they embalm people with."

"She's just doing her job. And in this case, it's a thankless one. They can't win."

Ty turned his roiling eyes on Angela. He would have started in—again—about hired-gun lawyers from New York City coming down to Texas thinking all they had to do was bullshit a bunch of good ole boys who'd never made it past eighth grade, but just then the clerk stepped out of the judge's chambers.

"Ms. Sanchez," she said to Angela. "Ms. Westin," to the blonde. "We have a verdict."

Across the hall, the blonde snapped her phone shut and dropped it into her purse, snatched her briefcase off the tile floor, and without looking at Angela or Ty, or anyone else for that matter, walked briskly through the massive oak doors and into the courtroom. Ty followed several paces behind, staring bullets in the back of her tailored navy suit.

Twenty minutes later they walked out again. A reporter from *Houston Tonight* stuck a microphone in Ty's face.

"The jury obviously believed you, Mr. Brown. Do you feel vindicated?"

I feel homicidal, he wanted to snarl. But the camera was rolling. "I'm just glad it's over," he said. "Jason Taylor dragged this out for seven years, trying to wear me down. He didn't."

He continued striding down the broad hallway, the reporter jogging alongside.

"Mr. Brown, the jury came back with every penny of the damages you asked for. What do you think that means?"

"It means they understood that all the money in the world won't raise the dead. But it can cause the living some serious pain."

"Taylor's due to be released next week. How do you feel knowing he'll be walking around a free man?"

Ty stopped abruptly. "While my wife's cold in the ground? How do you think I feel?" The man shrank back from Ty's hard stare, decided not to follow as Ty strode out through the courthouse doors.

Outside, Houston's rush hour was a glimpse inside the doors of hell. Scorching pavement, blaring horns. Eternal gridlock.

Ty didn't notice any of it. Angela caught up to him on the sidewalk, tugged his arm to slow him down. "Ty, I can't keep up in these heels."

"Sorry." He slowed to half speed. Even as pissed off as he was, Texas courtesy was ingrained.

Taking her bulging briefcase from her hand, he smiled down at her in a good imitation of his usual laid-back style. "Angie, honey," he drawled, "you could separate your shoulder lugging this thing around. And believe me, a separated shoulder's no joke."

"I'm sure you'd know about that." She slanted a look up from under thick black lashes, swept it over his own solid shoulders. Angling her slender body toward his, she tossed her wavy black hair and tightened her grip on his arm.

Ty got the message. The old breast-crushed-against-the-arm was just about the easiest signal to read.

And it came as no surprise. During their long days together preparing for trial, the cozy take-out dinners in her office as they went over his testimony, Angela had dropped plenty of hints. Given their circumstances, he hadn't encouraged her. But she was a beauty, and to be honest, he hadn't discouraged her either.

Now, high on adrenaline from a whopping verdict that would likely boost her to partner, she had "available" written all over her. At that very moment they were passing by the Alden Hotel. One nudge in that direction and she'd race him to the door. Five minutes later he'd be balls deep, blotting out the memories he'd relived on the witness stand that morning. Memories of Lissa torn and broken, pleading with him to let her go, let her die. Let her leave him behind to somehow keep living without her.

Angela's steps slowed. He was tempted, sorely tempted.

But he couldn't do it. For six months Angela had been his rock. It would be shameful and ugly to use her this afternoon, then drop her tonight.

Because drop her, he would. She'd seen too deep inside, and like the legions preceding her, she'd found the hurt there and was all geared up to fix it. He couldn't be fixed. He didn't want to be fixed. He just wanted to fuck and forget. And she wasn't the girl for that.

Fortunately, he had the perfect excuse to ditch her.

"Angie, honey." His drawl was deep and rich even when he wasn't using it to soften a blow. Now it flowed like molasses. "I can't ever thank you enough for all you did for me. You're the best lawyer in Houston and I'm gonna take out a full-page ad in the paper to say so."

She leaned into him. "We make a good team, Ty." Sultry-eyed, she tipped her head toward the Marriott. "Let's go inside. You can . . . buy me a drink."

His voice dripped with regret, not all of it feigned. "I wish I could, sugar. But I've got a plane to catch."

She stopped on a dime. "A *plane*? Where're you going?"

"Paris. I've got a wedding."

"But Paris is just a puddle-jump from here! Can't you go tomorrow?"

"France, honey. Paris, France." He flicked a glance at the revolving clock on the corner, then looked down into her eyes. "My flight's at eight, so I gotta get. Let me find you a cab."

Dropping his arm, she tossed her hair again, defiant this time. "Don't bother. My car's back at the courthouse." Snatching her briefcase from him, she checked her watch. "Gotta run, I have a date." She turned to go.

And then her bravado failed her. Looking over her shoulder, she smiled uncertainly. "Maybe we can celebrate when you get back?"

Ty smiled too, because it was easier. "I'll call you."

Guilt pricked him for leaving the wrong impression, but Jesus, he was itching to get away from her, from everyone, and lick his wounds. And he really did have a plane to catch.

Figuring it would be faster than finding a rush-hour cab, he walked the six blocks to his building, working up the kind of sweat a man only gets wearing a suit. He ignored the elevator, loped up the five flights of stairs—why not, he was soaked anyway—unlocked his apartment, and thanked God out loud when he hit the air-conditioning.

The apartment wasn't home—that would be his ranch— just a sublet, a place to crash during the run-up to the trial. Sparsely furnished and painted a dreary off-white, it had suited his bleak and brooding mood.

And it had one appliance he was looking forward to using right away. Striding straight to the kitchen, he peeled off the suit parts he was still wearing—shirt, pants, socks—and balled them up with the jacket and tie. Then he stuffed the whole wad in the trash compactor and switched it on, the first satisfaction he'd had all day.

The clock on the stove said he was running late, but he couldn't face fourteen hours on a plane without a shower, so he took one anyway. And of course he hadn't packed yet.

He hated to rush, it went against his nature, but he moved faster than he usually did. Even so, what with the traffic, by the time he parked his truck and went through all the rigmarole to get to his terminal, the plane had already boarded and they were preparing to detach the Jetway.

Though he was in no frame of mind for it, he forced himself to dazzle and cajole the pretty girl at the gate into letting him pass, then settled back into his black mood as he walked down the Jetway. Well, at least he wouldn't be squished into coach with his knees up his nose all the way to Paris. He'd sprung for first class and he intended to make the most of it. Starting with a double shot of Jack Daniel's.

"Tyrell Brown, can't you move any faster than that? I got a planeful of people waiting on you."

Despite his misery, he broke out in a grin at the silver-haired woman glaring at him from the airplane door. "Loretta, honey, you working this flight? How'd I get so lucky?"

She rolled her eyes. "Spare me the sweet talk and move your ass." She waved away the ticket he held out. "I don't need that. There's only one seat left on the whole dang airplane. Why it has to be in my section, I'll be asking the good Lord next Sunday."

He dropped a kiss on her cheek. She swatted his arm. "Don't make me tell your mama on you." She gave him a little shove down the aisle. "I talked to her just last week and she said you haven't called her in a month. What kind of ungrateful boy are you, anyway? After she gave you the best years of her life."

Loretta was his mama's best friend, and she was like family. She'd been needling him since he was a toddler, and was one of the few people immune to his charm. She pointed at the only empty seat. "Sit your butt down and buckle up so we can get this bird in the air."

Ty had reserved the window seat, but it was already taken, leaving him the aisle. He might have objected if the occupant hadn't been a woman. But again, Texas courtesy required him to suck it up, so he did, keeping one eye on her as he stuffed his bag in the overhead.

She was leaning forward, rummaging in the carry-on between her feet, and hadn't seen him yet, which gave him a chance to check her out.

Dressed for travel in a sleek black tank top and yoga pants, she was slender, about five-foot-six, a hundred and twenty pounds, if he was any judge. Her arms and shoulders were tanned and toned as an athlete's, and her long blond hair was perfectly straight, falling forward like a curtain around a face that he was starting to hope lived up to the rest of her.

Things are looking up, he thought. *Maybe this won't be one of the worst days of my life after all.*

Then she looked up at him. The bitch on wheels.

He took it like a fist in the face, spun on his heel, and ran smack into Loretta.

"For God's sake, Ty, what's wrong with you!"

"I need a different seat."

"Why?"

"Who cares why. I just do." He slewed a look around the first-class cabin. "Switch me with somebody."

She set her fists on her hips, and in a low but deadly voice, said, "No, I will not switch you. These folks are all in pairs and they're settled in, looking forward to their dinner and a good night's sleep, which is why they're paying through the nose for first class. I'm not asking them to move. And neither are you."

It *would* be Loretta, the only person on earth he couldn't sweet-talk. "Then switch me with someone from coach."

Now she crossed her arms. "You don't want me to do that."

"Yes I do."

"No you don't and I'll tell you why. Because it's a weird request. And when a passenger makes a weird request, I'm obliged to report it to the captain. The captain's obliged to report it to the tower. The tower notifies the marshals, and next thing you know, you're bent over with a finger up your butt checking for C–4." She cocked her head to one side. "Now, do you really want that?"

He really didn't. "Sheeee-iiiiit," he squeezed out between his teeth. He looked over his shoulder at the bitch on wheels. She had her nose in a book, ignoring him.

Fourteen hours was a long time to sit next to someone you wanted to strangle. But it was that or get off the plane, and he couldn't miss the wedding.

He cast a last bitter look at Loretta. "I want a Jack Daniel's every fifteen minutes till I pass out. You keep 'em coming, you hear?"

CHAPTER TWO

THIS CAN'T BE HAPPENING. Victoria Westin shut her eyes and counted to ten, opened them again . . . and he was still there. She'd actually believed that her day couldn't suck any worse, but now Tyrell Brown was sitting beside her, wrestling with his seat belt and cursing under his breath.

Up close like this, he seemed a lot bigger than he had in court. Maybe it was the jeans and cowboy boots, or the UT shirt stretched across his chest, showing off his arms. She'd only seen him in a suit, and while he'd been a lean and imposing six-foot-two, he hadn't looked like this, like he could snap her in half without breaking a sweat. Now he looked more than capable of it.

And if she was reading his body language right, that's exactly what he wanted to do.

Not that she blamed him. The person she blamed was her mother. Adrianna Marchand, of Marchand, Riley, and White, the premier civil defense law firm in New York City. Adrianna, who was a senior partner, had stuck her, a lowly associate, with an unwinnable train wreck of a case and then refused to let her settle it.

"The plaintiff has nothing but his own word to prove that the deceased ever regained consciousness before she died," her mother had said in her most pedantic tone. "Surely, Victoria, you can convince six jurors of questionable intelligence that he's highly motivated to lie. Nine million's a lot of motivation for a jerkwater rancher. Shake him up. Trip him up. If you can't think of anything else, then bloody well *smile* at him." She smirked at her daughter. "Your smile flusters any idiot with a penis. And frankly, after five thousand in orthodontics, it ought to."

But Adrianna had been wrong about all of it. The jurors were two doctors, a college professor, a newspaper reporter, a retired judge, and a grad student, all of whom were unquestionably intelligent. The "deceased," as Adrianna euphemistically termed Lissa Brown, had been a bright, young, universally loved, kindhearted rescuer of abused animals.

And the "plaintiff," who was sitting beside her right now, had a fifty-thousand-acre cattle ranch, a Ph.D. in philosophy, and the saddest eyes she'd ever seen. The sympathetic jury had hung on his every word. As a result, when Jason Taylor's five-year sentence for drunk driving and vehicular manslaughter was up next week, he'd have to sell most of what he owned to satisfy the verdict.

Her mother was going to kill her.

If Tyrell Brown didn't do it first.

SOMEHOW, WHILE SHE was brooding, they'd reached cruising altitude. Now the flight attendant, who was apparently friendly with Tyrell, asked for her drink order.

"Club soda with lime," she managed to get out.

Ty made a sound of disgust, then snarled at Loretta, "I'm still waiting for my Jack Daniel's."

"And you'll wait a little longer," she shot back. But her pat on his shoulder as she walked by belied the bite in her tone. Vicky shivered. Maybe Loretta would help him hide her body. They could probably fit her in a trash bag if they folded her up tight.

When Loretta returned with their drinks, she handed Ty his whiskey without a word. Passing Victoria her club soda, she smiled. "What brings you to Texas, honey?"

Victoria's hand shook. She covered it by taking a sip, then said, curtly, "Work," hoping Loretta would take the hint and quit trying to converse. She couldn't understand these Texans; they'd talk to anyone, poke their noses in anywhere.

"What's your line?" Loretta went on, undeterred.

Ty threw back his drink, waved the empty glass in front of Loretta's nose. "*Stewardess*," he sneered, "how about a refill here? You're not getting paid to flap your jaw."

Loretta arched a deadly brow. For a long moment, they eyed each other. Then, deliberately, she took the glass. "Be right back, honey," she said to Victoria, without once breaking glares with Ty. Then she turned, slowly, and walked away.

For an instant, just an instant, Victoria and Ty were united in their relief.

Then she opened her book and pretended to lose herself in it. He flipped through the SkyMall catalogue with the same intense concentration.

Of course, she wasn't really reading. How could she, bombarded by the waves of resentment rolling off Ty? He'd relived his worst nightmare on the witness stand, and it was clear to everyone in that courtroom, including her, that he'd never recovered from his wife's death. Even though he'd won his case, his heart had been raked over the coals in the process. And she'd been holding the rake.

From the corner of her eye, she watched him nervously. He was really putting away the whiskey. What if he got drunk and went postal? She'd be the first to go.

To her horror, his head whipped around as if he'd felt her watching him. She flinched.

Had she really thought his eyes were sad? Beautiful, yes, root beer brown shot through with gold. But they were murderous. She snapped her gaze back to her book, praying she hadn't set him off.

OF COURSE, TY wasn't really reading either. How could he, when Victoria Westin was sitting there in *his* seat, so cold and controlled. There was no heart in the woman, no heat, no compassion. Was she even alive? Maybe she was a vampire.

Still, he wasn't altogether proud that he'd made her flinch. As if he'd ever hit a woman. In his thirty years he'd been in more fights than he could count—fists, knives, even guns a time or two—and he liked to think he'd struck fear into a few hearts.

But never a woman's.

If he didn't hate her guts so much, maybe he'd apologize. But he did, and he wouldn't. He crossed his arms. Better yet, *she* should apologize to *him* for thinking he'd ever lift a hand to her. Sure, he *wanted* to twist her head off like a bottle cap, but he wouldn't really *do* it.

She had a lot of nerve making him feel like a bully.

Loretta finally showed up with a second Jack Daniel's, waited while he knocked it back on top of the first, then stalked off with the empty glass. He scowled at her receding back. For sure, she'd make him wait for the next one.

"BEEF FOR YOU"—LORETTA slapped it down on Ty's tray table—"and Ms. Westin, here's your vegetarian entree."

Ty gave her a grin. "Why, thank you, Loretta, honey." She ignored him, but he didn't mind. They were two hours into the flight and his jagged edges had smoothed out considerably. He'd gotten the wedding gift out of the way—matching massage chairs from the SkyMall catalogue—and while he was at it, polished off his third and fourth Jack Daniel's. Now, deep into his fifth, he was feeling more philosophical about life in general, and his situation in particular.

Glancing over at Victoria's steamed veggies, he wondered idly why anyone would pass up filet mignon for broccoli and rice.

Without meaning to, he asked the question out loud.

Victoria fumbled her cutlery. Cautiously, she turned her head to look at him. "I-I'm sorry, I didn't hear what you said."

Her wariness made him feel like a dick. And now that he'd gone and opened his big mouth, clamming up again would only make things worse. So he took a stab at his usual laid-back delivery.

"I said, why chew on leaves and twigs when this filet here melts like butter?"

"Beef's bad for you," she said, then flushed bright red.

Ty bit back a smile. She'd obviously just recalled that he owned a cattle ranch. Cocking one brow, he said lightly, "In Texas them's fighting words, but seeing as we're considerably east of Texarkana, I'll let it slide."

He forked another bite into his mouth, washed it down with a slug of whiskey. Then, because she was looking at him like she expected more, he aimed his fork at her club soda. "Liquor bad for you too?"

"I don't drink when I fly. It diminishes oxygen intake."

Ty's eyes widened. He broke out in a smile. "Well hell. I should be flopping around like a fish on land by now." He sucked down the last drops in his glass, caught Loretta's eye, and pointed to it.

VICTORIA PINCHED OFF a smile before it could form. She didn't trust this new, affable Tyrell Brown. True, the

whiskey seemed to have mellowed him. But he was unpredictable. He could strike out in an instant.

Still, she couldn't look away from him. His smile—
which she'd never seen in court—was an appealing flash
of full lips and white teeth that crinkled his eyes and
transformed his handsome face into a heart-stopper. With
his tawny hair, streaked like a surfer's, a little too long
and usually mussed, it was no wonder his attorney had
such an obvious crush on him.

Loretta appeared with his drink. "Loretta, honey," he
said, "tell this young lady here that you've got plenty of
oxygen on this plane."

Loretta tilted her head to one side. "Tyrell, am I gonna
have to cut you off?"

"I'm serious. She thinks"—he waved his glass at
Victoria—"that if she has some wine with her leaves and
twigs, she's gonna run out of air or something."

Loretta turned to Victoria. Deadpan, she said, "We've
got plenty of oxygen on this plane."

Victoria's smile slipped its leash. "What a relief."

"So"—Ty grinned at her—"what'll you have?"

She started to say that she didn't want anything, then
decided it would be simpler just to give in. "I'll have a
Cabernet," she told Loretta. After all, she could pretend
to sip it. At least she wouldn't seem like such a dork.
Beef's bad for you . . . liquor diminishes oxygen intake.
Good grief.

"I knew it," said Ty, "I knew you'd pick red wine. Antioxidants, right?"

She lifted one shoulder, a silent admission. God, she
really *was* a dork.

He nodded, smugly. "Yeah, I got this." He ticked it off
on his fingers. "Yoga twice a week for flexibility. Pilates
on the weekends for your core. Daily meditation, fifteen minutes morning and night, to keep you centered.

Monthly massage to release toxins and stimulate your immune system." He dropped his voice confidentially. "Or that's what you tell yourself. Truth is, it just feels good."

She laughed. He was funny. Handsome and funny, a killer combination.

And he'd nailed her routine. It sounded so . . . so regimented when he reeled it off in that laid-back drawl.

Loretta brought the Cabernet. Deliberately, Victoria took a big swallow, then another. So what if the airlines reduced the percentage of oxygen in the air to save money. Look at Tyrell. He was three sheets to the wind and he was breathing just fine.

Another glug, and she got up the nerve to say, "Core muscles, daily meditation. You've been reading your Oprah magazine."

He held up a hand. "Only for the articles. I swear I never look at the pictures."

She giggled, something she never did. She hadn't eaten a thing all day, and the wine had already gone to her head. She ate a quick bite of stir fry, too little too late.

Ty sipped his whiskey. "Met her once. Oprah, I mean. She had a sit-down with some cattle ranchers back when she stepped in a pile of shit, taking that dig at beef on her show. My daddy ran the ranch back then. He brought me and my brother along to hear what she had to say."

"And?"

He shrugged. "Seemed like a nice lady. Well-spoken. Sincere. I liked her. Even if my daddy didn't."

She took another long swallow of Cabernet. It was delicious. She really should drink wine more often. After all, it *was* loaded with antioxidants.

Another swallow, and she said, "I met Dr. Phil. On a plane, just like this." She flicked her hand back and forth between them.

"Dr. Phil? No shit. He give you any free advice?"

"He told me I should break up with my fiancé."

He held up two fingers to Loretta. Angled his body toward Vicky, just a fraction, and she noticed that she'd done the same, just a little bit, just enough to wrap the first delicate threads of intimacy around them. She took another sip.

"And did you? Break up with him?"

"Not right away. But I should have. He ended up cheating on me, which Dr. Phil predicted." Another swallow. "Of course, my mother blamed me for it."

Ty's eyes widened. "She blamed *you* for *his* cheating? Why?"

"Why does she blame me for anything?" She snorted a laugh. "That's what I should've asked Dr. Phil. Why does my mother hate me? And why do I keep trying to make her love me?"

And this, she thought, *is why I shouldn't drink.*

She went back for another sip anyway, realized her glass was empty just as another round arrived. Ty plucked the empty from her fingers and handed her a fresh one. She smiled at him. He had such expressive eyes. She couldn't imagine why she'd ever thought them murderous. They were maple syrup and butter, liquid and warm, and focused on her like she was the only woman in the world.

She angled a little more in his direction.

TY FORGOT HIS filet, let himself be pulled in. "What makes you think she hates you?"

"Where should I start?" She held up a hand. "Okay, I'll skip the formative years and go straight to college. I wanted to go to Williams—small, rural, with a great theater program. But no. According to my mother, as an actress the only line I'd ever have to learn is, 'Can I take your order?' "

She took a pull on her wine. "Just because her own mother took off for Hollywood and never came back, I can't be trusted anywhere near a stage. Apparently I'm too impractical, too"—she fluttered her fingers—"flighty to know what's good for me. So Mother decided my future for me. It had to be Yale, and it had to be pre-law so I could follow in her footsteps." She sipped, shrugged. "I gave in, of course. I always do."

Ty swirled his drink, tried to imagine his folks pushing him in a direction he didn't want to go. They wouldn't. And if they'd tried, he'd have dug in his heels. An hour ago, he'd have bet his ranch that confident, in-control Victoria Westin would do the same.

"You're an adult now," he said. "Tell her to whistle up a rope. Take yourself back to school and study what you want to."

She looked baffled. "What I *want* to? I don't even know what I want anymore." She shrugged again. "It's too late now. I'm stuck with the law, like it or not."

"Well, *do* you like it?" In the courtroom she'd seemed so cold and aloof, nothing like the warm-blooded woman beside him now. Even her blue eyes had heated up, from arctic ice to warm October sky. With her brow knit over them as she considered his question, she looked approachable and vulnerable and, well, pretty too.

"It has its moments," she said at last. "Probably like being a cop or a firefighter. You know, hours of tedium punctuated by moments of stark terror." When he chuckled, she said, "Okay, it's not life or death, but it's still months of boring paperwork and preparation, and then the trial—which is the terrifying part—is over in a couple of days."

She paused to hit the wine again, and it must have dawned on her that trials were bound to be a sore subject, because her eyes widened, her swallow turned into a gulp.

Ty could have told her not to worry, because after working hard to get there for the last few hours, he'd finally reached the zone he'd been striving for. He was, quite literally, mind-numbingly drunk. In this state, which he'd frequented many times in the past seven years, he could still carry on a conversation and even remember it in the morning. He could make jokes, wax philosophical, and fuck like a seventeen-year-old after the big game.

But he couldn't think of Lissa.

It was a programmed response that had probably saved his life, and he'd gotten the ritual down to a science. When his memories overwhelmed him, he'd drink whiskey steadily until his fingers started to tingle. Then, and only then, he'd let himself shut off the part of his mind where she lived and forget her for a while.

He'd reached that place half an hour ago, and while most men would be sliding under their tray table, Ty was in the bubble. For another half hour, he'd be good company. The best. Then he'd go down hard and sleep for eight straight.

He'd dream about Lissa, that was the downside. But when he woke in the daylight, he'd be able to deal with it again.

"So." Victoria changed the subject in a hurry. "What's in Paris?"

"An old girlfriend's getting married."

"You're going to an ex's wedding?"

"Weird, huh? Thing is, about three months in, we both figured out that we like each other a lot, but it wasn't going past that." He shrugged. "We did the friends-with-benefits thing for a while. Now we're just friends."

VICTORIA COULDN'T IMAGINE being friends with her ex. Aside from the fact that he'd crushed her heart like roadkill, Winston wasn't exactly fun to hang out with. They'd have to do whatever *he* wanted to do, just like always.

"How about you?" Ty asked. "What's in Paris?"

"Actually, I'm headed to a wedding too, in Amboise, a couple of hours outside the city. My brother. Well, technically my half brother, from my mother's second marriage."

"Second out of how many? Wait, let me guess." He closed one eye, calculating. "Assuming she's about fifty . . ."

"Fifty-four."

"Okay, fifty-four, and a looker, I'll bet." His smile said he meant it as a compliment, and her cheeks warmed in response. "A lawyer," he went on, "so she's financially independent, used to being her own boss. And based on her attitude about college, a control freak too, right?"

"Oh yeah, she's into control." She swallowed more wine.

He looked thoughtful. "Yeah, I'm gonna say she's on number four."

"Close." She bobbed her glass in salute, drank again. "Number four just got kicked to the curb. She's keeping his name, though, so she won't have to change the firm's letterhead again."

"Add practical to her list of virtues."

Victoria snorted, very unladylike. Her mother would disapprove. Then she shrugged one shoulder. "To be fair, she probably wouldn't be so hard to live with if my father hadn't died. He was her first husband. She really loved him." She looked down into her glass, swirled the last inch of wine. "The rest of her husbands, her boyfriends too . . . well, Dr. Phil would say she's trying to fill the hole Dad left."

"How did he die?"

"Cancer. I was only three, but I remember him. Helping me blow out the candles on my birthday cake, stuff like that. And the funeral, I remember that. Mother crying and crying like she'd never get over it."

The minute the words were out of her mouth she wished them back. Damn it, she kept stepping on land mines.

First trials, now tragic death and heartbreak. What next, drunk drivers?

"So, what do you do with your Ph.D.?" she blurted, hoping he was too anesthetized to notice another abrupt topic change.

TY NOTICED, BUT he rolled with it, untroubled by where the conversation had been and unconcerned with where it was going.

The truth was, in the slightly detached manner of the comfortably intoxicated, he was enjoying himself. Now that Victoria had come out of her cold hard shell, he kind of liked her. She had layers. He liked layers. He liked it when things weren't what they appeared to be on the surface. Must be the philosopher in him.

And honestly, with her hair around her shoulders and that curve-hugging outfit in place of her lawyer suit, she looked good. He didn't usually go for the pale, porcelain-skin type. Too fragile-looking. And he liked more meat on his women. Still, he was a sucker for blue eyes, and he had to admit that what meat she had was in all the right places.

Effortlessly, he shifted into flirting mode.

"Mostly I dazzle the ladies with Descartes." He wiggled his brows. "Empiricism's always a turn-on. And rationalism? Another aphrodisiac."

VICTORIA WIDENED HER eyes, playing along. "Philosophy's sexy? Who knew?"

His smile was smug. "Make fun if you want to. But I did my dissertation on the perception of sexual experience under those two competing doctrines, and trust me, a *lot* of women thought that was sexy."

Sure enough, she felt a frisson herself. She doused it with the last of her wine.

Propping her elbow on the armrest, she set her chin on her fist, scrunched her forehead into a pitying moue. "Please don't tell me that's your pick-up line. It's pathetic."

"But effective. Check it out." He closed his eyes, made a show of slipping into character.

When he opened them again, Victoria nearly gasped. Ty the joker had vanished.

In his place was this loose-limbed, sloe-eyed cowboy straight off the range. Lanky and sexy and in no hurry at all, everything about him said baby-I've-got-all-night-and-I'm-gonna-spend-it-fucking-you-right.

Taking his time, he dragged his gaze down her body, languid, smoldering, raising her temperature by ten degrees, then slowly dragged it up again, lingering on her breasts, her throat, her mouth, until he locked eyes with her. Then he smiled, a slow, bone melter of a smile.

Her heart thumped so loudly he should be able to hear it.

"Honey"—he spread his drawl like butter—"I got a favor to ask you." Reaching across the space between them, he drew one finger down her arm, tucked it into the crook of her elbow. The slight pressure on her pulse set it racing.

"I'm doing some research for my dissertation." He nodded slowly, encouragingly. "Yeah, that's right, sweetheart, it's college stuff."

She would have chuckled but her throat had closed tight. Flecks of orange glimmered in his tiger eyes. How had she missed those before?

His teeth caught his bottom lip, tugged lightly until it popped free. "I'm studying the perception of sexual experience under the competing doctrines of rationalism and empiricism." Drawing his finger up her arm again, he cuffed her wrist gently. "That's all right, sugar, you don't need to know what all those big words mean." His voice dropped to a husky whisper. "It's the sex I need your help with. Hours and hours. Hot and sweaty—"

She burst out in a shaky laugh. "Okay, I get it. Philosophy's sexy."

He sat back with an I-told-you-so smirk. "So, you want to know the upshot of all my research?"

Did she? "Uh-huh."

His lips curved in a wicked smile, and his eyes twinkled; she'd swear they did.

"I concluded that I'm definitely an empiricist—I absolutely believe that to truly understand what sex'll be like with another person, I can't just think about it like a rationalist would."

He paused a beat.

"I have to experience it."

CHAPTER THREE

VICTORIA HAD NEVER had sex on an airplane, but she had a feeling she was about to.

She checked her watch. Midnight. In under four hours, Tyrell Brown had readjusted her attitude from please-don't-kill-me to please-undress-me.

He was a dangerous man, all right. But not in the way she'd first thought. If he killed her, it would be by arousing her to death.

Taking her cosmetic bag from her carry-on, she smiled at him. "Excuse me a minute?"

He rose politely, waited in the aisle while she slid out of her seat. Walking away, she peeked over her shoulder, appreciating the way he folded his frame into his seat. God, he was built. Strong shoulders, flat stomach, narrow hips—all of it said riding and roping and stringing barb-wire, all the things cowboys did in the movies.

He caught her looking, flashed a smile that jacked her pulse up another twenty beats a minute. Jesus.

The tiny restroom made primping a challenge; nerves made it practically impossible. Fumble-fingered, she dropped her toothbrush in the sink, had to throw it away and pop an Altoid instead.

She noted the flush in her cheeks, the sparkle in her eyes. It stood to reason. She hadn't been so attracted to a man since, well, ever. And she'd never gotten so turned on with so little physical stimulation. Winston could've worked on her for an hour and not gotten her as wet as Ty's gentle touch on her wrist.

Ty wanted her too, she was sure of it. Nobody could flirt like that unless he meant it. It was powerful stuff. If he'd hit her with it in a bar, she'd be back at his place by now.

On an airplane, they'd have to make do. She couldn't quite picture how it would work, but Ty seemed creative, she'd trust him to figure it out.

In a distant part of her brain, a warning bell clanged. *Victoria Westin, you're about to violate every canon of ethics sacred to your profession.*

It was true. If she did this, had sex with her adversary, she'd be honor-bound to withdraw from the case. Another firm would have to handle the appeal. Her mother would be furious.

Yessss! Vicky fist-pumped in the mirror. She could hardly wait to tell her mother that she'd joined the mile-high club with Tyrell somewhere over Jersey. With any luck, she'd be fired.

Yessss! Another fist pump. She could go back to college. Join a small-town theater troupe. She grinned into the mirror. Maybe it wasn't too late to get out from under her mother.

And she'd start by getting under Tyrell Brown.

With a second Altoid sizzling her tongue and fresh gloss on her lips, she fluffed her hair one last time and stepped out into the cabin.

The lights had dimmed. Almost everyone was engrossed in a movie or settled down to sleep. She made her way down the aisle.

Ty's seat was reclined, the leg rest extended. You had to love first class. Maybe he'd pull her down on top of him, wrestle her clothes off . . .

Okay, she'd never had sex on an airplane, but it certainly required more discretion than that. More likely, he'd turn her on her side, then snuggle up behind her . . .

Stomach fizzing like champagne, she paused beside his seat, waited for him to welcome her in.

He didn't budge.

She leaned over, squinting in the dim light. His eyes were closed. Well, that explained it, he hadn't seen her. Then his lips parted slightly . . .

. . . and released a snore.

She snapped upright. He was out cold!

Feeling eyes on her, she glanced over her shoulder. A middle-aged man watched her with a sympathetic smile. He couldn't know she'd been counting on getting laid, but she flushed anyway.

Covering embarrassment with a shrug, as if merely inconvenienced instead of rejected and humiliated, she pretended to care about disturbing Ty while she climbed over him—landing an accidental kick on his shin, oops—and plopped into her seat.

Madder at herself than at him, she dug through her carry-on for her eyeshade and shawl, then jammed her finger into the recline button.

Her mother was right. She couldn't trust her own judgment. She couldn't read men at all. Tyrell Brown wasn't interested in her. At best, she'd been a diversion on a long and boring flight. At worst, he'd led her on so she'd feel exactly how she felt now. Stupid.

Flicking open her shawl—no way she'd touch those

germy airplane blankets—she pulled it up to her chin.
Behind her eyeshade, she was in the dark. The champagne bubbles were long gone. Her old friend anxiety was
back, a clenched fist in her stomach. Well, she'd slept with
it for years. She shouldn't have expected tonight to be any
different.

TY CAME TO slowly, slitting one scratchy eyelid at a time.

Shit. He hadn't been on a bender in more than a year.
He'd forgotten how bad the day after sucked.

And he couldn't even crawl bare-assed to the kitchen
and put on some coffee. Because he wasn't at home, he
was . . . where was he?

On an airplane. Right. An airplane. Heading to France.

Carefully, he swiveled his head. The bitch on wheels.
Christ, he'd been so fucked up he'd almost had sex with
her. Would have, if he hadn't passed out. What was he
thinking?

Sure, sound asleep, with her pink eyeshade and her
blond hair all mussed up, she looked sweet and vulnerable. But now that he was sober, he remembered why he
hated her.

The trial. Two days of hell. Stark terror, she'd called it.
Well honey, he thought, *you have no idea.*

Partly because he wanted to, partly because he had
to, he summoned it up, made himself remember every
minute of those two awful days.

The first had centered on the wrongful death claim—
hospital bills, and actuarial projections used to calculate
how much Lissa's life would have been worth in dollars
and cents if she'd been allowed to live it. Eighty years, she
should have had. She'd gotten twenty-three.

Then the second day—yesterday—they'd fought about
pain and suffering. The defense's theory was that Lissa's
estate wasn't entitled to damages for her pain and suf-

fering because she'd never regained consciousness after Jason Taylor plowed into her favorite mare, killing it and pinning Lissa, who was riding the mare, to the trunk of an oak tree with his Hummer.

Lissa was knocked out by the impact, then slipped into a coma at the hospital. Though she lingered for five long days, neither her doctors nor any of the staff ever saw her wake up.

But Ty did. He was at her bedside around the clock, and when she'd opened her eyes in the dead of the fourth night, he'd been looking right at her. His heart had jumped straight up into his mouth.

"Ty," she'd said, and he could still hear her thready voice. "Honey, you've got to stop this."

"Stop what?" he'd asked, disoriented.

"This." She slid her eyes to the right where a ventilator wheezed, pumping breath through the trach in her throat and into her damaged lungs, and to the left where an IV rack held seven bags of liquids, all running into the lines in her arms.

"I can't stop it, Lissa. They're keeping you alive while you get better. While you heal."

"I'm not healing, baby. I'm hurting." Her words puffed out on gusts of breath, timed to the ventilator's rhythm. "You've got to let me go. Let me go now, you hear?"

"Lissa, baby, I can't." Tears rolled off his cheeks. "I can't go on without you, sweetheart. You need to stay with me." He clutched her hand. "Just try to get well, now. Just a little bit better, so I can take you home to the ranch. I'll wait on you hand and foot, honey. You'll see. You'll be strong again before you know it."

A smile ghosted across her face. "I love you, Ty. I'll always love you. Remember that when you feel lonely." Her eyes closed again.

"Honey? Lissa baby?" He squeezed her hand, got no

response. She'd slipped back under. And left him alone.

His chest opened up, a hole that gaped from front to back, and a frigid wind blew through it. It sucked his breath out, and his heart, and left him empty. And oh so lonesome and cold.

Twelve hours later, he signed the consent to discontinue life support. He pulled the plug on his wife, the love of his life.

He'd managed to tell his story to the jury without breaking into a million pieces. But when Victoria Westin, on cross-examination, had asked him if it was possible that he'd simply *dreamed* that conversation, or perhaps *hallucinated* it—which would be completely understandable given the stress he was under, his fatigue, his grief—he'd fallen apart.

Just like that, after seven years, he'd crumbled.

Oh, the jury didn't see it, he held it inside. But he'd be putting himself back together for a long time to come. And he had Victoria fucking Westin to thank for that.

Unsnapping his seat belt, Ty shot his seat up and lunged out of it, a reckless move that made his head spin, but he was too mad to care. Momentum propelled him down the aisle to the restroom. He slapped the door open and kicked it shut behind him.

Christ, it was too much to ask of him. To have to sit next to her until they landed in Paris.

He plowed his fingers through his hair, breathed in, breathed out. Faced the mirror, the circles under his eyes. The agony in them.

"Fuck," he hissed. "Fuck fuck fuck."

Turning away, he unzipped his jeans, braced his hands on the wall, and pissed whiskey for a minute straight.

LORETTA WAS WAITING when he came out. "I was about to come in there after you," she said, not unkindly.

He looked down at her out of red-rimmed eyes, and the hurt there spoke louder than words. It hit her where she lived, that pain in his eyes.

When his Lissa was alive, Ty had been the fun-lovingest, good-timingest boy you could ever meet. The day she died, his light dimmed. And seven years later, he still hadn't gotten past it. Nobody understood why. Not his folks. Not his friends. But there it was.

She couldn't fix it, she knew that much. But she could damn well pour coffee on it.

Steering him into the galley, she pointed to a tiny fold-down seat attached to the wall. He opened it and sat down, forearms resting on his knees. Taking the ceramic cup she pushed into his hand, he gave her a weak smile. "I can sure use this."

She wagged her head. "Boy, you look like five miles of bad road." She tried to sound gruff but couldn't pull it off, covered it up by turning her back and digging through a drawer. "From my private stash." She tossed him a packet of Pop-Tarts. "Cures a hangover every time."

That pulled a genuine smile out of him. "Why, Loretta Jane Mason, I've never known you to tie one on. You got a secret life you're hiding from me?"

She drew herself up, started to deny it, then flapped a hand. "I wasn't always sixty, you know. And no," she cut him off, "no details."

Leaning one hip against the counter, she folded her arms and eyed him steadily. "Now tell me what's wrong with your seat."

His brows came down hard. "Not the seat. The blonde."

"Seems nice enough to me. A looker too. Figured you'd have her curled up in your lap purring like a kitten by now."

He made a face. "She's a lawyer. Taylor's lawyer."

Loretta dropped her arms, momentarily at a loss.

"Well," she said at last, "that's bad luck."

Ty snorted. "Bad luck's breaking your leg on vacation. Or forgetting to buy a Powerball ticket the day your numbers come up. This"—he waved in the direction of his seat—"this is the hand of a vengeful God."

She couldn't disagree, though why God would wreak vengeance on a kind, sweet boy like Ty was a mystery to her.

For a long moment she studied him. The whiskers shadowing his jaw, the tousled hair and rumpled shirt. The troubled eyes. She made up her mind.

"You can stay here till it's time to buckle up." She opened the drawer again, took out the new issue of *O Magazine*. "Drink all the coffee you want, but do *not* dribble on this. I haven't read it yet."

"Thanks, Loretta. I owe you one."

"I'll collect. Now stay out of my way while I get breakfast going."

THE LIGHTS WERE up when Victoria slipped off her eyeshade. Other passengers stirred, folding their blankets, sipping steaming cups of coffee.

Cracking the window shade on bright sunlight, she squinted down at puffy clouds, snow white against the blue backdrop of the ocean far below. She checked her watch, tried to calculate the time change, then gave it up until after coffee.

Ty was gone, presumably to the restroom. Folding her shawl, stowing her pillow, she fretted over how to greet him when he returned. There was no protocol for this situation. They'd almost had sex, but didn't, and yet they were waking up together the next morning. That didn't happen in the real world. If you decided not to have sex, you went home. You didn't face each other with morning breath.

It would be awkward, for sure. But Ty had been pretty

drunk. Maybe he wouldn't remember how close they'd come to doing it. That he'd basically stood her up.

God, how embarrassing.

She made her way to the restrooms. One was vacant; she assumed Ty was in the other. When she came out, that one was vacant too. She braced herself to face him.

But he wasn't in his seat. She glanced around the cabin. No sign of him.

She sat down, but couldn't sit still. Was he hiding from her, as embarrassed as she was? Why? *He'd* rejected *her.* What did he have to be embarrassed about?

Then a new thought occurred. Maybe he was ill. Had they moved him somewhere to nurse him? Was it food poisoning? Alcohol poisoning?

Concern squelched her anger. She waved Loretta down. "Have you seen . . . I mean . . . is he okay?"

"He's fine." Loretta's smile looked tight. "I'll bring you some coffee," she said, and turned away.

"LADIES AND GENTLEMEN, the captain's asked me to inform you that we're beginning our descent into Paris de Gaulle. At this time, I'll ask you all to return to your seats. The fasten-seat-belt light has been turned on."

Loretta hung up the handset, turned to Ty. "Time to suck it up."

"Shit." He rose stiffly, let the tiny seat snap up against the wall.

She took *O* from his hand, rattled a box of Tic Tacs at him. "Do us all a favor."

"Hell." He shook half the box into his palm, shot them into his mouth.

"Now go." And she shooed him out of the galley.

TY DROPPED INTO his seat like a ton of bricks.

"Good morning," Victoria said, the best she'd come up

with after an hour of rehearsing. It was innocuous, gave nothing away. Left it to him to set the tone.

He didn't waste any time. His head whipped around like a snarling dog's.

"Don't push me," he snapped. She jerked back. He bared his teeth. "Don't look at me. Don't breathe on me. Don't fuckin' talk to me." He slammed his seat belt together, locked his arms across his chest, and shut his eyes. Shut her out.

Victoria could only gape. Of all the reactions she'd anticipated, this wasn't among them. Snarling fury a hundred times worse than yesterday radiated from his spring-loaded body. He looked . . . lethal.

Afraid he'd feel her staring, she yanked her wounded gaze away, trained it out the window. The sky was cloudless now, as clear as crystal. Far below, the ocean caught the sunlight and winked it back at her.

Gradually, her pulse retreated. But her mind continued to churn.

She'd meditate, that's what she'd do. Center herself. Block his negativity. Knowing he'd sneer only made her feel better about it.

Closing her eyes, she summoned the image of a single candle. Slowed her breathing. Four counts in, four counts out.

Thoughts intruded, a procession of worries. The trial, her mother, Tyrell, the wedding. Gently, surely, she nudged each one out. The candle held her focus. Her mind settled.

"Ms. Westin." Loretta's voice cut through to her. "Ms. Westin, we're getting ready to land. Please put your seat up."

She peeled open her lids. Glimpsed Ty glaring murder at her.

But this time she was ready. This time, the injustice of

it pissed her off. Instead of flinching, she met him glare
for glare and had the satisfaction of seeing his eyes widen.
A dozen cutting remarks danced on her tongue. She bit
them back. It was enough that he knew she wasn't cowed.
A battle of words would bloody them both and she'd only
end up feeling guilty for hurting him.

But for what she'd done in court, she no longer felt
guilty. She'd had time to work through it, to accept that
even though Jason Taylor was a heartless son of a bitch
who thought his money should buy him out of any tight
spot, including manslaughter, he was still her client—or
rather his insurance company was—and she was sworn
to defend him. She, Victoria Westin, attorney at law, had
only been doing her job.

And damn it, she'd done it with a lot more compassion than any other lawyer would have shown. Not only
had she never once accused Ty of lying, something she
couldn't bring herself to do, and which, she'd rational-
ized, would only have won him the jury's sympathy, but
she was as sensitive as possible when she asked him if
maybe, just maybe, he'd imagined that conversation with
his wife.

She'd had no choice, the question had to be asked. It
would have been malpractice not to ask it. But where another attorney would have kept at him, circling around
from every direction, badgering, prodding, trying to wear
him down, to trick him into admitting that he couldn't be
sure, she'd asked him only once. Just once, and then she'd
left him alone.

Not that she hadn't tried to raise doubts through other
witnesses. She'd brought in a parade of doctors and
nurses, none of who saw Lissa wake up, and all of whom
testified that in their professional opinions it was unlikely
that she would have done so. She'd also put a psychiatrist
on the stand to explain how emotional and physical strain

could affect the human mind. How it might cause a grief-stricken man who was desperate for a last word with his beloved wife to imagine such a conversation. To believe with his whole heart that it had happened.

She was only doing her job, and she wasn't sorry about it. In the end, the jury believed him anyway. And she wasn't sorry about that either.

Last night she might have told him so. Now, forget it. He could think what he liked; she was done worrying about Tyrell Brown. Ten minutes after touchdown, she'd never see him again. And good riddance.

TYRELL WAS OF the same mind. Every muscle in his body itched to get away from the blue-eyed bitch on wheels. When the plane taxied to a stop at the terminal, he was the first one on his feet, yanking his bag out of the overhead, turning on his cell phone like every other idiot.

For something to do, he checked his voice mail while they waited for the Jetway. And he was glad he did. As always, Isabelle's flirty French accent triggered his smile.

"Ty! I can't *wait* to see you! Call *the minute* you get in. I scheduled a five o'clock fitting for your tux, so you'll have to go straight from the airport." His smile dissolved into a scowl. Isabelle giggled. "Stop frowning, I know you are! Trust me, you'll look amazing and all my girlfriends will go crazy for you."

He rolled his eyes. She'd surely set him up with one of them; she always did. Oh well. If tumbling a French beauty would make her happy, he'd be glad to oblige. After all, that's why he was here, to see that she was happy. And to check out her fiancé—Matthew J. Donohue III. They hadn't met yet, but Ty already knew he wasn't good enough for her. Nobody was.

The door opened and the first-class passengers began moving forward. Ty glanced at Victoria. She was standing up, carry-on in hand. Grinding his teeth at his own good manners, he took a step back to let her into the aisle in front of him.

And got a don't-sully-me-with-your-gaze-you-lowly-turd stare for his trouble.

VICTORIA KNEW HOW to sell it too. She'd learned from her mother, the expert at making people feel like she'd scraped them off her shoe. And it got to him, she could tell. She could almost hear the blistering curse run through his brain as he shuffled forward, foiled from striding away in disgust by the barely moving elderly couple in front of him.

Stepping smoothly into the aisle behind him, she had the satisfaction of staring at his stiff shoulders as they inched toward the door.

Loretta stood at the threshold. "Tyrell, you take care now, you hear?"

"I will," he said, dropping a kiss on her cheek. And then he was out, through the narrow doorway and into the wide-open Jetway.

He hit the gas and left her far behind.

CHAPTER FOUR

SIX FEET TALL, blond and blue-eyed like his sister, Matthew J. Donohue III grinned down at her. "Awesome place for a wedding, huh?"

Victoria gazed up at the massive gray stone walls of the Château Royal d'Amboise, the eleventh-century castle that lorded over the green banks of the Loire River and the classically beautiful French town.

Totally impressed, she tossed off a careless shrug. "I guess. If you can't get the VFW."

Matt laughed out loud. "You thinking what I'm thinking?"

"Uncle Rodney's third wedding. Eighty guests, twenty mounted deer heads, and Mother catching you in the broom closet with No-Pants-Nance."

He winced. "Ouch. I blocked out that last part."

"I'll never forget it. No-Pants was already a cougar at eighteen, and Mother was *not* happy to find her pouncing on her *innocent* fourteen-year-old son. I can still hear her raving, 'That's statutory rape, you mousy little slut!'" Victoria rubbed her palms together. "What a great story for the rehearsal dinner."

Matt didn't say a word, just held up his index finger, flexed it a few times, and her abdominals contracted reflexively. "Not that I'd ever tell it," she added quickly. She was insanely ticklish, and Matt exploited it remorselessly.

He grinned. "Come on, I'll show you the house where you're staying." He hefted her bags and set off across the plaza with his long, athletic stride. She fell into a familiar half trot beside him.

"How'd your trial go?"

"I lost. Big."

"How big?"

"Seven figures big."

"Ouch. Mom know yet?"

"I texted her. Then shut off my phone before she could call and ream me out." She darted a wary glance over her shoulder at the hotel, situated in the castle's shadow.

"She'll be on the next train," Matt said. "Her plane was late, or you could've ridden down together."

Victoria grimaced. "So there *is* a way my trip could've sucked worse."

"Bad flight?"

"The. Worst. Ever. I don't want to talk about it. I'm working on repressing the memory."

Together they trudged up a steep hill, talking of other things, honoring their unspoken rule to leave work at work. Vicky never discussed her cases, Matt never discussed his clients, and yet they never ran out of interesting things to talk about.

Turning right onto a side street, they passed several imposing chateaus, each set back on its own generous acre. Matt turned into a curving driveway and they followed its sweep up to the door of a sprawling two-story chateau built from the same gray stone as the castle.

"Beautiful," Victoria said, following him up the stone steps. "And ancient."

"Five hundred years old," he said, "and the decor is semi-authentic. You're gonna love it."

"Who wouldn't?" she murmured, stepping through the ornately carved front door and into the vaulted center hall.

Turning in a slow circle, she soaked it in; wide-beamed ceiling, plaster walls, faded tapestries, brass sconces. A curved staircase rose to the second floor. "It's straight out of an Alexandre Dumas novel."

Matt beamed. "We were kind of screwed hotel-wise, moving the wedding to Amboise at the last minute. But with everything Isabelle's got planned, renting this place actually works out better. It houses the whole wedding party, and then some. And hey, it's amazing."

"Yeah, it is." Wandering through an open door, she let out a low whistle. Bookshelves lined the walls, floor to ceiling. A large casement window set into the back wall poured sunlight across two leather club chairs.

"Don't bother," Matt said when she reached for a book. "They're in French."

"So? I took French."

"Yeah, in *tenth grade*."

She made a face, let him prod her out of the library and through another door across the hall. "This is the living room, or whatever they call it in French."

She ran her hand over one of the leather sofas that filled the space before the fieldstone fireplace, fitting comfortably into the medieval decor. "Imagine sitting here four hundred years ago, sipping brandy by the fire on a rainy evening while the wind rattled the shutters." She could see herself in that picture.

Matt snorted. "Last time you drank brandy you puked on Mom's white chaise longue."

She spared him a withering look. "I was sixteen, and that was the *first* time I drank brandy, not the last."

"Seriously? You could stomach it again after that puke-fest?"

"Winston's an aficionado. He dragged me to some tastings."

"Oh."

The fact that Matt left off teasing her spoke volumes about his feelings toward Winston. He still hadn't forgiven himself for introducing them at a Harvard alumni function, and she knew he was worried that she'd be miserable at the wedding, that it would remind her that she'd be married herself by now if Winston hadn't cheated on her.

She didn't want Matt dwelling on her problems. She wanted him to enjoy the weekend, so she'd do her best to convince him that she was enjoying it too. "Is Isabelle here?"

The mention of Isabelle brightened him again. "She's in Paris, meeting up with an old friend. They'll come in tomorrow." He waved as they passed another door. "That's the dining room. Kind of gloomy, lots of old portraits frowning down at the table." He kept her moving. "There's a conservatory out back. Kitchen, too, not that you need to know about that. You've got a cook. Maids too. The whole nine."

She blinked in surprise. "My, my."

"They come with the rental, so it's not as extravagant as it sounds, especially with the whole wedding party staying here. Except me, that is." He grinned. "I've got the bridal suite at the hotel. Groom's prerogative."

Unexpectedly, her throat tightened. He was a groom. Her hotshot stockbroker brother, one of Manhattan's most eligible bachelors, her defender, champion, and best friend, was a groom.

The wave of emotion that swamped her was lost on

Matt. "Come on," he said, loping up the sweeping stair-case, "you gotta see your room." At the top, he led her down a four-doored hallway. "These are all for the wedding party." He gestured to the first door on the right. "Isabelle's cousin Lilianne'll be in here. With her husband . . . Jack McCabe."

He paused to let it sink in.

Victoria's eyes bugged. "*The* Jack McCabe? No way!"

"Way." He grinned. "Isabelle's afraid we might get some paparazzi. Cool, huh?"

She had to admit that it was. Jack McCabe was a celebrity, having caught the media's fancy with his former band the Sinners. For almost two years, he and Lil had kept a low-profile living in Italy. But once in a while the press still caught his scent.

"What's he like?" she asked.

"Nice guy. Wouldn't want to piss him off, though. He made a point of telling me that Isabelle is family, and he takes care of his family. He was smiling when he said it, but I've got to tell you, it was a little intimidating."

He opened the next door. "This one's yours."

Stepping inside, she caught her breath. It was a room from a fairy tale. Flocked white wallpaper, white marble fireplace, white lace curtains framing casement windows. And a queen bed covered with a white chenille bedspread as soft as kittens.

Matt plunked her bags on the bedspread. "You can put your stuff in those," he said, nodding toward an antique armoire and bureau. "Your bathroom's through there." He waved at a narrow door. "It's the size of a closet, which is what it used to be." Then he crossed to the window, pushed it open. "Check this out. It's why I hoseyed this room for you."

Stepping up beside him, Victoria gasped again. Half an acre of magazine-ready formal gardens spread out below her window. At the center, Cupid rose from a marble fountain ringed by spring flowers in pink, white, and hyacinth blue. Velvety green lawn spread out in a wide swath around it, dotted with blossoming cherry trees that shaded a variety of wooden benches, all sprinkled with fallen petals. More flowerbeds, not yet in full bloom, lined the rose-covered fences that obscured the neighboring chateaus. "Wow," she murmured, dazzled by the colors.

Directly below her window, a flagstone terrace stretched the entire width of the chateau, holding a huge farm table that would easily seat twelve and had to be centuries old. Blazing pink azaleas framed the terrace, with more lining a flagstone path that led away from the terrace to a pergola blanketed in grapevines, utterly private and perfectly romantic.

"Gosh, Matt."

"I know. Crazy, right?"

She tore her gaze away from the gardens, eyed him narrowly. "Okay. Now give me the bad news. Who else is staying here?"

"Well, Ricky's across the hall from Jack and Lil." Ricky was the best man, wide receiver to Matt's quarterback through four years of varsity, and like a second brother to Victoria.

"The other groomsman's across from you. He's that old friend of Isabelle's I mentioned. More of a surrogate brother, I guess. I haven't met him yet, but he's friends with Jack too, going back to when they were kids—"

"Quit stalling, Matt." She stared him down. "I saw another hallway with four more doors."

He shifted from one foot to the other. "Well, Isabelle's in one room, obviously. And Annemarie, who's a friend of hers from high school—"

"Mother's staying here, isn't she?"

He swallowed. "Isabelle put her here without asking me."

Victoria plopped on the bed.

"I'm sorry, Vic. Mom looked at the hotel online and mentioned something about how small the rooms are. Isabelle panicked. She sent Mom pictures of this place and she loved it." He sat beside her, massaged her shoulder with one hand. "The good news is she's bringing a guy. He'll probably keep her busy."

She groaned. "They'll be doing it down the hall."

"Maybe not. He's getting a separate room."

"When has that stopped her? Remember the Hamptons?"

"SORRY," MATT SAID again, and he truly was. Their mother, who never gave him grief about anything, was unremittingly hard on her only daughter. Always disapproving, always critical.

And Vicky let it get to her, big time. No matter how well she did in school, what she accomplished professionally, how many people told her she was a star, the only voice she heard was her mother's.

Then that idiot Winston came along. How he wished for a do-over on that, so he could un-introduce them. But it was too late, the damage was done.

The crazy thing was, everything had seemed to be great between them. Winston acted like he really cared about her. And he was good for her. He got her out of her apartment, took her to new places. She seemed really happy when they got engaged, and she threw herself into the wedding plans.

Then the dick cheated on her, and to make matters worse, when she gave him the boot he went running to Adrianna, professing remorse. And unaccountably, Adrianna actually took his side, accusing Vicky of disappointing him in some way. She even badgered Vicky to take him back, to the point where Matt had intervened.

That was nothing new, he'd intervened often over the

years. But now he was getting married. With a wife and, hopefully, kids of his own, he wouldn't always be around to stick up for Vicky. Now, more than ever, she needed to stand up for herself.

He'd asked Isabelle's advice and, wretched over housing Victoria and Adrianna under one roof, Isabelle had decreed that what Vicky needed was a man who would boost her ego. An easygoing, fun-loving guy who wouldn't be fooled by the cool and distant woman Vicky often pretended to be. A guy who'd recognize and care about, maybe even love a little, the warm, funny person she really was.

And, Isabelle had assured him, she knew just the man for the job.

"TYRELL, WILL YOU *stand still*." Isabelle Oulette rolled her big blue eyes. "Raoul's trying to pin your inseam."

Ty threw her a look of distress, stage-whispered, "He's grabbing my nuts."

Raoul huffed. "In your dreams, monsieur."

Ty backpedaled fast. "Hey man, I was just kidding. Go easy with those pins down there, will you?" He mouthed to Isabelle, *You didn't tell me he speaks English*.

She mouthed back, *You didn't ask*, and stifled a giggle.

Isabelle giggled a lot. Which led people who didn't look past her blond curls, designer-clad curves, and occasional wide-eyed gullibility to mistake her for a scatterbrain. But those who knew her knew she was a force of nature.

She'd proven it once again by channeling her inner Napoleon to organize every detail of her wedding weekend with the relentless efficiency of a military campaign. As a result, she had nothing left to do on the Wednesday night before the wedding except to entertain, and be entertained by, the man she loved like a brother.

As usual, he was being a pain in the butt.

"Kinda tight across the shoulders, isn't it?" He flexed back and forth.

"It's a tux," she reminded him, "not a T-shirt. Vidal designed it exactly to your measurements. If you'd stop fidgeting, you'd be fine."

"But it's supposed to be comfortable. You promised."

"Comfortable for an *adult*. For a groomsman, not a toddler."

He managed to look hurt. She wasn't buying it. "I refuse to feel sorry for you, Ty. You look like a movie star."

Raoul stepped back for a moment to survey his work, and Ty made a break for it, hopping down off the tailoring platform. "You're right, honey. Looks good, fits fine. Now help me get it off."

Resigned, Isabelle slid the jacket off his shoulders and passed it to Raoul. When Ty continued to stand there, looking much too innocent, she folded her arms. "You can manage the rest on your own."

Turning her back on him, she caught sight of the cashier, a stacked brunette who'd sidled into the fitting room to ogle the tall, rangy American with the luscious smile. Isabelle pointed to the door. The girl slunk out grudgingly.

"Why'd you go and do that?" Ty griped.

"You don't need an audience to take off your pants."

"Maybe I'm practicing to be one of those Chippendales."

"Ha. The Chippendales wear tuxes every night."

"Yeah, but not for long." She heard the grin in his voice. "Probably wouldn't work out though. That G-string looks painful."

"How would you know?" She rolled her eyes again. "Did Oprah have the Chippendales on her show?"

"Maybe she did."

He stepped around in front of her, jeans in place, and

she had to admit they looked almost as good as the tux. All male, all Texan, Ty could sell stock in faded Levi's.

He grabbed his T-shirt off a hook, and while he tugged it over his head she allowed herself one long last look at the shoulders, the chest, the rippling abs that she'd never handle again. Then she put them out of her mind.

"Hungry?"

"As a grizzly."

Out on the sidewalk, he draped his arm over her shoulders, she wound hers around his waist, and they meandered through the bustling streets, finding their way to the Seine, then out onto the Pont Royal, pausing in the center of the bridge to lean on the wide stone rail and drink in the view. Twilight had given way to night. City lights glittered off the water.

Ty drew a deep breath. "I do love Paris in the summertime." He looked over at her. "You miss living here?"

She turned in a slow circle, soaking it up; the ribbon of river curving into the distance, traversed by a dozen bridges, the Parisians hustling home with baguettes under their arms or walking arm-in-arm toward the lights of Left Bank cafés, the Eiffel Tower spearing the darkened sky.

"Sometimes I forget how beautiful it is. There's nothing like this in Manhattan." She sighed. "Ah well. Once I'm married, I'll officially be a New Yorker."

He grinned. "You don't sound like a New *Yawker*. Still got that sexy-French-girl thing goin' on."

She elbowed him lightly. Then checked her watch. "It's time."

All at once, the white lights that sheathed the Eiffel Tower erupted into their insane twinkling dance, twenty thousand of them reflecting off every window and windshield in Paris, sparkling off the river's surface, multiplied a trillionfold.

For five minutes they watched, bedazzled, until the twinkling ceased. Then Ty sighed, a contented sound. "I never get tired of that."

Catching his hand, Isabelle tugged him toward the Left Bank. "Come on, I know a café where we can watch it all night. We'll drink wine and I'll tell you all about Matt."

He let her tow him along, but he let out a groan. "Just how a man wants to spend his evening, hearing about the guy who took his place."

"Hey, you dumped me, remember?"

"I remember the dumping as mutual."

"But you said it first."

"Only because you were too nice to say it."

She gave up. You couldn't win an argument with Ty.

They squeezed into a table just outside the door. It was intimate, with enough warm light spilling out to read each other's expressions.

Around them, couples and groups of young people conversed in animated French. Ty checked them out. "People sound more interesting when I can't understand them," he mused. "I can imagine they're talking about philosophy, or art. Or sex."

She cocked her head, listening. "Strange, I don't hear anyone discussing the perception of sexual experience under the competing doctrines of rationalism and empiricism." She fluttered her lashes at him, prompting a chuckle. "But those two"—she poked her chin at a middle-aged couple—"are married . . . but not to each other."

His ears perked up. "So they're talking about sex?"

"Yes, they are. And no, I won't translate."

His face fell. "You're a cruel woman, Isabelle. I love you, but you're heartless."

Unexpectedly, emotion swamped her. It happened at the oddest moments as the wedding drew near and her feelings ran high, triggered this time by the woeful look on Ty's face. He was joking, of course, but she'd seen real sorrow there too often to forget it. And now he was hurting all over again, thanks to the trial. He wouldn't say much about it except that he'd won and that the other lawyer was a bitch on wheels, but she knew it was heavy on his mind.

She also knew that she'd been his only real girlfriend in the seven years since Lissa died, so she was worried about how he'd handle her wedding, especially coming hard on the heels of the trial. Resting her fingers on the back of his hand, she said softly, "Thank you for coming, Ty. Thank you for standing up with me on my wedding day."

He turned his hand over, laced his fingers through hers. Replied just as softly, "Sugar, I wouldn't miss it for the world."

Then, predictably, he looked away. Beckoned to the waiter, and tried out his pitiful French. "*Vin rouge, un pichet, s'il vous plaît.*" He winked at Isabelle. "How'd I do?"

She squeezed his hand. Ty was more sensitive than any man she knew, but he liked to think it didn't show. She loved him too much to call him on it, so she winked back. "*Très bien, mon ami.*" Then she ordered steak frites for him, an omelet for herself.

"You look thin," she said after the waiter had gone.

He shrugged. "Lost my appetite for a while, with the trial and all. But I'm still big and bad." He rotated his wrist, making his biceps jump. "You can stroke that baby if you want to."

She jabbed it with a finger. "You always had the best arms."

"Uh-oh, sounds like past tense." He wagged his head mournfully. "Guess you found a guy with bigger guns. That explains a few things."

"Like what?"

"Like why you're sprinting to the altar when you just met him six months ago."

"Seven months." She giggled. "Actually seven months and eight days."

He rolled his eyes. "I guess you better tell me about him."

"Well, he's a stockbroker. Very successful, and soooo cute. He's tall—"

"Whoa. Not taller than me? 'Cause I'd hate to have to kill him before the wedding."

"You're taller," she assured him. Men's egos were so fragile. "Anyway, he has blond hair and blue eyes like me, so it's almost guaranteed that our children will too. He's sweet and funny and *brilliant*, and I just want to gobble him up!" She beamed like the sun.

OUT OF NOWHERE, it punched him in the chest. Jealousy. Not of Matt, but of the wholehearted, full-bodied love that radiated from Isabelle. Lissa had glowed that way for him. Now, with a yearning so deep and strong it took his breath away, Ty wanted to feel that again, that bright-as-the-sun love shining just for him.

Christ, it hurt like a broken rib.

He sucked a breath, shook it off. Reminded himself that tonight was about Isabelle.

"So, where'd you meet him?"

"At Tiffany's, how perfect is that? I was walking down Fifth Avenue and I happened to notice this really cute guy, and he kind of smiled at me too. And I went into Tiffany's just to browse, you know how I like to do that. And he came in too. He was looking for a gift for his mother, and he asked my advice."

Ty groaned. "Honey, you fell for that?"

Her blue eyes widened. "Seriously, Ty, he bought her a beautiful bracelet that I recommended. Anyway, by then it was lunchtime, so he asked if I knew a good place for

Thai, and of course I did, just a few blocks away. I explained where it was, but he got confused—he's terrible with directions. So he asked me to show him. Then he invited me to stay for lunch. And voilà"—she spread her hands—"while we were eating, I fell in love."

Ty started to laugh. The wine appeared and the waiter poured it, and still Ty laughed, holding his side. He kept laughing until she socked him in the biceps.

"It's not funny," she huffed. "It was fate. I always find something I love in Tiffany's, and that day I found him."

It was so Isabelle.

"Where's God's gift tonight?" For the first time, Ty was looking forward to meeting him.

"His mother arrived today. His sister too." She frowned. "They don't always get along, so Matt's having dinner with them. To keep the peace."

"So he's all that, and brave to boot. You did good, sweetheart." He sipped his wine contentedly. He'd laughed the jealousy out of his system. Now he could enjoy her happiness wholeheartedly. "So, when do the festivities begin?"

"Tomorrow night, with cocktails and a buffet for the families and the wedding party. A few friends too."

The food arrived and Ty cut into his steak, chewing the first bloody bite while Isabelle ticked off the schedule on her fingers.

"The rehearsal's Friday evening. Some of the guests are arriving that day, so instead of dinner with the wedding party, we're doing heavy hors d'oeuvres for everyone at eight. The wedding's at four on Saturday, with the reception afterwards. We'll have a harpist during the ceremony, then a band at the reception. I'm hoping Jack will sing a few songs." She lilted it into a question, which meant she was hoping Ty would ask him. He nodded, and she went on. "Then Sunday there's a brunch at noon before Matt and I leave for Greece."

He swirled his wine. "Lots of logistics. How can I help?"

"I'm glad you asked." She met his eyes with her big baby blues. "It's simple, really. I need you to make sure everyone has a good time. That's very important to me, Ty. The most important thing of all."

She blinked slowly a few times, a mesmerizing experience he could never resist.

"The thing is," she went on, "Matt's mother is . . . well . . . she can be hard to get along with. I'm hoping you can charm her. Keep her in a good mood."

"Got it." He pretended to make a note. "Number one, charm Matt's bitchy mama. What else?"

"Well, the person she's bitchiest to is Matt's sister. So I'd like you to make a special effort to be nice to her. You'll like her. She's smart and beautiful and really sweet."

"Number two, be nice to Matt's sweet, pretty sister. Sounds like work, but I'll give it a go."

She smiled innocently. "She's getting over a bad breakup. So if you want to be *especially* nice to her . . ."

He smirked. "A sweet girl on the rebound at a wedding. Why, honey, you're wasting my talents. Any amateur can hit that."

She dropped the smile, leveled a look at him. "That's exactly my point, Ty. She's vulnerable. I'm putting her in *your* hands because you'll be careful with her."

He scratched his head. "Now you're confusing me. Which is it? Do you want me to be 'especially nice' or 'careful'? 'Cause they don't always overlap, if you know what I mean."

Her frustrated hiss made him bite back a grin. "Just find the place where they *do* overlap and work with it. Seriously, Ty, it's important to Matt, and to me, that she has a good time."

He knew she wasn't worried only about Matt's sister. She was also worried about him, about his inability to move past Lissa's death and connect with another woman. He didn't want her thinking about that this weekend, and if it took faking a flirtation for a few days to make her happy, he'd do it with bells on.

He squeezed her hand to let her know he'd been teasing. "She will. Everybody will, I promise you that. You just leave it to me."

She kissed his cheek. "You're the best." Then she frowned again. "I wish she and her mother got along. It seemed like such a great idea for all of us to stay in the same house together—"

Ty held up a hand. "Whoa there, honey, what do you mean we're all staying in the same house? What about that five-star hotel you promised me?"

"Didn't I tell you? Papa rented a chateau." She shrugged a shoulder. "Moving the wedding at the last minute—"

"You moved the wedding?" His heart started to thump. "It's supposed to be here. In Paris."

"Oops." She giggled. "I guess I left you off the e-mail loop. Papa pulled some strings and we got permission to use the castle! It only came through two weeks ago, so I've been going crazy changing all the plans—"

"Isabelle. Honey." He hung on by a thread. "Where's the wedding gonna be?"

"About two hours from here—"

"What's the name of the town?"

"Amboise." She touched his hand. "Ty, do you feel all right? Are you going to throw up?"

CHAPTER FIVE

TY SHOULD HAVE loved Amboise. The cobbled streets, the mythical castle. The bare-legged French girls strolling in the plaza, drenched in lemony sunshine.

He had too much on his mind to appreciate any of it.

After pulling himself together at the café the night before, he'd gently questioned Isabelle and confirmed his fears—Matt's sister was none other than Victoria fucking Westin. Bridesmaid to his groomsman.

He hadn't told Isabelle, not after swearing an oath to make sure everyone had fun at the wedding. And he'd vowed to himself that if Victoria hadn't already discovered the connection, he'd force her to keep her mouth shut too.

If he had to wring her scrawny neck to make her do it, well, any excuse for a party.

The first order of business was to find out if she was expecting him. He got his answer the minute she laid eyes on him.

Skimming down the chateau's staircase in a sky blue sundress, her yellow hair swirling around bare shoulders, lips curved in a lighthearted smile, she spotted him at the front door and her eyes bugged out. Her jaw unhinged.

She slammed on the brakes, tried to turn around, tangled her feet, and toppled down the last two steps.

Matt and Isabelle, lip-locked on the porch behind him, didn't notice until she hit the floor. By then Ty had shot forward.

Dropping on one knee, he blocked their view. "Pretend you don't know me," he hissed under his breath. Her mouth flapped in confusion. "Just fucking do it," he snarled. "I'll explain later."

Then raising his voice, he crooned solicitously. "Honey, you took quite a tumble there."

Matt dropped down at his side. "Vicky! Are you okay?"

She didn't respond, just goggled at Ty. After a moment, Matt followed her gaze, suspicion narrowing his eyes.

Ty feigned concern. "She's just discombobulated. Isn't that right, Vicky?"

When Matt's gaze swiveled back to her, Ty bared his teeth. She blinked. Then her eyes narrowed. Her jaw hardened.

And she was back, the bitch on wheels.

"I'm fine," she said, sitting up. "Matt, would you get me some water?"

"Sure." Matt helped her stand, then headed for the kitchen. Isabelle followed him, throwing an encouraging wink at Ty.

Alone, Ty and Vicky faced off. "You've got ten seconds," she fired.

"Show me the gardens."

"*What?*"

"When they get back, offer to show me the goddamn gardens."

"I'm not showing you anything but the door!"

She started to spin away but he stepped in front of her. Forced himself to be civil. "Give me five minutes, for your brother's sake. Then you can tattle if you want to."

She glared at him. He glowered at her. Tension crackled. Then footsteps sounded.

Rocking back on his heels, Ty shifted from menacing to flirtatious. "Why sure, Vicky. If you're feeling up to it, I'd love to see the gardens. Isabelle told me about them."

She took the water Matt handed her, gave Ty the fish eye over the rim. He sweated while she sipped.

Then, deliberately, she said, "I need to talk to you, Matt. Don't disappear, okay? I'll be back in five minutes."

STRIDING DOWN THE hallway, Vicky could feel Ty breathing down her neck. She wanted to turn around and punch him.

Why the hell was he here, anyway? And what was this charade about? Did it have something to do with his *friendship* with Isabelle? Hadn't he said they were "friends with benefits"? Was he planning to cuckold her brother on the eve of his wedding? Did he really think she'd stand still for that?

With every step, fury built. When the back door shut behind them, she swung around. "Tyrell Brown—"

Quick as a snake, he clapped a hand over her mouth. "Keep it zipped till I tell you to talk." His glance found the pergola and he hauled her underneath where they couldn't be seen.

When he let her go, she slapped both hands on his chest and gave him a shove. "What the *hell* is *wrong* with you?" Mad enough to spit, she stepped in to shove him again but he cuffed her wrists and stuck his furious face right down in hers.

"I'll tell you what's wrong with me. You, that's what. You're like a goddamn parasite, or athlete's fucking foot. I can't get rid of you."

"Sure you can! Just leave! Because if you're thinking about boinking Isabelle under my brother's nose—"

"*Boinking* Isabelle?" He cast off her wrists, disgust on his face. "You can think what you want about me, but Isabelle wouldn't cheat on anybody, she's not built like that. And she's crazy about your stupid brother."

She set her jaw. "My brother is *not* stupid. He's perfect, and he deserves the best. So if you ruin this wedding—"

"The last thing I want is to ruin this wedding, which is why I'm standing here talking when I'd rather be choking you."

She folded her arms. "So talk."

He heaved a breath, visibly throttled back his temper. "Look, until last night I had no idea that Matthew J. Donohue the Third was your brother. And Isabelle never told me she moved the wedding out here. I thought it was in Paris." He plowed a hand through his hair. "Hell, if I'd known you and me were headed for the same place, I'd have jumped out of the plane."

She snorted. Did he think this was buttering her up?

He ignored the snort. "The thing is, Isabelle's got her heart set on everybody getting along and having fun this weekend. She asked me to see to it, and I promised her I would."

Vicky barked a laugh. "You, the life of the party? Puh-leeze."

His lips thinned. "Believe me when I tell you, you don't know jack shit about me and you never will. But on this one thing, I'm pretty sure we agree. We both want Matt and Isabelle to enjoy their wedding, which they won't do if they're worried about us killing each other. So I'm asking you to be nice to me. That's all. You don't have to mean it. And I'll be nice to you."

Be nice. Right. In the last forty-eight hours, Tyrell Brown had frozen her out, scared her senseless, gotten her hornier than she'd ever been in her life and then *rejected* her, snarled at her like a wolf, and now he was strong-arming her. And he expected her to be *nice* to him for the next four days? While he pretended to be nice to her? It was the stupidest idea she'd ever heard.

Still, she wanted Matt's wedding to be perfect.

"Even if I agreed to this idiotic scheme, Matt knows me better than anyone. I doubt I could fool him."

"Yeah, well, Isabelle knows me pretty well too. We'll just have to be convincing." He crossed his arms. "She expects me to flirt with you. And she'll expect you to flirt back."

"Impossible."

He curled his lip. "Trust me, I can flirt with a stump."

"Oh, that I believe." She curled her lip back at him. "I'm just not sure I can flirt with a moron."

So LITTLE MISS Smarty-Pants had some smartass in her. Good for her. Ty paused a beat, let her relish it. Then took her down with one cheap shot.

"I guess that's why Mommy sent you to law school," he drawled. "She knew you'd make a shitty actress."

Watching the color drain from her cheeks, he almost felt bad for her. Then, when she pulled herself right back together, he almost admired her. But when she pointed her chin at him, that's when he knew he'd suckered her in.

Still, her snotty comeback had him itching to strangle her.

"Anything *you* can do," she sneered down her nose, "*I* can do better." And she flipped him the bird and stalked off.

He wanted to go after her. Oh God, did he want to. Every instinct howled to shake her till her eyes jiggled, then flip her over his knee for the striping she had coming.

Heroically, he fought off the urge. Told himself he'd won the round.

But damn it, it grated that she got the last word in. The woman was unbearable. He hated her guts.

And the next time he saw her, he'd have to be *nice* to her. God help him.

TAKE THAT, TYRELL BROWN, Vicky thought for the ump-teenth time since she'd met him.

You watch. I'll win an Oscar, a goddamn Oscar, for my seamless portrayal of a young woman falling hope-lessly in love with a half-wit. I'll be so convincing that you'll believe it too. And then, when you fall for me, be-cause you will, oh yes you will, then I'll reject you. Ha! I'll dump you at breakfast on Sunday morning, in front of everyone, and I'll let them think it's because we slept together Saturday night—which we won't—and you were a crappy lover. I won't say it, I'll imply it, but everyone will think—

She stopped stalking in mid-stride and let out a groan. Everyone . . . including her mother.

Oh God, her mother.

Adrianna had ruined dinner the night before, picking apart Vicky's trial tactics until Matt finally put his foot down. Now Vicky had to tell her that the plaintiff would be rooming with them for the weekend. Adrianna would immediately realize that they risked being disqualified from handling the appeal, and she'd be pissed. Maybe pissed enough to cause a stink, get Ty tossed out of the house, and make Matt and Isabelle miserable.

She couldn't let that happen.

Matt was standing where she'd left him, at the foot of the stairs snuggling Isabelle.

"Have you seen Mother?"

"She's up in her room," he said. "You wanted to talk to me?"

"Uh, actually I wanted to say a proper hello to Isabelle."
She flashed a smile at her almost-sister-in-law.

Isabelle smiled back, then cut to the chase. "What do
you think of Ty?"

"Gorgeous." That much was true. "So, how do you
know him?" she asked casually, curious whether Matt
knew Ty and Isabelle had been intimate.

"Through Jack. They've been friends forever. To hear
them tell it, they tore up most of Texas." She giggled, then
must have worried she was hitting the wrong note, because she sobered abruptly. "Ty's very sensitive. He lost
his wife seven years ago, and he's never gotten over it.
But I think he'll settle down again when he finds the right
woman."

"Has he had any girlfriends since his wife died?"

"Only me. We dated for a few months, then decided we
were better off as friends."

So Matt was okay with it. She felt a little bad for putting Isabelle on the spot, but she'd do worse to protect her
brother. Even pretend she could stand Tyrell Brown.

Isabelle cleared her throat and got back on message.
"He has a huge ranch in the Texas Hill Country. Cattle and
horses, fifteen cowhands. He runs the whole thing from
horseback. And he's brilliant too. He even has a Ph.D."
She nodded along, trying to pull Vicky in. "His wife was
passionate about abused animals, so he's planning to use
this big verdict he won to start an animal rescue ranch in
her memory. Isn't that sweet?"

Yes, it was. She hated to admit it, but the man was interesting. A study in contrasts—philosopher cowboy, mo-
nogamous womanizer. Sensitive jackass.

"Sounds like quite a guy," she said, and Isabelle smiled,
so obviously pleased with her matchmaking that Vicky
found herself smiling back. Damn it, she loved Isabelle. If

it made her happy to think that Vicky and Ty were hitting it off, then the least she could do was fake it for four days.

"I have to talk to Mother," she said, though it was the last thing she wanted to do.

Matt rubbed her arm. "Want me to tag along?"

"No, I've got this." She grinned. "Go enjoy your last premarital sex."

"HERE?" ADRIANNA FROZE, her lips half glossed. She stared at Vicky in the bureau's mirror. "Tyrell Brown is here?"

Vicky had seldom seen her mother stunned, but really, who could have envisioned a coincidence like this?

"Yes. And he asked me to pretend I don't know him."

"You're joking."

"I wish I was." She explained the situation, watching Adrianna's eyes narrow in the mirror.

"Does Matt know they were lovers?"

Vicky nodded. "Everything's on the up and up in that respect. Tyrell's just trying to spare them the stress of knowing that we're adversaries. He thinks it'll ruin the wedding for them. And I have to agree with him on that." Although she hated to agree with him on anything.

Adrianna angled her head, a calculating look. "What's he willing to do to keep us quiet?"

Victoria stared. "What do you mean, what's he willing to do? Like, settle his case to avoid the appeal? Are you kidding?"

Adrianna blinked at her. "I didn't say that."

"But you thought it. God, Mother. That's beyond un-ethical. It's criminal."

"Oh please." Adrianna finished glossing her lips. "It was just a passing thought. And don't tell me it didn't cross your mind too."

"It most certainly did not." Vicky stalked to the window, stared out at the castle's battlements, simmering.

"Well." Adrianna capped her lip gloss, fluffed her platinum hair. "If I'm going to cooperate with this charade, I want something from someone. Since you're not willing to squeeze Brown, then *you'll* have to bribe me."

Victoria turned slowly. "Bribe you not to ruin Matt's wedding?"

Adrianna eyed her in the mirror. "Perhaps I'm uncomfortable deceiving my son."

Vicky dismissed that with a snort. "This is a new low, Mother. Threatening Matt's happiness to coerce something from me."

"A good attorney turns a setback into an advantage."

"We're not in court," Vicky snapped. "We're your children, for God's sake."

"Yes, and the well-being of both of my children is important to me." She ignored Victoria's eye roll. "If we're not careful here, we could end up having to pull out of the appeal. So I'm turning what could prove to be a professional and financial setback for myself and the firm into an opportunity to promote your happiness as well as Matt's."

"Oh really? And how, exactly, are you going to promote my happiness?"

"You'd be happy with Winston."

Vicky's fists clenched. "Don't go there, Mother. The weasel cheated on me. We were *engaged* and he *screwed another woman*."

"You have to understand that to Winston this kind of thing seemed like a normal part of married life. His parents had sexual issues, so his father satisfied his needs outside the marriage and his mother simply turned a blind eye."

Vicky stared at her mother. "And you think that's okay?

Going behind someone's back to have sex with someone else is okay?"

"Of course not. But Winston explained it all to me, and he'll explain it to you too if you give him a chance. Then the two of you can work out an arrangement you're both comfortable with."

"An arrangement? Like, where he's out screwing other women while I'm home watching *Dancing with the Stars*?"

"Whatever works. Maybe you could go back into therapy."

"*I* need therapy because *he* cheated on me?"

"Well really, can you honestly tell me you were giving him all he deserved? You're emotionally stifled, Victoria. Dr. Burns said so years ago. And as far as I can tell, you've never been particularly interested in sex." She spread her hands. "Should a man like Winston have to settle for half a loaf?"

Like air from a balloon, Victoria's self-esteem hissed out through the hole in her ego. Half a loaf. Her mother thought she was half a loaf.

"He's willing to take you back," Adrianna went on. "The two of you got along very well before. You even seemed to be in love. I'm sure you can move past this little setback."

Adrianna turned to face her, and if Vicky hadn't been crushed she might have recognized something like love in her mother's eyes.

"Victoria, Winston's financially secure. There's family money there and his business is thriving. If you marry him, you'll never have to struggle like I did after your father died. Right now you have the upper hand because he feels guilty. You can insist on a generous pre-nup so even if there's a divorce down the road, you'll never have to worry about money."

When Vicky didn't respond, Adrianna's jaw hardened.

"That's the deal," she said. "Promise me you'll give Winston another chance or I'll go straight to Matt and insist that he throw his fiancé's best friend out of the wedding."

Vicky stared at the floor. It was a given that her mother was ruthless. But how could she force Vicky to choose between Matt's misery now or her own misery later?

And then, through the gloom, she saw a loophole in the deal. Winston was in New York City. By the time she saw him again, the wedding would be over and her mother would have nothing to threaten her with. Then she could, and would, renege on her promise.

After all, a good lawyer like Adrianna would know that a promise made under duress isn't enforceable.

Careful to keep the triumph off her face, she raised her head and met Adrianna's eye. "You leave me no choice. If you keep quiet all weekend, I'll give Winston another chance."

Satisfied, Adrianna turned away and began poking through her jewelry case. "Cocktails at six in the garden. You can introduce me to Brown then."

"Sure. Will your guest be there?"

Adrianna slipped a diamond stud into her earlobe, angled her head to admire it. "Unfortunately, I only thought to invite him at the last minute. He had some appointments he couldn't reschedule, so he won't be here until Friday."

Vicky went to the door, paused with her hand on the knob. "By the way, Isabelle's got it in her head that Tyrell and I should get together. She practically ordered him to flirt with me. I told him I'd flirt back, for her sake."

Adrianna arched an eyebrow as she fastened the other stud. "Just don't get any ideas about taking it further than that. I understand from Terry"—Vicky's second chair at the trial—"that he's exceptionally handsome and quite the charmer." She smiled at herself in the mirror, then flicked her gaze to Vicky's. "Remember that you're handling the appeal in his case. Don't cross any lines with him that could jeopardize that. And don't forget that I can—and will—pull the plug on this scheme if it gets out of hand."

Vicky rolled her eyes. "Believe me, anything you see going on between us will be completely phony. I can't stand him and he can't stand me. And nothing that happens in the next four days is going to change that."

CHAPTER SIX

A SLENDER MAN in a tuxedo uncorked a bottle of wine, then lined it up with a dozen others on the portable bar the caterers had stationed on the terrace.

Maybe I should get plastered, Vicky thought, watching from her bedroom window. *Throw up on Tyrell. Better yet, on Mother.*

She rested her forehead on the cool glass, dreading every minute of the weekend.

Down on the terrace, Isabelle stepped into view. She spoke a few words to the bartender, flicked an assessing glance at the café tables dotting the grass. Then someone must have called to her, because she looked over her shoulder, breaking into a smile.

Ty emerged from the chateau, ambling toward her with that loose-limbed gait of his, the sun picking out streaks in his hair. He plucked a sprig of lavender from an urn, ran it through his fingers, releasing the scent, then tucked it behind her ear.

In her present mood, Vicky almost wanted to perceive something illicit between them so she could pull the plug on the whole miserable weekend. But she sensed only friendship, and a deep affection. Ty would do what was necessary to protect Isabelle, even fake a flirtation with a woman he despised.

Vicky pinched back tears. No one cared about her that much. No one but Matt. And now he was abandoning her to go off and start his own family. Leaving her to fend for herself with the likes of Tyrell Brown and Winston Churchill Banes and all the other heartless people in the world.

A sob hitched in her throat. It wasn't fair. It wasn't freaking fair.

Outside, Isabelle reached up and touched Ty's cheek, made some giggling comment, maybe about the bristles there, then patted it lightly and disappeared inside. Hands in his pockets, Ty watched her go, and on his face Vicky could have sworn she saw the same wistful longing that wrung her own heart. The yearning to belong to someone.

She straightened away from the window.

God, I'm pathetic. Imagining I have something in common with that idiot. I should stop feeling sorry for myself and just be happy that Matt's found someone. That I can finally do something for him for a change.

Squaring her shoulders, she drew a deep, even breath, exhaled it to a four count. Another one. Another.

She just had to get through the weekend. Then, on Monday morning, she'd be back in her own world. Maybe it wasn't all she'd dreamed of, but it wasn't so bad. At least she knew what to expect each day.

For the rest of her lonely life.

TY CRACKED HIS funny bone, let out an oath. The damn shower stall was tighter than a coffin. How was a man supposed to hose out his armpits when his shoulders spanned the walls?

Snaking one hand up, he worked his hair into a lather,

then ducked under the low-hanging showerhead to rinse. Jesus, these Frenchmen must be short and narrow. Wait'll Jack had to wedge his frame into one of these. Then there'd be some cussing.

The water went lukewarm so he shut it off. What the hell? Were they rationing the hot water? It was a damn good thing he liked a short shower, or he'd be pissed.

He tracked water into the bedroom, yanked a towel off the stack on the bureau. Why didn't they keep them in the bathroom? It was too tiny, that's why. He shook out the towel. At least it was man-sized. And fluffy. He scrubbed it over his chest, roughed up his hair, and dropped it on the floor.

Then he stretched out on the queen-sized bed and stared up at the ceiling. A nap would be good; he was still jet-lagged. But he might as well forget about it. The four-day festivities were about to kick off, which meant that in ten minutes he had to be down in the garden making himself agreeable to a bunch of folks he didn't know, and didn't want to know.

First, he'd have to tuck his tail and let Matt play alpha dog. It grated, but he'd do it for Isabelle.

Next he'd make nice with Matt's mother, a woman so horrible she made the bitch on wheels quake. Christ.

And to really make his night, he'd cozy up to the bitch on wheels herself. Flirt with her, God help him, when she made his skin crawl. When he could still hear her asking him if he was sure, absolutely certain, that Lissa had woken up.

Was he? The question gnawed at him, as it had for seven years. Was he sure she'd actually opened her eyes and asked him to turn off the machines? Or was he so desperate for justification, for absolution, that he only imagined it?

If he'd imagined it, there was no absolution. He'd have

to admit to himself that he pulled the plug on his wife for his own selfish reasons. Because he couldn't stand to see her like that, to think she was hurting and he was helpless to heal her.

Fuck it. He threw his feet off the bed, plowed his fingers through his hair. Fuck Victoria Westin and her stupid fucking question.

He strode to the bureau, pulled on some fresh blue jeans. Opened the armoire and yanked out a shirt, midnight blue with pearl snaps. A gift from Isabelle, her version of a cowboy shirt.

Hell, he'd give his eyeteeth to be going off cowboying now. Saddling up for a few weeks on the range instead of primping for cocktails in Amboise.

He stomped into his boots.

Fuck it.

EVEN WITH HER back to the door, Vicky knew the exact moment when Tyrell stepped onto the terrace.

Isabelle's friend Annemarie, who'd been describing to her and Isabelle in her charmingly halting English the challenges of balancing her graduate studies in anthropology with her weekend job as an exotic dancer, broke off in the middle of a sentence.

"Ooo la la," she breathed.

Glancing over her shoulder, Vicky rolled her eyes.

Ty stood just outside the door, wearing cowboy boots and a hokey Western shirt tucked into faded jeans, his sun-streaked hair as carelessly mussed as if he'd just come in from a hard ride across dry prairie. All he needed was a Stetson and he could pose for a Marlboro ad.

Isabelle giggled. "I told you."

"Yes, you did," murmured Annemarie, "but I thought you were . . . how do you say . . . exaggerating?" Her eyes raked him. "He is here alone?"

"For now," Isabelle hedged. She cut a glance at Vicky. "Although he might be interested in someone."

Annemarie licked her glossy red lips. "Ah, but he is. Me." And lifting another glass of champagne off a passing tray, she ditched Vicky and Isabelle and made a beeline to the terrace.

Isabelle let out a sigh. "I suppose I can't blame her. I had the same reaction the first time I saw him." She gave Vicky an encouraging smile. "She won't get anywhere, though. Ty's a one-woman man. When he's interested in someone, other women simply don't exist for him."

At that very moment, Ty's gaze latched on to the dark-haired beauty sashaying up the stone steps. His lips curved in an appreciative smile.

As Annemarie crossed the terrace toward him, hips swaying seductively, his gaze wandered down the length of her in that lazy way of his, then back up again until his eyes locked with hers, holding them while he took the glass she offered, pinged it to hers, and took a long swallow.

Isabelle's brows knit as she watched him give the lie to her words. Her lips turned down in an uncharacteristic frown.

And Vicky got pissed. On Isabelle's behalf, and her own. *Damn you, Tyrell Brown, this was your stupid plan! You're supposed to flirt with* me, *not spread it around to every big-boobed stripper who throws herself at you!*

Okay, maybe Annemarie had more going for her than boobs. But predictably, that's where his eyes kept straying. And who could blame him? Jacked up like she was on those four-inch stilettos, her double Ds were literally *under his nose*, exploding like mushroom clouds out of her skintight, siren-red dress.

As if that wasn't enough, she tossed her lustrous black

hair over one bare shoulder and licked her ruby lips so the gloss glistened wetly. Then, incredibly, she reached out to touch his chest, fingering the pearly snaps.

The woman had no boundaries!

And Ty, the idiot, ate it up with a spoon, brushing a knuckle down her arm as he whispered in her ear, laughing with her as they shared what was certainly sexual banter.

Glancing down at her own conservative dress, Vicky bit her lip. The white linen sheath had seemed just right—flattering but not overtly sexy—until Annemarie showed up with her cleavage. And flat sandals had seemed like a practical choice until she got a load of Annemarie's mile-high legs. How was she supposed to compete with that?

Her stomach knotted. Rejected again.

Then she reminded herself that this evening—this whole weekend—was not about her. Whether Tyrell found her attractive—which he obviously didn't—was irrelevant. He was a jackass anyway. Let him hook up with Annemarie. At least that would put an end to the stupid fake flirtation.

Turning her attention to Isabelle, she tossed out the first thing that came to mind. "So, how did you find this place?"

Isabelle dragged her eyes away from the train wreck on the terrace. "You mean this chateau? A friend of the family owns it. He usually rents it to upscale tour groups, but it happened to be free this week."

Matt came up behind her, chained his arms around her waist. "Another happy coincidence," he said over her shoulder. "Like us meeting in Tiffany's." He winked at Vicky.

Isabelle turned in his arms, smiling up at him beautifully. She said something soft that Vicky couldn't hear.

And Matt rubbed noses with her.

Yes, Vicky's macho brother actually rubbed noses with Isabelle. Vicky didn't know whether to laugh or cry.

Either way, she needed to get away from them. Their open affection stung like acid in the wound of her most recent rejection. Granted, that rejection was by a man she couldn't stand and hoped never to lay eyes on again. But still.

Easing backward, hoping to escape unnoticed, she took a step back, and . . . crunch . . . her heel came down on a toe.

"Shi—!" A gruff voice bit back the curse.

Tyrell, of course, who else?

Reacting instantly, Vicky shifted to her other foot. But she moved too fast and lost her balance. She crow-hopped on one foot, arms flapping, champagne spouting from her glass.

She prayed with all her might. *Please God, please don't let me fall* again*!*

Then a strong arm curled around her waist, hauling her back against a solid chest and pinning her like a bug. "Careful now, sugar." Ty's drawl rumbled in her ear. "You don't want to take another tumble, now do you?"

Her humiliation was complete.

Well, not quite. She gritted her teeth as he added in an aside, "She's got some balance issues."

"Ah." Behind her back, Annemarie's stage whisper sounded sympathetic. "Now I understand why she is having to wear those sandals. My *grand-mère*, she wears ortho . . . how do you say . . . orthopedic shoes too, since she broke her hip."

Vicky's head came up. Her eyes narrowed to slits.

Now *that* she didn't have to put up with. *That* was a game she could play and win. Adrianna Marchand's daughter was weaned on passive-aggressive insults. She ate them for breakfast. And was only too happy to serve them with cocktails.

Shrugging off Ty's arm, she took a moment to smooth her dress. Then she turned around, innocent smile in place.

"Annemarie, you're still here? You're not working to-night?"

Annemarie's brow puckered as much as Botox allowed. "No, I'm not. Why do you ask?"

Vicky ran an astonished eye over her getup. "Well, why else would you wear a pole-dancing outfit to a cocktail party?"

Ignoring Annemarie's huff, she shifted her attention to Ty, her expression morphing into a worried frown.

"Gosh, Tyrell, I hope I didn't scuff the alligator. I know how you cowboys are about your boots"—she dropped into her own stage whisper—"up there on Brokeback Mountain."

TWO POINTS FOR the bitch on wheels, Ty thought. His lips kicked up in a grin as he watched her sail away.

He had to hand it to her, she'd hit Annemarie where it hurt. Him too, with that Brokeback comment. He could laugh it off, though, because any red-blooded woman—or man—would know from a mile away that he was all male. All *hetero* male. Not that he had a problem with gays. He just wasn't one, that's all.

Isabelle touched his arm. He dragged his eyes away from Vicky to look down at her, and damn it, she was chewing her lip. That meant she was worried about everybody else—him, Vicky, and probably Annemarie too, although she was likely down some on the list at the moment—when she should be having fun.

He was falling down on the job.

Matt had moved away to talk with Isabelle's father, so Ty draped his arm over her shoulders, gave her a squeeze. "Isabelle honey, this is just about the prettiest party I've ever been to."

That got her to smile. "I notice you said 'prettiest,' not 'best.'"

"Well now, sugar, the night's young. Things might pick up." He laughed when she stuck out her lip. "Don't you worry about me. You stocked the pond with pretty women. If I can't fish one out, I've got only myself to blame."

Annemarie's laugh tinkled at that, a seductive sound. He almost threw her a wink, then thought better of it. Given his druthers, he'd flirt her into a frenzy all evening, then take her upstairs and let her show her stuff, stripping off that five-alarm dress.

But, unfortunately, that wasn't in his job description. Instead, he'd have to fake-flirt with the bitch on wheels and go to bed alone.

Still, there was no reason he couldn't have a little fun with the situation. Push Vicky's buttons. Get under her skin. She could fire off some real good shots when she got her panties in a bunch.

It wouldn't make up for hot stripper sex, and he'd have to be damn careful that Isabelle didn't catch on. But it sure would keep things interesting.

PIERRE OULETTE MADE fifty-five look like the prime age for a man.

The usual benchmarks of maturity, like the silver threading his thick brown hair and the creases his smile brought out around his blue eyes, only enhanced his tanned and angular face, making it more compelling.

Women must flock to him, Vicky thought as she shook his hand. Not only was he handsome, but his trim waistline showed he was more fit than most men half his age; he positively exuded confidence and well-being, his affluence resting as comfortably on his shoulders as his perfectly tailored sport coat.

And that French accent. Well.

"Matt tells me you're a litigator," he said, his diction almost perfect, "and that you've just completed a demanding trial."

Vicky smiled. "Yes, and I'm very glad to have it behind me."

"Do you enjoy your work?"

The situation called for a polite answer, so she simply said, "It has its rewards."

Matt chimed in helpfully. "Litigation runs in our family. Granddad was a litigator. And Mom still does trials, even though as a senior partner she doesn't have to." He glanced at Vicky's tight smile. "It's stressful work, though. A lot of pressure."

Pierre smiled at Vicky. "I hope you can relax and enjoy yourself this weekend."

"That would be nice," she said, knowing it would never happen.

To underscore the point, Tyrell swaggered up, grinning. "Hey, Pierre, long time, no see."

Pierre gripped his hand, smiling broadly. "It's good to see you, Ty. Are you well?"

"Right as rain. My folks send their regards."

"Are they still in Florida?"

"Just bought a condo in Key West. Hanging out with Jimmy Buffett, I hear."

Vicky flicked an inquiring glance at Isabelle, who'd also joined them. She rolled her big blue eyes. "Ty's parents are *really* enjoying retirement."

Ty gave a laugh. "That's putting a pretty face on it, honey. What they're doing," he added for everyone's benefit, "is recapturing their youth. They rushed down the aisle at seventeen, two steps ahead of my granddad's shotgun. Before they knew it, they'd put in thirty years riding herd on two hell-raising boys and a few thousand head of longhorns." He shrugged. "Now they're making up for lost time. And I'm stuck with the longhorns."

"What are these *longhorns*?" Annemarie mangled the word.

"Cows," Isabelle volunteered.

Ty looked pained. "They're *cattle*, honey."

"Oh yes! That's right." She smiled innocently. "Cows are girls, steers are boys."

Annemarie's light bulb went on. "Ah, boy cows. For steak, yes?"

Isabelle nodded. "And girl cows are for milk." She beamed at Ty, clearly expecting praise.

His aggrieved expression made Vicky bite back a grin. Couldn't he see that Isabelle was yanking his chain?

By his long-suffering sigh, this wasn't the first time. "You got the gist of it, honey, that's what counts." Then he glanced around the circle. "You all see that article about Isabelle in the *New York Times*?"

"Oh, Ty." Isabelle flapped a hand. "It was about Vidal, not me. I'm just his assistant."

"Just his assistant, nothing. You're the creative genius behind everything he's done in the last two years."

Vicky softened toward him, minutely but perceptibly. Believing that Isabelle had failed Cattle 101, he was determined to show her strengths.

Pierre must have recognized his effort too, because he dropped a friendly hand on Ty's shoulder and joined in. "Isabelle, Vidal has often said that you inspire many of his designs. He wouldn't give credit unless it was due."

"He's damn stingy with it, if you ask me." Ty was indignant. "He should've made you a partner by now."

Adrianna appeared and put in her two cents. "I couldn't agree more." She smiled at Isabelle. "You won't get the credit you deserve until you go out on your own."

Vicky bristled on Isabelle's behalf. Nothing was ever good enough for Adrianna.

Amazingly, it didn't ruffle Isabelle. "Thank you for the vote of confidence," she said, "but I still have a lot to learn."

And with no more than that, she shifted into hostess mode, introducing Adrianna to her father, then Annemarie and, last but not least, Tyrell.

Vicky held her breath as her mother smiled and extended her hand to Ty. He shook it briefly but didn't smile back. From a guy who handed out smiles like candy, it was an obvious snub. But no one else seemed to notice, and Vicky breathed easy again.

The staff began gently herding the guests toward the buffet table set up at one end of the terrace, and her group coupled up and drifted away, Pierre strolling with Adrianna, heads angled in conversation; Matt cuddling Isabelle against his side.

Annemarie tried to move Ty along too, one arm linked through his elbow, stupendous breasts prodding his arm.

He wasn't budging, though, and when he offered his other arm to Vicky, she took a dark delight in the irritation that flared in Annemarie's eyes. The woman was Isabelle's friend so she must have redeeming qualities, but Vicky hadn't seen them.

Linked together, the three moseyed toward the terrace at Ty's usual snail's pace, Annemarie gabbling away in her pidgin English, Ty making appropriate responses, and Vicky ignoring them both, her attention centered on the carving station. Thanks to Ty's surprise arrival, she'd had no appetite for lunch. Now her stomach growled loudly.

Detaching from the pair when they reached the food,

she loaded a plate with asparagus and fingerlings, piled on some thinly sliced rare roast beef—she deserved a guilty pleasure given all she had to contend with—then retreated to a private table behind the pergola where she could indulge in peace.

But it wasn't to be. The first tender bite of beef hadn't hit her tongue when Ty plunked his plate on the table. "I hate to tell you this," he said, dropping into the other chair, "but there's a rumor going around that beef's bad for you."

Meeting his smirk with a baleful stare, she deliberately placed a forkful in her mouth. Chewed it slowly. Followed with a long swallow of Cabernet.

"Beef," she then said in her most pedantic tone, "is a religion in France. It's impossible to avoid, and if eaten sparingly is an excellent source of protein."

He raised his glass. "And if washed down with a good Cabernet is damn delicious."

She didn't bother denying it. Instead she cocked her head. "You look different. Oh, I know what it is. You're not wearing your stripper."

He unfurled a lazy grin. "She's clingy, but that can be a good thing."

"Clingy? No, Saran Wrap is *clingy*. That woman is *shrink-wrap*."

"You're just mad because she insulted your shoes."

"And you're just dense if you think that crack had anything to do with shoes."

"Are you saying she was taunting you?" He looked astonished. "Now why in the world would she do that?"

"Gee, I can't imagine. Maybe she's just a meanie."

"Doesn't seem mean to me. In fact, she seems real nice."

"Uh-huh. I'm sure she'll be *real nice* to you all weekend if you ask her."

He leaned back in his chair, regarded her thoughtfully. "It pains me to say this, but I'm beginning to think you've got yourself a sarcastic streak."

"Who, me? Get out."

"I mean it. Those were some nasty comments you made back there. That thing about Brokeback Mountain. Us cowboys can get real touchy about that."

She let her amusement show. "You should've seen your face."

"I'm sure I looked stunned. Who'd have thought that in France, of all places, I'd be facing a juvenile crack like that?"

She smirked unrepentantly. "If the shoe fits . . . or in this case, the boot . . . Which reminds me, how's your foot?"

"Oh, it's fine, just fine." He eyed her mounded plate. "Though you might want to count up those calories before you pack 'em in."

That made her sit up straight. "What does *that* mean? You think I'm *heavy*?"

"*I* don't, but then I've spent my life around large animals. Cattle, horses. Like that. Your average East Coast man might have a different frame of reference, if you take my meaning."

She stared at him for a moment, then burst out laughing. Apparently, he didn't realize that he'd just set himself up for a thousand cracks about cowboys and their barnyard animals. They zinged through her brain so fast that she went momentarily speechless trying to decide which hilarious one-liner to get off first.

Before she could pick one, Matt and Isabelle appeared at their table. Seeing their grins, Isabelle cooed, "Ooh, you two look like you're enjoying yourselves. Don't they, Matt?"

"Mmm." He looked skeptical.

"And Vicky, you look just lovely. Doesn't she, Ty?"

"Pretty as a painted pony." The wide smile he gave Vicky was completely sincere.

Biting back a crack about ponies and the cowboys who love them, she flapped a hand modestly. "Honestly," she said to Isabelle, "if all Texans are as charming as Ty, I'm moving to Austin." *Not.*

Isabelle giggled, plainly pleased that her plan was succeeding. Matt looked less enthused. He studied Vicky with worried eyes.

To convince him that she was having fun, she smiled fondly at Ty. Tilted her head toward the quartet playing a waltz on the terrace. "I'll take you up on that dance now."

Without the least hesitation, Ty stood and held out his hand. "Don't you worry about your two left feet, honey. I won't let you fall."

TWILIGHT TRANSFORMED THE garden from simply lovely to intimately romantic. Fairy lights twinkled in the trees; candles flickered on tabletops. The buffet tables had been cleared from the torch-lit terrace, and several couples danced sedately around the flagstones.

Relishing the prospect of Ty embarrassing himself with the eighth-grade shuffle, Vicky gasped when he tugged her smoothly into his arms. His eyes caught hers, amused, as if he knew what she was expecting. Then his strong hand settled at her waist and he swept her into a waltz like she'd never experienced.

She wanted to be disappointed that he wouldn't humiliate himself, but how could she be, when they floated so lightly over the flagstones that their steps might have been choreographed, fingers laced together like lovers. She should have known he could dance. The man was supremely coordinated, moving through the world with his deceptively lazy stride, as comfortable in his skin as a cat.

A big cat. A lion. Under that tawny skin he was all lean muscle; it flexed under her hand where it rested along his shoulder. A fine thread of suppressed tension ran through his sinews. He camouflaged it well with his lackadaisical style, but she sensed the vibration. The same tensile quality that allowed cats, especially lions, to look relaxed, even slumberous . . . just before they pounced.

Apparently, it made for fine dancing too, because waltzing had never felt so effortless, so intuitive. So romantic.

After a few turns around the terrace, she did manage to say, "Don't feel bad, I'm sure you're a perfectly good line dancer."

His palm slid around to the small of her back and flattened there, pulling her in until her cheek rested against his chest. She almost stepped back, but it felt too good and she slid her arm around his neck instead, moving with him like water flowing in a stream.

"Isabelle's watching," he murmured. "Try to look like you know what you're doing. It's not Zumba class, you know."

She smiled. It was really too bad he was such a jerk or she might actually like him. He could be funny. And his chest was as solid as an oak tree.

TY WAS HAVING a hard time remembering that he hated the woman in his arms.

She danced like a dream, supple and sexy, letting him lead, moving with him like she was inside his skin. To tell the truth, even in Texas he'd admired how she moved. Her purposeful stride into the courtroom; her command of the space between the witness, the jury, and the judge.

He'd never admit it, of course, and just the thought of

the courtroom should have made him tense up. But he loved to dance, and this slender, pliant woman with her cheek on his chest didn't seem anything at all like a bitch on wheels.

It probably hadn't been the best idea to pull her up tight against him, but he hadn't wanted her to catch him smiling at her crack about line dancing, or staring at the shimmering ribbon of blond that escaped her neat French twist.

And he really didn't want her to see what he was trying so hard not to see himself—that if he didn't hate her so much, he might actually like her.

But holding her tight presented its own problems. Maybe she wasn't stacked like that bombshell Annemarie, but the way her body curved along his, well, there was no denying that her hipbone rocking against his groin was about to cause him some embarrassment.

Still, he didn't put any space between them. In fact, he let his hand slide a little lower on her back, until his pinky sensed the uppermost curve of her ass. His thumb stroked along the bumps in her spine, easily felt through the fine fabric of her pretty dress. He'd never tell her, but he liked it a lot more than that skin suit of Annemarie's. Jesus, he could see the pebbles on the woman's nipples through that thing.

He almost laughed at himself. He must be getting old if a skinny lawyer in a high-necked dress turned him on more than a pole dancer in heat. Jack would laugh his ass off if he knew.

The song ended, and without an excuse to hold on to Vicky any longer, he let her go. Took a step back. And watched her gaze travel down to his crotch.

Why in the hell had he worn his tightest jeans?

Then she looked up into his eyes and a smile spread across her face; her blue eyes crinkled in delight.

Damn it, he needed to nip this in the bud. His brows slammed together. "You should be ashamed of yourself," he said, "rubbing up against me like that. What did you think would happen? I'm only a man, a *heterosexual* man." He made himself look scandalized. "And you talk about Annemarie."

Her mouth fell open. "*You* were grinding against *me*," she shot back. "And . . . and *feeling me up.*"

"Feeling you up? How could I feel you up when your chest was mashed up against me like you were trying to climb inside my shirt?"

Outrage widened her eyes. "I was *not* trying to climb inside your shirt! And you were feeling up my *back.*"

He looked pitying. "Vicky, honey, it's not possible to feel up a *back.* It's sad to think your experience is so limited that you got turned on by my hand resting there, but believe me, that was not sex."

They'd kept their voices low but she was close to cutting loose, so he tugged her into his arms for another dance, waltzing her out of range of Matt and Isabelle, who'd joined the small group on the terrace.

She didn't pull away, but she hissed like a cat. "I didn't say it was sex!"

"Well, sweetheart, maybe the rules are different in New York, but where I come from, feeling up is foreplay. So is grinding your pelvis into the man you're dancing with. Now, as far as that goes, being a gentleman, I'm willing to make allowances for your sheltered upbringing. But if you want some advice, you'll be careful with those signals you're sending out. Another man might call you a tease."

Her chest heaved against his, because of course he'd pulled her in tight again. God, he got such a kick out of stirring her up.

"Tyrell Brown," she squeezed through her teeth, "you are either the dumbest man I've ever met, or the biggest fattest liar. Either way, I'm *not* attracted to you, and I'm *not* trying to tease you. That boner of yours—and yes, I can still feel it down there—is your doing, not mine."

"And it's turning you on, isn't it?"

Her breath caught, a sexy little sound of surprise that zinged through his groin. She started to raise her head, probably to bite out his heart and spit it on the ground, but his hand shot up and pinned her face to his chest. "Easy there, sugar. We can't have you pulling my clothes off out here in public."

"In your dreams." It came out "In your threamth" since her cheeks were flattened by his palm.

He swallowed a laugh, filled his voice with regret. "I know this'll be hard for you to hear, and I'm sorry about it, I truly am, but I can't have sex with you tonight." She sputtered into his shirt. "It's not that you're not pretty, in a skinny, smarty-pants kind of way. It's just that, well, under the circumstances we don't need the complications. You falling head over heels, I mean."

That did it. The fingers resting on the back of his neck, the same fingers that had toyed with his collar during the last song, turned into pincers. The Vulcan death grip shot a pain through his shoulder that made him drop his hand from her face. She reared back.

"You"—she gnashed her teeth—"are an idiot."

"Smile," he said. "Your brother's right behind you."

CHAPTER SEVEN

THE NERVE! THE insufferable egomaniac actually thought she wanted him!

So maybe, in a weakened moment, suckered in by soft music, romantic lighting, and a truly spectacular erection pressing precisely against an erogenous zone, she had, fleetingly, wanted him. That still gave him no right to *think* it.

This was what she got for letting her guard down for one minute around Tyrell Brown.

Matt tapped her shoulder. "Mind if I cut in?"

Sucking a steadying breath, she aimed a last, scorching glare at Ty, then turned around to smile at her brother. "Not at all."

Having danced together for years in the classes Adrianna had insisted upon, brother and sister fell easily into step. After a moment she no longer had to force her smile. "Hey you. Nice party."

He grinned. "It's all Isabelle. All I had to do was show up." He paused a moment. "You okay? Is Tyrell coming on too strong?"

"Of course not." And because she knew how much he

wanted her to enjoy the weekend, she made herself add, "He's a perfect gentleman. Why do you ask?"

He shrugged. "Just some stories I've heard about him and Jack. They ran together before Jack got married, you know. Never any shortage of women around."

"Is that so?" Jack McCabe was legendary for the women he'd gone through. But Ty had been married, and after that he'd been grieving. If she'd read him right on the witness stand, he still was.

"Isabelle claims Ty was crazy about his wife and hasn't gotten over losing her," said Matt. "Who knows how a person might react to that kind of grief? Maybe it helps to jump in and out of bed with beautiful women. I don't know, and I hope I never find out."

Against her will, Vicky searched out Ty, spotted him waltzing in the grass with Isabelle, dipping her lightly, grinning at her squeal of delight. Torchlight glinted off the gold streaks in his hair, and off his silver belt buckle, and off the pearly snaps on the Western shirt that fit him just right. From that distance, in that light, it was hard to cast him as a star-crossed lover. But that's what he was. He'd lost the love of his life.

And now his heart would be breaking again, because he was losing Isabelle to Matt. Oh, they'd always be friends. But he'd fallen to second place in her affections. Unfortunately, Vicky could sympathize with that.

As much as she disliked having anything in common with the jackass, as she shifted her gaze back to her brother, her very best friend, she knew exactly how Tyrell felt.

BITTERSWEET. TY HADN'T known what the word meant. Now, watching Isabelle walk away from him, letting go of a love that was wonderful and precious but had passed its time, he understood.

Bittersweet meant feeling joy and heartbreak at once. It swelled the chest and left a hole in it at the same time.

Shaking it off, he glanced around, not looking for Vicky. Which was a good thing, since she was nowhere to be seen. She wasn't on the terrace, where the quartet had left their instruments for a short break. Or on the lawn. Or at any of the tables. He took a few steps backward—just to stretch his legs—and glanced under the pergola. It was dark in there, but he didn't sense any movement.

Maybe he should go inside the chateau. Find the bathroom, or just wander around not looking for Vicky.

Then he spotted Adrianna Marchand striding toward him and he froze, filled with dread but unwilling to show weakness by fleeing like he wanted to.

"Mr. Brown," she said, closing in. "I hoped we might have a chance to talk."

Up close, she was stunning. Deep blue eyes, stylish blond hair, a body like her daughter's. Beautiful, for sure. But an iceberg. No wonder she'd caught four husbands. And no wonder three of them didn't stick.

He hooked his thumbs in his pockets, cocked his head to one side. "I can't imagine what we'd have to talk about," he drawled.

His indolent pose didn't seem to impress her. "I assume Victoria's already explained that she'll be handling the appeal in your case."

As a matter of fact, she hadn't. "Whatever," he said, putting on a bored face.

"I'm sure she also mentioned her fiancé."

He quirked a brow. "You mean the guy who can't keep his pants zipped? Yeah, she mentioned him. In the past tense."

"Their separation is only temporary, I assure you. Victoria will accept his apology."

"His apology? How will that go? 'Sorry you found out

I fucked around on you, Vicky. Next time I'll do a better job of hiding it.'" He wagged his head in disgust. "What kind of mother wants her daughter to marry a creep like that?"

Adrianna's eyes frosted over. "You know nothing about me, Mr. Brown. And despite your cozy display with my daughter on the dance floor, you know nothing about her either. She needs a man like Winston."

"No woman needs a man who cheats on her. Your daughter least of all. She's smart, gorgeous, and she's got a damn fine sense of humor. She can have anybody she wants."

"If you believe she'll want you, you're mistaken." She scraped cold eyes from his hair to his boots, twisted her lips into a hard smile. "You're not her type, Mr. Brown. Don't let this sham flirtation go to your head. When the weekend is over, you'll never see Victoria again."

Now that just pissed him off. Not that he had any notion of seeing Vicky again. Even if he was having fun tormenting her, that didn't spell long-term relationship. And anyway, he hated her guts.

But he wasn't letting her bitchy mama off that easy. Instead, he curved his lips into his patented bone-melting smile, let his eyes go warm and buttery. Her own eyes widened on cue.

He gave her a moment to think about it.

Then he dropped his head, shifted his weight slightly, so all of a sudden he was crowding her. Her breath caught, and he leaned in closer, until his lips almost brushed her hair. In a drawl as thick and sultry as sweaty sex on a summer night, he spoke into her ear.

"I wouldn't bet on that, honey, if I was you."

IT HAD TO hurt, having a pole up your ass like that. Made for good posture though. Ty had never seen a spine as

straight as Adrianna Marchand's as she stalked away
from him.

It occurred to him that he'd promised to charm her.
Well, there were only so many ornery, abrasive women a
man could be expected to dazzle in one weekend, and he
had his hands full with Vicky. Isabelle would have to find
someone else to sweet-talk Matt's mother.

He took another look around, not for Vicky. Which was
a good thing, since she still wasn't anywhere in sight.

Then his ears picked up a whisper beckoning from the
pergola. "Pssst. Pssst."

Had she snuck in there when he wasn't looking?

Casually, like he had no particular destination in mind,
he ambled over, stepped underneath. And out of the darkness, two arms pulled his head down and locked around
his neck. Pillowy lips vacuum-sealed his mouth. An
eager tongue speared inside. And a bolt of lust shot from
his brain to his cock.

Christ, Vicky really *did* want him! Without stopping
to question it, he closed his hands on her ass, yanked her
hard against his groin, and plunged his tongue into her
mouth with equal abandon.

He'd lost his mind, and he didn't care. Pulse pounding
in his ears, cock straining for freedom, he dragged her
down to the grass, aiming to take her hard and fast before
either of them could think it through.

She tumbled with him willingly, tangling him up in her
arms and legs. He pawed her dress up over her ass, shoved
his hands inside her thong, snapped it like a thread. She
moaned and squirmed, rubbing against his hard-on. He
dragged his lips across her jaw, buried his face in her
throat. And—what the fuck!—sucked in a noseful of
Annemarie's perfume!

He reared back, but her ankles chained his thighs. With
one hand she opened his jeans, snaked the other down

inside, and wrapped her fingers around his pulsing cock.

Goddamn him for a horny fool! If he'd thought about it for even a second he would have realized that the ass in his hand was too round to be Vicky's. The heaving chest was bigger too, three times bigger, and the frantic panting, at least the part not coming from him, had a definite French accent.

With superhuman willpower, he unfastened his hand from her bare breast—how it got there, he couldn't recall—and locked it around the arm she'd shoved halfway down his jeans.

"Slow down there, honey," he said against her swollen lips.

"But you're so hard," she moaned, making him harder.

"I sure am." He could hardly breathe. "And that's a real good grip you've got there." He tugged on her arm. "Come on, now, sweetheart. Let go before it's too late."

She held on, stroking expertly.

He changed tacks. "You don't want to waste a good hard-on, do you, honey? Not when we can put it to better use in one of those feather beds."

That slowed her down. "Now?"

"Soon." He tugged her arm again. If she didn't let go this time, it was all over.

Reluctantly, she released him. He gasped out a breath, part relief, part regret. Rolling onto his back, he lay still, afraid to adjust himself yet. The slightest touch might set him off.

Beside him, Annemarie rose up on her knees. His vision had adjusted to the faint light inside the pergola and he could see her naked breast, a creamy globe. He couldn't look away. Deliberately, she cupped it, took the weight. Licked her thumb and ran it across the nipple. Blew on it lightly so it stiffened, while his dry mouth went drier. Then she slipped it inside her dress.

A sexy sound in her throat pulled his gaze up to her mouth. Her tongue peeked out; she stroked it over her lips. Leaning down, closer, closer, until those lips were just an inch from his, she said in a smoldering accent that no man with a throbbing hard-on could be expected to resist, "Your bed? Or mine?"

He swallowed once. "Let's make it yours, honey. And hurry."

CHAPTER EIGHT

TY EXITED THE chateau through the front door, then crept around the side to the garden in the back. Hugging the shadows, he scanned the crowd, if twenty people could rightly be called a crowd.

Pierre and Adrianna danced on the terrace. Matt and Isabelle clustered around a table with a small group of friends. Others were scattered in twos and threes around the fountain or on benches under the trees.

No sign that he'd been missed.

Moving briskly across a narrow strip of grass to the pergola, he ducked quickly into its shadow, pausing just long enough to rake his hair into a semblance of order and give his zipper a final check. Then he hooked his thumbs in his pockets and strolled casually out into the torchlight.

He'd hadn't gone ten steps when Vicky came barreling down on him. She slammed on the brakes six inches from impact, nostrils flaring.

"What in the world did you say to my mother?" she hissed in a furious whisper.

He knew better than to break into a grin, but damn, he

loved to see her fired up. Catching her arm, he tugged her toward the terrace. "Come on, let's dance."

"*Dance?*" She dug her heels in. Literally, so they divoted the grass. "I asked you a question!"

"And I'll answer it. On the dance floor." He tugged again. She huffed out an aggravated sigh and followed him.

Up on the terrace, he gathered her in and they flowed seamlessly into the waltz. He let himself relax into the rhythm. Why did it feel so good to dance with a woman he couldn't stand?

Circling the flagstones, he kept one eye on the door. After having second thoughts on the way to meet Annemarie, he'd thrown himself on Isabelle's mercy. She'd promised to run interference, but since she'd already sent Annemarie off on one trumped-up errand that evening—which explained where Annemarie had disappeared to at dinnertime—there was no telling whether it would work again.

Which meant she might pop out that door any minute, expecting to cash in on his promise to bed her. He'd barely escaped their last encounter with his virtue intact; he couldn't risk being alone with her again. Which meant he had no choice but to stay glued to Vicky all evening. Whether she liked it or not.

At the moment, she wasn't so hot on it. "Well?" she demanded, blue eyes sparking under lowered brows. "What did you say to make my mother so mad? She's spitting nails, and she won't tell me why."

He'd already figured out that the only way to play it with Vicky was to turn the tables, keep her off balance. If he gave her an inch, she'd lawyer him into a corner he'd never get out of.

"The question you should be asking," he said tartly, "is what your mother said to me."

She glared some more. Then, "Okay, I'll bite. What did my mother say to you?"

"The first thing she said is that you're handling the appeal. Why didn't you tell me that?"

She lowered her eyes. Some of the starch went out of her. "I didn't think you'd want to talk about the case. And anyway, it's not really ethical for us to discuss it."

"Okay then, we won't." That suited him. "She also told me that you and Winston are a match made in heaven."

That put the starch back in her. Her head whipped up. "She said that?"

"Not in so many words, but that was her drift."

He could almost hear her teeth grind. "Do you know she made me promise to give him another chance, or else she'd tell Matt and Isabelle about you and me? What kind of mother blackmails her child? What kind of mother wants her daughter to marry a cheating swine?"

"That's exactly what I asked that got her all riled up."

Vicky's mouth fell open. "You did? You asked her that?" Her lips curved into a spontaneous smile.

It softened her, that smile. She looked so amazed and so vulnerable that he had to look away. Jesus, hadn't anybody ever stuck up for her before?

"That was . . ." She paused, cleared her throat. "I'm sure that's what got under her skin."

No need to add that he'd as much as told Adrianna he was planning to seduce her daughter.

"Yeah, she's got a temper," was all he said.

Vicky was quiet after that, her body swaying with the music, her cheek resting on his chest. He rubbed his jaw against her hair, not because it felt so silky, but because he had an itch. Her fingers fiddled with his collar again.

He was glad she wasn't letting his erection bother her, because it was there to stay.

IF ONLY THEY could keep dancing, Vicky thought.

If they kept dancing, she wouldn't have to face her mother's bullet-hole stare, or regret Matt abandoning her, or worry about running into Winston at some cocktail party in New York. She could let her head rest where it was, against Ty's broad chest.

He didn't seem to hate her so much when they were dancing. Oh, he made fun of her, obviously thought she was a tight ass. But he also smiled at her.

That smile mesmerized her. It was a loaded weapon. When he aimed it at a woman, he could make her do crazy things. Like drink too much wine. Care about the difference between rationalism and empiricism. Toss out her inhibitions and have sex on an airplane.

That last one still hurt, his rejection on the plane. But in truth she was partly to blame. She should have learned her lesson with Winston, and rejected Ty before he could reject her. She wouldn't be so foolish again. Not with him, or any man.

But she had the rest of her life to worry about that. Right now, just for a while, she'd pretend that Ty was holding her close because he liked how she fit in his arms. That the erection against her hipbone was more than a knee-jerk reaction to estrogen proximity—

"Ah, there you are, *chéri*!"

The sexy French accent cut into her daydream. Vicky lifted her head to see Annemarie steaming toward them, chest cleaving the small crowd like the prow of an ice-breaker.

Moving in on Ty like Vicky was invisible, she curled her arm around his waist, went up on her toes to "whis-per" into his ear. "Forgive me for deserting you, *chéri*. Isabelle begged me to do an errand for her. I could not refuse."

"Well now, honey, she's the bride, after all." Ty's tone was magnanimous. "If there's anything else you need to help her with—"

"No more." She slashed a hand through the air. "I have done my share. Others can take their turn now." She pointed a look at Vicky before turning back to drool on Ty. "You and I, we have . . . how do they say in the movies? Unfinished business."

The phrase hit Vicky like a cold blast from a hose. "Unfinished business" could only mean that Isabelle had interrupted an assignation between these two—which explained the hard-on that wouldn't quit.

Her whole body stiffened. While she'd been spinning a stupid romantic fantasy around him, the two-timing slime was only killing time with her until he could get Annemarie naked! Would she never learn?

Forcing her lips into a face-saving smirk, she tried to step back so they could get on with their rendezvous.

Unaccountably, Ty held on like a drowning man. He started to babble, unreeling a string of excuses about having an early day tomorrow . . . a round of golf . . . some nonsense about yoga, of all things. His drawl dripped with regret.

Vicky's jaw hardened. He must be punishing Annemarie for running out on him and his hard-on. Well, she was damned if she'd be a pawn in his stupid sex game. Slapping her hands on his shoulders, she gave him a shove.

He didn't budge. In fact, his grip tightened. One arm banded around her lower back, the other around her shoulders, all while he wagged his head dolefully at Annemarie, who could only stare back at him wide-eyed, as if she'd lost the ability to translate the excuses rolling off his tongue.

She recovered quickly, though, and promptly took matters into her own hands. Hooking her fingers in his belt, and putting her back as well as her well-developed quadriceps into it, she tried to yank him backward toward the door. But her efforts were useless too. He was stronger than both of them put together, and with his legs rooted and his arms locked, none of them was going anywhere.

The standoff might have lasted all night if Isabelle hadn't pealed out, "Lilianne! Jack!" All eyes swung to the door.

Wow, was Vicky's first thought, *they really* are *gorgeous*.

She'd seen a hundred pictures of Jack and Lil McCabe—on TV, in the *Post*, in her guilty pleasure *People*—but they were even more striking in person. Especially Jack, standing in the doorway in faded Levi's and a chest-hugging white T-shirt, with his jet black hair sweeping back from his chiseled face and astonishing jade green eyes.

Vicky's mouth actually watered.

Lil was a beauty too, of course, with her own raven's hair curling past her shoulders, framing lovely pale cheeks and big violet eyes. She wore a loose peasant top over her jeans, with Jack's arm—and what an arm it was—looped protectively around her waist.

A waist that was—stop the presses—sporting a definite baby bump.

Isabelle rushed forward to throw her arms around them. Matt shook Jack's hand, kissed Lil's cheek. And the next thing Vicky knew, the four of them were turning her way.

Predictably, four sets of eyes locked on Annemarie's hands, still latched in Ty's pants. From there they moved to Vicky's, pressed against his chest. Isabelle's mouth formed an O. Matt's jaw went rigid.

Only Jack and Lil looked unsurprised. Lil gave Vicky a sympathetic smile. And Jack got a load of Ty's rueful expression and busted out in a laugh.

"WELL, SHIT," TY muttered under his breath. It figured Jack would show up at the stupidest moment of his life. He'd never hear the end of it.

Resigned to the inevitable, he dropped his arms and let Vicky go, then calmly unhooked Annemarie's fingers from his jeans. Ignoring Jack, he wrapped Lil in a hug. "Hey, gorgeous. How you feeling?"

"Fat and sassy," Lil said with affection. She let her smile encompass Annemarie and Vicky, then quirked a brow at him. "Looks like you're in demand."

He turned his palms up. "What can I say? One of me just isn't enough."

Vicky let out a snort. He let it roll off his back. She didn't worry him at the moment.

Isabelle, on the other hand, worried him a lot. By the look on her face, she'd moved past astonishment to frustration, on her way to all-out fury. She'd be mad at him for a month, and he knew he deserved it. After promising to make sure everyone had a good time, so far he'd managed to outrage Adrianna, sexually frustrate Annemarie, aggravate Vicky, and piss off the groom.

And it was only Thursday.

CHAPTER NINE

PINK STREAKED THE eastern sky as Vicky unrolled her yoga mat on the cool flagstones of the terrace. A pair of early-rising sparrows twittered in the cherry trees.

In the pale dawn light, objects in the garden appeared in silhouette. The bulky pergola. The low-slung benches. Cupid rising from the trickling fountain.

It couldn't have been more tranquil.

Turning her face to the brightening horizon, Vicky spread her bare feet to shoulder width and filled her lungs with the cool, fresh air. Her palms came together as if in prayer. Then she raised her arms high, reaching for the sky, and moved fluidly into the first sun salutation of the day.

Tree pose followed, then downward dog. A few more sparrows joined the chorus.

In the solitude of daybreak, serenity reigned.

Lying on her back, she moved into the plow position, ass pointed skyward, toes touching the flagstones above her head. She heard the terrace door open. Assuming the staff was coming to clean up after the party, she managed to ignore the footfalls, maintain her focus.

Until—

"NICE *ASS*-ANA YOU got there, sugar." Ty appraised Vicky's butt with approval.

She whipped her legs down. Snarled up at him. "What in the world are *you* doing up at this hour?"

"Back at you, honey. Don't you need your beauty sleep?"

Her eyes narrowed.

He kept a straight face. After a shitty night tossing and turning, alternately hating and craving this very woman, he deserved some entertainment. "Not that you need it," he added belatedly enough to imply the opposite.

"I was here first." She sounded like a third-grader.

"Tough titties," he responded in kind. "I'm here now, so shove over and make room."

Her lips flattened. She stayed where she was, lying on her back glaring up at him. Daring him to do something about it.

He took the dare. Rolling out a lazy smile, he walked his eyes along her supine form, from her head all the way to her toes, lingering on her breasts, the cleft of her thighs, her long, lovely legs. And then he walked them back up again, just as slowly, all the way past her flaming cheeks to her stormy blue eyes.

Bad idea.

Sure, he'd embarrassed her, which was the whole point. But that body-hugging yoga outfit showcased every curve. Now he was fully, and conspicuously, aroused. Again!

Damn it, he did *not* want to be attracted to this woman!

Even worse than his cock saluting her was the unnerving fact that she actually interested him. She was a bundle of contradictions. Half the time she vibrated with tension. Other times, like when he'd stuck up for her with her mama, she melted like ice cream.

And she was so damn unpredictable. Like now. After he'd peeled her clothes off with his eyes, Little Miss

Wrapped-Too-Tight should have been scrambling for the door. Instead, she calmly assumed the lotus position and lobbed her first snark bomb of the day.

"Finished writing in your *gratitude journal* already?" Her wide eyes looked so sincere. "Hoping to *remember your spirit* by communing with the birds?"

He narrowed his eyes. "Pick on me all you want, but leave Oprah out of it."

"Maybe she'll give you your own column. The philosophical musings of a Cro-Magnon cowboy."

He couldn't hold a back a grin, so he turned it into a pity smile. "Your chakras must be out of alignment. It's making you snippy."

She raised one brow, didn't deign to reply. Instead, she did her own eye-walk, from his bed head, past his stubble, over his holey T-shirt and the yoga mat under his arm, down to his bare toes, and all the way back up again.

He had to hand it to her, she knew how to get it done. And she hadn't batted a lash at the erection tenting his sweats.

Now her eyes flicked back down to that growing problem. "Aren't you supposed to call a doctor if it lasts more than four hours?"

"That's only if you take a pill, honey. What you see here is all Tyrell." He leered. She rolled her eyes.

So much for running her off.

Okay then. With a snap of his wrist, he unfurled his mat a yard from hers. "Seeing as how you're a control freak, you can lead the class."

"Forward bend," she called out without missing a beat. "Legs straight. Lie forward over your knees." She paused. "Oops, I wasn't thinking. You probably can't do this pose with all that wood in your pants."

"I admit there's a lot of it, thanks for noticing. But

I'll work around it." Locking his hands on his ankles, he stretched forward until his flat stomach rested on his thighs, well aware that it would impress the hell out of her.

HOLY CRAP. IN hundreds of yoga classes, Vicky had never seen any man do a forward bend like that. Ty must have been practicing yoga for years.

Probably seven years, since Lissa died.

Why, she asked herself, must he keep blindsiding her with his stupid sensitivity?

She called another pose, and another, and together they flowed through a dozen more asanas, a weird kind of harmony evolving as they bent and twisted, stretched and rolled.

An hour later they ended the routine in the corpse pose, lying on their backs, legs relaxed, arms at their sides, their breathing naturally synchronized.

Turning her head, Vicky stole a look at his profile. With his eyes closed and without his smile to distract her, she could appreciate how unfairly handsome he was. Strong brow, bladed cheekbones, firm jaw. All suitable for stamping on a coin. Add the sexy touches—ridiculously lush lashes, thick golden stubble, sun-streaked hair that always looked like he'd just gotten laid—and you ended up with trouble.

The man was too good-looking for his own good. Even standing next to Jack McCabe, probably the hottest guy on the planet, Ty shone with his own light.

Not to mention that Cro-Magnon Cowboy was an accomplished yogi. Just another of the man's fascinating contradictions: new-age caveman.

So who could blame her for being attracted to him? She'd have to be gay not to want him. And though she'd sometimes wished she was—because having a relationship with another woman *had* to be less annoying, right?—she just wasn't.

Ty's eyes blinked open. As if he'd heard her thoughts, he turned his head and looked right at her. His lips curved into that smile that made her stupid, and sure enough, stupid ideas popped into her head. Ideas like rolling up against him and taking a bite out of his delicious bottom lip. Stuffing her hand down his sweats and grabbing hold of that hard-on she'd become so familiar with.

Then his eyes widened, his pupils dilated. His delicious smile deepened into something seriously irresistible. And she realized that her stupidity must be written all over her face!

It wouldn't do. It simply would *not* do.

She forced a smirk. "All done now? Or should we take a minute to tell each other *what we know for sure*?"

SHE WANTED HIM, that's what he knew for sure.

If Ty had doubted it before, he didn't doubt it now. And suddenly he knew exactly what his problem was. He'd made his whole attraction to Vicky too complicated, weighing it down with psychological bullshit when all he really needed to do was get her into bed and fuck her out of his system.

Yes, sir, that was the cure for what ailed him. He'd unwrap little Miss Wrapped-Too-Tight. And she'd enjoy every ever-lovin' minute of it.

The trick, though, was to make her think it was her idea. Rolling up on his side, he propped his head in his hand. "Okay, me first. I know for sure that you're not as prissy as you pretend to be."

That put surprise on her face. "How do you know that?"

He trailed his gaze from her eyes to her lips. "Your sassy mouth. You dress yourself up in conservative clothes, playing the part of the Ivy League lawyer. But you can't disguise your sassy mouth."

His gaze roved up to her eyes again, wide and blue. A light flush stained her cheeks. This was going to be pitifully easy.

He let his slow drawl do the work. "I like a sassy mouth. You never know what kind of trouble it'll get itself into. Keeps things . . . interesting."

Her color rose higher.

"Your turn," he said, curving his lips. "Tell me, Victoria Westin, what do you know for sure?"

Half a dozen expressions scrolled across her face. He waited to see where the dial would stop, which facet of this complicated woman would win out. Sexy Victoria? Smartass Victoria? Snooty Victoria? So many possibilities, each with its own attraction.

He could admit that now, the *attraction* part, because he was halfway to getting her underneath him, around him, wet and willing and smokin' hot—

"Victoria." Adrianna's frosty tone dropped the temperature twenty degrees. She'd snuck up like a storm cloud, tricked out in silver and black running gear. Ignoring him, she aimed her chilly gaze at Vicky.

"You're up early. I trust you slept . . . well." By "well" she clearly meant "alone."

Vicky showed some spunk. "Actually, I had sex with Tyrell all night. We're just taking a break before we go another round."

Adrianna never blinked. "If I didn't know how much you dislike sex, I might believe you."

Ty watched the wind go out of Vicky's sails.

"The men are golfing this morning," Adrianna went on as if she hadn't just punched her daughter in the gut. "I need to do some shopping. You can be ready by ten, can't you?" She ran a critical eye over Vicky, whose cheeks had paled. "Go light on breakfast. You have to get into your bridesmaid dress tomorrow."

And off she went, leaving the wreckage behind her.

Vicky stood and began rolling her mat, a cool, distant expression on her face. Ty forgot about seducing her, compelled to say something, anything to ease her pain.

"Vicky—" he began, but she cut him off.

"Here's what I know for sure," she said sharply, concentrating on her mat. "I have to deal with her insults because she's my mother. But I don't have to deal with yours."

TY WAS FURLING his yoga mat and grumbling under his breath when Jack ambled onto the terrace.

"Golf," Jack said through a yawn. "I fucking hate golf."

"Yeah, well, I fucking hate everything about this fucking weekend."

Jack grinned. "I guess counsel for the defense started the day by tying your dick in a knot."

"No, she did not tie my dick in a knot." He positioned his mat to cover up what she *had* done to his dick. "We were getting along fine until Cruella de Vil showed up."

"She the one who looks like the counselor, but older and colder?"

"Yeah, that's her. Wearing the puppy-fur coat." Ty's lips thinned. "She's a stone bitch. Hard to believe she's Vicky's mama."

Jack nodded sagely. "Busted up your little seduction, did she?"

Ty glared at him. Jack snorted out a laugh.

"Fuck you," Ty muttered, and holding his mat in front of him, he strode away.

"THANKS FOR TAKING Mom shopping, Vic. Isabelle's got tons to do, and I promised the guys we'd play golf."

"Please tell me you're not equating shopping with Mom

to spending a few hours on the golf course. They are *not* comparable."

He filled her coffee cup from the pot the cook had left on the farm table. "I know you're taking one—a really big one—for the team. I owe you."

"Yes, you do. And I'll collect."

He refilled his own cup. Poked through the basket of pastries meant to tide them over until a hot breakfast was served. Pulling out a *chausson aux pommes*, he sank his teeth in, pushed the basket toward her.

She pushed it away. His brows shot up in surprise.

She wrapped both hands around her cup. "I have to get into that dress."

He licked pastry flakes off his lips. "So?"

"So Mother said I look fat."

His brows came down hard. "Mom needs glasses. That trial took some serious weight off you. Isabelle's worried you're gonna swim in that dress." He shoved the basket at her. "Now eat a damn croissant."

Ty pulled out the chair next to her. "Hey, Matt. Where's your beautiful bride this morning?" He leaned across Vicky and poked around in the basket, helped himself to a croissant drizzled with chocolate, then fished out a second and dropped it on Vicky's plate.

Conscious of Matt's gaze, she smiled sweetly. "Thanks, Ty, but I'm really not hungry." She shoved the plate into the middle of the table.

He dragged it back. "Hunger has nothing to with it, honey. French pastry's all about pleasure."

She turned to eye him, her smile pasted on. "You're sweet," she said, and pinched his leg under the table so he'd know she didn't mean it, "but I don't want it."

"Sure you do." That was Matt, siding with Ty. "Don't listen to Mom. You look great."

"It's empty calories."

"They're the best kind." Ty bit into his flaky croissant. "You can't get pastry like this at home," he pointed out. "You're here for what? Four days? Why not relax a little? Enjoy some forbidden pleasures."

It sounded innocent enough, but she had a feeling he wasn't talking about croissants. She went in for another pinch, but he caught her hand and trapped it on his thigh.

To her disgust, a shiver tingled up her arm and found its way to her belly. Lust, for God's sake. What was *wrong* with her?

"*Bonjour*, everyone!" Isabelle sailed onto the terrace and dropped a kiss on Matt's waiting lips. "Why didn't you wake me, *mon ami*?"

"I looked in," he said, "but you were sound asleep. Too beautiful to disturb." He pulled her down on his lap. She curled her arms around his neck.

Vicky used her free hand to poke a finger in Ty's ribs. He sloshed his coffee, gave her a sinister look.

Let go, she mouthed.

Slowly, he shook his head. His hair was still damp from the shower and looked like he'd finger-combed it back from his face. He'd given himself a little scrape with his razor along the edge of his jaw. She wanted to touch it, damn him.

It really wasn't fair.

She tugged her hand. He laced his fingers through hers.

"Someone will see," she whispered.

"We're supposed to be flirting," he whispered back.

"*Flirting*, not *hand-holding*. If my mother sees—"

"What's she gonna do? Skin some more puppies?"

"*What?* My mother might be a hard ass, but she'd never hurt a puppy!"

"What are you two whispering about?" Isabelle asked.

Vicky's head snapped around. "Puppies," she stammered, "we were talking about puppies."

Isabelle cooed. "Ty loves dogs, don't you, Ty?"

"Yup, love 'em," Ty drawled agreeably. "In fact, I'm thinking about getting a puppy on the ranch. Neighbor's mutt just had a litter, and there's a pretty little black and white who's got her eye on me." He took a pull on his coffee. "Gonna call her Spot. She's got Dalmatian in her."

Vicky's lights went on. Dalmatian . . . puppy skins . . . She caught Ty's eye. He grinned, and her lips curved. *Cruella de Vil.* Why hadn't she ever thought of that?

A moment later, the villainess herself swept onto the terrace, Pierre one step behind her. Watching him pull out Adrianna's chair, Vicky wondered if she was looking at her next stepfather, and sincerely hoped not. After the inevitable divorce, family Christmases would be hell.

The coffee made its way down the table, along with the basket of pastries. Adrianna plucked out a *chausson aux pommes*, cracked it in half, and took a dainty bite.

Ty leaned back in his chair, eyed her appraisingly. She caught his look, raised her eyebrows a bare fraction, returning his stare.

"How many calories in that thing?" he asked, poking his chin at her pastry. No one was listening but Vicky. Her palms popped a sweat.

"I have no idea," Adrianna said stiffly.

He walked his eyes down to her waistline, then back up. He smiled blandly. "Just wonderin'."

Adrianna's nostrils flared, then pinched. For a long, pregnant moment, she stared wordlessly at Ty while Vicky held her breath.

Then Pierre touched her arm, asking a question, and, deliberately, Adrianna turned her back on Ty.

Vicky let herself breathe. Then Ty leaned in, touched his lips to her ear. "What I said last night about watching your weight? I was kidding. You know that, right? If anything, you could stand a few more pounds. Not that you need them. You're pretty much perfect like you are."

Her jaw dropped. Warmth flooded her chest. He was . . . amazing. With one speaking look he'd taken down Adrianna, and now he'd called her, Victoria Westin, perfect. She couldn't find any words.

He poured some orange juice, put the glass in her free hand. "Drink that." She took a sip. Then he leaned in close again, and quietly, he began to hum.

It took her a moment, but when she recognized Cruella de Vil's theme song, Vicky lost it. Orange juice spurted, dribbling down her chin. Ty started laughing. So did she, blotting her chin with the napkin he handed her, laughing until her stomach hurt. Her mother glared at her, of course, but everyone else laughed along with them, not knowing why, simply catching their wave of amusement.

Ty's fingers tightened on hers again. This time, she squeezed back.

CHAPTER TEN

"FOUR HUNDRED EUROS." Adrianna dangled a silky pei-
gnoir. "I could get the same thing for half that in New
York."

"Then you should have bought it in New York." Vicky
flipped through the rack. "I don't understand why you
waited until you were over here anyway. We could be sitting at a café now, drinking lattes and watching gorgeous
Frenchmen stroll by."

Adrianna arched one perfectly shaped brow. "Since
when are you interested in man watching?"

Vicky arched a brow back at her. "Since I was thirteen. Just because I didn't share it with you doesn't mean
I wasn't interested."

Adrianna continued to eye her. "Your attitude today
leaves much to be desired."

Ignoring her, Vicky pulled out a gauzy number, held it
up at arm's length.

Adrianna shook her head. "Isabelle is silk or satin."

"How do you know what Isabelle is? And isn't it a little
creepy for you to be buying fuckwear for your daughter-
in-law?"

Adrianna inhaled sharply. "Where did *that* language come from?" Her eyes narrowed. "It's that Tyrell Brown, isn't it? This foolish charade is throwing you together too much."

"Ty's never used the term 'fuckwear.'" Vicky said it again for shock value. "He's actually very nice." It was almost worth putting up with him just to get under her mother's skin.

Adrianna sniffed. "He's a *cowboy*. A *Texan*, for heaven's sake."

"He's also smart and funny. And he can be a whole lot kinder than the men I've met in New York." When he wants to be, she added to herself. When he wants to be, he can be amazing.

Her mother's eyes narrowed. "Do *not* get involved with him, Victoria. Remember that our client's appeal is on the line here. And remember that I'm tolerating this facade only on the condition that you reconcile with Winston."

"I haven't forgotten about the appeal." How could she, when it hung over her head like a storm cloud? "But *your* memory is obviously slipping, because I didn't promise to reconcile with Winston. I said I'd give him another chance to convince me he's not pond slime. If he doesn't succeed"—and he wouldn't—"we won't be reconciling."

"Victoria—"

Out on the plaza, the church bell began to toll noon. Vicky headed for the door. "I'll go tell Lil you'll be joining us after you pay for the fuckwear."

Outside, the plaza bustled with pedestrians crisscrossing the cobblestones, poking into shops, settling down for lunch under the brightly colored awnings that shaded the tables at every café. Brilliant sunlight bounced off windows, and off the tourists' pricey sunglasses.

They'd arranged to meet Lil at one of the cafés for lunch. Vicky found her in the farthest seat from the street, still wearing her hat and sunglasses despite being almost invisible in the awning's deepest shade. So far, she'd kept her pregnancy out of the press, but in a world where cell phones turned everyone into paparazzi, it was only a matter of time.

"I ordered sparkling water," Lil said, greeting her with a smile, "but please go ahead and order wine. I'm jealous, but I'll deal with it."

"Okay, twist my arm." Vicky signaled for a *pichet* with two glasses.

"Cute sundress."

"Thanks." It was daffodil with interlocking white rings, and white spaghetti straps that left her shoulders bare. Vicky shook back her unbound hair, enjoying the sweep of it across her skin.

"I remember sundresses," Lil said. "Like I remember wine. And coffee." She gave a rueful smile, shifted her hips into a more comfortable position. "So. Ty told Jack the whole story. The trial. The fake flirtation. How's it going?"

Vicky bit her lip, deciding how much to say. Lil seemed nice, but still. Ty was Jack's best friend, Isabelle's former boyfriend, and he was close to Lil as well. Vicky wasn't inclined to share her conflicting thoughts about him.

"I guess you could say I'm making the best of it. It really pisses off my mother, so that's a plus."

"Why is she pissed? Will there be a problem because of the case?"

"It's hard to say. She's afraid I'll succumb to Ty's charms, which would definitely be a conflict of interest. Completely unethical. We'd have to withdraw from handling the appeal. But since that isn't going to happen, the only possible problem would be if someone back in the States found out that we're sharing a house with him. That would create the appearance of impropriety—which is lawyer talk for 'It would look bad'—so we'd have to withdraw anyway." She shrugged. "But it's unlikely anyone will find out, so I don't foresee any problems on that front."

"Sounds complicated."

Vicky smiled. "Lawyers make everything sound complicated. That way we can charge more. But it boils down to this. Sharing a house *looks* bad; sex *is* bad. But since sex is *not* going to happen, there really isn't anything to worry about."

The waiter brought their drinks. Vicky took a sip of the delicious house red. "Mmm. Feels decadent to drink wine this early in the day."

"Not decadent. French." Lil cast a longing look at Vicky's glass, then poured more sparkling water. "So, if the case won't be a problem, why is your mother pissed?"

"Because she's afraid I'm going to fall for Ty, and she wants me back together with my former fiancé."

"The cheating snake oil salesman?"

Vicky sputtered her wine. "How'd you know?"

"That's how Ty described him. Why does she want you back together with him?"

It was a question she often asked herself. "She claims it's for financial security, so I won't have to struggle like she did. And she did struggle, I know that. My dad came from an old, established family that ran through its money a few generations ago. He was a lawyer and he gave us a nice life, but when he died, all he left was some life insurance. Mother had to get a job."

Vicky took another sip. "She grew up with the country club set. Never expected to work, much less support a child on her own. So she got married again pretty quickly—mostly for financial reasons—and used the life insurance to put herself through law school. When she graduated—summa cum laude—she went to work for the firm where my dad had worked. And she cut husband number two loose."

She shrugged a shoulder. "I know that sounds mercenary. But I can't judge her too hard because she did it, at least in part, for me." She twisted her lips. "But numbers three and four, they're on her. I could never understand why she married either one of them. All I know is that it wasn't for money. She's made plenty of her own by working hard and investing well."

She shrugged again. "Maybe she was lonely, I don't know. But whatever her reasons were, I keep reminding her that it's the twenty-first century and I'm already a lawyer. I don't need a man to take care of me. And I certainly don't need a cheating snake oil salesman."

She cut a glance at Lil. "Sorry to unload on you."

"Hey, I know what it's like when a parent interferes in your love life. My uncle Pierre wasn't always a fan of Jack's. He had someone else in mind for me, someone he thought would take care of me." She shrugged. "He came around eventually, and now we're closer than ever. I hope that happens for you and your mother too. Try to remember that she wouldn't be butting in if she didn't love you."

Vicky stifled a snort. "That's hard to believe when she's trying to control me. And she's *always* trying to control me." She glanced toward the lingerie shop. "Here she comes." She topped off her wine. "I like this drinking with lunch thing. Now if I can just get her drunk too . . ."

She filled Adrianna's glass, slid it in front of her as she sat down.

"Hello, Lilianne." Adrianna tucked her shopping bag between her feet, quirked that damn eyebrow at Vicky. "Wine with lunch?"

"When in France . . ." Vicky saluted with her glass, then took another pull.

"Hmm." Adrianna took a delicate sip. "Very nice. For house wine."

"The house wines are usually local," Lil said. "They're often as good as any on the wine list."

"I'm sure you're right, dear." Adrianna sounded anything but sure, and Vicky's jaw clenched. If her mother insulted Lil . . .

But Adrianna relaxed into her chair. The waiter appeared and they ordered omelets and frites. As he walked away, Vicky found herself staring at his ass. Nice and tight. Like Ty's.

Oh God, where did that come from? Maybe she should lay off the wine. Every time she got buzzed she started lusting after him. It wasn't fair that he was hot. Hot and annoying. Annoyingly hot.

She took another swallow.

Adrianna and Lil began talking pregnancy. She tuned them out, let her gaze wander around the plaza, soaking in the colors. Window boxes overflowed with geraniums in scarlet and salmon and white; parti-colored umbrellas shaded groups of tourists drinking wine and eating omelets at the tables across the way.

What a lovely way to spend an afternoon.

Then Adrianna mentioned Ty's name. Vicky's ears perked up. This couldn't be good.

" . . . close friends with your husband?"

Lil nodded. "Jack and Ty go way back. Jack's parents had a place in the hill country, not far from Ty's ranch."

"Yes, I heard about his ranch. Growing up in the East, I can't quite picture it." Adrianna's voice lilted at the end, making it a question.

"It's a big operation," said Lil. Vicky heard pride in her tone. "His parents built it up from practically nothing, with help from Ty and his brother, Cody. Then his folks retired and Cody left for med school—he's a doctor in Boston now—and Ty took over the whole thing. He runs a lot of cattle and about thirty head of horses, prime bloodstock. The ranch house is a hundred years old, very traditional and really lovely. He and Lissa were updating it when she died."

"Did you know her?"

"No, but Jack did and he told me a lot about her."

"But you're friendly with Brown? He seems like an interesting man." Adrianna lilted again.

Lil smiled. "If you've talked to Ty for ten minutes you know all there is to know about him. He's funny, loyal, hardworking—though he likes to pretend he's lazy. And he's brilliant. When he finished his Ph.D., UT offered him an assistant professorship. He thought about it because he really liked teaching, but in the end, he couldn't bring himself to leave the ranch. Even though he's lonely there." She looked down at her glass. "Maybe I shouldn't say that out loud, but it's not a secret."

No, it wasn't. With everything else Tyrell was—and Vicky could add a few things to the list, like sarcastic, irritating, and, okay, sexy—his loneliness underlay it all. Beneath his easygoing manner, he held himself just a little bit apart.

Except when they were dancing. Then he was fully present. Not to mention erect.

"So young to lose his wife," her mother was saying. "I know how hard that is. I lost my husband when I was twenty-seven. If not for Victoria, I don't know if I could have gone on."

Vicky's eyes widened. Her mother sounded sincere, even emotional. The wine must be hitting her, because she never spoke about her feelings. At least not to her daughter.

Lil bought into it, tearing up. "Sorry, I'm a faucet these days." She dabbed her eyes with her napkin, placed the other hand on her stomach, fingers spread protectively. "I cry over commercials. And forget the news, Jack won't let me watch it anymore. It takes him an hour to quiet me down."

"I was the same way with both of mine. It's the hormones, it passes." Adrianna patted Lil's hand as Vicky looked on, amazed. Who was this woman, and what had she done with Cruella de Vil?

"Anyway," Lil went on, "Ty's a great guy. The best." She smiled through misty eyes. "If I'd met him first, I probably would've fallen in love with him. He's sweet and thoughtful. One of those guys who treats every woman like a princess."

Vicky waited for the punch line. When it didn't come, she stifled a snort. At no time had Tyrell Brown ever treated her like a princess, at least not when he wasn't faking it for an audience. Maybe pregnancy was affecting Lil's memory.

Or maybe Ty really hated her. Maybe those fleeting moments when he'd been sweet were completely phony.

Maybe . . . no, *definitely* . . . she shouldn't believe a single word he said.

"NOT BAD FOR a guy who hasn't slept in twenty-four hours." Ricky handed off his clubs to the caddy. He'd arrived at the chateau just as they were leaving for the golf course.

"Saved our asses," Ty said, sincerely. He'd paired with Ricky, who'd led them to a three-stroke victory over Jack and Matt. "I never could play worth a damn, and I've gotten worse with age."

Matt was too pleased with life to care that his best man

had beaten him. "Get you next time," he said, clapping Ricky's back. "Let's head back to the chateau. The chef's whipping up some fancy sandwiches."

"What's the plan for tonight?" Ricky wanted to know.

"Rehearsal at six," Matt said, leading the way to the parking lot. "Hors d'oeuvres at eight at a restaurant in town. Open bar. Some kind of fancy cake. Isabelle set it all up, so it'll be great."

Back at the chateau, Ty grabbed a jambon and brie panini and a shower. Then he dug out his iPad and headed down to find a shady spot in the garden and check his e-mail. His foreman, Joe, ran the ranch with minimal interference from the boss, but occasionally things came up that Ty needed to know about. And he liked to keep tabs on his folks. Make sure they hadn't been arrested.

The day was unseasonably warm. Cutting through the kitchen, he got his hands on a cold beer, then ambled out onto the terrace.

And stopped in his tracks.

Annemarie lay stretched out on a chaise, sunning herself in a hot pink bikini the size of two Cheez-Its and a Triscuit. A half-empty pitcher of sangria sweated on the table beside her.

Spotting him before he could retreat, she sat up abruptly, breasts bouncing like basketballs. Expecting— okay, hoping for—a clothing malfunction, he froze, not daring to blink. But her spaghetti straps must have concealed steel cables, because they didn't snap like they should have under that kind of strain.

Eventually the jiggling subsided and he noticed that she'd pushed her lip out. "I have been waiting for you, chéri." She held out a tube of sunscreen. "You must do my back so I can turn over."

It was the oldest trick in the book, but what was a red-blooded man to do? He sat down beside her on the chaise and squirted some into his palm.

With both hands, she lifted her hair, and he smeared his hands across her silky shoulders, down her back, all the way down, to where her hot pink thong disappeared into the crack of her firm, round ass. Then up, up, and over the top of her shoulders, not quite as far as her breasts. Then down her sides, fingertips barely skimming the swells.

She was built for sin, and in his mind he was already halfway to hell when she reached behind her back to untie her top. That brought him to his senses. He caught her hand.

"Whoa there, honey. Let's keep it G-rated. Or PG, anyhow."

"But the string will leave a line," she pouted. "Men don't want to see a white line when I'm dancing."

"Believe me, sugar, when you're dancing, all eyes'll be up front."

"Then you should do my breasts," she said, and before he knew it, she'd pulled his greased-up hands around her and pushed them up underneath the Cheez-Its.

To his everlasting shame, he didn't pull them out. Not right away. Instead, he let his mind go blank. Didn't resist when her palms flattened over his and she slid them around, feeling herself up with his hands. Squeezing those jumbo jugs. Kneading them. Tweaking them.

And damned if they weren't the real thing! His lips curved smugly. The golf course money had been on silicone, with Matt promising to pry the truth out of Isabelle. Well, now he knew.

Annemarie looked over her shoulder at him, eyes smoldering, lips curving invitingly.

He knew he had to turn her down. But then she touched her tongue to her lips and he gave himself another minute.

Would have given himself a few more too, if laughter hadn't drifted through the door. It jolted him like a shot of adrenaline. Whipping his hands out of Annemarie's top, he jumped up like a schoolboy caught with his first *Penthouse*, sprinted for the farm table, and flung himself into a chair, pretending to read his iPad.

Lil came through the door first, followed by Vicky. No sign of Cruella. Thank God for small favors. They exchanged hellos with Annemarie, who was packing up her things in a huff. Then Lil pulled out the chair across from him and plopped down with a heavy sigh.

He tsked at her. "Don't let Jack know you tired yourself out."

She rolled her eyes. "Where is he?"

"Upstairs napping."

"Isabelle?"

"In her room. With Matt."

"Ah." She pointed at his iPad. "Can I check my e-mail?"

"Sure." He passed it to her.

"Eww. What's on it?" She set it on the table. "It's all greasy."

He wiped his palms on his jeans. "Must be mayo. I had a sandwich." The last part was true.

"Did you stick your hand in the jar? Because this thing is covered with it." She dug out a tissue, swiped the screen.

"You're smearing it around. Give it here." He stuck his hand up inside his T-shirt, used it to clean the screen. "There, good as new."

He eyed Vicky, strolling toward the fountain. She stumbled a step, and he said, "Guess you gals hit the wine at lunch."

"*They* did," Lil mumbled, scrolling through her messages. "Yours truly made do with bottled water."

Vicky picked her way through the flowerbed that

ringed the fountain, then sat down abruptly on the edge. Ty snorted. "Hell, I better go keep her from falling in."

That brought Lil's head up. "You be careful with her, Ty. She's got enough to deal with right now."

He put on a pained face. "Why does everyone assume I'm out to hurt her?"

"I don't think you'd *deliberately* hurt her. You don't have it in you to hurt anyone."

Now he tried to look offended. "I'll have you know, I've put my share of rednecks in the hospital."

"You know what I mean. Winston did a number on her. I'd hate to see her heart get broken again this weekend."

His offended look was sincere this time. "If it gets broken it won't be by me."

Leaving her with his iPad, he strolled across the grass and sat down beside Vicky, the narrow edge of the marble fountain digging into his butt. Behind them, water jetted from Cupid's lips, splashing into the pool. Droplets bounced up, speckling Ty's skin just above his jeans and dotting Vicky's sundress.

"You're getting wet," he said, sitting on his hand so he wouldn't brush the drops from her back.

She'd been smiling up at the fair-weather clouds. Now she turned to look at him, still smiling her dreamy smile. The blue of her eyes matched the sky above them. He really was a sucker for blue eyes.

"I don't mind," was all she said. Her eyes wandered down. "What happened to your shirt?"

He glanced down at the greasy smear. "Got some mayo on my iPad."

"Oh." In her present state, that seemed to satisfy her.

"Have fun shopping?"

She lifted her shoulders in an exaggerated shrug. "Mother bought Isabelle some fuckwear."

He snorted in surprise. "Fuckwear, huh? Get any for yourself?"

One corner of her mouth curved. "Wouldn't you like to know, Mr. Perpetual Hard-On."

He almost choked on that one. "How much did you have to drink, Victoria?" He sounded like Principal Danvers at the senior prom, but hell, she sounded like a drunken teenager. "Because if you're trying to shock me, forget it. I'm shockproof. Your mother, on the other hand, will lie down and give birth to a calf if she hears you talk like that."

She looked thoughtful. "Maybe that's why she went straight to her room. Think we should call a vet?"

"That does it." He hooked a hand under her arm and pulled her to her feet. "Time to go inside, honey. You need to sleep it off."

"But I like it here." Leaning over to drag a finger through the water, she would have toppled in if he hadn't had a grip on her.

"It's a pretty spot, all right," he said agreeably, humoring the drunk, "but there's nothing like a drowning to ruin a wedding."

He headed for the house, alternately towing and prodding her along with him. "Bye, Lil!" she called, waving as they passed her. He wagged his head in despair. Unless he was mistaken, she was actually getting drunker.

Wrapping an arm around her waist, he coaxed her up the stairs. "That's right, honey, one foot in front of the other." He maneuvered her down the hallway. "Here's your room."

She pointed at his door. "That's your room," she informed him.

"Don't I know it, sugar. And it made for a real long night, knowing you were right across the hall." He propelled her through her door.

"We could have a pajama party."

"Don't tempt me, honey." He sat her on the bed. It was bigger than his, and the bedspread was ridiculously soft. She flopped back, one arm above her head, hair floating in a silky cloud around her.

She smiled up at him. He smiled back.

Time slowed to a crawl.

His eyes trailed down her body. The column of her throat. Her chest, rising and falling.

Her sundress had hiked halfway up her thighs. His gaze traveled down her long, lean legs. Dancer's legs. Then wandered up to her face again.

She sure was a beauty, with her cheeks flushed pink and that come-hither look in her sleepy baby blues. He realized he was holding her hand, his thumb rubbing circles in the hollow of her palm. She blinked, slowly, her heavy-lidded eyes telling him she liked it.

They drew him in, those eyes. Next thing he knew, he was sitting on the edge of the bed. She gave his hand a little tug, almost imperceptible, but it brought him down on one elbow beside her. Her lips curved. She caught the bottom one between her teeth.

Releasing her hand, he drew his fingers lightly up her arm. Lingered on the pulse points, her wrist, the crook of her elbow. With one fingertip, he drew patterns on her shoulder. Her skin was softer than the bedspread, softer than kittens. He circled the shell of her ear, tapped her earring softly. Traced his finger along the line of her jaw.

Her eyes stayed on his. Her lips parted, glistening. She didn't look so dangerous now, his bitch on wheels. She looked like a woman who liked what he was doing and wanted him to do more.

He could do more. He could do lots more.

Cupping her cheek, he stroked her bottom lip with his thumb. Her tongue poked out, licked the pad, and she might as well have licked his cock. He went hard as iron. His own lips parted, and with his eyes locked on hers, afloat in that deep blue sea, he dropped his head and kissed her.

His kiss was gentle, not demanding, and she kissed him back the same way, toying with his tongue, stroking it, sucking it lightly, while his thudding heart thumped harder. Her fingers curled around his biceps; they jumped and quivered in response. Her thumb swiped over the curve of the muscle, and primal male instinct made him flex it so it bulged.

Her palm slid up, up, inside his sleeve, curving over his shoulder, exploring. Jacking his pulse even higher. Her lips moved with his, soft, eager, letting him lead, driving him crazy with one gentle hand, one tame kiss.

She rolled toward him, just a bit, just enough to encourage him, and he stroked his hand down her side, inch by slow inch, his thumb skimming the swell of her breast, his palm curving with the indent of her waist, then rising over the crest of her hip, sloping down to linger on her bare thigh, where the long, smooth muscles shivered at his touch.

Then back up he stroked, his thumb dipping under her hem, sliding her dress up, higher, until his palm covered her hip again, nothing between his skin and hers but a band of lace no wider than his finger.

Her hand coasted down his arm, nails lightly scraping along his triceps, following his forearm until her hand covered his. He stilled, waiting. But she didn't pull it away, she scratched it instead, and his pulse skipped. From deep in her throat came a humming sound; it vibrated through his body like a tuning fork.

His fingers slid up under the strip of lace so his wide palm splayed on her hip, then he followed the curve of her ass until one round cheek filled his hand. She lifted her thigh, hooked her knee over his hip, and he used his handful of ass to tug her against him. His breath quickened, his kiss deepened. His cock strained against denim, trying to reach her.

Then his fingertips touched liquid heat, and he lost his head completely.

Rolling on top of her, he ground his cock to her mound, lifting her hip as she locked her leg around him. His other hand drove into her hair. He tangled his fingers in yellow silk, fisting it like a caveman. Dragged his lips across her cheek, scraped her jaw with his teeth as she threw back her head, opening her throat to his starving mouth.

His teeth snapped the strap of her dress, peeled back the cotton, and exposed her pale breast, the pink nipple hard as a nail. She arched her back, offering it up, and he released her hair to palm it, sucking the nipple into his mouth, rolling it with his tongue. She rucked up his shirt, raked his back with her nails, moaning for more, more.

Yes, oh yes. He could give her more. He dropped his hand to his jeans, yanked open the button, dragged at the zipper.

And then Isabelle's laughter rang out in the hallway.

His hand froze. His lips too.

Isabelle had warned him to be careful with Vicky. Her definition of "careful" absolutely would not include drunk sex. If she found him here now, she'd skin him.

With superhuman effort, he pushed up on his hands. Took one long last look into the sex-glazed eyes staring up at him. Let his gaze roam down to the perfect breast that fit his palm like it was cast from the mold.

Then he heaved himself to his feet. Zipped his zipper. Buttoned his button.

The dreamy eyes clouded. The perfect brow knotted. "What—" she began.

He did Principal Danvers again. "You should be

ashamed of yourself, Victoria Westin, taking advantage of a man in my condition. Your brother must've told you I had some beers with lunch. You figured my defenses were down. That I'd lose my wits if you showed a little tit."

Her jaw dropped. He forged ahead. "Well, that might work on your city boys, sugar, but my mama taught me to respect myself, even when I've had a few."

He backed toward the door as he spun his bullshit. Reaching behind him, he found the knob. "Now you stay in here for a while, have yourself a time-out, and think about what kind of woman you want to be. The kind who shows compassion for a man who's drunk a little more than he should, or a hussy who tries to get into his pants. Because, honey, we both know which one you're acting like today."

And with a last disgusted wag of his head, he closed the door behind him.

HE WAS FULL of shit, and Vicky knew it. He wasn't one bit drunk.

But then, neither was she.

Well, maybe she was a teeny bit buzzed. But what in the world had possessed her to pretend she was really drunk?

Probably his smug expression as he swaggered toward her in the garden, perfectly male and supremely coordinated, after she'd almost nose-dived into the fountain when the heels of her silly but adorable sandals sank into the flowerbed.

Better he think her drunk than clumsy.

Then, unexpectedly, instead of teasing her about it, he seemed concerned. Caring. It made her go all warm and fuzzy inside. So she played up the whole drunk thing. Let him into her bedroom. Lured him down on her bed.

And when warm and fuzzy turned into hot and horny, well, it was easy to keep on playing drunk. To have an excuse for kissing him. After all, what harm could it do to see how he tasted? If his lips were as soft as they looked. If he smelled as good, felt as good as she thought he would. And he had. Clean and fresh, like a shower; hard and muscled, like a man.

And he tasted, oh, he tasted like . . . more.

She flattened her palm on her stomach. She could still feel his weight, pinning her to the bed. With her other hand she cupped her bare breast. Stroked her thumb over the nipple, still damp from his mouth.

If he'd gotten them naked, she would have let him inside. Taken him deep. She'd be riding him now, at this very moment. She squeezed her breast. Slid her other hand lower to cup her wetness. Sucked a ragged breath through her teeth.

She'd never, ever wanted anyone the way she wanted Tyrell.

The jackass.

She sat up abruptly, raked both hands through her hair. God, she was pathetic. After bending Lil's ear with her big talk about ethics, she would've shucked those very ethics right along with her panties if Isabelle hadn't shown up. Even now, when Ty had taken his lips and his hands and his hard-on and left her alone to contemplate her own weakness, her biggest regret was that she'd lost her one chance to do it with him without taking responsibility. She'd never pull off the fake-drunk act again. He'd catch on. He was an idiot, but he wasn't stupid.

The sad truth was that she'd missed her free shot. Now she'd never have sex with Tyrell Brown.

CHAPTER ELEVEN

TY DUG THROUGH his armoire, pulled out the tailored black suit Isabelle designed for him two years earlier and the sapphire shirt she gave him to go with it. It was all top of the line, red-carpet wear. Even the French would approve.

He tossed the whole pile on the bed.

Dragging his T-shirt up over his head, he blew out a weary sigh. He'd already changed clothes three times that day, from yoga gear to golf wear, then into his usual jeans and T-shirt, and once more thanks to the sunscreen smear that even he realized was unacceptable. Now it was cocktail party duds.

The only consolation was that Isabelle would get weepy when she saw him in the suit. And Vicky's mouth would water. He smiled. She'd only seen him in his court suit, the one he'd stuffed in the trash compactor after the trial . . .

The trial. His smile evaporated.

How could he have forgotten? How could he have forgotten that just forty-eight hours ago Victoria Westin—Victoria Westin of the perfect breasts and pink cheeks and sleepy blue eyes, the same woman he'd dry-humped just hours ago on her bed across the hall—accused him of cutting off Lissa's life support? Of letting her starve, letting her suffocate, for Christ's sake!

And now here he was, still half hard, dressing up for her, hoping she'd drool over him. Hoping she'd fuck him.

Self-loathing coated his skin like slime. It slithered down his back, soaked the roots of his hair. How could he live with himself? It was bad enough he had to *pretend* to be attracted to her; he couldn't let himself *actually* want her.

His cell phone chimed, the tone that meant Joe was calling from the ranch. He made himself focus. It had to be important for Joe to call.

"Hey, Joe. What's up?"

"Oh, hey Ty. How's it going?"

Joe was a slow talker, and Ty was short on patience. He started to pace.

"It's going great. Now what's up?"

"Um, well, I thought you'd want to know. Clancy came by this morning to look at Brescia."

Ty stopped walking. "What's wrong with Brescia?" She was his most loved horse, and Clancy was the vet.

"Well," Joe drawled out, "Clancy's not a hundred percent sure . . ."

Ty's patience snapped. "Damn it, Joe! Spit it out before I reach through this phone and pull it out."

Joe gulped audibly and got to the point. "Probably bloodworms. He took some samples, sent them to the lab."

"How the hell did she get bloodworms?" They could be fatal.

"Can't say for sure. But Molly Tucker's got them over to her place . . ."

Shit. Molly Tucker. He'd known that was a mistake even as he bent her over her sofa.

"Those two bay mares of hers'll be okay," Joe was

saying, "but the gray gelding, well, Clancy says he likely won't make it. He's got some age on him."

Ty swallowed. He'd left Brescia in the paddock with the docile gray while he'd been banging Molly. "But he can't be more than thirteen or fourteen."

Which was just about Brescia's age. Lissa had rescued her nine years ago, when Brescia was five or six. He'd always figured she'd live another ten years, or even longer.

Now she could die of some damn parasite. Because he couldn't keep his pants zipped.

He made himself ask more questions while guilt ate a hole in his stomach. But Joe was out of information. Ty let him ramble about other things for a minute, then cut him off.

His throat was raw when he barked out his parting orders. "You take good care of Brescia, you hear? And tell Clancy to call me the minute he gets the labs."

THE PRIVATE ROOM at Le Cirque was barely large enough to contain the fifty guests who'd arrived for what was shaping up to be a pre-wedding wedding reception. Except for the few who'd been at the chateau the previous evening, Vicky didn't know any of them.

"Hey, babe." Ricky dropped a brotherly kiss on her cheek. "You look like a million bucks."

"You think so?" She did a little spin that flared her cocktail dress, a shimmery scrap of black silk that fell two inches above her knees, held up by flimsy black-sequined straps. A narrow band of sequins edged the neckline too, curving just below her collarbones in front, then dipping daringly below her waist in back. Five-inch Manolo Blahniks jacked her up to runway height.

Ricky looked her up and down. "Nah, I was wrong. A billion bucks."

She laughed, feeling pretty. Her hair, loosely piled on

top of her head and strategically bobby-pinned to look like a casual afterthought, bared her neck and, not coincidentally, showed off diamond drop earrings so stunning that women actually gasped when they saw them, the only gift she hadn't returned to Winston when she broke their engagement.

She'd used a heavier hand on her makeup too. Not Annemarie-heavy, but she'd dabbed on some sooty eye shadow, a few swipes of mascara, and an extra stroke of blush, and dug out her seldom-used fuck-me-dead-red lipstick.

She gave him an exaggerated eye-walk in turn. "Look who's talking, Mr. GQ." As tall as Matt and all-American handsome, Ricky looked terrific in a dark gray suit with a barely detectable pinstripe. For the umpteenth time she wished she could have fallen in love with him back when he had a slavish high-school crush on her. He was long over it, and she was glad of his friendship. But sometimes she missed all that worship and devotion.

They stood together comfortably, sipping their drinks and scanning the room, commenting on the stylish French couples.

Then Ricky sputtered his beer. "Holy shit. Check that out."

Annemarie had made her entrance. Or rather her chest had made an entrance, stopping conversations around the room.

After a brief pause in the doorway for effect, she sailed forth like the *QE2*, effortlessly parting the sea.

"They can't be real," Ricky marveled. "They just can't."

"That dress is the eighth wonder of the world," muttered Vicky. Mostly gauze except for satin swaths covering ass and boobs, it somehow concealed a suspension system worthy of the Brooklyn Bridge.

"Underwire," Lil said, as she and Jack appeared beside them. "Isabelle tells me you can work miracles with it.

And keeping those up off her knees all night will definitely take a miracle."

Jack sipped his whiskey, said casually, "Isabelle happen to mention if they're real?"

Lil gave him the beady eye. "You've got money on this, don't you?"

Jack looked innocent. She stared him down until he shrugged. "Twenty on fake." With a pointed look, he threw Ricky under the bus too.

Vicky snorted. "Seriously? You *bet* on her *boobs*?"

Ricky tossed up his hands. "Don't look at me, I didn't start it."

"Who did?"

He jigged his head at Ty, who'd chosen that moment to cross the threshold.

Vicky's eyes slitted. Lil snorted. Jack grinned and waved him over.

Vicky tried not to watch as he ambled their way, handing out smiles to the other guests, looking unfairly incredible in a beautifully tailored suit. His sapphire shirt—which some woman must have handpicked for him—was open at the throat, setting off his tanned skin and sun-streaked hair. He could have been on a billboard advertising expensive whiskey, a slinky woman hanging from each arm, the image of privileged debauchery.

It wasn't fair. It. Was. Not. Freaking. Fair.

"Well, Ty," Lil said before he could get a word out, "where's your money? Real or fake?"

He didn't even have the decency to blush. "As a firm believer in a beneficent God, I put my twenty on the genuine article." Lil and Vicky snorted in unison. "I take that to mean you girls aren't believers. Well, it's not too late to put your money where your mouth is."

Lil reached into her purse and pulled out a twenty. Not to be outdone, Vicky opened her own purse. "All I've got is a fifty." She fanned it at Ty. "Too rich for your blood?"

"Not at all. You can give it to your brother, he's holding the bets."

"*Matt?*" She couldn't believe it. "He's getting married tomorrow!"

"He's still got eyes in his head. And in case you're wondering, his money's on fake too."

"So you're the only one betting on real?" She smirked. "Inside information?"

He smiled easily. "Years of experience."

That was undoubtedly true. He'd probably handled hundreds of breasts of all shapes and sizes. After all, he'd gotten his hands on hers less than twenty-four hours after he'd walked through the door. And she didn't even like him.

The look on his face said he knew what she was thinking. He dipped his head so only she could hear. "I knew yours were real."

Her cheeks heated, but she summoned a "duh" look. "When I decide to pay money," she said like he was a dunce, "I'll go bigger than B-cups."

His eyes flew wide open. His jaw unhinged. Then he grabbed her arm so quickly she gasped, and with a muttered "Excuse us," he hustled her across the room.

Too stunned at first to say a word, she found her voice as he propelled her into the lobby. "What the *hell* are you doing?" she hissed. "Let go of my arm!"

Ignoring her, he spotted the coatroom, unused on this balmy evening. He bustled her inside and shut the door.

She shook her arm free. "Are you *out* of your *mind*?"

"Are *you*?" he shot back. "You can't seriously be thinking of a boob job." He made it a statement.

In fact, she'd never once considered a boob job, but she wouldn't tell him that now. Instead, she glared. "And why not?"

"Because they're fine like they are, that's why not." His eyes dropped to the B-cups in question. His jaw hardened. "Shit."

Instinctively, she backed up. He followed her. Her back hit the door.

His left hand flattened on the door beside her head, half caging her. His gaze roved up, along her throat, to her lips, parted in surprise. "Fuck." He squeezed it out through gritted teeth.

He was wired, more tense than usual. Electricity sizzled just under his skin. She held her breath as his right hand came up. With the back of his knuckles, he grazed her breast through the thin silk of her dress. Her nipple hardened to a nub.

Over it he skimmed. Again, and again. Then he opened his palm and cupped her, his thumb drawing a tight circle over the peak.

Her breath hitched. She put out her tongue to wet her lips. And his eyes, already dark, went black. His mouth, those full and luscious lips, opened just a little. A whisper came out. "Fuck."

And then he was on her, kissing her, and it wasn't gentle like before, but hard and greedy. His hand kneaded her breast; his other hand dropped to her hip, fingers digging into her ass, yanking her pelvis against his rock-hard erection.

She knew she should stop him. Now, before it was too late. And she would. She would. But first she had to get her hands inside his jacket, slide them over the muscles bunching in his back, his shoulders. Oh God, he was hard everywhere, and she was burning up, kissing him like she'd never kissed anyone, putting her whole body into it, lips and tongue, grinding against him.

Releasing her breast, he flattened her to the door with his chest, his groin, his rigid thighs. His fingers dug into her hair, bobby pins pinging on the floor as he tore it apart. His other hand slid from her hip to her thigh, bunching her dress until he found her skin. His thumb hooked her panties.

This was it. She moaned in her throat.

He dragged his lips across her cheek, rasped in her ear. "Please tell me you've got a condom in that bag."

"No. No!" It was both an answer and a cry.

A shudder ran through his body. He muttered a curse, flattened his palms on the door.

And then he took a giant step back.

Her dress dropped into place; her arms fell to her sides. Furious, frustrated, she fisted her hands in black silk. "Damn you, Tyrell Brown! I can't believe you don't have a condom on you!"

TY RAKED HIS fingers through his hair, dragging it back from his face till it hurt.

"What do you mean, you can't believe it?" he squeezed out through his teeth. Jesus, he was hard as a spike.

"Aren't you supposed to be some big lover? You and Jack McCabe, cutting a swath through Texas? Girls tearing your clothes off whenever you turn around!" She waved her arms. "So why don't you have a freaking condom in your pocket?"

He steadied himself with a hand on the wall. Closed his eyes. Christ, he was actually in pain.

And Vicky, she was hyperventilating. She'd kept her voice down so far, but in a minute she'd be raving. A minute after that, Matt would be crashing the door, Adrianna right behind him.

He really didn't need that now, with guilt and worry gnawing his guts, and hunger for this woman strangling his balls.

Opening his eyes, he forced himself to look at her. And

the sight almost undid him. Flushed face, tumbled hair, wrinkled dress—she was so fucking hot. Another shudder ran through him.

With an effort, he grabbed ahold of his frustration, turned it into something he could use.

"As a matter of fact," he informed her, "I usually do carry a condom. But I didn't think I'd need one tonight. I thought you'd be able to control yourself."

"*Me?*" Her voice squeaked. "This is on *you*! You dragged me in here like some . . . some *caveman*, and started feeling me up, *again*, knowing full well that you weren't prepared. That's . . ." She flapped her arms again. "That's *irresponsible*!"

"*You're* calling *me* irresponsible?" He held up a finger. "First you fish for compliments by threatening a boob job. Then, when you've got me all worked up about it, you shove your tongue down my throat. As if you didn't know where *that* would lead." He pointed the finger at her. "And all along you knew you weren't prepared. Now *that's* irresponsible."

Red flags stained her cheeks. She filled her lungs to let him have it . . . and his eyes dropped to her breasts again. The angry points of her nipples thrust toward him accusingly.

"Shit," he breathed out. He took a step toward her.

She yanked the door open and ran.

LOCKING HERSELF IN a stall, Vicky opened her compact to survey the damage.

Oh God. Hair half up, half down; bobby pins askew. Puffy clown lips ringed with lipstick smears. And that was just the visible damage. The mirror didn't show her sexual-frustration stomachache or the soggy panties that would make sitting down impossible.

Galling as it was to admit, even to herself, Tyrell Brown

knew exactly how to get under her skin. He was a sexy menace, and if she didn't get a grip, she'd walk out of the ladies' room and drag him straight back into the coat-room.

Breathe, she told herself. In to a four count, out to a four count. In. Out.

Someone came into the room, peed, washed up, touched up, and left, and still she breathed. Another minute passed. Another.

Finally, when her heart slowed to normal, she began the business of putting herself back together; removing the rest of the bobby pins and finger-combing her hair into some semblance of order, wiping her lips with a clump of toilet paper and reapplying her lipstick.

Stepping out of the stall, she checked her dress in the mirror. Wrinkled, of course. But how could it not be, after Ty's long, hot body crushed her to the door . . . ?

She slapped her own cheek. Enough, already! Enough of behaving like one of his brainless bimbos, another helpless victim of his sexual mojo. For God's sake, he'd barely touched her breast and she'd kicked her vaunted ethics to the curb. How humiliating.

Well, she wasn't going *there* again. She was smart, she was savvy, and if she could just remember that and steer clear of him for the next thirty-six hours, she could still get out of France with her dignity—and her professional integrity—intact.

Striding into the party with her lawyer face on, she spotted him standing at the bar with Jack, looking like they'd both just stepped off a movie set. Calmly, coolly, in full possession of herself, she whirled in the opposite direction.

And walked smack into Winston Churchill Banes.

CHAPTER TWELVE

VICKY STEPPED BACK. Blinked. Got her bearings.

And then she got royally pissed. "What are *you* doing here?"

Before Winston could answer, Adrianna stepped around him. "He's my guest."

Vicky gaped. "You *invited* him? Why would you do that to me?"

"So the two of you can talk things out. You broke off your engagement without giving him a chance to explain."

"Explain what? Why he was standing between my secretary's legs with his pants around his ankles? For God's sake, Mother, she left her *ass print* on my desk!"

"Victoria—" Winston's tone was plaintive.

She rolled right over him. "Does Matt know what you've done?"

Adrianna waved it off. "It's none of Matt's concern. Winston is my guest."

"Okay, fine." Vicky's voice shook. "If he's your guest, Mother, then you entertain him. I'm done here." And before either of them could utter another word, she turned on her heel and stalked from the room.

Out in the hallway, her composure crumbled. Blindly, she turned right, ran down an empty corridor until she found the back door. Hitting the crash bar with both hands, she burst out into the parking lot.

Darkness had fallen; the lot was deserted. Pacing between the cars, she sucked air through her teeth, wheezing like an asthmatic.

Not a heart attack, she told herself. Anxiety. She tried yoga breathing, but for once, it failed her. Her heel rolled on a stone, she stumbled against a BMW and the alarm whooped out. She leaped backward and her ass hit the hood of a Porsche. That alarm shrieked louder. The restaurant door flew open; voices pealed over the racket.

And in a stark flash of insight Vicky saw her future, cuffed in a squad car, struggling to explain to stoic policemen in her high school French exactly why she was pingponging around the parking lot in fuck-me heels.

She couldn't bear it. She simply could not bear it.

Sinking to a crouch, she slipped off her shoes and duckwalked between the cars, careful not to touch them. At the end of the row, she stole a glance over the hood of an Audi. The commotion centered around the Porsche, a handful of men gesturing and blabbing.

Heart tripping like a thief on the lam, she darted around the corner of the restaurant, and ran.

TY HAD SEEN Vicky the minute she'd entered the room, face flushed, lips swollen, hair mussed up and bedroomy. He'd looked away before she caught him staring.

Disgusted with himself, he slipped a hand in his pocket and adjusted his junk. He'd be hard all night until he got back to his room and finished himself off like the goddamn teenager he turned into around her.

"If you want her so bad," Jack drawled out, "what's stopping you?"

"I can't stand her, that's what." He didn't sound convincing, even to himself. "Besides, she's too much trouble."

"Well, if it's easy you're looking for, the stripper's locked and loaded. Grab yourself a handful. And you can settle the bet while you're at it."

"Hell, I can already settle the bet. They're the real deal."

"Well why didn't you say so?"

"Because Matt'll kill me. Then Isabelle'll dig me up and kill me again. And it wasn't even my fault." He sounded aggrieved. "She shoved my hands up inside that excuse for a bikini. Out in the garden, no less."

Jack broke into a grin. "No wonder you're such a mess. All that tit in your hand and nowhere to go with it." He waved Lil over, jerked a thumb at Ty. "He settled the bet."

"There's a surprise." She favored Ty with a smirk. "When did you squeeze that in? So to speak."

"This afternoon." He gave her a toothy grin. "That was her sunscreen on my iPad."

She shrank back. "For God's sake, Ty, I'm pregnant!" As she spoke, she dug out a travel-sized bottle of hand sanitizer, squirted some in her palm. "If you infected me with your germy hands—"

"Heads up," Jack cut in. "Incoming."

Ty turned, expecting to see Vicky. But it was Annemarie, bulldozing through the crowd. He groaned to himself as she latched on to his arm.

"Tyrell," she purred, rubbing one of the breasts in question against his biceps. "So handsome in your suit." She fingered his lapel.

"You're cutting a swath in that dress yourself." He slewed a glance around the room. Jack and Lil had already deserted him, but he waved Ricky over. "Sugar, I don't think you've met the best man. Ricky, this is Annemarie. She's a friend of Isabelle's."

Annemarie unloaded a slow, seductive smile on Ricky,

who was having a hard time keeping his eyes up on her face.

"Annemarie's studying anthropology at the Sorbonne," Ty added, peeling her fingers off his arm and nudging her gently toward the best man. "And she's got a real interesting sideline too."

She dragged her sexy smile away from Ricky and brought it back to Ty. Slowly, languorously, she blinked her dark, exotic eyes. He eased back a step.

"Ricky's in insurance. One of those too-big-to-fail deals. I'm sure you'll have lots to talk about." Another step back . . . and then he was moving, heading for the door.

He glanced around. No sign of Vicky, which was fine, since he wasn't looking for her anyway.

He spotted her mama, though, doing the cougar thing with some guy who had to be twenty years younger. Ty gave him a once-over. Tall, dark-haired. Good-looking in an old-money, never-got-his-hands-dirty kind of way. Probably stayed in shape playing polo, or squash. Ty smirked. The dude looked too arrogant for his own good, exactly how he pictured Winston . . .

Ty stopped walking. Narrowed his eyes for a closer look.

Damn it, Adrianna wasn't flirting with him. The guy's shoulders were stiff, his jaw set. He was pissed; Adrianna was placating him.

And Vicky had disappeared.

Could Cruella really be evil enough to blindside her daughter like that?

One way to find out. Putting on his swagger, he ambled into the eye of their hushed conversation.

"Adrianna, honey"—he laid on the down-home drawl— "where's that gorgeous daughter of yours? She promised to buy me a drink."

"I have no idea where she is, Mr. Brown." Her chilly tone should have turned her lips blue.

Ty kept smiling, playing the clueless Southern boy. Sticking out his hand, he said to the guy, "Tyrell Brown. How you doing?"

The guy shook briefly. "Winston Banes," he intoned.

"The ex?" Ty's brows winged up. "Vicky know you're here?"

Winston looked down his nose, which took some doing since Ty was the same height. "That's none of your business."

"Told you to fuck off, didn't she?" Ty's shit-eating grin was as good as a chest shove.

Winston's jaw clenched. He set his drink on the table.

"You sure you want to do that, Winnie?" Ty wagged his head slowly, egging him on. "I'll hand your ass to you." And wouldn't that be fun? With all the testosterone pumping through his veins, putting Winston in the hospital was the second best way Ty could think of to burn it off.

Winston flushed dark red. "You ignorant hillbilly. Who do you think you are?"

Ty hooked his thumbs in his pockets. "As a matter of fact, Winnie, I'm the man who just had his hand up Vicky's skirt." He wagged his head again, inviting mayhem. "Mmm-mmm. You must be crazy, trading in a fine piece of tail like that."

"You son of a bitch!" Winston shoved Ty hard, knocking him back a step and surprising a laugh out of him.

"Not bad, Winnie, my man." Shrugging off his jacket, Ty tossed it at a chair, then curled his fingers in a bring-it-on wiggle. "Come on, boy, let's have some fun."

Around them, a circle quickly opened as folks caught wind of a fight. Adrianna was shuffled to the rear, her protests falling on deaf ears as guests and waitstaff alike jockeyed for position.

Ty's mishmash of conflicting emotions had crystallized into one uncomplicated desire: to beat Winston black and blue. Dropping his cuff links in his pocket, he cracked his knuckles, grinning like a kid at Christmas.

Then Jack's heavy hand fell on his shoulder. "Ty. Not the place."

Ty shrugged him off. "Sure it is."

"Uh-uh. Isabelle'll kill you dead. And Lil'll dance on your bones."

Ty flicked a look past Jack, saw Isabelle fuming. "Aw, hell." His shoulders slumped. Women. They just didn't understand that a good fight made a great party better.

CLAD FOR COMFORT in a baggy Yale T-shirt and saggy granny panties, her hair scrunched into a messy topknot, Vicky settled back against a pile of pillows, pulled the kitteny bedspread up to her armpits, and opened the National Book Award winner she'd bought at the airport.

Five minutes later she snapped it closed. It didn't hold her attention now any more than it had on the plane. "Why didn't I buy something racy?" she muttered. "At least I'd be *reading* about sex."

Thinking of sex made her think of Tyrell, of course. She flung an arm over her eyes. Good God, they'd almost done it in the coatroom. And the worst part of it was, despite her perfectly rational second thoughts and all the trouble it would have caused, she was sorry they hadn't!

And now, as if dealing with Ty wasn't bad enough, she had to contend with Winston too, which was a hundred times worse. Ty only humiliated her in private. Winston had done it the most public way possible.

Seeing him tonight, she couldn't for the life of her recall why she'd found him attractive. Yes, his face was handsome—dark eyes, patrician nose. But his hair. It *seemed* nice—thick and wavy—but it was always *exactly* the same length. And it always lay perfectly in place. He never touched it, never ran his fingers through it. Creepy.

And his body. Again, it *seemed* nice enough, but it was strictly ornamental. He couldn't *do* anything with it, like change a faucet or a tire, or even set a mousetrap. Thank God she hadn't married him! What if there was a massive earthquake, or a tsunami, or a pandemic? He'd be useless in the new world order, where the skills required to manage a hedge fund would have no value and diamonds would be worth less than a good piece of flint.

She smiled grimly. There she went, catastrophizing again. Her therapist said her end-of-the-world scenarios stemmed from losing her father at a young age. Well, no kidding. But that didn't mean the end of the world wouldn't really come. It couldn't hurt to be ready.

Footsteps sounded in the hall, and she stiffened. Then the door across from hers opened and closed. Ty was back. She let herself breathe, even smiled a little. He would have given a beautiful toast, hit just the right note, teasing Isabelle, maybe telling a funny story about her. And when Vicky didn't show, he would have risen to the occasion and said something nice about Matt too.

Yes, Ty was a jackass, but at least she could count on him.

A few minutes later Jack and Lil's door opened and closed. Soon afterward, a woman giggled in the hallway, high-pitched and quickly hushed. Ricky mumbled something, then the giggle squirted out again, cut off by the closing of a bedroom door.

How in the world had Ty managed to palm Annemarie off on Ricky? And why hadn't he kept her for himself?

In the further reaches of the house, doors opened and closed. Isabelle, Adrianna. Winston. Vicky shrank lower under the covers. Reminded herself she didn't have to deal with him tonight. She could hide in her room, safe behind her locked door.

A moment later, knuckles rapped on that door. Winston's stern voice vibrated through the wood. "Victoria, let me in."

Up came the blankets, over her head.

"Victoria. Stop behaving like a child. I came all the way from New York to talk to you." The knob rattled impatiently. "Don't make me get your mother."

She blinked into the darkness under the blankets. Held her breath.

A long moment passed. She listened intently.

Silence. Had he gone for Adrianna? Or was he lying in wait?

Barely breathing, she slipped out of bed. Padded barefoot to the door, pressed her ear to the crack. Nothing.

Carefully, she poked her head out in the hall. From around the corner came the rumble of his voice, followed by Adrianna's impatient reply. Then a door closed. The voices moved closer.

Panicking, Vicky didn't pause to weigh the consequences. She darted across the hallway, silently turned Ty's doorknob, and tiptoed into his pitch-dark room.

CHAPTER THIRTEEN

VICKY CLOSED TY'S door without a sound. Slowly, silently, she backed away from it.

Her eyes stayed riveted to the ribbon of light visible beneath it. When a shadow crossed it, she almost peed her pants.

Knuckles rapped her bedroom door. Pressing her palm over her galloping heart, she took another step back . . . and a hand reached out of the dark and grabbed her arm.

Scared senseless, she shot forward like a bullet, would have zoomed straight out into the hallway, but another arm around her waist pulled her back. A hand over her mouth smothered her shriek.

"Easy there, honey," Ty breathed in her ear. "You don't want your boyfriend busting down my door, now do you?"

She swallowed the shriek, shook her head. He released her and she spun around. "For God's sake," she hissed, "you scared me to death!"

"Honey, you're lucky all you got was a little scare, creeping around in the dark like a thief." He kept his voice to a whisper.

"I wasn't creeping around." She sounded sulky.

"You were so." He found her wrist in the dark, dragged her away from the door. "If I hadn't heard Banes at your door and figured out what was what, believe you me, you'd have gotten worse than a scare."

Giving up that argument, she circled back to the other thing he'd said that pissed her off. "Winston's *not* my boyfriend. He's a liar and an asshole and a snake in the grass."

"It so happens I agree with you," he said, "which is why I'm standing here in my underwear whispering like a girl instead of tossing you out on your ass."

"Oh." That took the wind out of her sails. "Well. Thanks." She tried not to think about his underwear.

Across the hall, Adrianna called out. "Victoria." She kept her voice low, but every syllable simmered. "Open the door."

Together, Vicky and Ty crept to his door, pressed their ears to the crack.

"The door's unlocked," they heard Adrianna say. She opened it and went in.

"She's not here," Winston clipped out.

"She's not in the bathroom either."

A conversation followed, too quiet to hear. Then they stepped into the hallway, closing the door.

A sharp rap on Ty's door made them both leap back. Vicky stumbled against Ty. He caught her arm. "Hide in the bathroom," he breathed in her ear. "I'll get rid of them."

Hands held out in front of her, she groped through the darkness. Then—wham!—she stubbed her toe on the leg of the bed. Air hissed out through her teeth, ending in a drawn-out whimper.

He was beside her in an instant. "Shhh."

"My toe," she breathed, an agonized whisper. "I think I broke it."

A heavier fist hit the door, louder and more impatient. Pulling her arm over his shoulders, Ty half carried her while she hopped on one foot.

When soft carpet gave way to cold tile, she felt around for the sink, grasped the rim. "I'm okay," she whispered. "Go."

And without a word, he closed the door and left her standing on one foot in the dark.

WEARING A SNUG pair of boxer briefs, an annoyed expression, and absolutely nothing else, Ty pulled the door open.

He waited a beat while Adrianna's gaze traveled instinctively from his jaw, down his chest, all the way to his crotch. When it flew back up to his face, he let his scowl fade and a slow smile curve his lips.

"Honey," he drawled, "I'm not up for a three-way, but if you lose the yuppie you can come on in."

Her jaw dropped. Speechless, cheeks crimson, she looked so much like Vicky—who'd often favored him with a similar look of sexually charged outrage—that he had to bite his cheek to keep from laughing.

Winston didn't find it funny. "We're looking for Victoria."

Ty smirked. "She run away from you again, Winnie?"

"She didn't run away from me," Winston ground out through his teeth. "She's overwrought because of the wedding."

Ty did confused. "Which wedding would that be? Her brother's? Or the one she would've had herself, if not for finding you up another woman's skirt?"

Winston's face went florid. His fists bunched at his sides.

At any other time, Ty would've welcomed the invitation. But unfortunately a fistfight wouldn't help Vicky, hiding in his bathroom, possibly with a broken toe.

So instead of throwing more gas on the fire, he stepped

back, held his door open wide. "See for yourself. No way-ward ex-fiancées in my bed tonight."

Winston's eyes swept the room. Adrianna stepped inside to peer behind the door. Before she could get any ideas about the bathroom, Ty laid on a silky smile. "Offer stands. Ditch Winnie and come on back around." He dropped his voice. "Truth is, I got a thing for cougars."

She scurried, actually scurried, into the hallway. "I don't know what Isabelle sees in you," she sniffed from a safe distance. "You are completely disgusting."

"Mmm-hmm," he hummed, a knowing sound. "If you change your mind, I'll be here." And he swung the door shut in their faces.

He listened as they moved down the hall, Adrianna's tone taut with insult, Winston's jagged with fury. Then he opened the bathroom door, flipped on the light. And got his first glimpse of Vicky.

She was a mess. Holey T-shirt, saggy underpants, bird's nest hair. And one extremely swollen big toe.

He wanted to eat her up.

"Well, hell," he said, making himself focus on the toe. "We've got to get you to the ER."

"Uh-uh." She shook her head and the bird's nest wob-bled. "I just need some ice. Can you go down to the kitchen and get some? And grab anything chocolate you see lying around."

He shook his head ruefully. "I'll be glad to wait on you, honey. But first you're going to the ER."

She hissed her impatience. "I don't need the freaking ER. It's just a sprain."

"Then you won't mind if I give it a squeeze, just to make sure." He took a step forward.

She hopped a step back. "Keep your hands off my toe."

"No can do, sugar. If you want to skip the ER, you gotta

let me play doctor." He took another step. She snatched up his shaving kit and threw it at his head. He caught it, tossed it on the bed. She chucked his toothbrush, his comb. He let them sail on by.

"I'm a lot bigger than you, sweetheart, and I'm gonna win this little standoff. The only question is how hard you're gonna make it on yourself." He couldn't help grinning.

"You're such an asshole," she seethed, blue eyes flashing. "I'm in *pain* here, and you're *laughing* at me!"

"Well, of course I am. Have you looked in the mirror? A man could turn to stone looking at that hair of yours. And I haven't seen panties like those since my sweet granny passed away. She used to hang a dozen pairs just like 'em on her clothesline."

He watched color rise up her neck until her face was as red as her toe. She tugged her T-shirt down to cover her underpants.

Poor Vicky. She was having a lousy night. He hated picking on her when she was down, but she was stubborn as a stump and it was the only way he could think of to make her quit sassing him about the ER. He took another step toward her.

And a big, fat tear rolled down her cheek.

His heart swelled up, filling his chest. "Aw, shit, honey," he murmured, and taking the last step, he wrapped her up in his arms.

VICKY'S PITY PARTY lasted about a minute. Then she wiped her nose on her sleeve, lifted her splotchy face to look up at Ty.

Even through puffy lids he looked great, gazing back at her with tiger's eyes. He didn't let go of her, and she didn't push him away. Instead, she propped her chin on the light mat of honey-colored hair that covered his truly awesome chest.

"So, what did Mother do when she got a load of your abs?" He had three rows. Vicky's throbbing toe hadn't struck her blind.

He shrugged. "She dummied up for a minute, which was a nice change of pace. Then she got all embarrassed because she eye-fucked me before she could stop herself."

Vicky let out a startled laugh, picturing Adrianna's expression.

"And Winnie," he went on, "he got an eyeful too. I expect he's back in his room thanking his stars that Isabelle stopped me from kicking his ass back there at the restaurant."

Her head came up. "Kicking his ass? Why would you do that?"

"Because he's got it coming, that's why." He brushed a knuckle across her damp cheekbone. "If he's smart, he'll keep out of my way all weekend. But lucky for me"—he flashed an outlaw grin—"he doesn't seem too smart."

Vicky blinked up at him, dazzled. Utterly beguiled.

"Okay," she said finally, "you can take me to the ER." It was the least she could do.

WHAT A PRODUCTION. First, Ty had to carry her downstairs. Then he had to wake up the maid. The maid had to call a cab. At the hospital, they had to wait around for a doctor. She didn't speak English. Neither did the nurse. Then he had to carry Vicky back upstairs to his room.

And they had to pull the whole thing off without waking any of the guests.

"There you go, honey." He laid her gently on his bed. The doc had doped her up good, and she lolled back against the pillows, a shiny drop of drool pooled in the corner of her mouth. He wagged his head. "Let's get you out of that snot rag."

Digging through his drawers, he found his last clean

T-shirt. "How can I be out already?" he muttered, trying not to think about what was really on his mind.

Undressing Vicky.

That's right, she'd be naked in his bed and, once again, he was helpless to do anything about it. She was practically comatose, had only come to life when he accidentally touched the ticklish spot on her ribs. Then she turned into a ball of worms in his arms. He'd almost dropped her on the curb getting out of the cab, and again while he was wrestling open the front door.

This was *not* how he'd pictured the wedding weekend. Back in Texas, he'd been too busy with the trial to think much about it, but to the extent he had, he'd assumed it would be fun, that he'd probably get a little emotional, and that he'd definitely get laid.

Well, so far fun was thin on the ground, his emotions were all over the map, and his prospects for getting laid were dwindling by the hour. Next door, Ricky's headboard banged the wall like a jackhammer. Ty's biggest thrill would be a glimpse of Vicky's tits while he changed her out of one ugly T-shirt and into another.

He sat on the edge of the bed. "Vicky. Honey. Sit up for me." She didn't move a muscle. He hooked her under the arms, pulled her upright. She sagged like a rag doll. He peeled her T-shirt over her head and let her plop back onto the pillows while he reached for the fresh one.

And then he gave himself a minute. Just a minute to look at her beautiful tits. Damn, they were perfect. Anger streaked through him when he imagined her inflating them with bags of silicone, but he couldn't sustain it, not with her nakedness before him. Her skin looked like satin.

Would it be so awful to touch her? After all, she'd let him do it before.

He reached out one hand, cupped her gently. A perfect

handful, not too much, not too little. His thumb brushed her nipple. It stiffened, and his eyes darted to her face.

Nothing. It was only a reflex.

It tickled his conscience that she was too out of it to know he was handling her, but he couldn't take his hand away. Anyway, it wasn't like he was feeling her up. He wasn't kneading or massaging. He wasn't squeezing. Or sucking.

His mouth went dry.

No. That would be wrong. Sucking, licking. Wrong, wrong, wrong.

He sat back. Pulled his hand off her breast. Drew a fortifying breath and held it while he wrestled her, very gently, into his T-shirt. Then he pulled off the sweats he'd loaned her, careful not to jostle her taped-up toe. Left the execrable panties in place and tucked the covers up under her chin.

Then he locked himself in the bathroom and took a very, very cold shower.

SUNLIGHT SCRAPED POINTY claws across Vicky's eyeballs. She turned her head away from the light. And blinked. Blinked.

Blinked, blinked, blinked.

Oh God. No matter how many times she blinked, Ty's head was still there, resting on the other pillow.

She'd done it, she'd actually had sex with him. And *she couldn't remember it*! The words wailed in her head. She *wanted* to remember!

Salvaging what she could, she let her gaze travel down his body. The brick wall of a chest, the paving stone abs. The package bulging inside his oh-so-snug underwear. Even semi-hard, he was impressive.

She'd really, really wanted to see him naked. And all the way hard.

Her eyes lingered there for a while, then moved lower, over long, lean legs to perfectly formed feet. Funny, feet usually bummed her out. She didn't even like her own. But she liked his.

She must have been thinking too loudly, or scrutinizing him too noisily, because he stirred. Whipping her head around, she snapped her eyes shut and pretended to be asleep. The bed shifted. A long moment passed while she felt his eyes on her face. She forced herself not to swallow.

Then, "I know you're awake. I can see your eyeballs jittering."

"They're not jittering," she said. "They're spasming. You're not so pretty first thing in the morning."

He chuckled, a warm and throaty sound that had all the little muscles between her legs twitching. A tingle zipped up her spine and actually made her shiver.

His tone shifted to concern. "Feeling all right? You don't have a fever, do you?" He laid his palm on her forehead, and it was so warm and dry that she moaned a little, deep in her throat. He drew his hand down so it cupped her cheek, turned her head to face him. "Open your eyes, sugar."

She did, to find him propped on an elbow, studying her face like a map.

"Well, your eyes are clear. You don't have a fever." He removed his hand. "How's the toe?"

Oh yeah, the toe. Everything came back to her. Every. Thing. She shut her eyes again, while a tsunami of humiliation swamped her.

Then his knuckles brushed her cheek. "Look at me, honey." His voice was soft, but his tone commanded and she obeyed, gazing up into his honey brown eyes. Concern shone there, and something more. Warmth and comfort, and kindness.

"About last night," he said, "here's all you need to

know. Winnie's a fuckhead. Your mama's a shrew. And your toe's broken in two places."

He stroked her cheek as he spoke. So gently, so sweetly. She didn't know how to deal with such compassion. A tear rolled down her cheek.

He brushed it away with his thumb, brought his lips to her ear. "And one other thing I almost forgot. Honey, you've got great tits."

She socked him. "Tyrell Brown, you're a complete shit! I can't *believe* you took advantage of me that way."

He rolled away from her flying backhand, choking with laughter. "Admit it, sweetheart. When you woke up you were checking me out, trying to remember if we did it last night. And you weren't too upset about it, either."

"You're an asshole." She crossed her arms. Her toe throbbed to a disco beat.

Whatever. She had bigger problems than Ty copping a feel. Like how she'd explain to Matt why she'd blown off the rehearsal party. How she'd get through the day without informing Winston that he was a fuckhead, or get down the aisle in the gorgeous Jimmy Choos she'd had dyed to match her dress.

And most of all, how she'd get out the words she needed to say to Ty.

Fast, that's how.

She covered her face with her hands. "Thank you for everything you did for me last night," she said into her palms. "I don't know what I would've done if you hadn't hidden me in here. I really appreciate it."

For a moment, he said nothing. Then, "Sorry," he drawled, "I couldn't hear you mumbling through your fingers like that."

She slapped her hands on the mattress. "You're impossible!" She swiveled her head to glare at him. He wore an innocent expression. Too innocent. "I said thank you," she squeezed through her teeth. Then she swallowed hard. "And I think I need some help getting to my room. If you don't mind."

"I don't mind at all." He swung his legs off the bed. "Probably best if I put some clothes on first, just in case your mama's waiting for you."

He picked up his jeans off the floor and pulled them on, left them open while he moved around the room, looking for his boots, scooping up yesterday's T-shirt and tossing it in the laundry.

She bit her lip. He was doing it on purpose, of course. Showing off his abs. His back. All that lean muscle rippling and bunching and stretching and flexing as he opened the armoire and fished around for a shirt. Even after he found one, he walked around with it trailing from his hand.

It was dangerous to stare too long at the sun, but damn it, she couldn't look away.

When he finally finished dressing, he walked to the bed. "Time to get up, sweetheart." He whipped back the covers, and that's when she remembered the most humiliating thing of all—she was wearing her ugliest panties.

WHEN VICKY TRIED to yank her T-shirt down over those nasty panties, Ty let out a chuckle.

"Don't worry, honey," he said, lifting her with one arm under her knees, the other under her back, "it'll be our secret. I can't have people knowing I slept with a woman in granny panties."

"We didn't sleep together," she huffed.

"What do you call it?"

"You know what I mean. We didn't *do* anything. Well, *you* did. You looked at my breasts."

"It was definitely the highlight." He tucked her into his chest. When she curled her arms around his neck, the breasts in question smushed against him and made him hard. Again.

"But you just looked, right?"

"That's right, we just looked."

She stiffened. "We?"

"Me and a couple of janitors at the hospital. They took some pictures, but I didn't let them touch you."

For ten seconds she was silent. Then, "Har har. You almost got me."

He laughed.

With a little help from her, he got her through both doors and into her room without bumping her foot. But then, just as he was lowering her to the bed, his fingers grazed her tickle spot. She yelped. Her body straightened like a ruler, then folded like a hairpin. And she squirted right through his arms.

"Damn it, Vicky!" He'd played varsity football—serious business in Texas—and in four years as a wide receiver he'd never had as much trouble holding on to a sleet-slicked football as he did hanging on to Vicky when she went into a tickle spasm.

She'd landed half on the bed, half off, and if her caterwauling was any indication, she'd bumped her broken toe on the way down. Scooping her up, he laid her gently on the bed. "Hush, now, before your mama comes running."

That threat worked. She simmered down to a whimper, which was even more pitiful than her yowling.

"Hang on, honey. I'll get you a pain pill."

He made the round trip to his bathroom in under thirty seconds. Found her calmer, but her face was tearstained. He'd seen it that way too often to suit him, and he could trace every teardrop back to Winston Banes. He should have hospitalized the fucker when he had the chance. Then Vicky never would've broken her toe.

Well, it was spilled milk now. He shook a pill into her

hand. She looked like she wanted to argue about it, but he menaced her with a look and she swallowed it down.

"Now let's get you dressed." All business, he strode to the armoire, rifled through the sundresses. "How's this one?" Huge white flowers splashed on a black background. He looked over his shoulder. She shrugged. He tossed it on the bed.

"I'll bet you want some new panties, too." He pulled open a drawer. And hissed a breath through his teeth.

It was like Victoria's Secret had disgorged its entire inventory, a wonderland of silk and satin just begging him to plunge in to his elbows. He didn't fight it, running his fingers through red lace, black silk, hot pink satin. "Shit," he muttered, angling his body to block her view.

"White," she called from the bed.

"White. Hmm." Sifting through zebra stripes and leopard spots, fingering every skimpy scrap, he untangled a white pair from the others, barely enough lace to cover his palm. He held them up. They had little satin bows on each hip. "These okay?"

"Fine. Now get your mitts out of my underpants."

He snorted. "Like I've never seen panties before." Tossing them at her head, he used the diversion to push a scrap of red lace into his pocket. "Now get yourself dressed while I get you some breakfast."

"I'll go with you. I have to apologize to Matt and Isabelle."

"I'll bring them up here."

"And I have to talk to Winston."

"What the hell for?"

"To pretend I'm giving him another chance."

At his snort of disgust, she held up a quelling hand. "Seriously, Ty, I didn't go through all this so Mother could ruin everything at the last minute." She glanced at the clock. "The wedding's in six hours. I can tough it out for that long. That pill will definitely help."

The smile she gave him slid a little off center.

Oh boy. "Vicky, honey, those pills knocked you on your ass last night. You couldn't even remember whether we had sex or not."

Her smile got loopier. "Maybe we did. Maybe I jumped you in your sleep."

Oh boy. Things were going downhill. Stepping to the bedside, he folded the kitteny comforter over her, gave her his badass stare. "You stay put. I'll bring you some food. And some coffee. Then we'll talk about going downstairs."

Out on the terrace, everyone except Ricky and Annemarie was seated around the table. The looks they gave him said they thought they knew what he'd been up to. Jack and Lil each lifted an eloquent eyebrow. Isabelle gave him a knowing smile. Matt thunked his mug down on the table.

Adrianna, who was speaking to Pierre, cut off in midsentence to glare. And Winston pushed back his chair. Two strides put him directly in Ty's face.

"You son of a bitch. What have you done with Victoria?"

Ty didn't even hesitate. He was short on sleep, sexually frustrated, and seriously caffeine-deprived. It all added up to a short jab to the mouth.

Winston staggered backward, barely keeping his feet. His hand went to his lip; he goggled at the blood. "You sucker-punched me, you bastard!"

Ty smirked. "What're you gonna do about it?"

"Kill you!" Winston roared, and charged.

He caught Ty in the gut with his shoulder, carrying him backward into the breakfast cart. Over it went. Croissants spiraled through the air, the coffeepot shattered. Ty landed in the middle of the mess, pinned on his back by one pissed-off preppie with murder on his mind.

Winston was stronger than he looked—and he looked plenty strong—but with a twist and a roll, a quick knee and a head butt, Ty managed to wriggle free. Gaining his feet, glass crunching under his boots and sticking out of his back, he grinned insanely.

Finally, he was having fun.

Winston scrambled upright. "Tell me where she is!" he roared. "Tell me, or I swear I'll kill you!"

Ty spread his arms wide. "Bring it on, Winnie, my man. Let's get the party started."

Winston curled his fists, eyes blazing with fury and indignation. Everyone waited, holding their breath. Both men balanced on their toes.

And into that tense silence, a feminine voice warbled out. "Good morning, everybody!" All eyes swung to the door.

Poised on one foot, arm looped around Ricky's neck, Vicky grinned out at her startled audience.

Forgetting about Winston, Ty put his hands on his hips. "What the hell are you doing out of bed? I told you I'd bring you some breakfast."

Winston rounded on Vicky. "You *slept* with him?"

She giggled. "Slept with him?" She giggled some more.

Winston went purple. Ty cut in sharply. "She's doped up, asshole, can't you see that? She broke her damn toe."

Winston's eyes dropped to her foot. "Is that where you were last night, Victoria? At the hospital?"

She rolled her eyes hugely. Giggled again.

"Yes, that's where she was," Ty snarled out. "I took her to the ER. They drugged her up and I put her to bed."

Winston's head snapped around. "Did you take advantage of her?"

Ty narrowed his eyes. "If by 'take advantage' you mean

did I screw around on her while we were engaged, no I didn't."

Winston's eyes darkened. He took a step toward Ty. And Jack spoke up from his place at the table.

"Listen up, Winston," he drawled mildly. "I've known Ty a long time. He might not look like much, but he'll shatter your jaw without breaking a sweat. Think about that. You really want to drink your meals through a straw for six months?"

Heavy silence followed. Winston simmered visibly, grinding his teeth, flexing his fingers. Ty baited him with a smirk, hoping bad judgment would carry the day.

The scales could have tipped either way.

Then a demented giggle cut the silence. "Look." Vicky pointed at his coffee-soaked crotch. "Ty wet his pants."

It shattered the tension as nothing else could have. Everyone laughed. Everyone but Winston.

Even Adrianna cracked a smile. "Oh, for goodness sake, Ricky, bring her over here. Let's get some coffee into her."

TY SCOWLED AT the T-shirt in his hand. It was one of his favorites, perfectly broken in. Balling it up, he hooked it into the trash can. Isabelle had picked the glass out of it—and out of his back—but what with the holes and the bloodstains, it was ruined.

As if that wasn't bad enough, she'd laid on a tongue-lashing while she was at it, harping on little things like broken crockery, which he rightfully tried to pin on Winston, and bloody lips, which he sincerely argued were well deserved. Not to mention Vicky's sorry condition. Like he hadn't spent half the night at the ER trying to help her out.

His explanations fell on deaf ears.

He slung his jeans onto his growing pile of dirty clothes.

The damn things were coffee-soaked from ass to knees. No wonder Vicky thought he'd pissed himself.

Of course, if she weren't so looped, she'd have known better. His conscience pricked him. It was his fault she was wrecked. Knowing what a lightweight she was, he should've halved the dosage.

At least she couldn't get into too much trouble out on the terrace. Winnie had gone to his room to lick his wounds, and Cruella had backed off too, probably realizing that even her venom was no match for Vicodin.

What Vicky needed was food, and he damn well hoped she was getting some. He peeked out the window, saw her sitting at the table, hair fanned around the shoulders of her black and white sundress, bad foot propped on a chair. Sure enough, Matt and Adrianna were plying her with croissants and coffee, but she was too busy to eat, gabbling away at Isabelle and Lil, probably implicating him in all sorts of crimes.

Good Lord.

Knuckles rapped on his door and Jack came in without waiting for an invitation. He walked straight into the bathroom, lifted the seat, and unzipped. "So, what happened last night? You sleep with her?"

Ty snorted loudly. "Not in any sense of the word. She was drugged up and dead to the world. And there was no chance of getting any *actual* sleep with Ricky banging the stripper six ways to Sunday till the sun came up."

Jack grinned. "So that's why you're loaded for bear."

"Damn right. That, and Brescia's sick." His throat tightened when he said it.

"What's wrong with her?"

"Clancy thinks it's bloodworms."

"Well, shit." Jack wasn't smiling anymore.

"Yeah," Ty said. Then he let it drop. There was nothing else to say. "Anyway, I was all set to take my shitty mood out on Winnie." He tugged yesterday's jeans on, aimed a surly look at Jack. "Why'd you have to go and spoil it?"

Jack zipped up. "Couldn't be helped. My wife's in a delicate condition. Can't have her exposed to wanton violence."

"Uh-huh," Ty grunted skeptically. "In other words, she told you to shut me down." He wagged his head. "Time was, you were the first one on his feet when a fight was brewing. Now you're whipped."

Jack slapped his shoulder, unapologetic. "You'll get another crack at old Winston. He's not giving up on your girl."

"She's not my girl."

It was Jack's turn to say, "Uh-huh."

Ignoring him, Ty pawed through his drawers, hoping he might find a T-shirt he'd forgotten about. "This whole fake flirtation was a stupid idea. I should've told Isabelle right off that I can't stand Vicky, and for good reason. Then, by God, it would've been me going at it with the stripper last night."

Jack's snort called bullshit on that. "If you wanted Annemarie, you'd have found a way to get at her. You don't want her."

"That's what you think. If you recall, it was me that got the first handful."

"Yeah, and you dropped it like a hot coal."

Giving up on the T-shirt, Ty yanked a white button-down out of his armoire, punched his arms through the sleeves. "If I did, it's only because I made a promise to Isabelle. Even though I'm not really keeping it, she thinks I am. I can't have Annemarie comparing notes with her about what a stud I am."

"Uh-huh." Jack wandered to the window, looked down at the terrace. Made a tsking noise. "Looks like you should've put more muscle behind that jab."

"What the hell?" Ty pushed in beside him. Winston had moved Vicky's foot and taken the seat beside her. By the looks of things, he was doing his best to get her attention by rubbing her arm and bending her ear. And the poor kid was too messed up to fend him off.

"For fuck's sake!" Stepping away from the window, Ty scrabbled with his buttons while he stomped into his boots.

Jack didn't attempt to conceal his amusement. "Isabelle'll skin you if you start another fight."

"Yeah, I got that message loud and clear. Doesn't mean I can't defend myself if he starts one." He plowed his fingers through his hair, the extent of his grooming. "Close up when you leave," he said over his shoulder, and strode out the door, the sound of Jack's laughter following him down the hallway.

WINSTON SAT WITH his back to the door, so he missed Ty's entrance, a thumbs-hooked-in-the-pockets amble that said he hadn't a care in the world.

Moseying over to take the seat across from Vicky, he spread an amiable smile around the table. Beside him, Isabelle spoke just two words. "Be nice."

He patted her arm. "Don't you worry, honey, I'm sure Winnie won't be instigating any more fights." He grinned at Winston, who glared bullets back at him.

"The name is Winston," he clipped out. "I'll thank you to remember it."

Ty tapped his temple. "Got it right here in case I ever need it. Winnie."

He shifted his smile away from Winston's clenching jaw and onto Vicky. "How you feeling, honey?"

"Hi, Ty." She giggled.

Winston fumed. "How much did you give her?"

Ty ignored him. "Sugar, you know you're supposed to

keep that foot up. Give it here." Reaching under the table, he hooked a hand around Vicky's ankle, propped it on his thigh.

"For God's sake!" Winston turned to Matt. "This hill-billy overdosed Victoria. Do something."

Matt glanced at Ty. "What's she on?"

"Vicodin. Five hundred milligrams, as prescribed."

Matt's eyes shifted back to Winston. "Vicky gets drunk on half a beer. You ought to know that, since you were engaged to her." To Ty, he added, "We should halve the dose."

"Way ahead of you."

Adrianna sniffed. "It's no longer your concern, Brown. You'll give the pills to me."

"No, I won't." Ty met Cruella's eyes. "When she's up to it, I'll give them to Vicky."

Steam shot out of her ears. "Victoria is *my* daughter. *I'll* take care of her."

"By shoving her at Winnie? Hell, that's child abuse in my book."

He felt a sharp pinch on his thigh. Isabelle again. But he'd had enough of being pulled in different directions. He rounded on her. "What do you want from me, Isa-belle? Who should I make nice to now? Vicky? Or her bitchy mama? 'Cause I can't do both."

She flinched like he'd slapped her. He felt instantly awful.

Damn it, his whole purpose this weekend was to make Isabelle happy. He was usually so good at that. Making people smile, putting them at ease. It should have been simple, but somehow he kept screwing it up. Now he'd lost his handle on it so completely that he'd just snapped at his favorite person in the world.

He was coming unglued and he didn't know why.

"I'm sorry, honey." He meant it from the bottom of his

heart, and Isabelle, the sweetest girl he knew, forgave him on the spot. Which only made him feel like a bigger heel. Could he possibly look any more despicable?

Then Vicky trilled a giggle. "Ty kisses really good."

He dropped his head in his hands.

CHAPTER FOURTEEN

STANDING ON ONE foot in her midget bathroom, Vicky plopped two Alka-Seltzer into a glass of water and glumly watched it fizz.

It probably wouldn't help, because even though her head weighed fifty pounds and her stomach quivered like jelly, this wasn't a normal hangover. She was coming down off a narcotic high, and she doubted whether any of the numerous over-the-counter meds she routinely carried when she traveled would help.

She fingered the Vicodin bottle. Another pill would get her over the hump . . .

And that's exactly how people got addicted to painkillers. She pushed the bottle away. She'd just suck it up.

The fizzing subsided and she took a sip. Ugh. She forced another. Anything that nasty had to help.

Hobbling out of the tiny bathroom, she plunked down at the dressing table and stared at the disaster staring back in the mirror: pasty skin, puffy eyes, dry scaly lips, all topped off by a rat's nest. A magnifying mirror was attached to the table by a swing arm. She made the mistake of looking into it. "Agghh!" Gaping pores, shaggy brows, fuzzy teeth. And she'd gone out in public like this! It was unprecedented. If she weren't in the wedding party, she'd grab a cab and head straight to a spa.

But she *was* in the wedding party. That was her dress hanging on the bathroom door: ivory lace over peach satin, strapless, cocktail length, as clingy as a mermaid's skin. Her five-inch peach-silk heels would have looked fabulous with it. Her open-toed "granny" sandals, not so much.

At a knock on the door, she squared her shoulders. Isabelle poked her head in. "Do you need help getting dressed?"

"Isabelle, you're the bride. I'm supposed to ask you that."

Isabelle inched into the room. "You don't have to do this, you know."

Vicky pointed a finger at her. "Don't you *dare* worry about me. Ty promised to carry me down the aisle if he has to." Like he'd carried her up to her room after she threw up her breakfast all over the terrace.

Good Lord, how could she face everyone after that?

She vaguely remembered making some embarrassing remarks too, but most of what happened before she tossed her croissants was a blur. Her only clear memories were snapshots of Ty. Cradling her foot on his knee. Scooping her up and delivering her here. Promising to help her get through the wedding.

That last had been extorted by tears. It turned out that he was helpless against tears.

"I think he likes you," Isabelle commented.

"Well, at least he doesn't seem to hate me anymore."

Isabelle cocked her head. "Why would he hate you?"

She could have kicked herself. "Don't mind me, I'm just feeling sorry for myself." She gestured at the dress. "That's the most beautiful bridesmaid dress I've ever seen. The most beautiful dress, period."

Isabelle beamed. "Vidal tweaked it, but it's my design, to coordinate with my gown . . ."

Vicky listened to her ramble on about it while she sipped at the Alka-Seltzer. It seemed to be helping after all. At least she didn't feel like puking anymore. Not that there was anything left in her stomach.

After a few minutes, Isabelle wound down and Vicky managed to shoo her out by convincing her that she could get herself dressed.

First, though, she had to get herself showered. Her head still wasn't up to hopping, so she hobbled into the shower on her heel, foot sealed in one of the handy Ziploc bags she always carried with her, and washed her hair standing on one foot. After toweling off, she wiped a clear spot on the steamy mirror and tried to call her reflection an improvement.

With plenty of time before she had to get dressed, she wrapped her hair in the damp towel and limped to the bed, hoping a catnap would deflate the bags under her eyes. Curling up in the kitteny comforter, she closed her eyes, just for a minute . . .

"Vicky! Open the damn door!" It was Ty, hammering it with a fist.

"Hang on already," she groused. "What's your problem, anyway?"

She hopped on one foot to the door, pulled it open.

He goggled at her. "What the hell are you doing? Why aren't you dressed?"

She hopped back to the bed and sat down. Yawned hugely. "What's the rush?"

"Are you nuts?" He stabbed a finger at the clock.

Three-thirty.

"Shit!" She leaped to her foot. "Shit, shit, shit! I fell asleep!" She hopped around in a circle, unable to decide which way to go first. The towel drooped over her eyes.

She whipped it off. "Oh God, my hair!" It hung in soggy ropes.

"Your hair, is right!" Ty practically shouted. Cinching her waist with his hands, he lifted her straight off the floor like she was five years old, rushed into the bathroom, and set her down in front of the mirror. Yanking the blow dryer off the hook, he pushed it into her hands. "Do something," he ordered, and sped out into the bedroom.

She fumbled the dryer, managed to get it going, and was making headway when Ty came in waving peach panties and a strapless bra. Snatching them out of his hand, she shot him a don't-get-too-comfortable-with-my-underwear look. He ignored it, racing out and closing the door behind him.

Her hair was a frizz bomb, but it couldn't be helped. As soon as it was dry, she shed her robe and, handicapped by the tiny room and her now-throbbing-again toe, struggled into her underwear. But when it came to getting into the dress, she quickly discovered that she needed help. And Ty was the only one around.

The time for modesty had expired while she napped, so without a second thought she opened the door and hopped out into the bedroom wearing only a peach thong and a miracle of engineering that shoved her B-cups up, out and together, serving them up like peaches on a plate so it looked like she had a lot more going on than she really did. Ty's eyes popped out of his head.

"Jesus Christ," he cried, "are you trying to give me a heart attack?"

"Down boy." No time to blush. "I need help with the dress, and you're it."

"No way. I'll get Lil." He tore his eyes away and headed for the door.

"You can't get Lil," Vicky called after him. "She's helping Isabelle. They're probably at the chapel already."

He faced her with an expression of utter male exasperation.

"Come on," she snapped her fingers, "just hold it down and open."

Muttering a litany of grievances, Ty knelt on one knee, holding the dress down where she could step into it. She gripped his shoulder, put her bad foot through first. But when she tried to balance her weight on her heel and lift her other foot, she wobbled like a Weeble. She tried to step back but her foot caught in the dress. She started to topple backward. Her arms pinwheeled.

Ty dropped the dress, wrapped both arms around her thighs. She grabbed his head, mushed his nose into her peach panties. His other knee came down on the dress. She heard the fabric rend.

"No!" she cried, shaking her foot harder, trying to free it from the shredding silk.

"I've got you!" Ty's voice was muffled. "Hold still!"

She couldn't. With the dress binding her foot and his arms binding her thighs, she felt like she'd been trussed. Every instinct shrieked to break free. She kicked out with her foot; the fabric rent more. Swung out with her arm; the bedside lamp hit the floor. And like a tree felled by an axe, she went over backward, helpless to break her fall.

Somehow, she landed on Ty. Face to face, chest to chest.

She lifted her head, dragged in a breath. Gazed down into his whiskey eyes. "What happened?"

"*What happened?*" He snorted a laugh. "You want me to summarize?"

She rolled her eyes. "I mean how did you end up underneath me? I was falling backwards . . ."

"Sugar, I couldn't face another trip to the emergency room with you."

So he'd spun her around and taken the brunt of the fall. The man liked to pretend he was molasses in January, but he truly had lightning reflexes. And damn it, it really turned her on. She let her palms spread out on his chest, that magnificent wall of muscle hidden under a perfect black tux.

Yikes! Tux! She hadn't even noticed that he was dressed for the wedding! And now he was lying in the shards of the lamp. She had to get off him right away.

Bracing her knee on the floor between his legs, she wasn't completely surprised to feel good old Mr. Hardon against her thigh. She couldn't even blame him for it, since she was laid out on top of him wearing page 42 of the Victoria's Secret catalogue, her naked ass cheeks cupped in his hands.

She had to admit, she liked the cupping. But still, it had to be said. "You can get your paws off my ass now."

He squeezed. "Honey, there *has* to be something in this for me." He squeezed again. "If I wasn't such a gentleman—"

He waited out her derisive sputter.

"If I wasn't such a gentleman," he went on, "I'd tell you that all your hours on the Precor have definitely paid off." His palms stroked her cheeks. Around and around. Then he spanked them lightly. "Now get up before I quit being a gentleman."

Okay, she had to admit this too: She didn't want to get up. She liked his hands where they were, rough palms grazing her smooth ass. She liked her bare skin against his satiny tux, wanted to rub along it like a cat. She liked his hard chest under hers. His flat stomach. The hot pressure of his arousal against the inside of her thigh. All of it together made her feel warm and slumberous and sexier than ever before in her life.

In the heat of the moment, her scruples, her ethics, her worries about the future all melted away. Without thinking, she slid her thigh along his erection. Up, and down.

He let out a moan. "You're killing me, sugar." His hands started roaming, one gliding up over the small of her back, along her spine; the other curling down and around, to her heated core. That one drew a humming from low down in her throat, a primal sound of seduction that had his arms tightening around her, his teeth scraping her collarbone. She squirmed her nakedness against him, her softness against his hardness.

"Honey," he managed, devouring her throat, finding her wetness with his fingers and smearing it up and around and back again to the source. "Honey . . . wedding."

"No!" she moaned from the bottom of her sex-starved soul.

"Later," he panted out as his fingers delved into her bra. "I'll fuck you later. All night."

Later wouldn't cut it, and no matter what he said, his hands, his lips, and his rock-hard cock were all about now. It wouldn't take much to push him over the edge.

Never once in her sadly limited sex life had she played the aggressor, yet this new, sex-crazed Vicky shoved her hand down between their writhing bodies, flicked the tab on his waistband, and unzipped him like a pro.

When she fisted him, he jerked. "Back pocket," he blurted. "Left side."

She dug out the foil packet with her other hand, ripped it open with her teeth. Straddling his hips, she sheathed him, wondering briefly how she'd take him all in. Then his thumb hooked her panties, pulled them aside, and his big hands closed around her hips, lifting her, guiding her. "Take it slow, honey," he got out on a strangled breath. "But not too slow or I swear to God it'll be too late."

She was so slick that he was inside her before she knew it, a tight fit, but she handled it. He held on to her hips, fingers digging in, eyes locked on hers, holding back while she adjusted to him. When she started to ride, he clenched his jaw, held himself still while her palms flattened on his chest.

For one long minute, a dozen deep, delicious strokes, she kept control, set the pace, while sweat beaded his forehead and his muscles twitched and quivered.

Then in one explosive move, he jackknifed up, a kind of forward somersault. She landed on her back, two hundred pounds of frustrated cowboy flattening her to the rug. Pushing up on his arms, his beach bum hair falling in his blazing eyes, he said, "Sorry, honey, I'll make up for it later," and drove into her, driving what little control she'd held on to right out of her head. With a will of their own, her legs locked around his hips, pulling him deeper. Her fingers clawed the rug. Her head wanted to thrash, but he shoved a hand in her hair. "Come with me, baby. Come with me now."

She couldn't. She absolutely couldn't come like this. She never had. Coming was a project best left to her own hands, in the privacy of her own room. She couldn't possibly—

And then she did. She did! Her eyes popped, she gripped his arms. "Holy shit!" she cried out, as everything in her, every muscle and tendon and drop of blood contracted down to one solitary cell . . . then exploded into a billion brilliant shards.

"Oh my God," she gasped out when she could speak at all. "Oh my God. Oh my God," on each heaving breath. "What in the world was *that*?"

Ty had collapsed on top of her, face buried in her throat. Now his laughter bubbled up, vibrating through his chest. He rolled onto his back, pulling her over on top of him. Cupping one big palm around the curve of her bottom, he used his other hand to brush the hair from her face, tucking it behind her ear.

"That," he said flatly, "was the best fuck I've had in years. Maybe ever."

He was grinning at her, his eyes twinkling, actually twinkling, and her stomach fluttered, an unfamiliar sensation. She grinned back at him helplessly, caught in his spell.

His fingers stroked her cheek lightly. Skimmed her shoulder, the swell of her breast. One fingertip tucked inside the top of her bra like he belonged there. Slid along the edge to the deep crevice in the center. "Perfect," he murmured, letting it rest there, snug between her smushed-together breasts.

Her skin heated up. The flush spread upward, from her nethers to her hairline. How did he do this to her, make her warm and fuzzy and horny all at once? Everything was different with him, she felt more like herself, for better or worse. And he turned her on until she lost all control. She'd attacked him, for God's sake! Pulled his pants down and ridden him like a cowgirl!

And then . . . then she'd had an orgasm *while he was inside her.* A real one, not a fake one.

What, oh what, was she going to do now?

TY TUCKED A long lock of blond silk behind Vicky's ear, let his gaze roam over her upturned face. She had the damnedest blue eyes. Like an October sky on a warm, breezy day when there wasn't a cloud in sight.

Right at the moment those blue eyes were glazed. Her lips curved up at the corners, a contented smile she probably didn't know she wore. Yup, his little cowgirl had taken a ride straight to heaven and she was having a hard time coming back down to earth.

Too bad he couldn't let her drift awhile, but they were already late. Isabelle would peel a stripe off him if they messed up her schedule. He'd make it up to Vicky later. Whisk her out of the reception and into his bed—where he wouldn't have broken light bulb sticking in his back—and rock her world all night long.

Finally, the weekend had taken a turn for the better.

"Vicky honey?"

She didn't respond. Her languid gaze had taken a turn of its own, and truth to tell, she looked kind of terrified. Color bloomed in her cheeks. But there was no time to smooth her feathers now. He got his hands around her waist, carefully avoiding her ribs—he didn't need a tickle fit with her knee resting on his nuts—and shifted her to the side so he could sit up.

"Sugar, we've got to go."

It took a minute to sink in. Then, "The wedding!" she cried, bouncing to her knees. They both started to stand, and—"Aghh!"—her toe whacked his knee. Tears welled in her eyes.

"Aw, sweetheart." Lifting her in his arms, he set her gently on the bed. She brought her foot up to cradle it, trying hard not to cry, and her eyes landed on her dress, flattened on the floor. The brimming tears spilled over.

He scooped it up, shook it out. "It's not as bad as it looks, honey. Just let me clean myself up and then we'll take it from there."

Closing himself in the bathroom, he took care of business, then did a quick check in the mirror. His bowtie was cockeyed but easily straightened. His jacket was fine once he brushed off the glass. And the torn tab of his trousers—that memory prompted a smile of male satisfaction—was easily concealed under the cummerbund, a device he'd previously scorned as useless but that now took on a whole new meaning . . . *cum*merbund. His smile widened to a grin.

Then he opened the door and got a load of Vicky, and his grin faded.

He went into crisis mode.

"Okay, honey. First thing you've got to do is wash your pretty face and get some stuff on it." Her nose was red as a clown's, and her lips, fetchingly puffy from having the hell kissed out of them, needed some color. Her red-rimmed eyes would probably take a miracle.

Hoisting her by the arms, he hustled her into the bathroom as fast as she could hop. Standing behind her, he met her eyes in the mirror. "You can do it," he said bracingly, and fled the scene of the accident.

Digging through the armoire, he came up with an iron. No ironing board, but one sweep of his forearm pushed everything on the dressing table back against the mirror. He went at the dress, and by the time Vicky emerged, it was wrinkle-free. His mama would be proud.

But there was one big problem.

"Honey, you got any safety pins?"

"What for?" she asked, rooting through her underwear drawer. She came out with some pale yellow panties that caught his eye. His gaze slid to the mangled peach ones she still wore.

"Um." He'd forgotten what he meant to say, and who could blame him? She had, without a doubt, an absolutely perfect ass. Smaller than he usually went for, but tight as a drum, round as an apple, and built to model tiny lace panties.

She glanced over her shoulder. "Well?"

He pulled it together. "I don't want you to panic, sugar, but we've got a little tear."

"What!" She flew across the room as fast as she could hop.

Their scorching quickie must have driven the rending sound that preceded it clean out of her head, because when he showed her the split seam—starting just below the zipper and running eight inches down over what would be the curve of her bottom—she muttered a curse and took off for the bathroom again, reemerging with a tiny sewing kit.

"Honey, I don't think we have time—"

She cut him off. "The fabric's too delicate for safety pins, especially at a stress point like the seat." She threaded a needle, all business. "Turn it inside out and hold it taut."

Quick as lightning, she stitched it up, although in his opinion it was a half-assed job. His mama would *not* have approved. But he wasn't about to say so at ten minutes to four. In the distance, the church bells tolled, welcoming the wedding guests. A bead of sweat rolled down his temple.

She bit off the thread, a show of teeth that for some reason got him hard again. Then she slapped her hands on his shoulders. "Down," she snapped out, "and try not to trip me this time."

"It wasn't my fault—" he began, but she cut him off again.

"Just *do it*."

Well, enough was enough. "I'll *do it* all right." And wrapping one hand around the back of her head, he kissed her hard on those swollen lips.

For one split second, she resisted. Then she let out a whimper and melted like butter. Her palms slid up his chest, over his shoulders, into his hair. She leaned into him, putty in his hands. He could take her again—and gladly would—if only they had more time.

With an effort, he gentled the kiss. Then slowly, a centimeter at a time, he pulled back, broke it off. And smiled down into blue eyes gone glassy again.

Now that was more like it.

Together, they got her into the dress and he zipped it up, saying a reluctant farewell to silky lingerie and silkier skin, already envisioning unzipping it again in just a few hours' time, when he'd put that lost-in-space look back into her eyes and keep it there for fourteen hours. Until he had to board the train and start for home.

The thought jarred him. Tomorrow he'd be going back to Texas, never to see her again. A couple of days ago that was his fondest wish. Now it felt . . . weird.

But there was no time for introspection. Vicky was checking her hair in the dressing table mirror. She'd piled it into a loose knot of some kind, with two tendrils curving around her cheeks like parentheses. She fiddled with it nervously.

"It looks great, honey. Let's go."

She shook her head, distressed. "It's a mess. I can't do a thing with it."

He paused. Took a moment. Caught a tendril and let it slide through his fingers. "I like it this way," he said, softly, and watched her eyes widen, then flutter. Nervously, she smoothed her hands down the dress.

"I like the dress too," he said. "You look like a movie star."

Her gaze fell, but her telltale skin flushed a pretty pink. He grazed a knuckle over her bare shoulder, and a shiver shimmied through her. The damnedest things about her got him hard. Her teeth on that thread. That little shiver. Christ, he hadn't been like this since . . . Lissa.

Her memory blew through him like an icy wind, chilling him to the bone. He dropped his hand. "Ready?"

She let out a breath, as if she'd been holding it. Hopped to the bed and picked up the tiny purse that matched her dress. "Ready."

He took a moment to look her over, coolly, just to verify that she was in one piece. And in spite of himself, warmth flooded his chest again. She looked so damn cute that he wanted to laugh at her, with her bad foot held up behind her, the drop-dead dress and fuck-me hair almost—but not quite—ruined by the granny sandals.

But on second thought, her knitted brow told him she expected to be laughed at. Or criticized. And he needed her to understand once and for all that he wasn't her mother, and he wasn't Winnie.

So he held back the laugh on the chance she'd misconstrue it. Gave her a sexy, slow smile instead.

"Come on, gorgeous," he drawled. "Your carriage awaits." And he scooped her up in his arms.

CHAPTER FIFTEEN

NO GRAND ROMANTIC gesture goes unpunished. The castle was farther away than Ty remembered, the steps up to the chapel narrower, and much, much steeper. And Vicky, well . . . "Honey, remember what I said about you being on the skinny side?"

She lifted her head from his shoulder, squinted at him dangerously.

He huffed out a breath. "Let's just say that I've come to appreciate it."

That made her laugh.

"And to give you fair warning," he went on, "when Isabelle gives me shit for being late, I'm telling her the truth. That you dragged me down on the floor and nailed me."

She whopped her bag against his shoulder. "You can't tell her that! What if Winston finds out? Or Mother?"

"What if they do? Before they can shoot off their mouths, the wedding'll be over." He paused a beat. "But if you're really worried, I might be persuaded to take the blame."

"What'll that cost me?"

His forehead crinkled like he was thinking about it.

"Historically speaking, a woman's best bargaining chip has always been sex."

"We just had sex!" Her color rose when she said it.

Biting down on a grin, he gave her a pitying look. "What we had, honey, was a quickie. It was nice—in fact, it was fucking fantastic—but what I'm talking about is the kind of sex that takes all night. The kind where you come a bunch of times and I come a bunch of times, and neither of us gets more than a catnap in between. The kind where we have to sneak down to the kitchen for snacks to keep up our strength."

She was quiet for a minute. He braced for the explosion.

Then she said, "Oh. Okay." And she let out this little humming sigh that stiffened his cock like a hit of Viagra. Sweat popped out on his brow. His gait hitched as he battled the urge to ditch the wedding and carry her straight back to bed.

In the end, he made himself walk the last fifty feet to the chapel, but he didn't trust himself to say another word.

VICKY CAUGHT HER lip in her teeth. To hell with her lipstick, she'd just committed to a sex-a-thon with Ty! *What was she thinking?*

Not that she didn't want to go through with it. She did. Oh boy, did she.

But insecurity racked her. She knew her way around the basics, but her only acquaintance with the advanced stuff came from books and, okay, a few movies. Compared to Ty's encyclopedic sex life, her experience wouldn't fill a pamphlet.

And that wasn't the worst of it. The worst of it was that she couldn't orgasm with a man. She needed privacy. She needed to concentrate. She needed to get it just right or it slipped through her fingers. So to speak.

Men just didn't understand that. They wanted to make

her come, to be the hero, and when they couldn't, they got pissy. They put the blame on her, and made condescending cracks to salve their egos. They called her uptight and frigid and sexually stunted, names that stuck in her mind like burrs and pretty much assured that she'd never be able to come with any man, ever.

Until Ty, that is. Wow, what a trip. Her insides still quivered. But it was probably just an aberration. She'd been carried away, rocked by passion like never before. Not thinking, just going with it, letting it happen.

Ty was different, she couldn't deny it. He wound her up, pissed her off, made her laugh, stirred her up in every way.

But *she* wasn't different. She was the same old Victoria. And when she got in bed with him tonight, all her neuroses and fears and deficiencies would come with her. What would happen then? Would she revert to form? Would he realize that she was only half a loaf and let her down easy?

Or it would it be like today, when she'd shed her hangups like last winter's coat and finally let herself go?

There was no way to know until it happened.

For the moment she had to focus on her brother's furious fiancée, waiting for them outside the chapel with arms akimbo. She fired both barrels at Ty.

"Where have you been?"

Seeing Isabelle's tight lips, the spots of color in her cheeks, Vicky knew she should feel guilty. But she couldn't muster it. After all, Isabelle had a lifetime of great sex ahead of her with Matt. Vicky's one quickie with Ty might be the best sex she'd ever get.

Now he worked his magic on Isabelle. "It's my fault, honey, and I promise to make it up to you." His smile would've disarmed a nuke.

Isabelle was no match for it. She flapped a hand. "Oh well. Weddings never go off on time anyway."

And that, Vicky thought, explained why their romance had fizzled. Isabelle was too nice for the likes of Tyrell Brown. He needed a woman who wouldn't fold like paper when he whipped out that killer smile. Who'd call bullshit on him when he laid on the charm. Who'd shake up his comfy little world and make him work a little.

Not that she had anyone particular in mind.

AN HOUR PAST sunset, the reception was in full swing. Dinner was long over, the cake had been cut and served, and the band was hitting its stride. Under the huge open tent, lit only by fairy lights and the votives that flickered on tabletops, bodies packed the dance floor.

Up on the dais, at the long table where the wedding party was seated, Vicky sat alone with her foot propped on a chair, watching the dancers. As "Blue Suede Shoes" came to a rousing close, Matt looped an arm around his new wife's waist and dipped her low. Flushed and glowing, she let her head fall back dramatically until Matt swept her up again as everyone, including Vicky, burst into applause.

The band signaled a break and the dancers drifted from the floor, the happy couple making their way to Vicky. Jack and Lil joined them a moment later, sweaty and smiling, then Annemarie, towing Ricky by the hand. An attentive waiter appeared with champagne. Matt raised his glass.

"To my wife," he said, looking, if possible, even happier than when he'd said, "I do." "Isabelle, the moment I saw you walk into Tiffany's, sparkling brighter than anything in the store, I knew you were the woman I'd marry. I fell in love with you that day, I love you even more today, and I'll love you for the rest of my life."

Isabelle's giggle tinkled like chimes. Looping her arms

around his neck, she whispered something in Matt's ear that made him laugh out loud, and Vicky's heart swelled. He deserved every bit of happiness Isabelle brought him.

Fingers grazed her shoulder as Ty sat down beside her. His hand came to rest on the back of her chair. Together they watched the newlyweds whisper back and forth, oblivious to everyone else.

"They're a family now," Ty murmured. "They come first with each other."

"I'm glad for them." Vicky meant it, but her voice held the same wistful note. They both felt the loss, and sharing it relieved some of the ache in her heart. She angled toward him. "We were lucky to have them for as long as we did."

Surprise lit his eyes. Hadn't he known she was lonely too?

He lifted a hand, traced her jaw with one finger. "Honey, I'm feeling pretty damn lucky right this minute."

The tenderness in his tone caught her off guard. It set butterflies fluttering in her stomach. Rendered her speechless.

A slow smile touched his lips, telling her he'd read her mind again. Telling her he was going to kiss her.

She wanted him to kiss her.

Before he could make good on the promise, Isabelle spoke up, her voice full of mischief. "So, Ty, would you like to explain why you were late for my wedding?"

He dragged his gaze from Vicky. For a long, slow moment he blinked lazily at Isabelle, while first one side of his mouth, then the other, kicked up in a smile. Another long, slow moment passed and he didn't say a word, leaving them to divine the meaning of his smile while heat bloomed up Vicky's neck. Then one by one, their gazes flicked to her. Matt's brow furrowed. Isabelle's lips pursed knowingly. Jack grinned. Lil rolled her eyes.

And Annemarie did something under the table that drew Ricky's attention back to her.

Another long, slow moment later, Ty leaned over and spoke in her ear, his voice pitched low so only she could hear. "Remember what you owe me for this," he drawled. Her butterflies swooped and plunged. Then he leaned back in his chair and said, truthfully, "Isabelle, honey, it's embarrassing to admit, but a clothing emergency came up, a bad one. So bad it required a needle and thread which, as you can imagine, I didn't have on me."

He stroked a thumb along Vicky's shoulder. "Luckily, Vicky here had a couple dozen of those little sewing kits you get in nice hotels. She stitched things up quick as could be, but still and all, it held us up. I'm real sorry about that, but believe me, sugar, it beat the alternative." He rolled that smile over Isabelle again. "Didn't figure you'd want anybody's ass, no matter how fine, hanging out in the wedding photos."

Isabelle stifled a grin, and it occurred to Vicky that her new sister-in-law was likely conjuring up a memory of Ty's fine ass. And who could blame her? It was eminently memorable.

Gently, his thumb stroked her shoulder blade, back and forth. Something so simple, so G-rated, shouldn't be so sexy. But it was. Her lips curved of their own accord. He smiled back at her, whiskey eyes crinkling irresistibly.

The sound system took over for the band, a change in tempo from Elvis to Chopin. Ty's smile deepened. His palm, warm and lightly callused, cupped her shoulder, making the butterflies turn somersaults. "Dance with me?"

"I wish I could," she said, and meant it from the bottom of her heart. She would have given anything not to be hobbled by her toe, because when she danced with Ty, all of their sharp edges smoothed out. As if their bodies

knew the secret of compatibility that their brains were
just learning.

"Trust me," he said. He lifted her foot off the chair,
lowered it gently to the floor, then pointed to his own feet.
"Climb on." She gave him a skeptical look. He grinned.
"Sweetheart, if I could lug you through the cobblestone
streets of Amboise, I can sure as hell cart you around this
itty-bitty dance floor."

"But your boots look . . ." Ignorant of cowboy boot lore,
she searched for the appropriate adjective. "Expensive?"

"You got that right, honey. So I won't argue if you want
to leave your shoes under the table."

Her bare feet molded to his boots. Balanced like that,
she couldn't help but cling to him. He held her just as
tightly, arm strapped across the small of her back. The
music carried them around the floor, and if they weren't
as graceful as they'd been on the terrace, they were more
in tune in other ways. Less antagonistic; more horny.

"I see you brought your friend," Vicky smirked, refer-
ring to the now-familiar erection sandwiched between
them.

"Wouldn't go anywhere without him." He rubbed his
cheek against her temple. "You seemed mighty fond of
him yourself a few hours ago."

His words, and the silky, sexy tone he uttered them in,
sent a bolt of heat due south. She had to swallow twice
before replying. "Anthropomorphizing your penis? What
would the philosophers say about that?"

"Fuck the philosophers." His breath was hot in her ear.
"You started it, honey, and when it comes to sex, I can go
along with most anything. You want to think of it like a
three-way—you, me, and my cock—that's okay with me.
As long as both of us get to fuck you, it's all good."

Her breath hitched. Dirty talk as foreplay was a new

experience. Her college boyfriend had lacked the imagination for it, and Winston, her only other lover, hadn't
bothered much with foreplay of any kind.

She had to admit, she liked it. And she was determined
to give it a try.

"Sounds interesting." Her lips had gone dry. She
touched them with her tongue. "Who gets to be on top?
Out of the three of us, I mean."

He pulled her closer, if that was possible, caught her
earlobe in his teeth. "It's a long night, sugar. We'll all
take a turn."

His voice was honey heated to the boiling point. Her
heart did a double thump, then broke loose into a gallop.
His teeth tugged at her earring, possessive, not painful.
His bristled jaw scraped her cheek, a thoroughly mas-
culine sensation that triggered answering spasms in her
pelvis.

Oh yes, she liked this dirty talk. She couldn't match
his steamy drawl, but the heat coursing through her veins
infused her voice with a sexual rumble she hardly recognized as her own. "Me first," she growled close to his ear.
"Then you and your friend can do whatever you want to
me for the rest of the night."

She scored big with that one. His teeth bit down; his
arm clamped her to his hard-on.

But she never got to enjoy it, because a sharp intake of
breath made her look up over Ty's shoulder, where Adrianna gaped at her. From her appalled expression, she'd
overheard Vicky's remark. And Winston, her partner,
stared at Vicky too. His expression was harder to read,
but mingled with rage and disdain was definite interest.

The look on her own face must have been as
spectacular—shock, dismay, a fiery flush—because Ty
spun them in a circle to follow her gaze. Seeing Winston

and Adrianna, both frozen in their tracks, he unloaded a slow smile.

"Winnie," he drawled, "you don't want to sneak up on me like that. I might get twitchy. Give you another bloody lip."

Fury flushed all other emotion from Winston's face. "Let's take it outside right now, *cowboy*. We'll see whose jaw is wired shut."

Ty's smile widened to a grin. "Tempting as that sounds, I've got other plans." He shrugged. "Maybe in the morning. If I can drag myself out of bed."

Winston sneered. "Yeah, now that the trial's over you can quit pretending to mourn your wife and get back to fucking anything with tits."

Ty's jaw tightened but his smile didn't falter. "If you're afraid I'll show you up, Winnie, that horse already left the barn. You have a good night, now, you hear?"

Vicky was sure her own face was flushed as dark as Winston's. She couldn't look at her mother, whose jaw had fallen.

Ty danced her across the floor to their table. She sat down dumbly, staring at her lap. He sat beside her, stroked a knuckle along her jaw.

"Vicky." He sounded more serious than he usually did. "I'm sorry, honey, I shouldn't have said that. He pissed me off and my tongue got out in front of my brain. But sweetheart, you haven't done anything to be embarrassed about." His knuckle kept up its slow cruise, curving under her chin, tilting her head up until she met his eyes. "You're a beautiful woman, and you have a gorgeous body. It's yours to do with as you please, and what pleases you is nobody else's business."

His thumb brushed her cheek. "Your mama will recover, she's no fainthearted virgin." A slow smile crossed his lips. "And Winnie, well, Winnie'll be lying awake to-night, jerking off and wishing he was me."

That surprised a laugh out of her. "Gee, thanks for putting that picture in my head."

Grinning now, he dropped a kiss on her smile. "Give me five minutes to find the men's room and then I'll carry you home."

Ty was barely out of sight when Winston descended. Looming over her like a storm cloud, he hissed through clenched teeth. "Are you out of your mind, Victoria? Did you actually have sex with that jackass?"

Up came her chin. "Yes, Winston, I'm completely out of my mind. I lost it four hours ago during a quickie on my bedroom floor, and I expect to stay out of it *all night long.*"

His eyes narrowed with each word she uttered. "Your mother told me you wanted to start over! That's why I'm here, Victoria. I'm a busy man and this trip has already inconvenienced me. So if this thing with Brown is some ploy to make me jealous, then you need to get it through your head that I don't have time for your shenanigans."

"My *shenanigans*?" She pushed back her chair, made room to stand up to him, even if only on one foot. "If it was any of your business, Winston, I'd tell you that having sex with Tyrell has nothing to do with *you*. It's all about *me*!"

"*You?*" He laughed, incredulous. "Do you really think he cares about having sex with *you*? He's doing it to get at *me*."

"Oh, please." She waved that off as egomaniacal claptrap.

His incredulity mutated to scorn. "Have you forgotten that you're frigid, Victoria? Do you honestly think he won't notice?"

His aim was true, a direct hit to the heart of her insecurities. She flattened her lips against the pain. And he went in for the kill.

"Do you have *any idea* how many women he's fucked? Do you think any of *them* were frigid?" His laugh scraped her skin like nails. "You'll be lucky if he doesn't throw you out of bed and go looking for that stripper." He leaned in closer, breath hot on her face. "That's what men do when a woman disappoints them in bed. They go find another one."

It hit her like a punch in the chest, knocking her back a step, stealing her breath. Her gumption ran out through her fingers like sand.

Humiliation this extreme had to be fatal, so like any wounded animal, she had no choice; it was flee or die.

Reaching behind her, she felt for her purse, knocking it on the floor in her distress. Cursing her clumsiness, she whirled away from him, then made it worse by jamming the table with her hip. Wineglasses upended, forks clattered against plates. And, last but not least, just as she bent over to grope for her purse, an empty carafe toppled onto its side and rolled off the edge of the table.

OCCURRING AS IT did during a break between songs, the explosion of glass drew every eye to the dais, all of them centering on Vicky's bent-over ass . . . at the exact moment when her amateur sewing job ruptured.

From across the tent, Ty watched with the rest of them as the seam burst wide open, exposing her ass cheeks to the world and to Winston, with only the flimsy strip of yellow lace that was caught in her crack preserving the tiniest measure of modesty.

Naturally, she was the last to know. Intent on searching the floor, she cluelessly swung her ass like a compass, giving every person under the tent a full-moon view, until, finally, a breeze must have struck her, because she snapped upright, flattening both palms over her cheeks.

Ty's heart wept for her as she spun toward the sea of upturned faces, mortification staining her face cherry red. She swooned back a step, bumping the table, setting off another crash.

And Winston, the asshole, didn't even reach out to steady her.

Ty couldn't take any more. He had to get to her. To get her away from that fuckhead Winston. Shouldering through the speechless crowd, he vowed to make the bastard pay. When he finished with him, he'd be nothing but a bloodstain on the floor.

But first he had to get Vicky out of here. Make her smile. Convince her, somehow, someway, that she'd look back on this and laugh.

It would require all of his powers of persuasion.

He leaped up on the dais, but her brother reached her first, leaving Ty flatfooted. His empty hands curled into fists. Damn it, this whole debacle was his fault. He'd provoked Winston, and then he'd left Vicky alone and vulnerable. And now he couldn't even get his arms around her!

Frustrated beyond reason, furious beyond measure, and with a bubbling brew of jealousy and fury and guilt and shame all churning through his heart and his head, he did the only other thing he could think of.

He shoved Winston off the dais and onto the table below.

The explosion of glass and crockery made Vicky's bursting carafe sound like a pin drop. The table collapsed like a movie prop with Winston splayed out in the center, a look of utter astonishment on his prep school face.

Now that was more like it.

Stripping off his jacket, Ty slung it around Vicky's shoulders, then, grinning like a lunatic, he jumped down from the dais into the great big beautiful mess he'd made.

Winston, meanwhile, had scrambled to his feet. Picking his way from the ruins, he wiped the soles of his shoes on the tablecloth, leaving streaks of chocolate cake on the crisp white linen. Gobs of frosting studded his hair. His jacket and trousers were smeared with it.

"You're a dead man, Brown," he hissed through his teeth. And tossing his jacket aside, he lunged at Ty like a lineman.

Winston was strong and gutsy, but Ty had it all over him on speed and agility. Sidestepping lightly, he used Winston's momentum against him, grabbing a handful of his expensive white shirt to help him further along on his trajectory. As he flew past Ty, his body got ahead of his feet and he pitched headfirst onto another table, bringing that one down too, pancaking at the feet of the gaping guests who'd risen to watch the spectacle.

Winston Churchill Banes face down in chocolate cake was a beautiful sight, and Ty laughed his glee out loud. Like a kid in a lunchroom food fight, he megaphoned his mouth and bugled like a ten-year-old, "Have a nice trip, Winnie, see you next fall!"

It had the expected juvenile effect.

Winston lurched to his feet, homicidal and adrenaline-fueled. With a blur of speed even Ty couldn't match, he rammed his head into Ty's gut, goring him like a bull and wiping the smile clean off his face.

Guests scattered like leaves as Winston drove him backward onto yet another table. Ty's shoulders hit the table, the table hit the floor. And then Winston, the fucker, hit him in the jaw with a sledgehammer of a right cross. Stars spangled his vision, the ocean roared in his ears, and for a split second it occurred to him that he might have underestimated old Winnie.

In fact, he might just get his ass kicked.

Then, over the shouting and squealing and general cussing that surrounded him, he heard Jack's drawl as plain as day. "Shit, Tyrell, this city boy's spanking you."

It was unthinkable. He'd never live it down.

Galvanized, he grabbed a fistful of Winston's shirtfront and yanked, bringing the son of a bitch down onto his own chest like an anvil, knocking the wind out of his lungs. Undeterred, he wrapped both arms around Winston's trunk, locked his wrists behind the asshole's back, and squeezed.

Hard.

At first it barely slowed Winston at all. He boxed Ty's ears, mashed his lips. But Ty kept squeezing, and when his arms tired, he juiced himself by picturing the misery on Vicky's face as Winston loomed beside her, not deigning even to offer a hand when she could hardly stay on her feet. Well, a few broken ribs would teach the shithead some manners. Winnie'd cry like a girl before he was through with him.

It took longer than it should have, but at last Winston's body seemed to go lax. Ty's lips curled in a savage smile. Scenting victory, he relaxed his hold the slightest bit, just enough to let some blood flow to his hands.

And Winston threw himself sideways, taking Ty along with him.

Winston, it seemed, had been playing possum, and as he rolled onto his back, crushing Ty's hands underneath him, Ty cursed himself for an amateur. Now Winston had the advantage, wriggling like a snake, deliberately grinding Ty's knuckles into the tabletop until he had no choice but to let go. Then he shoved Ty off, sprang to his feet, and shot out a kick at his head.

Ty's reflexes saved him by a bare inch. He rolled left, gained his own feet in a hurry, then faced Winston across the tabletop wreckage.

Damn it, this city boy should have been no match for him, but the fucker had lost his mind, and now he was powered by the strength of a madman. He seethed at Ty, pawing the earth like a bull, and Ty knew he had to get serious *right away* if he wanted to get out of this in one piece.

Ignoring his injuries, he ripped open his cuffs, scattering cuff links. Then he raked his hair back, and with eyes glued to Winston, taunted him with a grin while he circled like a panther waiting to spring.

Winston didn't like being stalked; impatience was written on his face. Instead of waiting for Ty to pounce, he charged instead.

But he only had one trick in his bag, and this time Ty was ready for it. When Winston dropped his shoulders for the head butt, Ty skipped aside, hooked an arm under his neck, and captured him in an upside-down headlock.

Winston roared his fury, windmilling his arms, trying to catch Ty's legs. But Ty was on his game now, and lightning fast; Winston couldn't get a grip. Around the floor they staggered, weaving and bobbing like drunks, while Ty gloated, knowing that whenever he wanted to, he could sweep Winnie's legs out from under him, crack his head on the floor, and plant a sweet right hook on his kisser. He'd be down for the count.

The problem was, it was almost too easy. For the first time in months, Ty was living in the moment. Blood and sweat, pain and property damage; it was freaking fantastic, and he didn't want it to end. So, like an idiot, he let Winnie rampage around, bent at the waist, head locked under Ty's armpit, while he poked a few jabs to the son of a bitch's ribs.

Yes sir, he had things well in hand. Until he broke the cardinal rule of fistfighting. He let himself be distracted.

Glancing up at the dais to see how Vicky was enjoy-

ing the show, he caught a glimpse of Isabelle. The wrath
of God blazed in her eyes. Steam whistled out of her
ears. And suddenly all the blood and sweat and property
damage didn't seem like such a good idea.

He glanced around. The few tables still standing had
been knocked askew, either by the brawlers or the guests
who'd fled them. Spilled wine stained white tablecloths
and pooled on the floor around broken glass and shattered plates. Chocolate cake smeared napkins, tuxes, and
satin chair covers. And the flowers, all those beautiful,
expensive arrangements, hand-selected by Isabelle herself, lay trampled on the floor. Only the dais had escaped
ruination.

He was in big, big trouble.

Winston must have sensed his distraction, because he
gave a mighty heave that broke Ty's grip. And then he
lunged straight at Ty.

Ty managed to keep his feet, and for a moment they
grappled awkwardly, sliding on tablecloths, skidding in
frosting, until they ended up in a bear hug, each of them
squeezing the other with all their might as they revolved
like dancers around the floor.

Ty struggled to shut Isabelle out of his mind, but the
more he tried not to think of her, the more stubbornly she
appeared. He'd never seen such fury on her lovely face,
much less directed toward him. And to make matters
worse, to guarantee the complete and utter destruction of
her entire wedding reception, it was becoming horribly
clear that Winston's gyrations were steering them ineluc-
tably toward the dais.

Ty tried everything to change their trajectory. He hol-
lered in Winston's ear, stomped on his foot. But inexo-
rably, inevitably, the pigheaded bastard circled, ignoring
his pleas, disregarding even his last-ditch attempt at sur-
render.

It was no use. Ever closer they came, a juggernaut of muscle and sinew, stubbornness and stupidity. At the last minute, Matt leaped from the dais, hauling Vicky and Isabelle with him. Ty caught one final glimpse of Isabelle's furious face. If he read her lips right, she was swearing to never, ever, *ever* forgive him.

Then he and Winston barreled into the dais, shoving it off its foundation. It collapsed into a pile of kindling.

CHAPTER SIXTEEN

VICKY PRESSED HER ear to her door.

"... *happiest day of my* ..." "... *brawling like a drunken* ..." "*Do you have any idea* ..."

Even at full volume, Isabelle's voice was softer than the average woman's. Vicky could catch only snatches of her tirade. But Tyrell, trapped in his room with Isabelle, surely heard every word.

Imagining his woebegone expression, his abject contrition, she let out a bubble of laughter. He deserved Isabelle's wrath, there was no question about that. The wreckage was epic. And though he'd promised to pay for everything, which would set him back a chunk, he could never truly compensate for trashing the wedding.

Opening her door, Vicky stuck her head into the hallway, the better to hear Isabelle blast him. Jack and Lil were doing the same. Ricky too. They exchanged wincing smiles as Isabelle hit her stride.

"*Do you know, Tyrell Brown, that videos of your debacle are* already *up on YouTube? Matt heard from someone he works with! They'll be watching them at his office on Monday! Laughing at him! Laughing at me!*" She got shriller by the second. *"And if anyone on either side of the Atlantic happens to miss it, half the guests were posting pictures to Facebook* in real time!"

Ty must have had the poor judgment to comment on guests who would do such a thing, because Isabelle dug down and found another decibel. *"Don't you dare . . ."*

Vicky couldn't take any more. She closed her door and hopped into the bathroom, the only place where she couldn't hear Isabelle shouting.

Two days earlier she would have reveled in Ty's come-uppance, but at the moment she felt quite charitable toward him, because after the damage was done and the dais in pieces, he'd pulled himself together and given Winston a final thrashing.

Yes, indeed. Ty would be nursing some injuries of his own, but Winston was on his way to the hospital.

Still and all, she couldn't wholly regret Isabelle's tongue-lashing, because between that and his own injuries, Ty was unlikely to be interested in sex. And that was a huge relief. Not because of the appeal on his lawsuit. Oh no, that ship had sailed. By making love to him on this very rug, she'd already forsaken her professional integrity and virtually guaranteed that the firm would have to withdraw from the appeal. And she couldn't bring herself to regret it.

No, she was relieved because Winston had quite effectively reminded her what a disappointment she was between the sheets. Better that she and Ty part ways tomorrow without him discovering it for himself. And possibly rejecting her when he did.

She'd finished washing up when she heard a knock on her door. "It's Tyrell, honey. Open up."

Tying her robe, she pulled the door open a foot. He stood in the hallway, barefoot, shirt open, looking like he'd been run over by a truck. He swept one glance from her bare feet to her towel-wrapped head, then pushed the door wider and limped inside.

Shutting the door, she said, "What happened to you?"

He widened blackening eyes. "What *happened* to me? If you missed it, check YouTube. I hear the video's gone viral."

"Yeah, I heard about that." She tipped her head toward the door. "Isabelle was kind of loud."

"That's one word for it." He plopped on her bed.

She didn't hold his surliness against him. "What I meant was, why are you limping?"

"Because your stupid ex-boyfriend stomped on my ankle, that's why. It's so swelled up I probably won't get my boots on tomorrow." He tugged up the leg of his trousers.

Vicky eyed his ankle skeptically. It looked normal, but she said, "Let me put some clothes on and I'll get you some ice."

He reached out and caught her arm. "I don't need ice, and you definitely don't need clothes. Now come over here and pay your debt to society."

Her heart thumped harder. She couldn't have sex with him. She wanted to. Oh, she wanted to. But she couldn't.

She tried to make light of it. "Don't you think you've had enough action for one day, cowboy?"

"The only action worth talking about was the quickie we had right here on this rug. As good as that was—and honey, it was real good—I didn't nearly get my fill of you." He tugged her down on his lap, hooked an arm around her waist to hold her in place. With his other hand, he cupped her cheek, stroked his thumb along her cheekbone.

She tried to turn her face away, afraid to meet his eyes, afraid of how much she wanted him, but the gentle pressure of his palm brought them face to face, his warm whiskey eyes just inches from hers.

"Now, sweetheart," he said, his drawl deep and beguiling, "you promised me a long night of hot sex. And if ever a man needed one, I do. So these second thoughts you're having, you need to put them out of your mind."

His thumb moved lower, rubbing her lips, lingering at the corner, then slowly, gently, tracing the seam. Goosebumps shivered up her spine, prickling her neck. Her lips parted, an instinctive reaction that let his thumb in to stroke along the wetness inside her bottom lip. His nail clicked across her teeth, and before she could stop herself, she nipped him, holding on lightly.

A smile curved one corner of his mouth, spreading like sunrise across his lips. "That's right," he murmured, "show me some teeth. Do your bitchy lawyer thing for me."

"I'm not a bitchy lawyer," she said around his thumb.

His eyes crinkled as his smile deepened. "Oh yeah you are. All buttoned up in your suit of armor, hair twisted up in a don't-fuck-with-me bun. And those lips, mmm, those lips. Bloodred, like you just sucked some poor bastard dry."

She had to smile at the picture he painted. "You don't like red lipstick?"

"Oh, I love red lipstick, sugar." He brought his chin down, came in for a bite, tugging her lower lip with his teeth. She hissed a breath, surprised, aroused. Then he sucked on her lip, and every cell in her body lit up.

Winston's poison forgotten, she released his thumb and kissed him, pushing her tongue inside, tasting his, tangling them up. Her hands dove under his shirt, raced over his back, so broad and deep. He wrapped one hand around her head, splayed the other on her back to plaster her breasts to his chest. She squirmed against him, stiff nipples scraping hard muscles through the silky fabric of her robe.

He dragged his lips across her cheek, breathing hard. "Tell me how you want it." His tongue licked her ear, and she let her head fall back, offering her throat, begging him to take it. "I can strip you down." His fingers hooked her neckline, pulled it down over her shoulders. "Tie you up. Lay you out."

"Whatever you want," she gasped, hardly recognizing her own voice. Desire made it raspy, and when his tongue swept along her throat, his teeth fastening on the tender spot where it curved to her shoulder, such a wave of liquid heat gushed through her, igniting her blood, melting her bones, that she hardly recognized herself at all.

"This one's your call, sugar." His breath came ragged now, his lips moving under her chin, along her jaw, devouring her like chocolate. "I can take you on the bed. On the floor. Up against the wall with your legs wrapped around me. I'll fuck you any way you want, and I won't stop until you're screaming my name, coming on my cock while I'm coming inside you."

His words were dynamite, blowing apart every inhibition. She shook like a leaf. Nothing, no one, had ever made her feel like this, like she owned her body, every sinew, every cell, and could make demands with it. Demands that wouldn't be denied.

Shoving her hands against his chest, she pushed him back, raking him with greedy eyes. "I want . . ." Her voice shook. "I want *all of it.*"

His body twitched when she said it. His eyes glazed. The heat of his skin blazed through his shirt, scorching her palms. God, he was as turned on as she was.

Already, she'd soaked through her panties, a scrap of black lace she'd put on in case he showed up. And she was glad she had, because his hand slid up her thigh. When his fingers touched lace, he sucked a breath. Flicking her robe aside, he dragged his gaze away from hers, fixing his eyes on the tiny triangle. "Jesus," he breathed, "there's nothing to them."

Slipping a finger under the edge, he ran his knuckle

along the crease of her thigh. "Soft," he whispered. "Soft and pretty." Then he dipped it down, letting out a groan when he hit the slickness between her thighs. "You're so wet for me," he got out on a rasp.

"You're so hard for me," she murmured, wriggling on the iron rod beneath her. His breath hitched. He ground up against her and, too lost in lust to wonder at her wantonness, she let her legs fall open in invitation.

Never before had she felt this way; gorgeous as a supermodel, lust-worthy as a porn star.

Heady with the power of her own sexuality, she drove her fingers into his hair, pulled his head down to take his mouth, and kissed him with pure abandon.

TY WAS COMING unglued. The woman in his arms was on fire. And so was he, hanging on by a thread, dangerously close to throwing her down and taking her hard, harder even than he had six hours ago when at least he'd still had some control over himself. Now she was in his head, under his skin, wrapped around his lungs, squeezing the air out so he could hardly breathe for wanting her.

So many nights in the last seven years he'd tried to forget Lissa by burying himself in another woman's body. He used them, but he seldom felt guilty about it. He always showed them a good time and, with a few notable exceptions, managed to leave them with a smile.

Vicky, though, she had him by the balls. At the moment, he wanted her so bad he'd have done anything to get inside her. Scaled the Eiffel Tower, naked. Sold his ranch for a dollar. Let Winston Churchill Banes take a free shot at his head. Anything.

But, thank God, drastic measures weren't called for. Her panties were drenched, she'd spread her legs to let his hand in, and she was kissing him like her life depended on driving him out of his ever-loving mind.

Her hands were everywhere. Fisting his hair, raking his shoulders, scratching his arms. Then they moved lower, pushing the cummerbund aside, working his zipper. Wiggling into his trousers and freeing his cock. Jesus, her palm felt like satin, like she was stroking him with a pair of those incredible panties. He pushed his fingers inside her and her moan was so deep, so hot, that he almost came in her hand.

He couldn't take any more. He broke the kiss. "Call it, honey." He could barely form words. "Bed, floor, wall. Now."

"Wall," she mumbled, and brought her lips down on his again. He could have eaten her alive. Her lips were delicious. He had big plans for those lips. They'd be swollen when he was done.

He stood them both up without breaking the kiss. Turned her toward him and caught her thighs, hoisting her up to his waist so her long legs clamped around him. Three quick steps put her back to the wall, and then, by God, all that wetness did what nature intended, easing his entry into one very tight pussy. He slid in to the root, drawing another moan from her, long and low.

That moan undid him. Just yesterday he'd still believed she was a bitch on wheels. Now he knew she was just the opposite, sweeter and more innocent than he'd ever dreamed. He wouldn't hurt her for the world. Fighting down the primal instinct to take her without mercy, to mark her as his own, he broke their kiss once more and turned his face into her throat, hiding his grimace, compelling sinews that were strung like wire to hold perfectly still while she adjusted to him.

When her muscles released, just a little, just enough, he lifted his head. Her eyes were passion-glazed, her lips puffy, cheeks pink. "Go ahead," she breathed, "fuck me."

God, yes. For hours, he'd craved this. Now he went at her with all that pent-up desire, taking her hard and fast, long and deep, while she met every thrust, her head back against the wall, her nails drawing blood. When his legs threatened to fold at last, he slipped his hand down between them, touched the place that drove her wild. Her eyes rolled back, she shouted "Yes!" And together they came, gasping for God, bodies quaking, a fucking amazing climax that he would never forget if he lived to be a hundred.

"THAT WAS NICE," Vicky murmured.

"*Nice?*" Ty lifted his forehead from her shoulder. "Honey, you just got fucked against a wall. If it was *nice*, I wasn't doing it right."

She smiled lazily. It was so easy to get under his skin, she didn't even have to try.

He walked to the bed and tossed her into the middle, then crawled forward on top of her, propping himself on his elbows. His face was flushed with exertion. He grinned down at her smugly. "Tuckered out?"

"Not a bit," she replied. A drop of sweat trickled from his temple. She licked it off. "You did the hard part. No pun intended."

He laughed. "You're right, I did. And I promise to keep doing the *hard* part for the rest of the night. But, honey, I'm an injured man. I'm afraid you're gonna have to do some of the work."

She shrugged a shoulder. "Like they say in the song, save a horse, ride a cowboy."

He chuckled, and her smile widened. She, Victoria Westin, was engaging in sexual banter.

It occurred to her, suddenly, that sex and fun could, possibly, coexist. After all, Ty made sex seem like play, not work. She felt comfortably sexy, not miserably self-conscious. And if that was true, well, maybe her sexual problems weren't hers at all. Maybe she wasn't frigid.

Maybe, just maybe, she hadn't been with the right man until now.

Ty pushed up on his hands, kicked off his trousers. Then with one hand, he opened her robe. "Mmm," he hummed. "Now *that's* nice." Appreciation glowed in his eyes, warming her skin, tickling the hairs on her nape.

His hand closed over her breast, his palm lightly callused, rougher than her own. The abrasion brought her skin to life. She liked knowing that his hand did more than shuffle papers and tap a keyboard. It turned barb-wire, roped steers, branded calves. Or at least she imagined it did, based on the Westerns she'd seen.

Still and all, Tyrell Brown was no ordinary cowboy. He was sharp as a dagger, and it behooved her to keep her wits about her.

He lifted his eyes to hers, said very seriously, "For the record, honey, *this* is what it means to get felt up." He squeezed, his thumb stroking over her nipple, tightening it to a point.

Her voice sounded breathy, but she played it cool. "How about this?" She cupped a handful of his butt, gave it a squeeze. "What's this called?"

"That's called grab-ass. As in 'The boys and girls played grab-ass on the class trip to the zoo.'"

She burst out laughing. "Where did *that* come from? Personal experience?"

"It's the best teacher. All my sexual knowledge comes from personal experience and, sweetheart, I'm giving you a crash course tonight. Kind of a sexual Berlitz."

"What makes you think I need you to educate me?"

He dipped his head down, stroked his tongue across her nipple. Then he blew on it, smiling as it gathered to a nub.

Looking up again, he said in a voice as warm as it was matter-of-fact, "Honey, somewhere along the line you got some wrong ideas about yourself. You keep trying to fit yourself into them, but it's like squeezing a round peg into a square hole. It's not gonna go. Even so, you keep on trying, and all that trying's got you tied up in knots."

He lowered his head again to drop a line of kisses between her breasts. She hardly felt it. She was frozen, barely able to swallow over the lump in her throat.

How could this man see into her soul?

He moved his head slowly, gently, rubbing his nose along the inner swell of first one breast, then the other. "Now, I can't solve all your problems for you," he said as he nuzzled her. "That's a tall order for just one night. But honey"—he lifted his head, his eyes glowing—"I can sure as hell show you how to enjoy the body God gave you. It's gorgeous, and baby, it's hot as a pistol. There's nothing frigid about you, just the opposite. You're liquid fire."

She stared at him, lips parted, amazed. Then everything inside her welled up, a tsunami of emotions, bitter and blissful, old and new. It swamped her utterly, took her breath away. It came damn near to drowning her.

And then it sucked back out to sea, leaving her blinking and gasping, and so, so glad to be Victoria Westin, alive and well and in bed with Tyrell Brown, in the city of Amboise, France.

From deep down in her belly, she released a laugh. It rolled through her gut and on up through her chest, and as it went, she felt the knots untie, the bars come down.

I'm free, she thought, delirious. *I'm free.*

CHAPTER SEVENTEEN

FREEDOM HAD A price. Pain. Pain in her broken toe, her calves, her cheeks—all four of them—and most of all, pain in her previously underutilized private parts.

Around four a.m., Ty predicted that they'd both be black and blue come morning. Five hours later, Vicky knew he was right. And she'd never felt better in her life.

"You awake?" he whispered in her ear.

"Mmm-hmm." She snuggled her bottom against his groin, smiled when he hardened.

"How do you feel?"

"Like a cat on a sunny windowsill."

He chuckled. "I mean, are you sore? *Too* sore?"

"Probably. But pain is the price of freedom."

He hesitated. "Um, are we talking about the same thing here?"

"I don't know about you," she said with a laugh, "but I'm talking about sex. And I'm ready if you are."

Untangling herself from his arms, she stretched languidly, unconcerned when the covers slid off. He'd al-

ready seen every inch of her, from every conceivable
angle. For the first time in her life, no inhibitions con-
strained her. Rolling toward him, she hooked her knee
over his hip. "Ride 'em, cowboy," she said.

And then—whoa!—she got a look at his face.

Mussed hair, stubbled chin, tiger's eyes roaming over
her appreciatively. All of that was good. But Lord, he
looked like a mug shot. The black under one of his eyes
had spread out in a raccoon ring. His jaw under the sexy
stubble was dark purple and swollen. And he had a cut on
his lip she hadn't noticed before.

Had she done that? With her teeth? She didn't know.

His chest looked okay, spectacular, in fact, except for
some scratches that were definitely her doing. But his
ribs. Ouch. She touched the bruise. "This looks like a
footprint."

He shrugged. "Old Winnie landed a kick or two."

How could he be so casual about it? "He could've
broken your ribs!"

"He was trying. But he didn't." He grinned, his teeth
gleaming whitely among the grape-colored bruises. "I'm
pretty sure I cracked a few of his, though."

She should feel badly about that, but she didn't. After
all the horrible things he said to her just before . . .

"Oh God!" she gasped, and clutched a fist to her chest.
How could she have forgotten?

"It's all right, honey." Ty cupped a hand over her fist. "I
know what you're thinking, and you have to believe me
when I say you have the prettiest ass I've ever seen."

She gaped at him. "I don't care if it's *pretty*! I was *exposed*! My dress split open like a banana and my whole
ass, my *practically naked ass*, hung right out through the
hole!"

"Well, think about it, sweetheart"—he sounded perfectly reasonable—"just imagine if it was riddled with cellulite. Then you'd really have something to feel bad about."

She saw him bite down on the inside of his cheek, trying not to laugh. "It's not funny, you jackass!" Barely restraining the impulse to slug him, she resorted to the torture Matt used on her to this day. She flicked him. In the side of the head, just above the ear.

"Ow!" He rubbed his head. "Why'd you go and do that? For Christ's sake, woman, you owe me a favor!"

Her eyes bugged. "A favor? For *what*?"

"For starting a brawl, that's what! For beating on Winston and ruining Isabelle's reception and busting every damn thing in sight until the whole goddamn tent came down on my head and *everybody forgot about your ass*!"

She went still. He had a point. Once the blood had begun to spill, her ass was old news.

She owed him for that, and she was big enough to admit it.

"You're my hero, Ty." He eyed her sweet smile suspiciously. She wriggled in closer, dropped light kisses around his eye. "Thank you." She sprinkled them across the bruise on his jaw. "Thank you." His lips curved in a smile. She kissed the cut there. "Thank you." Kissed his ribs. "Thank you." Moved her lips lower . . .

He sucked a breath through his teeth. Let his eyes drift closed. "Oh, you're welcome, sugar," he murmured. "Any old time."

TY WOKE ALONE in Vicky's bed. Bright sun streaked through a gap in the curtains. His stomach growled and he checked the clock—11:05. Brunch on the terrace in an hour.

Raising his arm to stretch, his ribs brought him up short. He twisted his head around. Yup, the bruise was definitely shoe-shaped. He didn't care, because he happened to know that old Winnie had one just like it, and it probably hurt a hell of lot more.

In the bathroom, the shower came on. He smiled smugly. Plenty of time yet for shower sex. He'd give her a chance to lather up before he surprised her.

Meanwhile, he had to take a leak.

Inching out of bed like his arthritic grandpa, he bent over painfully, plucked his trousers off the floor, and eased into them. Every muscle in his body ached, and not all of them from fighting. It wasn't that he was getting too old for marathon sex, not at all. The problem was that Vicky was insatiable. How in God's name could anyone think she didn't like sex? Christ, they'd done everything but swing from the chandelier, and that was only because there wasn't one in the damn room.

Hobbling like a quarterback on Monday morning, he crossed the hallway to relieve himself in his own bathroom. Did Vicky a favor by brushing his teeth, then took a minute to admire himself in the mirror, first one side of his mottled face, then the other. None too pretty, but he'd seen worse.

A soft knock on his door had him grinning at his reflection. Damn, the woman was impatient. He'd tease her about that just as soon as—

"Ty? Are you awake?"

Isabelle. His face fell. She must have thought of a few more names to call him.

So much for shower sex.

He opened the door, expecting the worst. But she took one look at him and clapped her hands to her cheeks. "Oh my God!" Tears welled in her eyes.

"Don't you even think about crying," he said. "Nothing's broken. I'll be good as new in forty-eight hours. And all this purple stuff'll be gone in a month."

She dropped her hands. "That sounds like the voice of experience."

"It is. I've been beat up worse, and you can verify that with Jack if you want to. It's temporary."

Her hands went to her hips. "I don't know why you and Jack think fighting's the answer to every problem."

"It's not the answer, honey. It's an excuse. I like to fight. It reminds me I'm alive." She'd never understand that, so he added, truthfully, "Doesn't hurt that I got to beat up on a guy who needed his ass kicked."

Instantly, her face softened. "I can't blame you for that. After all, I set you up with Vicky. Of course you'd want to defend her honor."

Was that what he'd been doing?

His cell jangled. He would have ignored it, but suddenly, guiltily, he remembered Brescia.

"Honey, can you hold your thought for just a minute while I see what's going on back at the ranch?"

"Of course." She touched his arm. "Jack told me about Brescia."

He checked the number, skipped the small talk. "Clancy, thanks for calling. What's the word?"

"Got the labs back." Clancy paused. Ty started to pace, knowing as surely as if he was standing in front of him that Clancy was tucking a pinch of Skoal into his lip. No force on earth could make him continue until he'd packed it in place with his tongue.

"It's bloodworms," the vet finally went on. "And lots of 'em. We'll have to treat her aggressively."

"All right." Ty stopped at the window, stared blindly at the garden. "I'll be home tonight. What do we do?"

"I worked up a treatment schedule." He laid it out while Ty grunted along.

"You'll get her started today?"

"Already have." Clancy paused. "Listen, Ty. We had to put Molly's gray down last night."

Guilt clawed Ty's throat. By exposing Brescia to the gray, he'd put her life at risk too. He tried to focus on Molly. "How's she taking it?"

"You know Molly. She's tough." Clancy paused again. "But it's always hard to see 'em suffer."

"Is Brescia . . ." He couldn't finish the sentence.

"Not yet. But I won't lie to you. You might have a tough decision in front of you."

Whether to euthanize his beloved horse. Inject the drugs into her veins that would stop her brave heart and close her trusting brown eyes forever.

Squeezing his own eyes shut, Ty forced his voice to sound normal. "Thanks, Clancy. Talk to you tomorrow." He closed his phone.

"Ty?" Isabelle's voice was full of concern.

He made himself turn to her. Managed a smile. "Clancy says she'll be fine," he lied. He let a little sadness seep into his voice, just enough to be convincing. If he acted carefree, she'd be on to him instantly.

And he couldn't bear her sympathy. Not the tears, the hugs, the love she'd shower on him from the bottom of her heart. He didn't deserve them. If, once again, life and death were placed in his hands, he didn't want anyone's pity. He didn't want anyone to know what it cost him.

She must have swallowed his act, because she didn't cross the room and throw her arms around him. Instead, she gave him a relieved smile. "I'm so glad. And I'm so glad it's working out between you and Vicky." Isabelle was relentless when she had a point to make. "I knew you'd get along. You're both so bright and funny. And you look so good together."

He cleared his throat. "She's a beauty, all right." And he

was a slut who let her blue eyes and hot body push Brescia clean out of his head. He'd also conveniently forgotten that she'd accused him of callously pulling the plug on his wife, and that she'd be making that same argument on appeal, trying to convince the court that Jason Taylor and his insurance company shouldn't have to pay for Lissa's suffering.

Isabelle must have misread the emotions playing over his face, because she stepped closer. Setting a hand on his cheek, she said softly, "It's time, Ty. It's time to let go of the past and move on."

He froze. "Whoa there, honey. Vicky's a nice girl and all, but I'm out of here in two hours and I don't expect to see her again."

"Oh, Ty." She shook her head sadly. "Anyone can see that you're perfect together. Don't you think Lissa would want you to be happy?"

He took a full step back, putting distance between them. "This has nothing to do with Lissa." Cold sweat popped out along his spine. "This is about me. And I'm not looking for a relationship."

She started to speak but he rode right over her. "Don't tell me you're surprised, honey. You know from experience that I'm not a good bet. You never should've hooked us up if it was going to be a problem."

She turned her palms up, helplessly. "I don't understand you. Vicky's obviously crazy about you. And you can't stay away from her. You're like Spencer Tracy and Katharine Hepburn. Everything you've said about Lissa tells me she'd want this for you."

"You're in no position to say what Lissa would want."

He'd meant to sting her to silence, but she wasn't buying it. "Maybe I'm not. But even Jack says so."

That was what he needed, a target for his anger. "You tell Jack he's got a lot of fucking nerve talking about me and Lissa! Just because he's walking the straight and narrow doesn't make it his business to tie me down too." He stepped around her. "Never mind, I'll tell him myself."

She flung herself at the door, pressed her back to it. "Please, Ty! It's my fault. I pestered him to talk about her. Please don't make a fuss. Lil's already uncomfortable. Everyone's on edge from last night—"

He held up his hands. "Okay, okay."

"I'm sorry." She brought her hands together, twisting them in the way that meant she was deeply distressed. "I thought I was helping. Vicky's been so unhappy. She's been unhappy as long as I've known her, even before everything with Winston. And you're so wonderful. You make everyone laugh and feel good about themselves. I thought you'd make her feel good too. And you do. She laughs all the time when you're around."

Her eyes pleaded for understanding. "And you're so lonely. You are," she added when he waved it off. "For whatever reason, you've sentenced yourself to live alone, and Ty, you're not a loner. You need people. You need someone special. I know you and Vicky are different. She's uptight and you're . . . not. She's a lawyer and you hate lawyers. She's a city person and you love your ranch."

"Listen to yourself, Isabelle. Why in the world would you think we're a good match?" He tried to sound like himself, but a giant hand was crushing his throat. He barely squeezed out the words through his narrowing windpipe.

She shrugged one shoulder. "I don't know. But I was right. You two light each other up. That's the only way I can express it. You light each other up. And it's beautiful."

Vicky's words echoed in his ears, telling him he was her hero. But he wasn't anybody's hero. He'd let his own wife down. Let her get hurt. Let her die. Now Brescia's life hung by a thread. Hell, he couldn't even take care of a horse, how could he ever trust himself to take care of a woman?

Guilt ate a hole in his chest. He never should've gotten involved with Vicky. He hadn't wanted to care about her, and he sure as hell hadn't wanted her to care about him. Now he'd fucked that up too. He was going to let her down. Because there was no future for them. No future for anyone with him.

The kindest thing he could do for Vicky was to end it fast. Rip the bandage off with one yank. No long, sweet good-byes, no promises he'd never keep. Leave her thinking he was an asshole so she'd forget about him and move on. Find someone who could give her what he couldn't. While he went back to his ranch alone.

Alone. Just the thought tightened the hand on his throat. And if Brescia died, if he lost her too . . . The hand closed in a stranglehold. He couldn't speak. Sweat trickled down his sides.

Once before, he'd come undone like this, when his ornery horse had tossed him off a cliff. By a miracle, he'd caught hold of a scraggly sagebrush just a few feet over the edge. But as his feet scrabbled for purchase, he made the mistake of looking down. And he panicked, nearly ripping the sagebrush out by the roots in a frenzy to climb away from his doom.

Jack had saved him that time, tossed him a loop, wound the other end around his saddle horn and dragged him over the rim. But panic had almost killed him.

So yeah, this was panic. He was about to crack.

He had to get rid of Isabelle, and there was no polite way to do it. Reaching around her, he yanked open the door.

Then he took her shoulders, backed her into the hallway, and closed the door in her astonished face.

"WHAT A PRETTY sundress," said Isabelle.

Vicky smiled happily. "Thank you, Mrs. Donohue. It's my favorite." Bright yellow flowers on a baby blue background. She glanced around the terrace where the caterers were laying brunch. "Have you seen Ty?"

"Um, he's in his room. Taking a shower, I think."

Phew. Silly to have panicked when she found her room empty. As if he would've up and run away after the amazing night they'd shared.

Then Isabelle touched her arm. "About Ty," she began. Vicky gave her her full attention. "He can be—" Isabelle searched for the word. Before she could find it, one of the caterers signaled. "I'll be right back," she said to Vicky, and followed him to the kitchen.

A moment later, Winston limped through the door, heading for the coffee cart without noticing her. She almost wimped out and snuck away. Instead, to make a point, if only to herself, she lifted her chin and hobbled up beside him.

He looked, literally, twice as bad as Ty. Two black eyes, two visible bruises on his jaw. And the elbow he kept pinned to his side shouted cracked ribs from the rooftops.

She met his eye, refusing to shrink or to dwell on her split seam. His brows rose slightly. He looked her up and down. She expected derision, anger, insults. He surprised her utterly by stepping closer, running a finger lightly up the back of her arm.

For a moment, she froze. She used to love it when he did that. She'd believed it was affection. Now she knew it was affectation, probably cribbed from a manual on women's erogenous zones.

Too bad he'd quit reading after chapter one.

He moved closer still. "Victoria," he murmured, his voice low and deep.

She couldn't believe it. He was hitting on her!

She wanted to laugh, but kept a straight face. "I just spent the night with the man who did that to your face. The competition's over. He won. You lost."

He took a step back. His split lip curled. "You stupid cow. Don't you know he only screwed you to get to me? He's jealous of me."

God, he was an idiot. What had she ever seen in him? "Believe me, Tyrell Brown is not jealous of you." She'd bet her 401(k) on that.

"Of course he is." His sneer turned nastier. "Why else would he bother fucking an uptight bitch like you when that stripper's panting after him, dying to spread her legs?"

If he hoped to shock her with his language, he failed. She cocked her head. "If I'm such an uptight bitch, then why are *you* so interested?"

"I'm *not* interested, not anymore. You look hot, Victoria, but you're cold where it counts. Between the sheets. And you're dull too," he added for good measure. "Boring. You don't know how to have fun, in the sack or out of it."

His words hurt, but not as much as they used to. And knowing as she did that wounded pride was behind them, she didn't let them stop her.

"You're right," she said disarmingly, "I didn't have fun in bed with you. But I *definitely* had fun last night. It's amazing how great sex is with a man who's good at it. How *satisfying*."

Winston's jaw tightened. "Don't blame your frigidity on me."

There was that word again. She held on to her temper, barely. "Any problems we had were yours, not mine."

He leaned in, his face lobster red. "Bullshit! You can't even come!"

"Are you sure, *Winnie*? Maybe I just need more than *sixty seconds* to get there!"

Coffee sloshed from his cup. His eyes bulged, throwing sparks of fury as she met him glare for glare.

Then Matt appeared at her side. "Vicky, come have some breakfast."

She glanced over at the table. People were gathering. "Okay. Sure."

Matt aimed a cold stare at Winston. "You can take yours to go."

For a moment Winston blustered, a thwarted bully. Then he slammed his cup down on the cart and stalked inside.

Jack and Lil had taken their seats, Pierre too, but before Vicky could join them, Adrianna appeared. She pounced immediately.

"I hope you're happy." Her voice was low and taut.

Vicky mimed looking thoughtful. "Hmm. Yup. Pretty happy at the moment."

"And tomorrow? How will you feel tomorrow, when we have to withdraw from the appeal?"

"Relieved, that's how I'll feel. I never wanted to go to trial anyway. The case was a loser from the get-go. The appeal will be a loser too. I'm glad I don't have to deal with it." It was all true. The case never should have gone to a jury.

Adrianna's lips formed a line as thin and flat as a dime. "I suppose you've deluded yourself that this thing with Brown has legs."

Vicky shrugged, more nonchalant than she felt. "I guess I'll find out."

"He'll break your heart, Victoria."

Vicky did a double take. "You almost sound like you care, Mother."

"Of course I care. Brown's reputation precedes him. He may have loved his wife, but since she died he's been up every skirt in Texas. Him and that Jack McCabe." She

flicked a glance at the table, where Jack had a hand on
Lil's belly, his awed expression saying louder than words
that the baby was kicking against his palm.

Vicky grinned. "Yeah, *that* Jack McCabe. He's a real
monster."

"Don't be naïve, Victoria. You wear your heart on your
sleeve, where everyone can see it when it breaks."

"Look, Mother. I appreciate that you're worried about
me." And she really did. Not that she was about to share
her hopes and dreams about Ty, even if she knew what
they were. But Adrianna didn't usually express positive
emotions, even in this backhanded way, so she didn't
want to discourage her. "I'm fine, though. I really am.
Tyrell Brown isn't going to break my heart." Not after the
connection they'd made last night.

Isabelle emerged from the kitchen and waved them
over to the buffet. Starving from her sexathon, Vicky
mounded a plate. The maid brought out two pitchers of
mimosas that Isabelle got moving around the table. A few
minutes later, Ricky and Annemarie appeared, showing
all the signs of another all-nighter.

But there was no sign of Ty.

Vicky was halfway through her omelet before he sur-
faced. She tried to catch his eye to wave him into the seat
beside her, but he headed straight to the buffet, then sat
down with Jack and Lil. When he fell into conversation
without meeting her eye, a chill wind blew through her.

Her appetite vanished; she set her fork on her plate.
Even when he'd hated her, Ty had at least acknowledged
her existence.

At last, he looked up and she caught his eye. Heart thudding uncomfortably, she managed an inquiring brow lift.

He smiled . . . politely . . . and turned back to Jack and
Lil.

Uh-oh. Polite was one thing Ty had never been toward

her. Suddenly, she couldn't swallow the sip of juice she'd taken. It pooled on her tongue.

Something was very, very wrong.

Then logic kicked in. He wasn't blowing her off. He didn't know that her mother had already figured out that they'd spent the night together, so he was simply playing it cool, keeping the change in their relationship quiet so Adrianna wouldn't make a stink.

She got the juice down. Everything was fine. Just fine.

She managed to make small talk with Isabelle for the longest twenty minutes of her life. Then Matt tapped his spoon on his glass. "Thanks, everybody," he said, coming to his feet. "It's been a great weekend, but now I'm going to take my *wife*"—he took Isabelle's hand, smiling hugely—"to Greece for a couple of weeks. We'll be busy"—his smile stretched even wider—"so don't worry if you don't hear from us for a while." As applause broke out, he tugged Isabelle to her feet. "Safe trip, everybody," he called over his shoulder.

And with that, the horrible, wonderful wedding weekend was over.

Talk turned to train schedules and flight times as everyone drifted away from the table. Vicky stayed behind, sure Ty would linger until everyone left, then make his way to her.

But he didn't. He walked off with Jack without a backward glance.

Okay, now that was taking the whole sensitivity thing too far. It was sweet that he wanted to protect her from Adrianna, but the fact was, they'd shared an incredible night of teasing, laughter, and mutual orgasms. She'd already spilled the beans to Winston, and now that Matt and Isabelle were safely on their way, she didn't care who else knew about it.

Hobbling into the chateau, she cut through the kitchen

and into the foyer, planning to hop up the stairs after Ty.

But he was already heading down, suitcase in hand, furtive look in his eyes. He stopped at the bottom when he saw her.

"Hey," he said, lamely.

She swallowed, barely, around the lump in her throat. "I guess you're leaving."

"Yup." He hefted his bag uncomfortably.

"No good-bye? Just . . ." She fluttered her fingers. "Just . . . gone?"

"Got a plane to catch." He dropped his eyes.

She nodded slowly. "Okay. Well. Don't let me keep you." Her voice sounded thin, like she wasn't getting enough air in her lungs to push it out. She took a deep breath, tried to beef it up. "Have a safe trip." She hobbled around him, hopped up two stairs before he said her name.

She stopped. Turned. Got one last look into warm brown eyes shot through with gold before he dropped a peck on her cheek, quick and dry-lipped. Sexless and final. And then he walked out the door.

She stood alone, all alone, and watched him go, watched the door fall closed behind him. That icy wind blew through her again. She shuddered, actually shuddered, in pain.

And out of the library stepped Winston, leather tome in his hand, odious smirk on his face. He'd obviously heard every word.

She turned and fled as fast as her broken toe could carry her.

CHAPTER EIGHTEEN

IT HAD TO be a hundred and twenty degrees inside Ty's truck.

He snarled at himself. If he hadn't dawdled around after the trial like he always did, then he wouldn't have run so late for his flight to Paris that he had to park his truck outside to roast in the sun for four days.

He slung his bag into the bed and sat his ass on the blistering seat. Scorching air blasted from the AC. Too ornery to wait for it to cool down, he dropped the windows—for all the good it did in the Texas heat—gripped the red-hot steering wheel and peeled out of the lot.

The flight home had been pure hell. After pulling the biggest dick move of his life by running out on Vicky without even telling her why, first class was wasted on him. Whiskey didn't help. Filet didn't help. He couldn't sleep. Not to mention that every inch of his body throbbed from Winston's pounding. To add to his misery, he'd had a bitch of a layover in D.C., then gotten bumped to a red-eye for the flight to Houston. Now his neck had a crick that meant a trip to the chiropractor.

All in all, it had been the very worst part of a very shitty weekend. The sooner he got back to the ranch—and Brescia—the better.

He drove like a bat out of hell, the memory of Vicky's wounded eyes chasing him all the way, but still it was mid-afternoon before he pulled up the dusty driveway. The low-slung ranch house, with its wide front porch shaded by two pecan trees, was a sight for sore eyes. Stopping the truck in the wide spot that passed for a parking area, he flicked a glance over the barns, the paddock, the bunk-house with the tiny business office at one end. It looked hard-used and sturdy, like it had stood for a hundred years and would stand for a hundred more. He couldn't under-stand why he'd ever left it, even for a weekend. If he had his way, he'd never leave it again.

He grabbed his bag from the bed and headed for the office. Joe came out to meet him. "Hey, boss. How was the wedding?"

"Pretty as a picture." He sounded surly and didn't care. "Where's Brescia?"

"Clancy said to keep her in her stall for now."

Ty dropped his bag and strode off toward the barn.

Brescia had prime accommodations near the sliding double doors that opened into the paddock, specifically selected by Ty so she could keep an eye on things even when confined to her stall. She must have heard him coming, because she poked her head over the half door and snorted out a welcome through her nose.

A dun-colored beauty with a black mane and tail, she was so pretty it was easy to forget that she had some age on her. "Hello, baby." He stroked her velvet nose, fished in his pocket for the cherry Life Savers he usually car-ried for her, then remembered he was wearing his travel-ing clothes. "I'll bring you a treat later, pretty girl." He reached around to scratch her jaw. "Now what's all this about bloodworms?"

She butted his shoulder with her heavy head, then let it droop. He couldn't believe it. Just over a week ago they'd ridden a hundred miles, camping out in the hills before the trial. Now her coat was dull, her eyes bleary.

His chest constricted; tears welled in his eyes. He couldn't lose Brescia too. He couldn't.

He heard Joe clomping through the barn. Blotting his eyes on his sleeve, he called over his shoulder, "Go and call Clancy, will you? Tell him to swing by on his way home."

"Sure thing." Joe clomped away.

Ty stepped into the stall, closing himself in with Brescia. Gently, he ran his hands over her coat, pausing when he felt the swelling in her belly. Dropping his forehead against her warm, sturdy neck, he let the tears come. His whole body shook with them.

"Please, Brescia." He choked the words into her mane. "Please don't die."

"GODDAMN IT, CLANCY, how the hell did we get bloodworms in this neck of the woods?"

Clancy pulled out his pouch, spent a long minute packing his lip.

Ty bit down on his cheek. Why hadn't he ever noticed how looooooong it took Texans to get to the point? It must've driven Vicky nuts when she was down for the trial.

Clancy adjusted his dip with his tongue, tucked the pouch back into his pocket. "Bloodworms aren't uncommon, Ty. You're lucky to have avoided 'em this long."

"You check my other horses?"

"Except the ones out on the range. They're clean." Clancy gave him a bland look. "I expect Brescia picked 'em up over at Molly's place. That new chestnut she brought in has 'em bad. I'm headed over there to dose him now."

Guilt shoved its barbed point a little deeper in Ty's belly. He should've expected that Clancy would know about him and Molly. The vet was a regular at every ranch in the Hill Country. Nothing got past him.

"You got a copy of that treatment schedule?"

"Yup." Like a man moving through molasses, Clancy ambled to his truck. Took some papers off the front seat. Sifted through them. "Here it is." He handed a sheet to Ty. "You'll have to keep a close eye on her. And if she pulls through, you'll have to watch out she doesn't get re-infected." Climbing in, he favored Ty with a last weighty look. "You go visiting Molly again, you'd best bring your truck and leave your stock at home."

"TYRELL, HONEY, CLANCY told me you were back."

"Come on in, Molly." He opened the screen door to let her inside, took the casserole she handed him. "Smells good."

"Chicken divan. My specialty. Well, *one* of my specialties." She batted big green eyes. He'd already sampled her other specialty, the fifteen-minute, deep-throat, porn-star blowjob.

Why, oh why, had he ever gone there with her? Not that she wasn't a great girl. Smart and sexy and full of fun, with glossy black hair that swung in loose, lustrous waves around her shapely shoulders. She'd had a crush on him since ninth grade. He'd never had occasion to do anything about it in high school, and by the time he came home from college, he was with Lissa, and Molly had married the other high school football star.

But four months ago, on the day her divorce became

final, she'd celebrated by asking him over to dinner. And like an idiot, he'd accepted.

It went about like he expected, except Molly was a lot more enthusiastic than he ever imagined. Said she was on a mission to fuck in every room of her house; a cleansing ritual, she called it. So they did. It took all night and he'd had a real good time, but even as he rode Brescia home in the breaking dawn, he was already regretting it.

Because Molly was definitely looking for a new husband, and he was definitely *not* looking for a new wife.

Now she set her hands on her hips and did a slow turn, checking out his kitchen.

Given that avocado appliances had gone out in the seventies, it needed some updating. But it was clean and cozy. He liked it. And Lissa had loved it.

Molly, not so much. "Your grandma must've ordered these out of the 1960 Sears catalogue." She smiled at him, taking any sting out it. "If you want, I can help you pick out something modern. Maybe stainless steel."

"That's nice of you, but I'm sort of attached to these." He smiled too, taking any sting out of it.

He really didn't want to discuss his kitchen, especially when he could tell she was mentally redecorating it to match her dishes, so he set the casserole on the counter. "You're a sweetheart to drop by, but I was just on my way out."

"But you just got home!" She looked hurt. "Honestly, Ty, I haven't seen you in months, what with you being in Houston all the time for the trial and then jetting off to France." She sauntered toward him, swinging her shapely hips. "Why, the last time I saw you—"

"—I had a real nice time." He cut her off politely but firmly. "And in case I didn't tell you, you're a heck of a cook, honey." Cupping her elbow, he steered her gently toward the door. "Don't tell my mama I said so, but your beef stew is the best I ever had." He kept her moving out onto the porch. "And your lemon meringue pie, well, you be sure to enter it in the pie-baking contest come Labor Day. I'm judging this year, and I don't see how you can lose." He tucked her into her red Mustang. "I'll give you a call, honey, and we'll get together real soon. Bye, now."

Watching the rooster tail of dust rise up behind her, he blew out a sigh. He'd have to let her down gently, and soon, but between an epic case of jet lag and everything else that was chewing at him, he just plain wasn't up to the task today.

Trudging back to the house, he daydreamed about kicking back in his recliner with a cold one and falling asleep to the ball game. But, for sure, Molly would drive by later just to verify he'd gone out. So after checking on Brescia one more time, he climbed wearily into his truck and headed for Fredericksburg to scare up a burger at the Horseshoe.

In the last few years, Fredericksburg had become a mecca for tourists, with gift shops and froufrou eating establishments popping up around town. But the Horseshoe hadn't changed a bit. It was, and always would be, a classic Texas roadhouse.

He pushed open the door and Hank Williams met him halfway, "Your Cheatin' Heart" crooning from the jukebox. Up on the low plywood stage, Jimbo and the boys were setting up, the usual Monday night band. A fly-specked poster on the wall behind them advertised 357, an old band of Jack's. Back in the day, they'd played the Horseshoe a hundred times and gotten into a hundred fistfights. Ty had loved every minute of it.

Bellying up to the bar, he slapped down a fifty and called

to the bartender. "Buster, bring me a longneck, will you?"

Buster swung around, all six-foot-seven, three hundred and ninety pounds of him, and broke out in a grin. "Tyrell fuckin' Brown, where the hell you been, boy?"

"Paris, France. At the nuptials of our sweet Isabelle."

"No shit!" Buster plunked a frosty Bud on the bar. "Always thought you two would get hitched." He wagged his head. "She shore is a pretty little thing. Don't know nothin' 'bout music, but we coulda educated her."

"I doubt she'd ever have taken to country music." Ty sucked down a swig, wiped his lips with the back of a hand. "But you're right about the rest of it. She sure is a pretty little thing."

The crowd was thin, it being a Monday. On the flat screen above the bar, the Astros trailed by five. Ty watched the game on and off as he worked through a burger with everything and a side of cheese fries, washing them down with another beer. He ordered some leaves and twigs too, in the form of a salad, causing Buster's eyes to widen in surprise, and he picked at it between bites of juicy beef.

Down the bar, a Texas cutie in skintight jeans and snakeskin boots was making eye contact. He called Buster over. "What've we got here?"

Buster leaned on an elbow, lowered his booming voice. "That, my friend, is the brand-new third-grade teacher. Been in town a couple months. Drops in every Monday night to tap her toes to Jimbo's band. Orders a turkey club and eats half. Sucks down two vodka martinis." He grinned at Ty. "She's been looking, but she ain't seen nothing she likes. Until tonight."

Ty glanced down the bar. Met her eyes and gave her a slow smile. No time like the present to start putting Vicky behind him. "Set her up with another one of those martinis, Buster. On me."

IT WOULD BE so easy. Jessie's place was right around the corner, as she'd made a point of dropping into the conversation twice already. If Ty wanted to, he could peel her jeans off by ten and still be home in time to catch the end of the game.

But he wasn't into it. And it was a damn shame, because she was a nice, normal girl with no apparent hang-ups. She didn't seem worried that two drinks might kill her, or that the bacon on her sandwich would cause brain cancer.

She was real pretty, too. Blue eyes. A lighter shade than Vicky's, but warm and bright. Blond hair. Not straight and silky, and it didn't fall like a curtain around her shoulders. But it was thick and wavy and would probably be soft if he ran his fingers through it. And she had the big, ripe breasts that men drooled over.

She even got his jokes, which wasn't the case with every woman. Some of them wouldn't know sarcasm if it waved a banner and sang "Yankee Doodle." But she didn't have any jokes of her own. No snappy comebacks, no razor-sharp put-downs. No witty banter at all.

Basically, she bored him.

He knew he wasn't giving her a fair shot, comparing her to Vicky like he was. But he couldn't help himself. Vicky was one of a kind, and the truth was, nailing the schoolteacher wouldn't help him forget her. Vicky'd stuck in his mind like a burr, and there was no unsticking her.

He stood up. "Jessie, honey, it's been real nice meeting you." He signaled to Buster, tapped a finger on the fifty.

She sat up straighter. "You're leaving? But the band just started up. I thought maybe we could dance." She gave him a bright smile, all white teeth and cherry lips.

He did a rueful headshake. "Got a sick horse at home, sugar. I need to tuck her in."

"Where do you live?"

He cut that off at the pass. "With my mama. She'll be

waiting up for me." He smiled easily, the good son. "We like our hot chocolate together before we turn in."

Her expression was priceless. Taking advantage of her shock to scoop up his change, he left a ten on the bar, called out to Buster, "I'll tell Mama you'll be dropping by."

Buster's brows shot up but he was quicker than he looked. "Next Sunday after church," he called.

Ty dropped a neighborly kiss on the schoolteacher's cheek and went home to sleep alone.

CHAPTER NINETEEN

"SO . . . HOW was the wedding?" Madeline St. Clair, Vicky's best girlfriend and another associate at Marchand, Riley, and White, poked her head into Vicky's office and jiggled her eyebrows expectantly.

Vicky propped her foot on the polished wood of her desk. The gleaming white bandage poked out through the toe of her sandal.

"Ouch."

"Exactly." Vicky swung her foot to the floor. "That pretty much sums it up."

"Bummer." Maddie perched on the leather chair across the desk from Vicky. "I was hoping you'd meet Prince Charming and elope to a tropical island."

Vicky snorted. "Hardly. And to top it off, Mother brought Winston along as her guest."

"Get out!" Maddie popped to her feet again. "I know she's your mother, but holy shit, that's just cruel."

"Yeah, that's her. Cruella de Vil." It brought a pang, but a smile came with it. Ty's humor was irresistible.

Maddie planted a fist on her hip. Anti-Winston from the

outset, her misgivings had been proven true when she and Vicky returned from lunch to find him boinking Vicky's secretary on this very desk. Ferociously loyal, Maddie had shoved a stunned Vicky aside, kicked the swine out of the office, and fired the secretary on the spot. And then, in a truly heroic act of friendship, when the partners, including Adrianna, had refused Vicky's request for a new desk, Maddie had personally disinfected this one with half a squirt bottle of 409.

Now she was royally pissed on her friend's behalf. "Tell me you didn't fall for that asshole's tricks."

"I was civil to him, for the most part," Vicky said, "but that's it." She tried to block out their last mortifying encounter, but it stomped into her brainpan like the proverbial pink elephant. Even so, she kept it to herself. Jetlagged and heartbroken, she wasn't up for telling Maddie about Ty. Someday she would, when it didn't still hurt like a stab wound. But not today.

Then Maddie said, "I heard about Tyrell Brown."

"What? Who told you?"

Maddie blinked. "Walter." That would be Walter Riley, one of the partners. "He said Brown was in the wedding so we had to dump the appeal." Her eyes slitted. "What's the problem?"

Vicky could have kicked herself. An ultra-petite size 0 with a pixie-ish wisp of strawberry blond hair, Madeline might look like Tinker Bell, but they called her the Pitbull for a reason. When she got her teeth into someone, she shook until they either snapped in half or gave up.

Vicky knew she was toast, but she gave it a shot. "There's no problem. I mean, except dumping the appeal. Mother wasn't happy about that. Like it was my fault, or something." She cleared her throat, tried rolling her eyes. "It's a loser anyway. It comes down to whether the jury believed Ty . . . I mean, Brown . . . or not. And he was very convincing."

Silence. Vicky shifted her gaze away from Madeline, tapped her keyboard rudely, as if her e-mail had suddenly become pressing.

More silence, while she scrolled through her messages. Then, simply, "How was he?"

Vicky tried disinterest-tinged-with-slight-annoyance. "He'd just won a seven-figure verdict, how do you think he was?"

"I think he must have been pretty damn good or you wouldn't be working so hard to convince me you didn't sleep with him."

Vicky did offended. "Are you saying I'm slutty?"

Maddie wasn't fooled. "Do I have to call Matt?"

"Do *not* call Matt."

"Then I want deets." She sat down.

Vicky threw up her hands. "God, you're a pain in the ass." Kicking back in her chair, she let out a sigh. "We didn't want to ruin the wedding, so Tyrell and I made a pact not to let on to Matt or Isabelle about the trial, or even that we knew each other. We pretended we just met."

"Thoughtful guy." Madeline cocked her head. "How long did your charade last?"

"All weekend. They still don't know."

Madeline steepled her fingers. "Adrianna must've made you pay for that. I suppose Winston was part of the deal."

"She wanted me to consider reconciling. I had to pretend I would."

"Must've been tiring, all that pretending." She ticked it off on her fingers. "Pretending you might forgive Winston. Pretending you didn't know Brown." She left it hanging, waiting for the rest of it.

Vicky sighed again. "I also pretended to flirt with Ty.

Actually, we pretended to flirt with each other, to humor Isabelle. She had some notion that we'd be good together."

"And were you?"

She shrugged. "Yes and no."

"I'll have to ask you to be more specific."

Vicky pinched the bridge of her nose. God forbid she ever had to take the witness stand against the Pitbull.

She told her everything, and when she was finished, Madeline summed it up in three words. "Shitty weekend, Vic." Then she shrugged. "Except for the sex, that is. It's about time you got some of the good stuff. I've been telling you for months . . . Well, whatever. Here's the takeaway." She counted on her fingers again. "Forget Winston, he's a jerk. Forget Brown, he's an immature jackass. Forget Adrianna, she's missing the mommy gene."

She used her other hand. "*Don't* forget that you're a beautiful, intelligent, *sexy* woman. *Don't* forget you deserve a man who'll treat you like a princess, give you *many* orgasms, and love you until you both wither up and die of old age in each other's arms." She aimed one finger at Vicky. "Got it?"

"Got it." As usual, Maddie had put it into perspective for her. Maybe she had a crush on Ty, but it wasn't *love* or anything. And she was already getting over it. She'd even told the whole story without collapsing into tears.

Of course, it could be that she'd wept them all into her whiskey on her flight across the Atlantic. And she didn't even *like* whiskey, she'd only ordered it because it was *his* drink.

To add insult to injury, Loretta-from-Texas had been the one to serve it to her. Somehow, the woman had divined that Ty had broken her heart—perhaps because he'd broken so many others?—and she'd tried to console Vicky. Well, Vicky had made short work of that. The last thing she wanted was to hear excuses about Ty's own heartbreak, especially not in that lazy Texas drawl that sounded so much like his.

Madeline stood up. "Drinks at six-thirty at Steve's. Chuck'll make you one of his special cosmos. Then dinner at Mama Ritz's, on me." She nodded once, firmly. "Pasta cures everything, even a broken heart."

"Okay." A soak in the tub and a Lifetime movie sounded a lot better, but Maddie would never let her get away with wallowing. And anyway, the worst was over now.

Now she could sit back and lick her wounds while her life, such as it was, got back to normal.

NOT TEN MINUTES later, her phone rang. Madeline. "Listen, girlfriend, Cruella just stormed past my office, heading for yours. I don't know what's up, but there was smoke pouring out of her—"

Vicky disconnected as her door flew open without a knock. Adrianna's face was puce. She slammed the door and strode to Vicky's desk.

Vicky arranged her face into a slightly bored, mildly inquiring expression. "Can I help you, Mother?"

Adrianna slapped the *Post* down on her desk. "Page four. And five." Vicky raised her brows half an inch. Without waiting, Adrianna flipped it open and shoved it across the desk.

The headline spanned both pages—"They Went to a Fight and a Wedding Broke Out." Vicky's heart sank. She skipped the text, went straight to the pictures.

The first showed Jack and Lil dancing sedately at the reception, with an arrow pointing to Lil's baby bump and a note to check the sidebar story; the second showed Ty and Winston locked in battle, devastation surrounding them.

"Poor Matt," she said.

"Poor *Matt*? *All of us* are mentioned in that story! The *firm* is mentioned! Brown himself is named. We may never live this down." She stalked to the window, glared down on Fifth Avenue, fingers clenched into fists.

Vicky kept quiet. No use pointing out that Jack and Lil were the real story. If they hadn't been at the wedding, no one would care. By tomorrow, all the attention would focus on the pregnancy. The wedding brawl would be forgotten.

"Tyrell Brown," Adrianna fumed. "That *cowpoke* has been nothing but trouble for us. First we lose the trial." A glare for Vicky. "Then he shows up at the wedding and seduces my daughter so we have to recuse from the appeal. And to add insult to injury, he brings shame on us all by brawling like a . . . like a . . . I don't know what!"

Pacing before the window, she flung her arms dramatically. "Who fights with their fists? He's a throwback. A caveman. Why wasn't he born ten thousand years ago? Then he'd be someone else's problem."

"Calm down, Mother." Vicky had never seen her so agitated.

"Don't tell me to calm down!" Her voice cracked at the end. She dropped into the chair once more, put her fingers to her lips, and stifled a sob.

"Mother." Vicky sat forward in her chair, starting to worry. "Mom. Why are you taking this so hard? It's just a stupid gossip rag. They'll be hounding someone else tomorrow."

The intercom buzzed. Vicky hit the button. "Roxanne, hold my calls, will you?"

"Um, Vicky. It's not for you. Walter's looking for Adrianna. He said it's urgent."

Adrianna let out a groan, plucked a tissue from Vicky's

box. "Roxanne, please tell him I'll be right there," she said. Then she turned to Vicky. "Darling, I want you to listen carefully."

Vicky blinked twice, once at the unprecedented endearment, the other at her mother's suddenly serious tone.

"I want you to pack up everything personal from your desk and put it in your purse. Copy any personal information from your computer onto a flash drive, then delete it from your desktop. And do it without delay."

Vicky's mind reeled. "Mom, what the hell is going on?"

Adrianna stood, ran her hands down her suit, smoothing the wrinkles. "I expect you know that we use a clipping service. They track any references to our clients or our competitors in the news or on the Internet." Vicky nodded. "Well, it's safe to assume that our clients and competitors do the same. It stands to reason that by now the insurance companies and lawyers involved in Brown's case have seen this story and are crying conflict of interest."

"But we withdrew from the appeal this morning."

Adrianna shook her head. "That won't be enough, under the circumstances. You know that the appearance of impropriety is more important than the facts. And your . . . relationship . . . with Brown looks very bad. We could be looking at a new trial."

Vicky's heart sped up. Her palms began to sweat. "But we didn't have a relationship until *after* the trial. And anyway, how could they find out about it?"

Adrianna leaned over her desk, dropped one finger on the picture of Jack and Lil. Vicky looked closer. And there it was. The appearance of impropriety.

In the background, small but crystal clear, she danced in Tyrell's arms.

That alone might not have damned her, but the looks on

their faces sealed the deal: she gazed up at him, he gazed down at her, and anyone with a nickel to his name would bet that they were lovers.

Fascinated, she stared at their image, remembering how he'd held her on his feet and twirled her among the other couples as smoothly as water flowing around stones. Had he really been looking at her like that? Like he absolutely adored her?

"Walter will have heard about it by now," her mother went on. "He gets the clippings first. Bill will find out shortly, if he doesn't know already."

"But—"

"They'll cut you loose, Victoria. Immediately. It will be their two votes against mine."

Vicky swallowed. Put a hand on her stomach. Then she looked up and met her mother's eyes. "You'll vote to keep me?"

"Of course I will. You're my daughter." Her voice cracked. Vicky rose instinctively, wanting to hug her. Wanting to be hugged. And for a brief, precious moment they clung to each other, mother and daughter.

Then Adrianna stepped back, moved briskly to the door. "Do as I told you," she said, the hard-nosed attorney again. "I'll hold them off as long as I can, but it won't be more than twenty minutes." Then she stepped out, closing the door softly behind her.

For a long moment, Vicky stood like a statue, staring blankly at the sterling silver nameplate on her desk, the only sound the pitiless tick-tock of the grandfather clock that presided over her tastefully appointed seating area.

Then a knock sounded on the door and Roxanne walked in waving two pink phone message slips. "Rodgers wants your vouchers for Houston ASAP. I told him you just got back, but you know what a prick he is. And Madeline wants you to call her right away." She paused in front of Vicky's desk. "Are you okay?"

Vicky looked up. Her gaze focused. "Roxanne, you're the best secretary I've ever had. And I'm not saying that just because the last one did my fiancé on this desk."

Roxanne's eyes widened. "Um, thanks?"

"I mean it." She should have said these things long ago. Now she was almost out of time. "You're punctual, your skills are top notch, and you always go the extra mile to make me look good. And you smile a lot. That's under-rated, you know. A smiling face makes the day a hell of a lot more pleasant."

"Oo-kay. Well, thanks. I'm glad you appreciate me." She smiled.

"Good. Now I need your help. In fifteen minutes the partners will be down to fire me."

"*Fire you?* Why? You're a brilliant attorney, everybody says so."

"Well, that's debatable. And either way, it's beside the point. All you need to know is that I didn't do anything wrong. Everybody knows that, but a few things happened this weekend that put the firm in a bad light. The easiest way to solve the problem is to sack me."

Roxanne sputtered. "But . . . can't your mother do something?"

"She already did. She warned me." The knowledge of that warmed her, a bright spot in a very dark day. "Now grab your steno pad. I'm going to give you the quick and dirty on some of these files while I pack my things."

When the partners arrived, they brought the security guard who would escort her from the building. Vicky sent Roxanne out and came around from behind her desk to face them.

Walter, gray-haired and gray-suited, wielded the axe. "I'm sorry, Victoria. We have to let you go."

Even though she'd known it was coming, the blow took her breath.

"It's the Brown case," he went on. "Waxman"—the insurance company she'd represented at trial—"has already severed its connection with us. Their in-house counsel called five minutes ago to inform us that they're moving for a new trial on the ground that your involvement with Brown was a conflict of interest. There's bound to be a hearing on the motion, so you should expect to be called to testify."

Vicky started to object but Walter held up a hand. "I know it's bullshit but it will still be a mess. There'll be a lot of scandal, a lot of bad press. All in all, it'll be easier for the firm to weather it if you're no longer with us."

"So you're sacrificing me to save the firm some bad press?"

"It's not only that. Waxman's deciding whether to sue us for malpractice. It might appease them if you're out of the firm."

Adrianna spoke up from her position behind the others. "Victoria, I want you to know that I disagree with this decision. Apart from the fact that it shows an appalling lack of loyalty to one of our trusted employees and will have a commensurately negative impact on morale, I think that firing you weakens our legal position and makes us all look guilty."

Vicky's gaze tracked to Bill. "You're with Walter on this?"

He couldn't meet her eyes. It was common knowledge that he'd long had a crush on her, but hadn't acted on it due to their respective positions in the firm. "I'm sorry, Vicky." He sounded miserable. "It was a tough decision, but we have to put the firm first. A lot of people depend on us. The attorneys, the staff. Their families." He turned his palms up, a silent appeal.

"We've agreed on a substantial severance package," Walter cut in. "It should tide you over while you decide what to do next."

She hadn't even thought about that, but she thought about it now. And felt the first inkling of panic. "No other firm will hire me with this hanging over my head."

"I wish I could disagree." Walter set a hand on her shoulder in his avuncular way. "You should also know that Waxman's filing a complaint against you with the Committee on Professional Standards."

Bill groaned. "Jesus, Walter. Do you have to dump it on her all at once?"

"It's best she have the whole picture." Walter patted her shoulder. "We all know it won't come to anything in the end. But in the meantime, the complaint will be a strike against you if you apply for a law job."

Full-blown panic kicked in. "What will I do? How will I live?" She cast a wild look around at all of them. "For God's sake, I never wanted to be a lawyer in the first place! But it's my career, goddamn it! You can't just take it away from me!"

But they did. Five minutes later she was out on the street.

"GIVE ME A mocha latte, Johnny. Full fat, triple shot, double whip."

Johnny's eyes bugged. Then he burst out laughing. "Jeez, Vicky, you had me going for a minute." He called to the other barista. "Green tea, no sugar, no nothin'."

Vicky leaned over the counter. "Hold that order." Then, "Johnny, I'm serious. Unless there's something with more fat, sugar, and caffeine?"

He slapped his hand on his hip. "Why you messin' with me, girl? You always get the green tea. For the antioxidants."

"And where have those antioxidants gotten me? No

place, that's where. So I'm trying something different. Something . . ." She churned her hand through the air, searching for the word. "Something *bad* for me."

He snorted. "Hard to find somethin' really bad for you at Starbucks." He leaned on the counter, dropped his voice. "How bad you wanna be? 'Cause I can hook you up."

"Thanks, but I'll stick to abusing legal substances. Like sugar, fat, and caffeine."

Her phone jingled. Maddie. The only person she could stomach talking to.

"Hey, Mad. Guess what I'm doing?"

"Signing up for unemployment?"

"Funny. Ordering a full-fat, triple-shot, double-whip mocha latte."

"Uh-huh. And a pig just flew by my window."

She gave Johnny a big tip and an air kiss, took her calorie bomb to a window seat. "I'm serious. Listen." She sucked whipped cream off the top.

"My God!" cried Maddie. "What did those animals do to you?"

Thank God Maddie could always make her laugh. Even in the heartbreaking aftermath of Winston's betrayal, she'd found ways to make it funny. She was sort of like Ty that way.

"Actually, they took it pretty easy on me. Mostly laid on a guilt trip, then had security escort me out of the building."

"Security? You're kidding me."

"Standard procedure, so they can assure the clients that I didn't steal any files on my way out. I'm a dangerous person now that I'm being investigated by the committee."

A snort of disgust came through the phone. "I hope you're planning to fight this bullshit?"

Vicky sipped her decadent latte. "I've got more immediate problems. Like how I'm going to make the mortgage payments on my co-op when I'm basically unemployable."

"Rodgers told me they cut you six months' severance. Stingy bastards."

"I can't blame them. The firm lost one of its biggest clients, and it's at least partly my fault. If I hadn't been dancing with Ty, our picture wouldn't have been in the paper and none of this would've happened."

"Don't even *think* about blaming yourself! If your mother hadn't shoved Winston down your throat, you wouldn't have broken your toe. If you hadn't broken your toe, you wouldn't have gotten so close to Brown, and you certainly wouldn't have been dancing on his feet." She summed it up neatly: "This is on Adrianna."

That was one way to look at it. But Vicky knew she bore some of the blame.

Maddie softened her tone. "Vicky, sweetie, you're always so hard on yourself. Please, just for today, be nice to you. Do something fun."

"There's a one o'clock yoga class at the gym."

"I was thinking more like a spa day. Maybe a movie. And don't forget we're on for drinks and pasta."

Vicky sighed. None of it appealed to her. But she didn't have anything else to do, did she?

SHE SHOULD HAVE trusted her instincts. Two cosmos and a glass of Chianti, even cushioned by half a pound of ziti and a slab of tiramisu, only served to add a queasy stomach and spinning head to Vicky's list of troubles.

Shuffling into her apartment at half past midnight, she dropped her purse on the Duncan Phyfe table inside the door and let her shoulders droop.

Tomorrow did not look promising in any way.

Toeing off her flats, she hobbled into her living room, dubbed "the sanctuary" by Maddie. The rest of her apartment reflected the fussy English style her mother approved of, but this space Vicky had designed for relaxation, from the restful taupe walls to the rich ivory curtains to the thick beige rug and mellow mood lighting. No computer or television intruded, no traces of her law career, no pictures of her mother. Nothing to disturb her tranquillity.

With a single remote, she ignited a fire in the black marble fireplace, activated the tri-level fountain in the corner, and engaged the iPod nestled in its docking station. Cocooned in moody light, with the trickle of water over stones and the quiet strains of Chopin to soothe her, she wilted onto the creamy beige sofa and released a shuddering sigh.

Most evenings, just walking into this room was enough to calm her spirit, and for those times it wasn't, she kept a yoga mat tucked under the sofa. Twenty minutes on the mat usually restored her equanimity.

But tonight nothing could console her. The pressure behind her eyes, pressure that had mounted all day long as tension, pain, and fear demanded their tribute in tears, could be denied no longer. Too tired to sob or wail or wring her hands, she simply laid back her head and let the tears seep silently down her cheeks.

She cried for Ty, because he'd hurt her and because she missed him in spite of it. She cried for her future. Her looming financial peril, her suddenly uncertain prospects, and the injustice of it all.

And she cried because she felt so wretchedly, achingly alone.

CHAPTER TWENTY

TY STORMED INTO the office. "Goddamn it, where the hell are my gloves?"

Joe looked up from a stack of bills. "Your gloves?"

"Isn't that what I just said?" Ty glared at him until Joe turned red.

"I-I don't know, Ty. I don't usually keep track of your personal items."

Ty's jaw hardened. "You don't want to sass me, Joe."

"I'm not sassing you, I swear it. It's just . . ." Joe's Adam's apple bobbed. "You're always so easygoing, and now you've been pissed at me since you got back from France." He turned his palms up. "I swear, I don't know how Brescia got infected. I racked my brains, but honest, Ty, I really don't think it's my fault."

Ty blew his stack. "Did I say it was your fucking fault? I'm the fucking idiot who brought her to Molly's! It's my fucking fault!"

He stomped across the paddock toward the barn. Brescia poked her head out to watch him come, and his heart swelled. She was everything he wasn't. Placid and even-tempered. Accepting of her fate.

Well, he couldn't accept it. If she died because of his selfish, slutty stupidity, he wouldn't be able to live with himself.

He'd already talked to Molly, told her he wouldn't be coming around again. She was prickly at first, but he'd had years of experience playing it's-not-you-it's-me. He laid on the sugar with a trowel, complimented everything from her hair to her toenail polish, and let her down so easy she hardly felt the bump.

He grimaced, mildly disgusted with himself. Those were his skills. Flattery, teasing, making people laugh. Skating over the surface of real emotions. Yup, he sure was good at convincing everyone he was easygoing. They all bought it, too, except Jack and Isabelle. And Vicky. She'd seen right through him.

He shoved that uncomfortable thought away. He'd rather think about Molly, which said a lot about how very little he wanted to think about Vicky. Not that he could help himself. Even after seven long days and nights, the look on her face when he abandoned her still twisted his guts like a corkscrew.

And that wasn't all that haunted him. Damn it, he couldn't even jerk off without reliving their sexathon. Imagine that asshole Winnie telling her she was frigid. Hell, the woman was hotter than—

Enough! He'd go nuts if he didn't quit thinking about her. It was all he did, that and worry about Brescia. And in some ways, worrying about Brescia was simpler. She was right here where he could touch her and care for her, try to make amends for letting her come to harm. Vicky, though, was two thousand miles away. He wanted to touch her too. He ached for it. But she was out of reach, and it was driving him absolutely batshit crazy.

Outside the barn, he made himself pause, take a few deep breaths. Brescia didn't deserve to deal with his shitty mood. Neither did Joe, for that matter. He'd apologize to him later. Or give him what passed for an apology—an extra day off. It was the least he could do after chewing his head off three times a day for the last week.

When he was as calm as he was going to get, he strolled inside. "How's my girl?" She raised her head for him, but her eyes drooped. Her tail swished listlessly.

He stroked her nose. She didn't seem to be getting any better. With bloodworms, an aneurysm was the greatest risk. She could drop dead at his feet without a moment's notice.

He kept his voice soothing. "Doc Clancy's coming by to see you today. I think you're his favorite patient. And who could blame him for falling for a beauty like you?" He stepped into the stall. "How about a little exercise?" He clipped a lead to her halter. "You want to keep your girlish figure, don't you?"

He led her around the paddock at an amble, talking to her quietly, the way he did when they were alone in the hills. He'd already apologized for getting her into this fix. Now he filled her in on his troubles, how he could fall asleep all right, but then he'd wake up in the middle of the night with all kinds of crazy thoughts running around his head.

"The problem is, there's this girl," he told her. "She's a real pain in the ass. A lawyer." He said it with distaste. "I know, I know, you don't like lawyers. Neither do I." He paused, then shrugged. "She made me laugh, though. And she's quick. It's real important to stay out in front of her, 'cause she's got a razor for a tongue. Peel the skin right off you."

He glanced over at Brescia where she plodded beside him. "I wasn't gonna mention her, because I'm trying to put her out of my mind. But I can't lie to you. She's what's keeping me up at night." It was a relief to say it out loud.

"Now, I know you don't like hearing too much about my sex life—and believe me, there's plenty I don't tell you—but me and Vicky, we tore up the sheets. I been at this for"—he counted in his head—"sixteen years, and nothing compares. Except Lissa, of course."

Or at least he thought Lissa compared. After seven years, he couldn't honestly remember.

He fought with his conscience. "Brescia, honey, I wouldn't tell this to another soul, but something about Vicky—maybe it's because I'm getting older, I don't know—something about the way she got me all worked up every time she opened her mouth made the sex even hotter. Is that weird?"

He nodded thoughtfully. "Yeah, you're right, it's weird. I mean, I like my girls rambunctious, but in a playful way. Vicky's rambunctious, for sure, but in a tear-your-throat-out way." He shrugged. "I'll be honest, though. I miss her. A lot. And if things were different—hell, if *I* was different—I'd go straight to New York City and get her."

That's what he wanted to do. Find her and bring her back to the ranch. Take her riding through the bluebells, and sappy shit like that. She'd probably hate it at first, being a city girl. But underneath her lawyer layer, she was real sensitive. Once he got her out under the stars, made love to her by campfire light, she'd come around.

Yes sir, if only he could believe that it wouldn't all go to shit eventually, he'd go after her in a heartbeat. But he just couldn't let himself believe that. Because if the past was any measure, at best he'd disappoint her. And at worst, he'd let her die.

"VICTORIA JANE WESTIN, it's time to get your head out of your ass and start thinking about your future." Maddie was in tough-love mode. "You're hitting three yoga classes a day, *jogging*, for crying out loud, meditating more than a monk, and you're a bigger mess than you were a week ago when the storm troopers marched you out of the building."

Vicky hit the button on the blender to give herself a moment's peace.

As soon as she shut if off, Maddie started in again. "I don't know how you can stomach another smoothie. Remember the latte? How good it tasted? How decadent you felt?"

"I tried decadence, Madeline. You should remember, since you're the one who had to pour me into a taxi. All I got out of it was a hangover."

Maddie crossed her arms. "Getting shit-faced on the night you got fired doesn't count as experimenting with a new lifestyle."

Vicky glugged some smoothie. She truly was sick of them, but she wasn't about to admit it. "Being out of control isn't a lifestyle. It's a disaster waiting to happen."

"Sweetie, the disaster *already* happened. You couldn't control it then, and no matter how many smoothies you force down—and I can see you're having trouble with that one—you can't control the future either. The only thing you can control is your reaction to it."

Vicky raised her glass in salute. "That's exactly what I'm doing. I'm reacting by being disciplined. Focusing on my health. As my best friend, I'd think you'd be glad I'm not sticking my head in a bottle or hopping into bed with a different guy every night."

"Maybe I would be, if it was working."

Maddie had her there. It wasn't working at all. At least twenty times a day she needed yoga breathing to stave off a panic attack. The rest of the time, she couldn't concentrate enough to read or even follow a television show. She'd finally resorted to reality TV, with its short spurts of action and total lack of plotlines. Speaking of which—

she flicked a glance at the clock—in twenty minutes she'd find out which of last night's couples would be voted off *Dancing with the Stars*.

Coming out from behind the counter, she tried herding Maddie subtly toward the door. "I'm fine. I just have to process things in my own way."

Maddie stood her ground. "Have you talked to Brown? Does he know what happened to you because of him?"

Vicky stood perfectly still. Breathed in to a four count, out to a four count. "No, I haven't talked to him. And I doubt he'd feel bad that I've been fired. Don't forget, I'm the one who had him on the stand. I tried to make the jury believe he was delusional. Or worse, a liar who pulled the plug on his wife and then tried to profit from it." She breathed in, out. "No wonder he dumped me."

Maddie wasn't buying it. "You were doing your job. And anyway, he won."

"He won money, though even that's up in the air now." She held up a registered letter. "Three weeks from today, I'll be back in Texas for the hearing on Waxman's motion for a new trial." She let out a feeble laugh. "I can hardly wait to raise my right hand and swear that I'm a slut. 'That's right, your Honor, I never met Tyrell Brown before the trial, but three days later we had hot monkey sex all night long.'"

Maddie simmered. "It'll serve Brown right if the verdict's overturned and he has to go through a whole new trial."

"I'd hate to see that happen. But thanks." Vicky smiled. "They say your best friend isn't the one who pats your arm and tries to cheer you up. She's the one who grabs the baseball bat and says, 'Let's get the bastard!'"

That made Maddie grin. "Just point me at him."

"Turn left when you get to Texarkana." Vicky chugged the last of her smoothie, set the glass on the counter.

"He'll be the guy with my red lace panties sticking out of his pocket."

CLANCY RESTED A hand on the door of Brescia's stall, looking in on her with troubled eyes. "I don't like it, Ty. It's been two weeks, she should be improving by now."

Ty turned his hat in his hands. "What else can we do? Is there someplace I can take her? Some new medicine to try? I don't care what it costs."

Clancy shook his head. "The problem we're having with bloodworms is that they keep evolving, developing resistance to everything we've got. The best we can do is try a new combination of old medicines. It's been known to work, though I haven't had much luck with it myself."

"Let's try it anyway. You got them with you?"

"In my bag." He headed toward his truck, Ty dogging his heels.

"How about alternative therapies? Vitamins? Acupuncture? I'll try anything."

Clancy pulled his bag from the cab, headed back toward the barn with Ty in tow. "There's a guy down Galveston way, I'll get you his name. But I don't want you to give up on traditional medicine. There's time yet to turn things around."

After Clancy left, Ty hung around the barn, stacking hay and keeping Brescia company. He was still out there when his cell phone jangled. Checking the number, he broke into a smile.

"Isabelle, honey, how was the honeymoon?"

"Wonderful!" She launched into a ten-minute description.

He grunted, "Uh-huh" at the appropriate times, let out a few long whistles, and flicked bits of hay off his sweaty chest. When she wound down, he told her how pretty her wedding was, how it brought a tear to his eye to see her riding off into the sunset with another man, and what a nice time he'd had, all things considered.

Then he waited for it.

"Tyrell Brown, I don't understand you at all. Why didn't you tell me about the trial? Why did you let me push you and Vicky together?"

"You had plenty to worry about, honey, without adding me to the list."

"But you got along so well." She sounded miserable. "When I think of the things I said to you Sunday morning . . . I'm so sorry, Ty."

"Isabelle, you quit it right now, you hear me? Vicky and me got along fine most of the time. She's a nice girl, for the most part, and I never would've known that if we hadn't faked it for a few days." He let his fingers slide into his pocket to rub the panties he'd swiped from her. Every morning he told himself to leave them behind, but every morning he stuffed them in there, like an addict pocketing his pills.

"She is nice, Ty. I'm glad you realize that now."

Her voice had softened like she was on to him, so he whipped his hand out and tried to change the subject. "How's the groom taking to married life?"

She giggled. "He's madly in love with his new wife." A pause. "But he isn't so happy that the wedding made the papers. You saw the pictures?"

He grinned. "I like the one where I'm giving Winnie an armpit-wedgie with his shirt."

"I suppose you know about the backlash?"

His grin faded. "Yeah, Angela filled me in. Taylor's insurance company filed a motion for a new trial. We've got a hearing in two weeks to clear it up."

"I know. Matt and I were summoned to testify."

"Aw, shit." Ty slapped his hat against his thigh. "I'm sorry, honey. Angie didn't tell me that."

"She must have mentioned that Vicky will be there too."

"Yeah, I figured that much out for myself."

Thinking about seeing Vicky again made him antsy, so he started toward the house. "I wish it hadn't come to this, honey. It's a pain in everybody's ass, and I'm sorry about that. But since I didn't know Vicky from a hole in the ground before the trial, Angie thinks it'll come out all right in the end."

"Well, I'm glad there won't be any problem for you. I really am. But Vicky—"

He didn't want to talk about Vicky anymore. "Honey, I'm out on the range now, and you're breaking up."

"Okay, I'll call you later." She shouted it, making him feel like a heel. But he really didn't want to go there.

"I'll be out . . . few days . . . see you in Houston . . ." He closed the phone, plopped down on the porch swing and stared blindly at the pink roses climbing the rail.

He'd been in a sweat for a week, since Angie'd told him about the hearing. One minute he was filled with dread at the thought of seeing Vicky; the next he was hard as a nail. Damn it, he couldn't even do yoga without remembering her ass in the air. And remembering her ass made him picture her tiny little panties, dozens of them, like Victoria's Secret had exploded in her drawer.

And thinking about her panties made him remember her bras. Bras that matched her panties, in tiger stripes and leopard spots and pretty pastels and bright jewel tones. Every color a woman had ever sinned in.

His fingers dug into the cushion, because he could see her in those bras and panties. In the peach satin, hopping one-footed out of her bathroom just before they made love on her floor. In the lemon lace she'd replaced them with, stepping into her bridesmaid dress with her cheeks still rosy from coming underneath him. In the black silk she'd worn later that night, giving herself to him so sweetly, letting him take her, and take her . . .

He shot himself out of the swing. Goddamn it, this had to stop!

Marching into the kitchen, he yanked open the fridge, glared inside, then shut it again without touching a thing. He couldn't go on this way. He had to do *something* to get her out of his head.

Maybe he needed a girlfriend.

The idea took root. Yeah, a girlfriend. Not a *serious* girlfriend, of course. His experience with Jessie told him he wasn't quite ready for sex.

He just needed someone to distract him from brooding about Vicky 24/7. Someone he could take out to a movie. Who'd believe him when he told her he wasn't looking to get married. Ever. Because that way lay loss and unbearable heartbreak. Why, even the specter of losing Brescia undid him. He couldn't handle another wife.

But a casual girlfriend, that was a horse of a different color. Leaning back against the avocado stove, he crossed his arms and mulled it over.

He could take a ride into Austin; he still had friends at UT. Maybe find himself a nice grad student, too busy with her studies to make demands on him. Planning to move on after graduation and pursue her career in a faraway land.

On second thought, that sounded like a lot of work. Commuting back and forth to see her. Cozying up to her friends. Listening to her rattle on about paleontology or genetics or, God help him, drama. No thanks.

Scratching his jaw, he considered the locals. There was Bette Davison, he'd always had an eye for her. But she had two kids now. He didn't want to break up with kids too, when he inevitably split up with their mama.

Patty Jo Mason had just moved back to town. She was a looker, and they had some hot history. But rumor had it that she was batting for the other team now.

Outside, gravel crunched in the driveway. A car door slammed, then heels clicked across his front porch and a feminine voice sang out.

"Tyrell, sweetie, I brought you my beef stew and a slice of lemon meringue pie."

He lifted his eyes to heaven. Seriously? Molly?

Well hell, if God was trying to tell him she was the answer to his prayer, who was he to ignore Him?

She poked her head in the door. He mustered up a smile. "Molly, honey, how about we take in a movie tonight?"

VICKY SIPPED HER coffee. "I don't want to talk about me," she said. "I want to hear about your honeymoon."

"I sent you the pictures," said Matt. "They tell the story. Unless you want to hear about the sex." She put her fingers in her ears. "Didn't think so."

"Where's Isabelle this morning? Is she sick of you already?"

"Mom wanted to have breakfast with her."

"And you let her go alone? I thought you loved her!"

He laughed. "Mom likes Isabelle. And she likes Isabelle's father too."

"Oh no." She clutched her head. "She wants Isabelle to do more matchmaking."

"I don't know, I'm staying out of it. Now tell me how you're spending your days."

"Well, I really like the new yoga instructor at my gym, so I've been taking a lot of her classes. I went to the zoo the other day for the first time since my sixth-grade class trip. There's a Renoir exhibit at the Met—"

He cut in. "How about looking for a job? It's been two weeks. What've you done about that?"

She frowned. "You sound like Mother."

"She's worried about you. So am I."

"Why?" She spread her hands. "I'm taking my time. Weighing my options. Figuring out what color my parachute is."

He stared her down while the waiter delivered their eggs. Then, "I can get you a job at Waverly"—the brokerage firm where he was a superstar—"working with one of the brokers. It's not a law job, but it'll hold you until this bullshit blows over and you can go back to the firm."

"I'm not going back to the firm." The words popped out unexpectedly, surprising her. Yet instantly, she knew they were true. She wasn't going back to Marchand, Riley, and White.

"Well then, until you can get a job with another firm."

"No, I'm done with the law." Another surprise. But it felt so right. She drew a deep breath, felt her shoulders relax, her stomach unwind.

Matt rolled his eyes. "Come on, Vic. The law's your career. It's how you pay for your co-op. Not to mention your Beemer."

By that he meant her BMW 325i convertible, her greatest luxury purchase, the consolation prize she'd given herself for her shitty job and disappointing life. She loved it. But not enough to go back to the firm.

"Is that all there is to life?" she said. "Making money to pay for stuff I don't need?"

"Listen, I know you're not crazy about being a lawyer—"

"Then why are you pushing me? Why would you want me to be unhappy every day? Stressed out? Miserable? Why would you want me to go back to that?"

He leaned back in his chair, stared at his coffee cup as he turned it with his fingers. "You're right," he said after a moment, "I am pushing you. I suppose I feel guilty." He raised his eyes to hers. "I wish you'd told me about Brown."

She shrugged. "I wanted your wedding weekend to be perfect."

"I appreciate that. But we would've dealt with it. And we could've avoided all this."

"That seems obvious in hindsight, but really, who could have imagined it would go nuclear? And anyway, if it hadn't happened I'd still be at the firm, mainlining Maalox." She smiled at him, her beloved brother, her best friend. "Honestly, Matt, it didn't sink in until now, but this whole thing was a blessing in disguise."

For a long, quiet moment he studied her face. Then he returned her smile, ruefully. "Okay, I'm a married man now, I know how to compromise. I won't mention it again until the hearing's over and we all get back from Texas. But if you change your mind before that, the offer stands. Some breathing room while you figure out what comes next."

"Thanks, I'll think about it," she said, even though she knew she wouldn't take the job. She knew it with the same bone-deep certainty that she knew she was done with the law. Done with wearing suits and carrying briefcases.

Such an apocalyptic turn of events should have precipitated a panic attack. She waited for it, but it didn't come. Instead she felt lighter, looser. The future yawned, scary but exciting, hers to do with as she pleased.

It was an utterly novel feeling.

"PRICE IT TO sell," Vicky told the realtor. "The sooner the better." Matt was right; without her lawyer's salary, she couldn't afford to keep her co-op.

"Not a problem. In this neighborhood, we'll be beating them off." The slender woman with Asian features and an Upper West Side accent moved efficiently through Vicky's apartment taking notes on an iPad. "What about the furnishings? Except for these things"—she halted in the center of Vicky's sanctuary—"I can probably sell everything along with the property."

"That would be great. Unload anything you can." Less for her to hassle with.

The woman's gaze cruised around the room. "I'm setting up a pied-à-terre for an artist in the Village. His friends will be using it most of the time, so he doesn't need brand-new. I could use some of this stuff there."

Vicky didn't hesitate. Not over her creamy sofa, her Bose sound system. Not even over her fountain. "All I need is the yoga mat. Give me your best offer for the rest."

When the woman left, Vicky went into her bedroom and started pulling things out of her closet, tossing them on the bed in two distinct piles. Into the reject pile went her suits, every last one of them. Her work shoes too, even some of her lingerie. Anything she'd ever worn in a courtroom. Later, she'd deliver it all to the battered women's shelter where she'd done pro bono work. The women there often fled their homes with only the clothes on their backs. They'd put her things to good use as they tried to rebuild their lives.

Into the keeper pile went everything else; a few nice dresses, her jeans, her favorite funky shirts, and all of the sundresses she'd worn in Amboise. Those sundresses gave her a pang, like everything that reminded her of Ty. She lingered over them, and for the hundredth time since she'd returned to New York, she tried to imagine what he was doing at that moment.

She'd never been on a ranch, so the pictures she conjured had a Hollywood sheen. In her favorite frame, Ty sat tall in the saddle, sleeves rolled, jeans taut over long lean legs, sun glinting off shaggy blond hair as he tipped his ten-gallon hat to some pretty little lady. In another vignette, he hefted hay bales, tossing them down from the wagon bed where he stood outlined against a sapphire sky, denim shirt flapping open over his sweaty chest, straw stuck to his cobblestone abs.

Oh, she was pathetic, no doubt about that. But picturing him in movie star roles didn't hurt as much as remembering him in real life, waltzing her across the terrace, carrying her through the plaza to the chapel, pressing her into the coatroom door. Making love to her all night long. *Those* were the images that kept her awake, trembling with need, touching herself in a watered-down version of the skin-searing, mind-melting things he'd done to her body.

She heaved a sigh. She was pathetic, all right. One week, that was all she'd spent with him, half of it in the courtroom. So why did she feel like her life hadn't really gotten started until she met him? Why did he stir her up, heat her up, make her want to bite him?

What she *should* be recalling was what a jerk he was. How he'd manipulated her into going along with his stupid scheme. How he'd pissed her off, made her homicidal, baited her, insulted her, and generally tormented her to distraction. How he'd walked away from her without a backward glance.

Those were the things she'd need to remember in two weeks' time, when they met again in Texas. Those were the memories that would help her keep her head when she looked into his tiger eyes.

CHAPTER TWENTY-ONE

HOUSTON BROILED LIKE a steak under the August sun. Sidewalks sizzled, plants and people wilted. By noontime the mercury hovered at a humid one hundred, and it was only going up.

Meanwhile, inside the courthouse, the AC piped air straight from the Arctic Circle. A Popsicle wouldn't have melted on the marble floor.

Pacing the familiar hallway outside the courtroom, Vicky chafed her bare arms. Her cap-sleeved dress seemed a good choice when leaving her hotel that steamy morning, but she should have remembered from the trial that the courthouse was a meat locker.

Angela's frosty gaze dropped the temperature another twenty degrees. In front of the judge, she'd played sympathetic and understanding, but here in the hallway, she wanted Vicky dead.

Her jealousy seemed absurd to Vicky, because Ty's demeanor made it painfully clear that what had happened in France, stayed in France. He'd barely acknowledged her before the hearing began. During his testimony, he never met her eyes.

Now, waiting for the judge's ruling, he chatted casually with Isabelle, seemingly oblivious to Matt's simmering dislike, and patently uninterested in Vicky.

His indifference stung like salt in her weeping wounds. But still, she had to admire his insouciance with so very much at stake. Not only did the seven-figure verdict and the punishment it would inflict on Jason Taylor hang in the balance, but the simple fact was, if he lost this motion, Ty would have to endure a new trial. He'd have to testify again. Open a vein and let the blood pump out.

Vicky, more than anyone, knew what it would cost him. And no matter how miserable he'd made her and was making her still, she would never wish that upon him. She could never be so heartless.

HEARTLESS, THAT'S WHAT Victoria Westin was.

Ty shoved his hands in his pockets to keep from strangling her. After all they'd been through together, the trial and the flight and the crazy wedding weekend, she treated him like a total stranger. Why, she'd barely spoken to him all morning. Never looked at him while she was testifying.

Now she paced the hallway, checking her watch like she had someplace else to be. Someplace more important.

"Ty." Isabelle touched his sleeve. "Are you okay?"

He slid his smile back into place. "I'm fine, honey. Just ready for this to be over and done with."

"I'm surprised the hearing went so quickly."

"Mmm-hmm." He was only half listening. His gaze strayed to Vicky. She had her phone out, scrolling through her e-mail.

Un-fucking-believable. Here he'd been mooning over her for a month, missing her, lusting for her, agonizing over hurting her feelings when he left her in France. And she didn't even care!

"Angela warned us it might take a couple of days," Isabelle went on, "so we booked our flights for tomorrow night."

That caught his attention. It was barely noontime. He couldn't abandon them for a day and a half. He'd have to stick around, take them out to dinner. It was the least he could do, the least Texas hospitality required.

But an afternoon of Matt's ominous silence and Vicky's cool indifference wouldn't be fun for anyone. Surely Isabelle would see that and make some excuse to let him off the hook.

"I was thinking," she began, and he waited for his out, "that since we don't have any plans and it's too hot in the city to do anything outdoors, we should come home with you for the night."

He blinked. "To the ranch?"

She smiled brightly. "I've told Matt all about it. He's dying to see it."

He cut a glance at Matt. No help there. His expression begged for five minutes alone with Ty in a dark alley, but his silence said he'd go along with whatever his new bride wanted.

"Uh." Ty groped for a lifeline. "Honey, the ranch is four hours from here. You'll have to drive all the way back tomorrow." He scratched his head. "You can't change your flight?"

"The best I could do was noon tomorrow out of San Antonio. That's only about an hour from the ranch, isn't it?"

"Uh."

Before he could pull a good excuse out of his ass, the clerk stuck her head into the hallway. "You can go in the courtroom now. The judge will be right with you."

MOTION DENIED.

Vicky's eyes were on Ty when the judge made her ruling. She waited for him to break into a grin, throw his arms around Angela. Do a fist pump, blow a kiss to the judge.

Nothing.

Pasty pale, he took Angela's briefcase from her hand and followed her from the courtroom.

Waxman's lawyer went out behind them, throwing Vicky a dirty look. She controlled the urge to stick out her tongue. He'd thrown everything at her on the stand, insisting that she'd conspired with Ty from the outset because she was either weak and blinded by love, or evil and motivated by greed. Thankfully, the judge hadn't bought it, and it was a sure bet that her ruling would satisfy the committee too.

For Vicky, at least, the whole miserable business was almost over.

Outside the courtroom, Angela huddled with Ty, probably talking about the appeal. It could go forward now, the last remaining threat to the verdict. Still, Ty had won a major victory today. So why wasn't he on top of the world?

Down the hall, Isabelle was waiting near the courthouse door. She beckoned to Vicky. "Matt went to get the car. We're going back to the hotel to get our bags. We'll get yours too."

"But I thought you said we couldn't get a flight out today."

"We can't." Isabelle smiled brightly. "Ty invited us to go home with him."

Vicky blinked. "To the ranch?"

"You'll love it there. Joe's so sweet. All the boys are. Most of them are out on the range, but you can meet Brescia, she's Ty's favorite horse." She kept up her stream of chatter while Vicky stared, speechless.

Then she waved Ty over. Vicky watched him come at a crawl, the dread on his face reflecting her own, and she finally understood why he wasn't celebrating. Isabelle had roped him in too.

"Ty, can you give Vicky a ride to the ranch? Matt's taking me to Tiffany's." She giggled. "Isn't he sweet? Wherever we go, he buys me something at Tiffany's. Oh, there he is. Bye!"

And she was gone.

"How does she *do* that?" Vicky wondered aloud.

Ty stared out at the curb, where Isabelle was ducking into the rental car. "She's a force of nature." It didn't sound like a compliment.

Vicky checked her wallet for cab fare. "I'll catch them at the hotel, tell them I'll meet them at the airport tomorrow."

His lips curled up on one side. "Right. That'll work."

"Got any better ideas?"

"Yeah. Get in my truck."

She looked up at him, and for the first time all day, he met her eyes. Gold flecks sparked in the sunlight, and her heart thunked hard against her rib cage, a warning shot that should have had her running for her nice safe room at the Marriott.

He shrugged one shoulder. "She's not gonna let either of us wriggle out of this," he pointed out. "Besides, back in France you said you wanted to see my ranch."

How dare he bring that up? "That was *before*."

"Actually, sugar," he said, his familiar smug smile spreading over his face, "that was *during*."

TY WATCHED HER blue eyes widen, then narrow, and he bit back a laugh. So she wasn't heartless after all. Maybe Isabelle was doing him a favor. Giving him a chance to get right with Vicky so he could get her off his conscience and out of his head.

Before she could get her footing and launch a counterattack, he took her elbow. "Come on, honey, let's get you outside in the good Texas heat." And he propelled her through the door.

Out on the street, she shook off his hand. "There's nothing good about this heat. It's got to be a hundred degrees."

He peeled off his jacket, loosened his tie. "Yup. Kind of cool today. It'll be downright chilly out at the ranch."

"I'm not going to your stupid ranch."

"You'll break poor Isabelle's matchmaking heart."

"Tough."

He shrugged like he was giving up. "Okay. Just tell her it was you, not me." He stopped at his truck, parked by some miracle in the building's shade. "I can drop you at your hotel."

He watched the struggle play out on her face. She wanted to tell him to suck it, but the Four Seasons was eight sweaty blocks away. Her dress was already stuck to her chest.

Idly, he bounced the keys in his hand, tempting her like Eve with the apple.

"Fine," she said snottily, like she was doing him the favor. He opened the door for her, took a good long look at her legs as she hiked herself up. "For crying out loud, you need a ladder to climb in here!" She plopped her butt in the seat.

He stalled around while she shimmied her dress down over her thighs. Then he shut the door without a word, climbed in behind the wheel.

And banged a U-turn in the middle of the street.

She rocked against the door. "Hey, jackass. You're going the wrong way. The Four Seasons is *behind* us."

"I know where the Four Seasons is." He took a hard right, then a left.

She grabbed the dashboard for support. "Jeez, slow down, will you?"

"Buckle up, sweetheart. We've got a long ride."

She got it then. "Seriously? You're *kidnapping* me?"

"Honey, if this was a kidnapping, you'd be hog-tied and gagged." He cut her a look that said it wasn't out of the question.

"Just try it." She aimed a viper's stare back at him.

"Is that a dare? 'Cause I got some rope right here." He whipped a coil out from under the seat, slapped it down between them. "And a nice sweaty bandana I can stuff in your mouth."

"You're bluffing," she shot back, but she didn't sound so sure.

He let a wicked smile curve his lips. "The way you're prodding me, I'm starting to think you're into it. Got a bondage fantasy you want to share?"

"You're disgusting." She didn't sound so sure about that either. In fact, the little squirm she did in her seat told him she liked the idea as much as he did.

He trained his eyes on the road, weaving through traffic, avoiding red lights. She was just ornery enough to jump out.

"For your information," he drawled out, "I'm trying to save us both from one of Isabelle's tongue-lashings. Maybe you haven't had that pleasure before, but I have, more than once."

"Gee, I wonder why. Maybe because you're an *idiot* who does *idiotic* things like *kidnap* people."

He wagged his head. "Sugar, this is a side of you I haven't seen. One minute you're asking me to tie you up, and now you're just begging for a spanking."

She balled her fists. "Take me back to the Four Seasons. This minute."

He hit the ramp onto the highway. "Sorry, honey, you should've mentioned your bondage thing sooner. But there's a Super 8 up ahead." He patted the rope. "I usually go for handcuffs, but we'll make do."

VICKY GLARED OUT the windshield at Interstate 10. How the hell did she end up trapped in this gas-guzzling monster truck with the person she hated most in the universe?

And worse than that, how did he keep outscoring her in the smart-ass department? Every time she opened her mouth, she set up another shot for him!

No more. She aimed below the belt. "Okay, I'm in."

His eyes popped. She almost laughed.

"There's the Super 8." She pointed up ahead.

His throat bobbed. "You're serious?"

"Absolutely. Get off here." She snickered. "Get it? 'Get off here'?"

He laughed, hoarsely. Took the ramp.

She almost changed her mind as he pulled into the parking lot. "You've done this before?"

"Um. Once or twice," he said. A bead of sweat rolled down his temple, and it wasn't from the Texas heat.

This was going to be hilarious.

She stuck her arm through the coil of rope, set her hand on the door handle as he put it in park. "Then you won't mind going first, will you?"

His head snapped around. She smiled sweetly. "Well, you're experienced, right? It won't freak you out if I tie you to the bed and gag you. I mean, what could go wrong?" She batted her lashes. "You trust me, don't you?"

He threw it in drive, squealed out of the lot. "You're evil, you know that?"

"Aw, what's the matter? Does Tyrell have a hard-on?" She smirked. "Silly question. Tyrell *always* has a hard-on. He *is* a hard-on."

"And you're a goddamn tease!" He gripped the wheel, clamped his jaw.

She let out an evil laugh, then sat back and pretended to enjoy the scenery.

While the bondage itch she hadn't known she had went unsatisfyingly unscratched.

THE WOMAN WAS a menace. Completely untrustworthy. Ty simmered while the miles rolled under his wheels.

Half an hour ticked by. He'd been doing his best to look relaxed, lounging against the door, driving one-handed. Now he tried to relax for real, subtly rolling his shoulders, circling his neck.

"I can drive if you're tired."

"I'm not tired," he snapped, annoyed that she'd caught him. "Like I'd let you drive my truck anyway."

"Like I'd want to. It's an environmental disaster on wheels."

"It's no Prius, I'll grant you that. But it's no Hummer either."

"Well, in that case." She laid on the sarcasm.

He got defensive. "There's lots worse things on the road than this truck."

Her laugh was more of a derisive snort. "If it gets ten miles to the gallon, I'll eat this rope." She flicked it with her fingers. "Admit it. This truck is all about status. It gives you cowboy cred at every redneck roadhouse."

That hit close to home, so he turned it back on her. "Why, Victoria Westin, I do believe you've been listening to your country music." He punched the radio and Miranda Lambert came on, singing about blowing a hole in her abusive boyfriend. He started to change the station but she batted his arm.

"Leave it. I like that one." She hummed along.

"Got a violent streak, do you?" Why wasn't he surprised?

"Let's just say I can sympathize."

"I guess old Winnie should be careful."

"I wouldn't waste a bullet on him."

"So you've got someone else in mind?"

She smiled. Tapped her fingers on her thighs, singing along.

He pulled off his tie, ran it through his hand. "Maybe I should tie you up after all, for my own protection."

"Unless you're planning to keep me bound for life, I wouldn't advise it." She turned up the radio, fiddled around until she found Carrie Underwood slashing the tires on her cheating boyfriend's big-ass gas-guzzler. Ignoring him, she sang along.

Damn it, she was smart-assing circles around him. He needed to take control again. Catch her off guard. And there was no better way to do it than with the truth.

He turned down the radio. Put an extra dollop of honey in his drawl. "Vicky, honey." He waited till he felt her attention on him. "I appreciate you coming all the way out here to testify. Angie told me you could've just sent a sworn statement, but it wouldn't have had the same impact." He met her startled gaze. "You saved the verdict, and I'm as grateful as I can be."

She turned away, stared out the windshield. "Well. We didn't do anything wrong. I mean, *legally* wrong."

"Yeah, I know, but that might not have mattered." He paused. "I didn't know you lost your job until you said so on the stand. Is there anything I can do to make that right?"

She softened up. "Thanks, but I was fired to prevent the firm getting sued, not because they think I did anything wrong."

He shook his head, sincerely apologetic. "It's my fault. If I hadn't started that brawl with Winnie and torn up the wedding, I doubt it would've made the papers."

"Maybe not. But Winston wouldn't have gotten two black eyes either."

He glanced at her, and for the first time all day, she was

smiling at him. His heart lifted, suddenly as light as air. "Honey, I only wish he had four eyes so I could've blackened them all for you."

She laughed at that, as he'd meant her to, and he grinned, loving the sound. He hadn't felt this good in a month.

The road was straight as a ruler, he hardly needed to watch it, so he let himself steal a long look at her. Her blue eyes had gone all warm and melty. Her lips were parted, moist and inviting. She'd angled herself toward him just a little bit, and without thinking about it, he stretched his arm across the back of the seat, brushed a finger over her shoulder.

Yeah, now *this* was how things were supposed to be. She was his, all his. He could reach out and take her.

There was just one last hurdle to clear.

"Honey," he said, his heart in his words, "walking away from you in France was the biggest mistake of my life. I'm sorrier than I can say."

She jerked like he stabbed her. Went to battle stations in a blink, brushing off his hand. "Thanks for reminding me why I hate you."

"But—"

She cranked the radio up.

He slapped it off. "I'm trying to apologize!"

She covered her ears.

He tugged on her arm. "Listen to me, goddamn it!"

She popped her seat belt, opened her window, and leaned out into the rushing heat. Waving both arms at the car they were passing, she yelled, "Help! I'm being kidnapped! Call the police!" The wind caught her words, but there was no mistaking her meaning. The driver's eyes widened in shock.

"Jesus Christ, Vicky!" Hauling on her dress, Ty yanked her back inside with one hand while he raised her window with the other, engaging the child locks, all while driving with his knee. Glancing in the rearview, he saw the driver on her phone. "Goddamn it, the police'll be after us. Don't you realize this is Texas? They could shoot first and ask questions later!"

"As long as they aim at you, I'm good with it."

He set his teeth.

A siren wailed in the distance.

TWO HOURS LATER when they pulled into the ranch, Ty still wasn't speaking to her. And she really couldn't blame him. She had a lot to answer for.

But honestly, who could ever have imagined that the police would drag him out of the truck at gunpoint? Or throw him against the side to frisk him. Or cuff him face-down on the broiling pavement.

And it wasn't like she just stood there watching. She'd tried everything to convince them that she wasn't some battered woman too afraid of her abusive man to press charges against him.

When nothing else worked, she finally called the judge to vouch for them. It was totally humiliating.

Not that Ty had appreciated her efforts. Filthy, sweaty and with a welt rising on his cheek where it hit the side of the truck, he'd spent a long, torturous moment considering the cops' offer to prosecute her before he finally shook his head, and, grim-faced, pointed to the truck. She'd climbed in meekly, tried to apologize until he shot her a look at her that said he might change his mind yet.

After that, silence had prevailed all the way home.

Now, as Ty got out of the truck, the skinny cowboy who'd started walking toward them stopped on a dime. His eyes tracked down from Ty's tar-blackened shirt to the hole in his knee to the scuffed toes of his boots, then shot back up to the welt.

"Shit, Ty! What happened to you?"

"Victoria Westin, that's what." Ty jerked his thumb toward the truck, where she still sat in the cab. In a drawl that dripped poison, he added, "Give her a wide berth, Joe, or you're liable to end up with a black eye, like every other man who gets near her."

Well, that was going too far. Clambering down from her seat, Vicky strode toward the dumbfounded cowboy.

He eyed her like she'd rolled out of a Dumpster. And no wonder. Her wrinkled dress was stiff with dried sweat. Her pricey suede pumps were gray with road dust. Her makeup had melted off of her face. And her hair, well, her hair had unraveled when she stuck her head out the window. Now it hung in dreadlocks that would take hours to untangle.

She wasn't deterred. Marching up to Joe, she stuck out her hand. "I'm Vicky. Ty's mad because he kidnapped me and almost got arrested."

"I didn't kidnap her," Ty ground out, talking to Joe but glaring at her. "But I might kill her. If I do, call the cops in Harwood. They'll testify that it's justifiable homicide." And he stalked off toward the house.

"Uh, Ty," Joe called after him. "Clancy came by. He said Brescia's doing better."

That brought Ty up short. The angry lines around his mouth disappeared as he broke into a smile. "What else did he say?" he asked Joe, changing direction for the barn. Joe tagged along, chattering about test results. For lack of anything better to do, Vicky followed at a safe distance.

The barn was cavernous and blessedly cool compared to the roasting sun. Ty and Joe disappeared into a stall. Over the half door, a horse's head poked out. Liquid brown eyes turned Vicky's way, bright and interested, and a velvet nose extended, inviting her closer. When she stepped up to the door, the warm, heavy head settled on her shoulder.

Cheek to cheek with the horse, Vicky closed her eyes. Breathed in, breathed out. Peace descended. She felt calmer than she could remember, as if the horse's quiet presence had drawn the worry and aggravation from her mind like poison from a snakebite.

"Look at that, Ty," Joe said in hushed tones. "Brescia likes your friend."

"She's not my friend," Ty grumbled, but Vicky heard the trace of surprise he tried to suppress.

"Well, Brescia likes her anyway. And you know she's not much on women."

"Which makes her the smartest horse I've ever had."

Vicky let herself smile. Ty was trying to keep on playing gruff, but he couldn't sustain it. His pleasure at Brescia's improvement had all but wiped out his foul mood.

"She's beautiful," Vicky said. "She's . . . magical."

Ty snorted, but without conviction. "She's one of a kind, I'll say that much."

Which was more than he'd said to her in the last two hours. She opened her eyes. He was watching her, his expression unreadable. She widened her smile.

"I'm in love," she said, and meant it.

TY'S BODY STILLED.

He couldn't have heard her right. Even Vicky, who could change with the wind, couldn't have gone from hate to love in the last five minutes.

As startling as that was, even more shocking was his own reaction. He wasn't running.

He was smiling.

Well, why not? She turned him on. Made him laugh. Kept him on his toes. The truth was, in the last month, he'd imagined her on his ranch so many times that it didn't seem weird to see her here in the flesh. It didn't even seem strange that she was talking about love. In fact, it felt natural. So natural that he couldn't remember why he'd fought his own feelings so hard—

"I always wanted a horse," she continued, threading her fingers through Brescia's mane. "Mother wouldn't get me one, or even let me take lessons. But I promised myself I'd get one when I grew up." She rubbed cheeks with Brescia while his ego shriveled like a raisin. "I'll trade you my Beemer for her, straight up. What do you say?"

He cleared his throat, put some vinegar in his voice. "She's not for sale. Or swap. Or loan, either. So you can quit cozying up to her. You'll only break her heart when you go."

He elbowed past Joe and pushed open the door, breaking up their hug-in. That made him feel mean-spirited, which only made him pricklier. He sniffed the air. "There's a shower in the downstairs bedroom. You ought to use it." And taking hold of Brescia's halter, he walked her out of the stall.

As he headed for the paddock, Vicky called after him. "At least I don't smell like I was lying in the garbage on the Interstate. With a jackboot on my ass."

He shot a glare over his shoulder. Joe had his hat off, scratching his head as he watched Vicky flounce toward the house, spiky heels divoting the dusty path to his porch. Then the screen door slammed. Joe made for the office. And Ty, disgusted with himself, trudged around the paddock in his ruined clothing, blistering Brescia's ear about the irresponsible, pigheaded *lawyer* she'd taken such a liking to.

CHAPTER TWENTY-TWO

HALF AN HOUR LATER, leaning against the stove with one ice-cold beer down and another in his hand, Ty was feeling considerably less homicidal. Brescia had calmed him down, as usual. As soon as he finished his beer, he'd strip down and shower off. Then he'd feel all the way human again.

Meanwhile, he had to quit picturing Vicky in the shower. In the past month, he'd fantasized approximately two hundred times about the shower sex they'd almost had in Amboise. Now she was down the hall, and he could see her all too clearly in his mind's eye, standing in the avocado-colored tub, warm water sluicing over her naked body.

He took another pull on his beer, rolled the bottle across his forehead.

Christ. He should shoot himself now, because he was too dumb to live.

He set the bottle on the counter. Took the first step toward the bedroom. And noticed a Post-it on the door.

KEEP OUT, JACKASS

That did it. He ripped it down, balled it up, and tossed it over his shoulder. Then he opened the door without knocking and walked in.

She wasn't in the bedroom. The bathroom door was closed, but he didn't hear the shower. He put his ear to the crack. Smiled. She was singing. Vintage Springsteen. He rapped with one knuckle. Then two. No response.

Slowly, he pushed open the door. Stuck his head in. And swallowed.

She was stretched out in the tub, eyes closed, ear buds in, bopping to her iPod. Bath-bubble islands drifted on top of the water, so he couldn't see much. But he knew what was hiding under the surface.

Taking a quick look around, he spotted her panties in a roll on the floor. Leopard spots. His favorite. The matching bra dangled from the doorknob. He reached around and snatched it . . . just as she opened her eyes.

"Hey! Put that back, jackass!" She started to sit up, saw his eyes zero on her breasts, and slid down deeper. Her knees stuck up through the bubbles. "What're you doing in here?"

He brazened it out. "I was gonna wash your clothes so you'd have something to wear. I knocked but you didn't hear me."

"Do I look stupid?"

"Is that a rhetorical question?"

"You're in no position to smart-ass me." She stared him down. "Do you always spy on women in the bathtub?"

He snorted, trying for derision. "Do I look like a Peeping Tom?"

"Is that a rhetorical question?"

He went for offended. "I was doing you a favor."

"I'll pretend to believe you, because otherwise I'll have to call the police. Again. Now put my bra back."

She shouldn't have mentioned the cops. He fluttered it in the air. "Come and get it."

Then he waltzed right in and scooped up the rest of her clothes, waltzed out again and closed the door on her fury.

Then he sat down on the bed to wait.

It didn't take long. There was splashing and thrashing, a muttered string of swearwords, then the door flew open and she charged out in nothing but a towel.

She stopped short when she saw him. "Why you—"

He waved her bra, a red flag to a bull.

When she lunged for it, he wrapped an arm around her waist and pulled her down on top of him.

VICKY LANDED IN Ty's lap, his arms strapped around her, not so tight she couldn't breathe, but snug enough to immobilize her.

Resistance was pointless with her arms pinned; it would only dislodge her towel. So she went still instead, putting all her rebellion into her eyes, diamond points of fury that should have drilled through his skull and out the back of his head.

Except that he'd reverted to annoyingly unflappable Tyrell, the Ty with the lazy drawl and the buttery eyes and the easy smile that scraped like jagged fingernails across her overwound psyche.

He turned all those weapons on her now. "Honey, I'm tired of fighting with you. Let's call a truce."

"A truce? When you're holding me prisoner?"

He loosened his arms, but kept them looped around her. "There. Now I'm not holding you prisoner, I'm just holding you." He angled his head. "Is that better?"

Better? It was scary how much better it was. He was

dirty and smelly, with his surfer's hair stuck to his sweaty brow. But he still felt better than anything she'd felt in the last lonely month. Better than anything she'd hoped to feel ever again.

"No, it's not *better*," she said, tart as a lemon. "*Better* would be my air-conditioned room at the hotel. Which is where I'd be if you hadn't *kidnapped* me."

He swam past the bait. "If you'd stayed at the hotel, sugar, you wouldn't have met Brescia." He smiled sweetly. "She sure took a shine to you."

That was the first thing he'd said that she didn't want to argue with. Brescia had gone straight to her heart, an instant connection she'd never felt with any other creature. "What's wrong with her? Will she be okay?"

"She's got bloodworms," he said, and he told her about them, all the risks and the worries. Then he took her through the treatment, Clancy's visits, the new meds. She hung on his words.

"But she's doing better now? Clancy thinks she's improving?"

"She's not out of the woods. But she's going in the right direction." He lifted a hand, tucked a clump of damp hair behind her ear. "It's nice of you to care so much."

A lump rose in her throat. "Brescia's beautiful, inside and out. I felt it the minute I saw her."

"She's been good company this past month. When I was missing you."

Her head came up. She must have misheard him.

"Maybe you can stay on awhile. Get to know her. I can teach you to ride."

Her heartbeat picked up. "You're kidding, right?"

He slid a finger along her jaw. "Honey, you're trouble with a capital T. But I can't seem to get enough of you."

For a moment she just looked at him, while he looked back at her with a question in his eyes. He was asking her to come along with him, to leave the bullshit behind and get back to the good stuff.

Her head tried to resist. But her heart and her body were already with him; the battle was lost before it began. He'd summed it up perfectly, the push and the pull. Even when he got under her skin, she couldn't resist him. He hit every button—passion, anger, humor, sadness. He made her feel fully alive.

She laughed, at herself, at the foolish leap she was taking, and her laughter felt lighter than air. It bubbled up from deep down, lifting her heart as it rose.

Setting her palm on his cheek, she skimmed her thumb over the welt. "Have you considered the risk? One of us always ends up needing an ice pack."

"I'll stock up." His fingers slid into her hair. "For now, you can kiss it better if you want to."

Her eyes locked with his. She leaned in, slowly, surely. Stroked her tongue across the swelling.

That was all it took. The towel hit the floor. Her back hit the mattress. Rolling on top of her, he kneed her thighs apart, ground against her as she arched up to meet him.

"Honey." He got the word out on a pant. "I need to get inside you *right now*."

Her breath hitched. "Yes. Now." She reached for his belt.

He caught her hand. "Condoms," he gasped. "Upstairs." He straightened his arms, raked tiger eyes down her body. Then pushed off from the bed, shedding his shirt as he ran.

She couldn't lie still. Her breath hitched. Her heart drummed.

She sat up, ran her hands through her hair. And her restless gaze hit a photo, framed on the bureau.

It stopped her cold. A reality check. Sunny day, white church. Beautiful bride, handsome husband. Laughing and loving, looking past the lens to a future sparkling and bright.

Vicky's eyes scanned the room, her first real look around. Lissa was everywhere. In other photos, pinning a blue ribbon to Brescia's bridle, at a party with Jack's arm around her, the two of them grinning drunkenly at the camera. In trophies and ribbons, lining a shelf.

She went to the closet. Here were Lissa's clothes. Her cowboy boots. Her leather jacket, worn soft as butter. Ty had kept it all.

Closing the closet, she leaned back against the door.

Isn't it possible, Mr. Brown, that you simply dreamed *that conversation with your wife, or perhaps* imagined *it—which would be completely understandable given the stress you were under, your fatigue, your grief?*

It was a good question, artfully crafted to raise doubt in the jury's mind while also showing compassion for his heartbreak. He'd borne up well until then, and she doubted anyone else in the courtroom knew how that question affected him. But she was standing a few feet in front of him. She saw the sick fear flicker over his face.

Reading it there, understanding what it meant, she did something she'd never done before. She abandoned her training, her judgment as a lawyer, and went with her instincts. She walked away from him, riffling her papers, drawing the jury's gaze to her and away from his suffering.

Stuffing two pages of follow-up questions under her notebook, she ignored her co-counsel's startled stare. He knew she'd pulled her punches, hadn't gone for the kill.

But Ty, she knew, had no idea. She'd touched on his deepest fear, and that made him believe she was cold and heartless, a lawyer in the most hated sense of the word.

Given that belief, how could he ever forgive her for asking that question? Wouldn't some part of him always see her as the enemy?

The things he'd said just moments ago, the way he'd looked at her, touched her, all made her believe that he wanted more from her than another quick lay. But if he didn't confront that part of himself that still saw her as a threat, how could they ever get back to the good stuff? Wouldn't it always be the elephant in the room, poised to stomp on her if she said the wrong thing, triggered the wrong thought in his head?

Footsteps thudded down the stairs. She moved back to the bed.

"Had to hunt for the good ones," he said, bursting into the room. He tossed a handful on the bed.

She sifted them through her fingers. "You're an optimist."

He grinned, stripping off his pants. "You're insatiable. And I aim to satisfy." He crawled up the bed until he caged her in. "Now, where were we?"

He dropped his head to kiss her, but she made herself plant a hand on his chest. "Not so fast, cowboy. I've got a question for you."

He rolled onto his back, pulling her over on top of him. Their legs twined like fingers. "No, I don't have any handcuffs," he said. "But I promise to get some."

She dropped her head on his shoulder, let out a laugh. If only it was that simple.

His hands stoked over her back, palms slightly rough, one gliding down to cup her ass, the other moving up, under her hair, to cradle her skull possessively. Desire dulled her brain. Why would she do anything to ruin this perfect moment? Why?

She lifted her head. His eyes glowed golden brown. His lips curved deliciously, prelude to a kiss.

"Why did you walk out on me in Amboise?"

His smile faltered for an instant, then firmed again. "Honey, I told you I'm sorry."

He started to roll her over, to put her on her back again, but she pushed against his shoulder. "I believe you. But why did you do it?"

He didn't answer, tried to roll her again, but she strad- dled him, planting her palms on his chest. "Stop trying to get on top of me."

His smile turned playful, determinedly so. "Honey, if you want to play cowgirl, just say so." He caught her waist and lifted her up, poised above his erection.

"Don't." That was all she said. His smile faltered again.

He set her down on his chest, blew out an exaggerated sigh. "Sweetheart, this is exactly what I meant when I said you were trouble." His lazy drawl made it sound like a tease. "Here I am trying to get my rocks off, and yours too I might add, and you're going lawyer on me, turning into your mother."

It was a cheap shot, throwing Adrianna at her. That he'd stoop so low meant she was close to the bone.

"I think I know why," she persisted. "You went back to your room and started thinking about Lissa."

"We're not talking about Lissa." No teasing tone now; his voice was stone cold.

"Her things are all over this room, but we can't talk about her?"

"Let's not talk at all." He flipped her onto her back. His mouth came down on hers, and this kiss wasn't playful. It wasn't gentle or sexy or fraught with passion. It was hard and hurtful, meant to dominate.

She turned her head away, and he didn't force her. In- stead, he spread her legs with his knees, would have plunged in, but she simply said, "No," and he didn't force that either. Pushing up on his hands, he glared down at her.

"Why the fuck are you doing this, Vicky? Just leave well enough alone."

"It's not well enough." She held his fiery gaze. "If you

won't tell me why you walked out on me, how do I know you won't do it again?"

"I said I was sorry." His growl was menacing, nothing like his easygoing drawl. But then, he wasn't as easygoing as he liked to pretend. Now he was hurting, and to some degree, she was the instrument of his pain. Until they got that out on the table, they could never be together.

"I know you're sorry, Ty. I'm telling you that's not enough."

In one motion, he levered up off the bed, grabbed his pants from the floor, and shoved in a leg.

Her throat squeezed. She forced out the words. "So you're walking out again. So I was right not to trust you."

He whipped around, fury darkening his face. "You want to know why I walked before? Why I'm walking now? Because you're a high-maintenance, pain-in-the-ass bitch on wheels who won't be happy till I'm on my knees. Well, I won't do it. I won't do it for you or anybody else, you understand?"

He turned his back on her, scooped his shirt from the floor.

Holding back tears, she managed to say, "Yes, Ty, I do understand."

Then he slammed out the door.

HE STOPPED IN the hall to stamp into his boots. Thought she understood, did she? She understood *nothing*. Not a goddamn thing.

He stomped through the house and out the back door, making for his truck. But he'd forgotten the keys, and going back to get them was too much to ask when the world was folding in on him. Hunched on the seat, he fought for control. His throat was so tight he couldn't swallow. An elephant stood on his chest; his lungs wouldn't fill.

Goddamn it, he was worse than Vicky, having a fucking panic attack. At least she could deal with them when they came on her. He was helpless, clutching his head like a lunatic. He'd fucking faint if he couldn't fucking fill his lungs.

"Ty? You okay?"

He couldn't take it, he couldn't face Joe. Bolting from the truck, he headed for the house. If he could just get his shoulder under Vicky's head again, then maybe he wouldn't faint. She'd do that thing where she traced his abs with her fingertip. It tickled, but he liked it. And he'd be able to breathe.

He found himself outside her door. He sucked a deep breath, the first in five minutes. Pushed it open and stepped inside.

She lay on the bed where he'd left her, face streaked with tears, crumpled tissues on the pillow.

He leaned back against the door, heart pounding, sweat rolling down his sides. "I killed my wife," he blurted. "I killed Lissa."

He waited for the sky to fall. For God to smite him. For Vicky to turn away.

None of those things happened. Instead, she opened her arms.

He went into them, let them close around him as he buried his face in her breast. Tears rose up from his heart, from the shreds of his soul, and her arms tightened, fingers threading his hair, holding him close as they poured forth. He sobbed as he'd not sobbed in seven years, since he'd laid his head on Lissa's breast and felt her breathe her last breath on this earth.

It took a long time to wring himself dry. Eventually, he lay quiet. Vicky's heartbeat thumped evenly in his ear. The rise and fall of her chest soothed his fever.

Slowly, he sat up, as groggy as if he'd been sick for a week. With a handful of tissues, he blotted his tears from her breasts, avoiding her eyes until she giggled. Then he looked up.

"It tickles," she said, smiling at him. Her eyes were red too. She'd cried along with him.

He tried to smile back at her, but he couldn't. "You were right," he said, "I'm not sure if she asked me to let her go. I used to be sure. But for a while now I've been wondering if maybe I imagined it because I couldn't stand to see her like that. Maybe I made it up in my mind. Pulled the plug on her to make it easier on myself."

Her smile faded. Compassion filled her eyes. Not pity, he couldn't have stood pity. But this was understanding, it was caring.

"Tyrell." She cupped his scorching cheek in her cool palm. "Whether Lissa asked you or not—and I truly be-lieve that she did—letting her go was a kindness. If it lessened your heartache for a time, that was incidental, and nothing you need to feel guilty for." Her soft voice fell like cool water on his overheated mind.

"What happened to your wife was tragic, but it was over long ago. What's happening to you is another kind of tragedy, and it's time for it to end too. You didn't kill Lissa. Jason Taylor killed her. You released her from the pain that he trapped her in, and whether she actually spoke to you and asked you to do it, or whether you knew her and loved her well enough to understand that it was the right thing to do, either way, you did it for her."

He wanted to believe her. He wanted it more than his own life.

She must have seen the doubt in his eyes, because she cocked her head and asked him one more question, just one.

"Would you do it again?"

Would he? Would he do it, knowing what he knew now about the sleepless, doubting nights, about the pain in his chest, just under his heart, that never went away? About his inability to move on, to have another relationship, a wife, children? Would he, knowing how seven years of suffering felt, wondering if he'd done the right thing, if he'd killed his wife in a misguided attempt to ease his own pain? Would he risk all of that again?

"Yes," he breathed out. "Yes, I'd do it again. I'd do it for Lissa. I would've done anything for her."

CHAPTER TWENTY-THREE

TY WOKE UP the next morning with a bug up his ass. A bug named Matthew J. Donohue III.

He kicked off the covers, stared sourly down at his morning wood. "God*damn* it." Vicky could've put that wood to good use and started both of their days off right, if Donohue hadn't locked her in her room in a chastity belt.

True to form, he and Isabelle had shown up at the worst possible moment, when Ty and Vicky were seconds away from epic makeup sex. He'd had to rabbit from her room like a guilty teenager.

It wasn't quite the end of the world, though, because they had a long, pleasant evening of making eyes at each other, building up to what should have been a long, hot night of scorching sex. But just when Ty was faking a yawn and getting ready to show Vicky to the upstairs guest room—har har—Donohue lowered the boom.

He decreed—that was the only word for it—that Vicky and Isabelle would share the downstairs bedroom, and he'd sleep on the couch at the foot of the stairs.

Ty gave it his best shot, making the case for everybody having a bed. But Donohue was on to him, and he wouldn't be budged. He crumpled his six-foot frame onto the five-and-a-half-foot couch, and Ty was left out in the cold.

All in all, he'd barely stolen five minutes alone with her since her brother arrived, and that was only when Donohue was in the can. He'd used the time to try to convince her to stay, but she claimed she had business to wrap up in New York, and they'd swapped phone numbers and left it at that.

He hadn't given up, though. Donohue would have to take a shower this morning, and Ty meant to use that time to lock Vicky down.

Downstairs, he found Isabelle fiddling with the coffee-pot. He nudged her aside and got it going, then enjoyed a moment's satisfaction when Donohue unfolded himself from the couch and limped toward the bathroom looking every bit as surly as Ty felt.

Taking Isabelle's arm, Ty steered her out on the porch, where he found Vicky on the swing, looking fresh as a daisy in a bright yellow sundress with pink and black flowers sprinkled over the skirt. His day improved instantly.

"Well, hello, beautiful."

"Morning, Ty." Her wholehearted smile lifted up his heart and rolled it clean over in his chest.

"Coffee's on," he got out past the lump in his throat. "Bring you a cup?"

"Love one."

He lingered a moment, gazing into her blue eyes with a dopey smile he couldn't begin to control. Then Donohue pushed through the door, grunted something that might have been "Good morning," and plopped down on the top step to chaperone.

Ty let it go. Once he had Vicky back here—alone—

they'd have sex all the time, everywhere. And little brother could go piss up a rope.

Bringing Vicky's coffee in one of his mother's china cups, Ty got another of those smiles in return. "You like pancakes, honey?" He could whip them up from scratch, float them in real maple syrup. "Why don't you give me a hand?"

Matt started to rise too, but Vicky waved him down. "We'll be right inside, Matt. You can hear everything we say."

"Yeah, Matt," Ty put in. "If I need you to rescue me, I'll holler." He let the screen door slap behind him.

Inside the kitchen, Vicky looked like a sunbeam, brightening up the tired avocado decor.

"I'm planning to update," he found himself saying as he pulled what he needed from the faded cabinets.

"Really?" She did a little spin, flaring her skirt. "Maybe some fresh paint, but I kind of like it otherwise. It feels homey."

"It does now, honey." He measured the flour, sifted in the baking powder. "What color paint are you thinking?"

"Yellow," she said without hesitation. "So it always looks like the sun's shining in here."

"I don't know. Yellow can be tricky." He heated the griddle. "I'll need help picking out just the right shade."

She smiled over her shoulder at him. He smiled back. Forgot about the pancakes for a minute.

Then Isabelle poked her head in the door. "Anything I can do?"

He pulled his gaze away from Vicky. "Not a thing, honey. Go on back out and keep your husband company." *Before he comes in here.*

Vicky must have thought the same, because she picked up the coffeepot. "I'll top him off." And she disappeared onto the porch.

Ty whisked his batter. He hadn't made pancakes in years, not since Lissa died, but he could do it blindfolded.

As he poured perfect silver dollars on the sizzling griddle, a car door slammed outside. Funny, Joe was supposed to be off today. Well, the more the merrier, there was plenty of batter. Spatula in hand, he stepped out onto the porch to call him in.

And the words died on his lips.

In the driveway sat a siren red Mustang, its raven-haired owner on a march toward the house.

For a moment, Ty couldn't process what he was seeing. He'd forgotten all about Molly. She'd never once crossed his mind. Now he stared at her like a man trapped in a dream, powerless to move his limbs or cry out a warning, as she arrowed like a missile at his fragile new future.

At first her expression was simply curious, wondering who his friends were, pleased to meet them. But as her eyes swept the porch, she did the math, and the numbers didn't add up to her liking.

Matt and Isabelle had "couple" stamped all over them, so she zeroed in on Vicky. Without breaking stride, she climbed the steps to the porch. "Morning, y'all," she said, hitting the down-home note. Heading straight to Vicky, she stuck out her hand. "Hi there, I'm Molly."

"I'm Vicky." She gave Molly a wide, clueless smile. "Do you work here?"

Molly waited a beat, while dread iced Ty's veins.

Then she widened stunning green eyes, put surprise on her face. "Why, Vicky, didn't Ty tell you about me?" She sashayed to his side, curled her arm around his waist.

"Honey, I'm his girlfriend."

VICKY'S PHONE CHIRPED. Another text from Ty. She ignored it.

She'd read the first one in the car, his bullshit apology. How does a man *forget* he has a girlfriend? Please.

He was Winston all over again. She was done with him.

Emerging from the bathroom stall, she found Isabelle waiting at the sink. "Our flight's on time," she told Vicky, trying hard to sound cheerful. Vicky's phone chirped again. Isabelle wrung her hands. "Maybe you should answer him."

"I did." Vicky lathered her hands. "I told him I hope Matt's right cross knocked out a few of his pearly whites. And I told him to stop texting me because I'm not going to read them."

"He won't give up."

Vicky rinsed the soap from her hands, dried them under the blower. *Chirp.* "You know, I'm beginning to think you're right." She fished her phone from her purse, walked back into the stall, and dropped it in the toilet.

Isabelle gasped.

Vicky flushed. Down it went. She dusted off her hands. "There. Now I'm finally finished with Tyrell Brown."

CHAPTER TWENTY-FOUR

"YOUR CO-OP SOLD already? But the real estate market's in the toilet."

"Funny story about toilets." Vicky gave Maddie the short version of how her phone ended up in the San Antonio sewer.

Maddie boiled it down even more. "Brown's an asshole. If there's any justice, Mustang Molly will make him miserable for the rest of his pathetic life."

Vicky shrugged, refusing to dwell on Ty. "On the bright side, Isabelle felt so guilty that she bought me an iPhone at the airport. And," she added with a smile, "my mother doesn't have my new phone number."

Maddie handed the bartender a twenty, left five for a tip, and clutching their two-for-one happy hour martinis, they inched through the girth of suits circling the oval bar at Maddie's new favorite downtown haunt. When they'd settled at a tiny table along the wall and Maddie had pronounced her martini as dry as the Sahara, she got back to the co-op.

"How did you unload it so fast?"

"I priced it to move. They're taking most of my furniture

too, and the realtor's taking the rest. Even so, there won't be much cash left over, because I bought in the bubble." Vicky smiled. "Just enough to pay off my Beemer."

Despite her big talk to Matt about "money" and "stuff," after much extremely optimistic number-crunching, she'd decided to keep it, even though she'd have to park it at her mother's house in Connecticut because she could no longer afford a parking space.

"Are you sure about this? Going from the decision to sell to the closing in two weeks seems—"

"Decisive?"

"Impulsive."

Vicky shrugged. Maybe it was impulsive, and it certainly left a lot of unanswered questions, but she felt lighter already.

"Where are you planning to live?"

That was one of those unanswered questions. "I guess I'll stay at Mother's for a few days while I look for a place."

"Not a chance. You're staying with me."

Vicky smiled again. "It won't be for long. I'll figure something out."

Maddie held up a finger. "Hang on, I just remembered something. My trainer's brother wants to sublet his place until the end of the year. He's a professor at NYU. Teaching abroad this fall."

"How much?"

"That's the best part. It's NYU housing, subsidized by the university, so it's dirt cheap. And it's in a great neighborhood down in the Village."

"Too good to be true. He'll have found someone by now."

"Let's find out." Maddie whipped out her phone. Ten minutes later it was a done deal; Vicky would move in next week. She couldn't believe it had been so easy.

"This must be what Joseph Campbell meant about 'hidden hands.'"

Maddie squinted in puzzlement.

"You know," Vicky prompted. "The 'follow your bliss' guy. He said that when you're on the right path in life, things fall into place as if you're being helped by hidden hands."

Maddie held up her own hands, waggled her fingers. "Some credit here?"

"Point taken," Vicky said with a laugh. "Thank you, Madeline, for finding me an apartment, and for everything else. When the shit hits the fan, you learn who your friends are. And how sucky life would be without them."

"Same goes," said Maddie, warmly. She raised her martini. "To BFFs." Their glasses clinked. They sipped in unison.

And into that moment of love and good feelings, friendship and warmth, Winston dropped like a wrecking ball.

"Well, well." He loomed over their table. "If it isn't America's Most Wanted Lawyer."

Vicky's heart sank. She'd expected to run into him sometime, but why did it have to be now, when she'd been back from Texas for less than a day?

Across the table, Maddie set her glass down with a thump, already morphing into the Pitbull. Vicky warned her off with a glance. She'd handle Winston herself.

Looking up, she recognized at once that he'd been happy-houring for more than an hour. His eyes were bloodshot and his jaw was mean. She acted pleasantly surprised to see him.

"Hello, Winston. I saw your picture in the paper." She glanced at Maddie. "Did you see it? He was the one with his shirt strangling his armpits." She wrinkled her nose at him. "You really need a new trainer, or at least some self-tanner. You know what they say, if you can't tone it, tan it."

Red flags stained his cheekbones. "You're a bitch, Victoria," he snapped back without his usual aplomb. "I hope the committee yanks your license. In fact, I'm going to file an affidavit telling them how you and Brown went at it like rabbits. Until he realized you're *frigid*."

His voice had risen, drawing attention. Vicky's body vibrated with an invisible hum. Maybe she shouldn't have taken him on, but she was in it to win it now.

She kept her voice sweet and light. "Lenore called me last week." Her former secretary. "Believe it or not, she was hoping to get her job back. When I reminded her how I found you two screwing on my desk, do you know what she said?" She pushed her voice up for the spectators' benefit.

"She said that sex with you wasn't worth losing a job as a Wal-Mart greeter, much less a high-paid secretary. And she said that not once in the *six or seven times* you did it, did she ever have an orgasm. *Not once.*"

She leaned back in her chair, assumed a thoughtful air. "You know, I'm thinking of posting that on Facebook."

Winston's hand fell like a slab on the table. "Don't you dare. Don't you dare post one word about me." His face had gone florid. His lips were pressed flat.

She sat up straight. "Then stay out of my face, you lying, cheating, arrogant horse's ass." Her voice rang with authority. "Send whatever you want to the committee, I don't care. But stay away from me!"

His eyes bulged. His jaw ticked. With a last slap of the table that set their drinks rocking, he whirled and stormed off, disappearing in the crowd.

Maddie whooshed out a breath. "Holy shit. You were amazing." She looked hard at Vicky. "But who are you, and what have you done with my best friend?"

Vicky managed a shaky laugh. "I can't believe I'm not having a panic attack right now."

"Good for you, but you almost gave *me* one. Please, *please* warn me the next time you're going to rip someone a new one, so I can have my inhaler ready." Maddie drank off the rest of her martini in one gulp, set her glass down with a thump. "So, did Lenore-the-whore really call you, or did you make that up?"

"She really called, and she really said all of it, even the part about the Wal-Mart greeter."

Maddie let out a laugh. "That's classic. You don't have to post it, because I will!"

Sparkling with high spirits, she turned her attention to their closest neighbors, four thirtysomething MBA types unwinding after a hard day of moving millions. Cuffs rolled up, ties loosened, they had the vaguely predatory air of out-of-town-businessmen-at-large-in-New-York-City.

They'd been openly amused by the scene with Winston; now they zeroed in on the women at the heart of it. Maddie offered an encouraging smile.

"Don't," Vicky murmured under her breath. "I'm off men for the foreseeable future."

Maddie looked appalled. "Are you kidding? You finally unleash your inner slut and now you want to cut yourself off?"

One of the men, tall, with dark hair and a tan that made his crisp, white shirt look whiter, stood and ambled over to their table. "You ladies look like you need more martinis," he drawled with an unmistakable Texas twang.

Vicky rubbed her temple. What next? Locusts?

Tracking sparkling green eyes back and forth between them, Mr. Lone Star unloosed a devastating smile. "What can I getcha? Gin or vodka?"

Damn all Texans to hell, with their stupid drawls and

ridiculous smiles and idiotic courtesy. Why couldn't they all just stay in Texas?

Even Maddie, whose hard-shelled cynicism she could always rely on, fell hard for the twang. Her long lashes fluttered, and she smiled her wood-sprite smile. "Gin, please. With a twist for me and extra olives for my friend."

Then, with her foot, she pushed out the extra chair at their table. And, naturally, the rest of the long-limbed, white-toothed, too-polite-for-New-York-City Texans un-limbered their lanky six-foot frames from their chairs and joined them.

CLANCY ROLLED HIS chaw from one cheek to the other, fired a stream at a lizard sunning itself by the barn. "I'd give her about a month," he drawled. "Maybe three weeks."

Ty's heart hit the ground. Brescia seemed so much better, he'd been sure she was getting well. He dropped his head, stared at his boots. He couldn't speak without crying, so he pressed his lips tight.

"Play it by ear," Clancy went on, "but you want to break her in slow. None of those two-week trail rides you're so fond of."

Ty's head came up. "Huh?"

"I said take it easy on her, let her get her strength back. I figure it'll be a month before she's up to anything strenuous."

"You mean . . . you mean she's on the mend?"

Clancy looked surprised. "I told Joe that yesterday, didn't he tell you?"

"Yeah, but I was afraid—" He stopped talking as relief swamped him. Now he wouldn't have to make the awful decision to put her down. Thank God. Thank you, God.

"You all right, Ty? You're pale as paint."

"I'm good," he got out. "I'm real good."

When Clancy's truck disappeared in a cloud of dust, he went into the barn to have himself a little cry and give Brescia the news. She nodded along like Mr. Ed, but he didn't attach much significance to that. She always nodded when she felt frisky.

Stopping in the office, he told Joe too, then added, "I'm hitting the trail for a few days. Dash could use the exercise."

"Sure thing, Ty. I'll round him up."

Heading to the house to pack his gear, he said a prayer of thanks for Joe. The man never hassled him about riding off for days, even weeks, at a time. He'd been doing it since Lissa died. In the early years, when his grief was still as sharp and hard as a diamond, it kept him sane. Later, when doubt and guilt ate at his mind, it kept him alive.

Now, with Brescia finally recovering, he wasn't wasting any time. He was in the saddle in under an hour, supplies for a week in his saddlebags, Dash's nose pointed toward the hills. Up there, he'd be able to listen to the silence, clear his head so he could figure out how to make things right with Vicky.

As the ranch fell away behind them, he started explaining the situation to Dash. The big gelding wasn't the gentle listener Brescia was, but as they talked it out, Ty started to see things from a different perspective.

"Sure, the thing with Molly looked bad," he told Dash. "Hell, it *was* bad. But Vicky didn't even give me a chance to explain. Why, just the day before, we had ourselves an emotional moment, you know? We connected, and it was fucking amazing. And I gotta tell you, Dash, I was getting all kinds of crazy ideas. Romantic ideas, if you want the truth. Then, at the first little bump in the road, she was off and running."

He lifted his hat, blotted his forehead with his sleeve. "Vicky's not the only one who's been done wrong here, you know. If she'd just stuck around, I could've explained to her that Molly's more of a buddy than a girlfriend. Somebody to have a few beers with. Watch the game at the Horseshoe. Hell, Molly and me haven't even had sex since I got back from France." He patted Dash's neck. "I know what you're thinking, I'm sure you've seen her rack. But I wanted to see how we got along without giving my dick a vote.

"Anyway, it's been clear for a while now that she's taking things more seriously than I am, and I'd pretty much decided to pull the plug. But what with the hearing and all, I hadn't gotten around to telling her yet. And I couldn't exactly break it to her with everyone standing around on the porch, could I? Then Donohue hit me with that haymaker." He rubbed his jaw. "By the time I woke up, they were gone."

As they climbed higher into the hills, indignation and the first seeds of anger took root in his breast.

"She should've given me the benefit of the doubt. She should've let me explain. But do you think she'd even answer her phone? Or text me back?" He snorted. "Oh, she fired off a parting shot, but that was it. Next thing I knew, her number was disconnected. She cut me off completely."

Stopping for the night by a narrow ribbon of a stream, Ty stomped around, setting up camp, building a fire, all while he worked up a bigger head of steam.

"You know what I think, Dash?" he said over his shoulder as he took a long leak on a flat rock. "I dodged a goddamn bullet. And from now on, I'm staying out of the line of fire."

THE PROFESSOR'S APARTMENT was large by New York City standards, and furnished comfortably, if blandly. All Vicky had to do was move in.

Well, that wasn't all she had to do. She also had to figure out how to pay for it. Her severance would only go so far. To stretch it, she needed a job.

Sipping a compromise latte—low fat, single shot, no whip—at the Starbucks around the corner, she stared out the window at the people streaming along the sunny sidewalk; students trickling back into the city before the start of the school year, couples holding hands, working stiffs staring straight ahead, intent on getting home.

For once, she wasn't one of them. She was a bystander, an aimless people watcher with nothing pressing to do and no place she had to be.

It wasn't as great as she'd imagined when she'd sat at her desk, buried under paper.

She pulled her gaze back inside, where a sign on the counter caught her eye. Without conscious thought, she found herself rising, making her way to the barista at the end of the counter, the one who called out the finished drinks.

Vicky pointed to the sign. "What're the hours?"

"Morning rush," the girl said, digging under the counter. "Here. Fill this out and bring it back to me."

Vicky took the application to her window seat, mentally editing as she filled it out. She omitted her law degree, made it sound like she'd held a clerical job at the firm—not because she worried that her current troubles would keep her from being hired, but because high-priced lawyers didn't pour coffee at Starbucks. And for good reason. Who'd want to work with them?

She handed it to the girl, who handed it to someone else, who glanced over it, then crooked a finger at Vicky. The interview took ten minutes. She spent the next twenty sipping her now-cold latte and figuring out how to set the alarm clock on her new phone, because she had to be at work at—gulp—five a.m.

Catching her reflection in the window, she smiled at herself. *Be careful what you wish for, Victoria. You just might get it.*

THINGS *FINALLY* SLOWED down around ten-thirty. Vicky leaned back against the counter, rotated one stiff ankle at a time. In all her years of drinking Starbucks, why had she never considered that the baristas stood on their feet *all day long*? She'd have left bigger tips.

Gerard, her boss, called out. "Take your break, Vicky. Be back in fifteen."

She limped off to the ladies' room.

Pausing at the mirror, she tucked a few loose hairs up into her French twist. They promptly fell down again, so she pulled out the clip. Why not? It wasn't like she'd be called into court at a moment's notice. She turned her head from side to side. She should get more interesting earrings. If she never saw another one-inch gold hoop, it would be too soon.

She checked her watch. Funny, she'd never had to time herself in the bathroom before. Peeing took longer than she would have guessed.

Back at the counter, another barista had appeared, skinny as a snake, with tattoos starting at her wrists and disappearing under the sleeves of her green Starbucks polo. Her hair was dyed black with magenta streaks, kohl ringed her indigo eyes, silver skulls and crossbones ringed her fingers, and she was pierced in places that made Vicky shudder.

"Hey there!" Her wide, friendly smile clashed wildly with her gothness. "You must be the new girl. I'm Josie."

From the back, Gerard started whistling "Josie and the Pussycats." Both of them did identical eye rolls, then burst out laughing. And that quickly, a friendship that Vicky couldn't have imagined a month ago was born.

"I'm Vicky. I started today."

"Cool. I've been here a year. That makes me an old-timer."

"It's hard on the feet."

Josie lifted a foot, showing off bulky clogs. "They're ugly as shit, but they help a lot. I'll show you where I got them. What time you off?"

"Twelve-thirty."

"I'm on till three. Meet me outside. I'll bring you a latte." She grinned. "Free coffee's the best and only perk of this job, so you might as well start sucking it down today."

Gerard barked from the back. "I hope you're restocking while you're yakking."

They rolled their eyes again.

By four o'clock, Vicky had a pair of the ugly clogs in her backpack, and she was parked on a bench in Washington Square Park, soaking up the sun with Josie.

"So what's your story?" Josie asked. "You go to NYU?"

"Not yet." But she might. Seeing all the students around had given her an idea. "I'm thinking of signing up for acting classes."

She flushed as she said it, feeling ridiculous. But Josie perked up. "Seriously? You want to act? Because that's why I'm in New York. I'm an actor. This rig"—she swept a hand down her body from her hair to her toes—"is for a play I'm rehearsing. I'm a gothed-out runaway surviving by her wits on the streets."

"You're an *actor*?" Vicky gaped. "In a *play*?"

"Uh-huh. We've got this little troupe, just five of us. We've been together for a year, done a couple of one-act plays in very tiny, very out-of-the-way venues." She gave Vicky a look to emphasize "tiny" and "out-of-the-way." "Got some good notices, mostly on Internet sites. Just enough to get a teensy bit of funding." Her thumb and forefinger parted enough to slide a paper through. "So we're putting up a play by one of the guys in the troupe. He was a runaway himself, so it's gritty."

She put a hand to her chest, fluttered her lashes dramatically. "I'm the star."

"Wow." Vicky goggled. "I'm so envious. I always wanted to act."

Josie's brows pinched. "Why didn't you?"

"My mother wouldn't let me." God, that sounded ridiculous. What was she, seven? "Anyway, I'm out from under her thumb now, so I'm giving it a try."

Josie cocked her head, gave her a long, searching study, her gaze inching down from Vicky's four-hundred-dollar haircut to her Gucci loafers. "Hmm."

"Hmm?"

"Hmm." Digging in her voluminous bag, Josie drew out a sheaf of dog-eared pages held together with a binder clip. "Take this home tonight and read it. We haven't cast the older sister yet. If you're interested in reading for it, I'll bring it up with the troupe."

Vicky clutched Josie's arm. "I'm interested! I'm *totally* interested!"

Josie laughed. "Okay, I'll talk to them tonight. They'll think I'm crazy, but what the fuck. I'm warning you, though. They're hard-asses. Hypercritical, overly judgmental, and definitely heartless and mean."

Vicky let out a snort. "Please. You just described my mother." She leafed through the script. "What's the older sister's story?"

"She's a Wall Street type," Josie said. "Straitlaced, kind of prissy."

Vicky managed not to laugh. "I think I can pull off that part of it."

Josie nodded. "Yeah, you've got the look. The challenge is that she's searching for me in the underbelly of the city. She's completely out of her element, dealing with the homeless, destitute, desperate people she used to cruise past in a limo without even knowing they existed."

A challenge, indeed, for an Ivy Leaguer from Westport.

"She has to let go of the way she's always done things," Josie added. "How she's approached people. Even how she saw herself fitting into the world." She shrugged. "It's not a huge part, but it's pivotal, because she changes the most during the course of the play. She has to convince the audience that she can readjust her narrow take on the world, think outside the box she's always lived in."

Vicky looked up from the script. Her lips curved slightly. "That'll be harder to pull off, but I'd like to give it a try."

VICKY DROPPED THE top for the drive to Connecticut. Her mother had summoned her to dinner, and since the lease on her parking spot expired at week's end, she was using the opportunity to move the Beemer to Adrianna's house.

She enjoyed the ride, but dreaded the dinner table conversation. Matt had undoubtedly told Adrianna that Vicky intended to give up the law, sparking the summons. Since her mother would certainly express—stridently— her opinion on that, and would probably drag Winston and Tyrell into it too, the evening was destined to end in shouting and tears.

Parking in the driveway of Adrianna's estate, Vicky let herself in through the garage, deliberately avoiding the cavernous foyer with its marble floor, stupendous chandelier, and copious arrangements of fresh flowers, designed to announce to all who passed through the front door that the occupants were Important People, wealthy enough to waste five hundred square feet of floor space on absolutely nothing.

Making her way to the kitchen—large enough to film

a cooking show—she sniffed appreciatively at the roast chicken Adrianna's latest housekeeper had left warming in the oven, then poured a fortifying glass of icy Chardonnay before going in search of her mother.

As usual, she found her in her office, phone pressed to her ear. Spotting Vicky in the doorway, she held up one finger. Vicky pointed outside, then cut back through the kitchen and out the double doors onto the adjoining patio.

Breathing deeply of the expensive Connecticut air, she looked out over the sweeping back lawn to the rolling meadow beyond, dotted with a dozen well-bred hunters belonging to Adrianna's horsey-set neighbors.

And she thought of Brescia. Beautiful, powerful, placid. Everything she wished she was.

Then she thought of Ty. The son of a bitch. For a few fleeting hours, she'd actually believed they had a future. That there was a place for her on his ranch and in his life.

But that was behind her now. She sipped her wine. She was over him. She truly was.

"So you've thrown over your law career to become a barista."

Like any good predator, Adrianna snuck up on her prey.

"The tips are surprisingly good." Vicky turned to face her with a silky smile. "And my boss likes me. I don't think he'll fire me unless I actually do something wrong."

Her mother's gaze didn't waver. "So you'll mop up coffee with your law degree to spite me."

"I've never done anything to spite you, Mother. Just the opposite. I got that degree to *please* you. I never wanted it. I still don't."

She skirted around Adrianna, went into the kitchen, and collected two place settings, brought them out to the patio and arranged them on the round glass table. She kept expecting to feel the familiar resentment. But she didn't. She was charting her own course now. Her mother's criticism had lost some of its power.

Adrianna brought the platter of chicken and roasted vegetables to the table, and for a few blessed moments they ate in silence. Vicky's mind wandered to the script. She'd read half of it before leaving the city; she was anxious to get home and read the rest. Josie had told her to select a scene for the audition and they'd run it together beforehand.

"You were always my responsible child."

Vicky's head came up. "Me?"

"Yes, you." Adrianna waved a hand. "Matt was a natural, he excelled at everything. Top of his class, captain of every team. And every bit as good-looking as the cheating bastard." Meaning Matt's father, Adrianna's despised second husband.

"But for you," she went on, "nothing came easy. You worked for everything. You *applied* yourself. You never settled for less than the best." The distress in her tone took some of the sting out of her words.

"Mother, I applied myself so hard because you pushed me so hard. I worked my ass off so I wouldn't disappoint you. I agonized over every test. Forced myself to practice the piano. Did everything you wanted me to, until I turned into a neurotic, anxiety-ridden, uptight, psycho nutcase. And I ended up disappointing you anyway." She gave a weak little laugh. "I should've done what I wanted to do all along. At least one of us would've been happy."

Adrianna set her fork down, took a long sip of wine. She gazed at her plate, wouldn't meet Vicky's eyes. "What will you do?"

"I'm going to take some classes."

Adrianna looked up hopefully.

"Acting classes."

Her shoulders drooped. "How will you live?"

"On a very tight budget."

"Matt said he could—"

Vicky cut her off. "I don't want to work on Wall Street. I want to be on the stage." Saying it out loud sent heat rushing up her neck to her face, but she didn't let it stop her. "I know that everything you've said about acting is true. The chances are that I won't make it and I'll still be pouring coffee when I'm seventy. But I want to try."

"This is my fault." Her mother's defeated tone was so out of character that Vicky almost felt sorry for her. "I should've gone to Matt straightaway and told him about Brown."

"No. Keeping quiet was the right thing to do. Your only mistake was forcing Winston on me."

Adrianna fiddled with her wineglass. Then she let out a sigh. "You're right."

Vicky's jaw dropped. "Did you just say I'm right?"

"He's a snake. You're too good for him."

Her fork clattered onto her plate. "Then why did you shove him down my throat?"

"Because he was the first man you'd shown any interest in since that pothead in college. Because I want to see you financially secure. Because I want *grandchildren*, for God's sake, while I'm still young enough to enjoy them."

Vicky stared. "You've never mentioned grandchildren before."

"What would've been the point? But when Winston came along, well, I thought if I encouraged you to overlook some of his . . . shortcomings . . . that you'd finally settle down." She lifted one shoulder, let it fall. "It was a miscalculation, and it ended in disaster. Especially for you. I apologize."

And the shocks just kept on coming. "Well. Thanks.

But it hasn't actually been a disaster. If things hadn't gone to hell, I'd still be at the firm, miserable, instead of . . ."

She hesitated. Adrianna could ruin this with a few choice words.

She took the chance. "Instead of auditioning for a play."

Adrianna blinked a couple of times. "Auditioning for a play." She repeated the words carefully, as if sounding out a foreign phrase. *Where are the restrooms? Où sont les toilettes?*

Vicky immediately downplayed it. "It's just a small troupe, completely unknown. The role I'm up for wouldn't be that challenging—an uptight MBA." She laughed nervously. "I shouldn't have a problem with that, but I haven't done any acting since high school, so I probably won't be any good, they probably won't want me—"

Adrianna drew herself up. "What do you mean they won't want you? Honestly, Victoria, I don't understand why you always put yourself down. If they have a brain between them, of course they'll want you."

Again, Vicky's jaw fell.

"I haven't a doubt," Adrianna went on, "that you'll work every bit as hard at acting as you've worked at everything else. And if you put your heart as well as your back into it, I'm quite certain you'll succeed."

"You are?"

"Of course I am." She waved a dismissive hand. "That's never been the problem. It's the *lifestyle.* The uncertainty. The utter lack of responsibility."

Now they were getting down to it. "I'm not like your mother," Vicky said with genuine compassion. "I won't run off to Hollywood and disappear."

"I wasn't thinking of my mother," Adrianna said stiffly.

"Of course you were. And why wouldn't you? She deserted you and you've never forgiven her. But Mother"—

Vicky reached out and touched her hand—"you just said I'm the responsible one, and you're right. I could never walk away from my family. Not from Matt. Not from you."

For a long moment, Adrianna's gaze rested on Vicky's hand where it covered her own. Vicky waited for her to pull away, as she always did. But this time when her mother raised her eyes, she left her hand where it was.

"You won't make any money, most actors don't. But you'll work, I'm sure of that, and working steadily counts for success in that field."

"So . . . you're okay with this?"

"I most certainly am *not* okay with it." Now she withdrew her hand, reverted to form. "But what more can I do? For ten years I've tried to steer you away from penury and into a financially secure profession." She spread her hands. "Yet here you are, auditioning for a play. Obviously, you won't give up until you follow this . . . this *dream* of yours to whatever impoverished end it might lead." She folded her hands. "No, Victoria, I am most definitely not okay with it. But as your mother, I have no choice but to support you."

Vicky lifted her jaw off the table. "You'll support me?"

"I just said I would. Why are you so stunned?"

No good could come from answering that question. Instead, Vicky simply said, "Thank you." Her smile was tentative, but hope spread tender shoots through her heart. "I'll try to make you proud."

Adrianna arched one speaking brow. "I'm sure you'll do your best."

THE PHONE WAS ringing when Ty stepped up on his porch. Dropping his saddlebags, he rushed inside, checked the caller ID.

Not Vicky.

Good, he never wanted to talk to her again anyway.

He picked up the phone. "MaryAnn Raines," he drawled with genuine pleasure. "How the hell are you?"

"Pregnant."

"Don't look at me."

She laughed. "How's it going, Ty?"

"Fair to middling." He took the phone out on the porch, propped a shoulder against the post. "I hear you're in New York City now. Never thought you'd leave UT."

"NYU offered me a full professorship. I couldn't turn it down."

They talked for a while about their time at UT, where she was his favorite philosophy professor and he was her favorite student. Then she said, "You still luring girls into bed with that rationalism/empiricism line?"

"If it works, don't fix it. You still hopelessly devoted to your husband?"

"I'm afraid so. We've been trying to get pregnant forever. Wasn't until we gave up and looked into adoption that I finally got knocked up . . . with twins, no less."

"They're lucky kids. You'll be a great Mom." He batted down a stirring of jealousy. Not for MaryAnn, they'd only ever been friends, but for her happy marriage and growing family. If Lissa had lived and he'd had his way, they'd have five kids by now.

"I hope so," she said, "but forty-five's a little old to be getting started. Especially with twins. The doctor wants me to start my maternity leave early, so I won't be teaching this fall."

"Probably a good idea. First things first." A fly buzzed him and he swatted it, started thinking about a hot shower and a cold beer.

Then she said, "That's why I'm calling. I'd like you to fill in for me."

He blinked, too startled to respond.

"I know it's short notice," she went on. "You'll have to

start in three weeks. But it's only two courses, both of them right in your wheelhouse."

"I haven't taught a class since grad school." He'd enjoyed it, though. All those fresh faces staring up at him like he knew what he was talking about.

"You're a natural. The students loved you. The faculty too. Heck, Ty, you'll have these New Yorkers eating out of your hand. And you'll like living in the city."

That made him laugh. "What in the world would make you say that?"

She was quiet for a moment, and he had a creeping sense that she was more perceptive than he'd given her credit for.

"You're brilliant, Ty," she said at last. "You write beautifully, persuasively. You enjoy the stimulation of other intellectuals." He made a derisive noise, but she persevered.

"I know you love your ranch, that it's part of you and always will be. And maybe if things had turned out differently, your life there would be full enough. But as it is, you're bigger than the box you've built for yourself."

"MaryAnn." He put just enough frost in his voice to show that the ice was thin. "I appreciate you thinking of me, but I'm happy right here in my little box."

She didn't apologize, that wasn't her style. "It's one semester, Ty. Granted, it's fifty-fifty that I won't come back. But all you'd be committing to right now is the fall."

He started to tell her thanks, but no thanks, when a red Mustang appeared in the distance.

God*damn* it! He'd broken things off with Molly before he left for the hills, but the woman wouldn't take no for an answer!

He kicked his saddlebags across the porch. Maybe he did need a bigger fucking box.

"I TOOK A wrong turn," said Vicky. "A wrong turn in life. That's why nothing ever worked for me. I was on the wrong road, heading someplace I didn't want to go. Then this . . . this *bomb* dropped in the middle of the road and suddenly I had to choose a new road. I had to take a chance. And look how it turned out."

Madeline leveled a look. "If you utter the words 'leap and the net will appear,' I'm leaving."

Vicky laughed. "I know I sound like a pop psychologist. But seriously, it's the most amazing thing."

Her eyes followed the teens skateboarding around the fountain in Washington Square Park, but she wasn't actually seeing them, or any of the other people enjoying the last warm and sunny afternoon before the Labor Day weekend proclaimed the unofficial end of summer. In her mind she was back at the audition.

"I totally rocked it, Mad. The rest of the troupe *applauded*!" Her smile was brighter than the sun. "Can you believe it? I'm *in*! In the play. In the troupe. Rehearsing on a real live stage. I mean, the theater's super-tiny, basically just an unused storage room in an old warehouse in Hell's Kitchen. It couldn't be more off-off-Broadway. But still!"

"I'm really happy for you." Maddie's smile was sincere. Then she shrugged one shoulder. "I miss you, though. Don't get me wrong, I'm loving all the free coffee." She waggled her cup. "But I wish you had time for martinis."

Vicky touched her friend's arm. "I miss you too. It's just that we're rehearsing every night. Then we usually hang out with some actor friends at this dive in the Village—"

She caught herself in midsentence. Maddie's smile had collapsed. Damn it, she'd wanted to wait until she was more comfortable in her new life before cross-pollinating it with the old one, but her own insecurities paled in the face of her best friend's hurt feelings.

"Why don't you meet up with us tonight?" she added casually. "I'll text you when we're heading over."

Maddie brightened. "Okay. Any cuties I should know about?"

"The playwright—Adam—he's got great eyes and a killer smile."

"Mmm, sounds interesting. Do you have dibs?"

Vicky shook her head. "Still off men."

"You mean you're still stuck on Brown."

She could deny it, but why bother? Maddie knew her too well. And anyway, as an actor she should face her emotions honestly so she could learn to channel them into her work.

"You're right. I fell in love with Ty, and it's going to be a long time before I stop comparing every man I meet to him."

Maddie's eyes went wide. "Whoa. I thought it was just great sex."

"No, it was all of him. He made me homicidal, but he also made me laugh. A lot. He stuck up for me with my mother, which almost made me cry. And God, Maddie, he beat up Winston! He'd probably say he did it because Winston's an asshole, but Ty doesn't go around beating up every asshole he meets. He did it for me. That alone would make me love him."

She'd rendered Maddie speechless. But it felt good to say it out loud. Now maybe she could move on.

"None of that matters," she went on, speaking as much to herself as to Maddie. "Ty's in Texas, I'm in New York. We might as well be in different solar systems. And even if our paths ever cross again, which I suppose might happen given his connection to Isabelle, he'll never forget what I put him through on the stand. And I'll never forgive him for almost cheating on Molly with me. Cheating on both of us, really. It's Winston all over again."

Checking her watch, she stood up and tossed her cup in the trash. "I've got to go. Josie has a friend in the registrar's office at NYU who can finagle me into Spike Lee's seminar if I register today."

"Oo-kay," Maddie said.

She looked so befuddled that Vicky leaned over and kissed her cheek. "See you tonight," she said, and walked away smiling, well aware that she'd left her friend wondering, again, who'd kidnapped her uptight, emotionally repressed BFF and left this much better adjusted, if annoyingly optimistic, clone in her place.

CHAPTER TWENTY-FIVE

NEW YORK CITY was okay, Ty decided, once you got used to the smell.

He'd take pungent manure over exhaust fumes any day, but still, by the middle of September he was ready to admit that apartment living had definite advantages over his ranch, like freeing up all the time he usually spent patching roofs and fixing porch steps and changing leaky faucets.

Much of that newfound time he devoted to his thirty-six students, along with the handful of philosophy majors he'd been assigned to academically advise. They trickled into his office between his morning and afternoon classes, eager to discuss everything from esoteric questions of metaphysics and epistemology to how they could earn a few points of extra credit. He never turned them away, but even adding in the time he spent making notes for his lectures, it wasn't exactly heavy lifting.

So if he felt a little stressed, it was his own fault for not showing up until two days before classes began and staying out too late every night since then. Well, the staying out too late wasn't entirely his fault. A handful of grad students—okay, *female* grad students—had made it their mission to take the new cowboy in town everywhere worth going, which meant clubs, bars, and even a strip joint.

Still, as busy as he kept himself, he hadn't stopped thinking about Vicky. Just the opposite. Being in the same city, he found himself looking for her everywhere he went, doing a double take whenever a slender blonde with a sweep of straight hair and a great ass sidled by.

The problem, he decided, was that he wouldn't rest until she heard him out on the Molly thing. She owed him that much, damn it. But since directory assistance insisted she didn't have a landline, he'd have to call Isabelle to get her new cell number.

And it would be ugly.

He'd never returned Isabelle's calls, and the last message she'd left warned him in pointed terms never to contact her again because he was an insensitive horse's rear and she was disowning him forever.

He didn't believe that for a minute, but she'd make him suffer for ignoring her calls. Even worse, when he admitted that he'd been in New York for two weeks, she'd peel a strip off him and pour acid on it. And then she'd really let him have it.

He sucked it up and dialed anyway.

She made him sweat through eight rings before she answered. "Well. If it isn't Tyrell Brown," she said in bitter tones.

"Now, honey," he went straight for the charm, "I know you're mad at me and I don't blame you. I'm a shit heel for sure. But sugar, you have to understand. My feelings were hurt."

She took the bait. "*Your* feelings? How in the world did *your* feelings get hurt?"

Stacking his heels on his desk, he laid out all of his

grievances against Vicky. When he finished, Isabelle was silent.

Then, "You know, Ty, I'm starting to think Vicky's right about you. You're an idiot."

His heels hit the floor. "What do you mean? She's the one who took off without letting me explain!"

She sighed as if he was hopeless. "Did you forget about Winston? Did you forget how he cheated on her?"

As a matter of fact, he hadn't thought about Winston in months. A seed of doubt imbedded itself in the hard earth of his self-righteousness.

"Did it ever occur to you," she went on, "that Vicky might see you cheating on Molly and decide you're no better than he is?"

"I just told you, I wasn't cheating on Molly." His protest lost some of its force.

"That's debatable. And you're missing the point, which is that you looked completely untrustworthy. Honestly, Ty, I couldn't even defend you this time. If I was Vicky, I would've flushed my phone down the toilet too."

So that's what happened to it.

"I used to think you were sensitive. Kind. Empathetic." She'd hit her stride now. "I'm so disappointed in you. And all this time you've been feeling sorry for yourself. It's inexcusable. I don't know what I ever saw in you."

"Whoa, there, honey. Don't write me off so quick." He got up, began pacing his office. "Now that you've pointed it out to me, I can see how it might've poked a sore spot with Vicky."

How had he missed it before? He'd been so caught up in his own disappointment that he'd quit thinking about how she might have felt. He really *was* an idiot.

"It so happens, honey, that I was calling you up to get her number."

"Why? So you can torture her some more?"

"Isabelle. Sugar." He worked his drawl. "You don't really think I'm a bad person, now do you?"

She let him squirm. Then, grudgingly, "I guess not. But Vicky doesn't want you to have her number. That's why she changed it."

He couldn't reach through the phone and shake it out of her, so he snapped a pencil in half instead. "Help me out here, honey. At least tell me she's doing all right, and that she's got a job." Then he could track her down at her office.

"She's working at Starbucks."

"Which one?"

She huffed. "What difference does it make? They're all two thousand miles from Texas."

Oh man, was she gonna be pissed.

TY HAD VISITED Vicky's Starbucks half a dozen times, but always in the afternoon. Isabelle said she worked the early shift, so the next morning after his nine o'clock class, he screwed up his courage and headed over there.

Pausing outside, he pretended to fiddle with his phone while he peered through the window. Two slender girls moved around behind the counter, using the post-rush-hour lull to restock the shelves. His eyes skipped over the one with pink and black hair and settled on the blonde.

She had her back to him so he couldn't see her face, but her sheet of silky hair and sweet ass looked familiar. His heart thunk-thunked against his rib cage.

Arranging his lips into a lazy half smile, he pushed through the door and sauntered toward the counter. The pink-haired girl caught him in her headlights. But he was all about the blonde.

He couldn't take his eyes off her. A bead of sweat

inched down his spine. He wet his lips. Why hadn't he thought beforehand about what he'd say?

Then she stretched her arm up to take something off a high shelf, and her shirt rode up, separating from her hip-hugging jeans. Naturally, his eyes riveted on the swath of creamy skin . . . and then his heart sank like a stone.

Unlike Vicky, whose satiny skin he was intimately familiar with, this girl—whoever she was—had a big old tramp stamp poking out of her pants.

Looking closer, he noticed other differences too. This girl wore a dozen silver bangles on each arm, and four-inch silver hoops poked out through her hair, where Vicky was strictly the gold-watch-and-diamond-studs type.

And Vicky—his demure Vicky—wouldn't be caught dead in skin-tight jeans that barely covered her crack and left nothing, absolutely nothing, to the imagination.

His shoulders wanted to slump with disappointment.

Coffee sounded awful now, but what else did he have to do? For once, he couldn't face the line of students who'd be waiting outside his door. He didn't want to go back to his apartment, either; it suddenly seemed empty and cold. And the streets, so vibrant and busy, were even less appealing.

For lack of any better idea, he kept walking toward the grinning goth girl.

"YEEHAW," JOSIE WHISPERED over her shoulder. "Look who just rode in off the range and straight into my heart."

Vicky winced. She made a point of avoiding all things cowboy—easier said than done when every good-looking Texan who happened to pass through New York found his way into her Starbucks—but with just one "yeehaw," visions of sun-streaked hair and warm honey eyes waltzed through her head, stabbed her in the heart, and just generally pissed her off.

Shouldering a twenty-pound bag of beans, she turned around to glare at whichever wayward Texan had wandered into her path today . . .

And holy shit! Her lungs seized.

Tyrell Brown swaggered toward her, tall and lanky, with trouble and heartbreak written all over him, from his alligator boots to his slim-fitting jeans to his familiar pearl-snapped, midnight blue shirt.

His stride hitched as their eyes met, barely noticeable to someone who didn't know his prowling pace like she did. Otherwise, he showed no sign of surprise.

She broke out in a sweat.

Josie hogged the counter. "Hey, cowboy." She was practically preening.

"Hey, goth girl," he drawled. "Nice smile."

Leave it to Ty to zero in on the genuine Josie. She lapped it up like cream, and that was even before he aimed his own luscious-lipped smile back at her. It put a breathy catch in her voice. "Nice smile yourself, cowboy. Nice everything."

Then she dropped into a spot-on imitation of a B-movie saloon girl. "Haven't seen you around these parts before." She drawled it out, batting her lashes.

He played along. "I'm new in town, honey. But you'll be seeing a lot of me from here on out."

She pressed her arms together, a subtle move that drew his eyes to her breasts. "Gonna clean up the town for us, Marshal? Wave your big gun around?"

That did it. Vicky dropped the beans, elbowed her aside.

"What can I get you?" she asked, as if he was any other customer. But he wasn't any other customer. He was the man who'd loved her and left her, who'd touched her heart and then smashed it like a china cup on a cold stone floor.

After six weeks of meditation, she'd finally convinced herself that she'd forgiven him. But it turned out that was easier to do from two thousand miles away. From across the counter, it was a different story. Now she couldn't bring herself to acknowledge him by anything more than the hot flush rising up her neck, heading for her hairline.

Disconcertingly, he didn't acknowledge her either, which pissed her off more than if he had. As usual, he knew just how to get under her skin.

"Give me one of those mocha lattes, honey. Nonfat, double shot, no whip. Gotta watch my figure."

Josie pushed in again. "How about *we* watch your figure instead?" She twirled one finger, the universal sign for show-me-what-you-got.

Vicky knew all too well what he had. Clamping her jaw, she shut her mind to cobblestone abs and went to work on his latte while they kept up their insipid banter.

She drowned out most of it by humming Coldplay loudly in her head, but when he dropped his change in the bulging tip jar, she heard him say, "Couple of pretty girls like you two must do all right," and his drawl scraped across her nerves like ragged fingernails. She smacked his drink down on the counter hard enough that it squirted through the little hole in the lid.

Josie jumped in to dab it with a napkin. "Sorry about that." She threw Vicky a WTF look, then eye-fucked Ty as she slid the drink across the counter, leaving her hand around it until his fingers brushed hers.

Vicky hung on to her temper by a thread. The torture was almost over . . . he had his coffee . . . any minute now he'd turn and walk out the door . . .

And then he did the unthinkable. From a stack on the counter, he picked up a flyer advertising the play.

Panicked, Vicky grabbed for it, but he turned aside casually, moving it out of her reach without seeming to notice her.

Shooting her another WTF look, Josie piped up. "That's

our play. It opens tonight at the Shoebox Theater. And,"—
she reached into her back pocket, whipped out a ticket—
"it's your lucky day, because this is the very last ticket."

"Sold out, is it?" He smiled all over Josie again. "Must
be getting good buzz."

"Well, some. And also, they don't call it the Shoebox
for nothing."

He laughed, and Vicky gripped the counter's edge.
God, she loved his laugh. She loved it so much she wanted
to stuff it back down his throat, choke him with it, and
then toss him on a boxcar bound for Texas.

With his eyes on Josie, he tipped his head toward Vicky.
"Your friend in the play too?"

Josie nodded. "I'm the star, but she's got a juicy part.
It's her first role, and she totally kills it." She waggled the
ticket. "You really want to come. Then you can say you
knew us when."

"Sugar, when you put it like that, how can I resist?"

Vicky followed his hand as he reached out and took the
ticket. The gleam in his eye made her fists clench helplessly.

With a last lingering smile for Josie, he slid it into his
pocket and ambled out of the shop.

Josie clutched her chest. "Oh. My. God. He's coming to
the opening!"

Vicky grabbed a rag, started wiping the counter. "So
what?"

Josie stared. "*So what?* Did you *see* him?"

"I saw his hokey cowboy shirt."

"Are you kidding? He totally rocked that look! He's
one-hundred-percent-authentic grade-A-prime cowboy
steak. And I want a bite."

Vicky breathed in to a four count, out to a four count,
taking note of the fact that she hadn't needed her yoga
breathing technique in, oh, almost six weeks. Since

shortly after the last time she laid eyes on Tyrell Brown.

"You know who he looks like?" Josie went starry-eyed. "The Sundance Kid. From that old movie with Robert Redford. He's got that same windblown look, like he hasn't combed his hair since he rode into town. And he's got Sundance's smile too. Slow and wicked, like he's thinking about all the ways he could make you come."

Vicky rubbed at a stain that would never come out.

Josie sighed. "I wonder what brought him to New York City? And how long he's staying."

So do I, Vicky snarled to herself, *and I'm damn sure going to find out*.

IF LOOKS COULD kill, he'd be a dead man.

Ty let the door fall shut behind him before he busted out in a belly laugh. Damn, she looked cute as hell with steam coming out of her ears. Good thing they'd been in a coffee shop instead of a roadhouse. With access to glass bottles, he was pretty sure she would've smashed a long neck and raked the jagged end across his throat.

Sucking down some mocha latte, he marveled that only minutes ago he'd thought he was off coffee for life. Now he couldn't imagine anything more delicious. His whole outlook had changed. The sun shone brighter; people looked friendlier. His muscles felt loose and limber, like he'd just done a good hour of yoga.

For the first time in months he didn't feel like hitting anyone.

Spotting a florist, he ducked inside. "Honey, I need three—no, six—dozen of your biggest, reddest roses. Tie 'em up in two bouquets with lots of pretty ribbons."

He hit the wine store next, shilly-shallied over Cristal or Dom Perignon, then bought one of each.

Even the line of students outside his office didn't faze him. He feigned interest in each of them in turn, nodding along with their ideas, commiserating with their woes, and dispensing advice as needed. But all the time his mind was back at Starbucks, going over every detail of his encounter with Vicky.

He'd stunned her, for sure. She was still lawyer enough to hide it from her friend, but he'd seen it in her expression and in the flush that burned her cheeks.

There was nothing lawyerly about her new look, though. Not her hair that swung halfway to her waist, not the bangles that jangled when she moved her arms, or that coaster-sized tattoo peeking out above her jeans. Jeans that were so tight he could practically pinpoint the tiny birthmark on her butt, shaped, as he'd told her, like the great state of Texas.

Well, he'd be revisiting Texas soon enough. Because now that he'd seen Victoria Westin again, he understood exactly why he'd obsessed about her these long last months: He was absolutely fucking crazy about her. And if he was any judge of women, the irritation, aggravation, and exasperation written all over her pretty face meant she was crazy about him too.

Of course, she wasn't thinking about it like that at the moment. She still thought she was mad at him. But once he reminded her how good they were together, then she'd forget about the whole Molly thing and they could pick up where they left off before everything went to shit.

"That's real interesting, Bristol." He rose from his chair before the earnest young woman could really hit her stride. "Why don't you think about how you can expand on that idea in your final paper? Then come on back next week and show me what you got."

Herding her into the hallway, he glanced both ways. That was the last of them. Closing himself inside, he grabbed the phone.

"Hey there, Sandy, this is Tyrell. I know you just

cleaned my apartment last week, but I'd appreciate you giving it another whack this afternoon. I've got company coming and I'd sure like it to sparkle. And while you're at it, honey, will you do me a favor and change the sheets? And make the bed up pretty with all those pillows I chucked on the floor."

Tipping back in his chair, he stacked his heels on his desk, crossed his arms behind his head, and grinned at the portrait of John Locke hanging on the opposite wall.

"Man, I'm with you," he said to Locke, "an empiricist all the way." He threw a wink at the stony-faced codger. "I'll have her naked by midnight."

CHAPTER TWENTY-SIX

JOSIE RUSHED IN, grabbed Vicky's arm in a vise. "Jack McCabe's out there! *Jack McCabe!*" Her eyes pinwheeled.

Vicky patted her hand. "It's okay. My brother's married to his wife's cousin."

Josie was too freaked out to follow the intricacies, but she latched on to the theme. "You're related to Jack McCabe? Why didn't you tell me? I *love* him! I *worship* him! I went to *every Sinners' gig!*"

"Calm down. I'll introduce you after the show."

"Oh God. Oh Jesus." Josie paced their tiny dressing room, wringing her hands. "I don't think I can hold it together with him out there."

Vicky ignored her. She had worries of her own. The Shoebox Theater held forty seats, all packed with the troupe's friends and family. It was a friendly, forgiving audience, perfect for her debut.

Until Ty showed up.

She'd prayed he wouldn't come, but when she peeked through the side door minutes ago, there he was, big as life, sitting in the fourth row with Jack, Lil, Isabelle, Adrianna, Maddie, and Matt.

Isabelle must have orchestrated the seating, because Ty sat at the opposite end from Matt, safe, for the moment, from her vengeful brother. But he didn't get off scot-free, because even though Jack buffered him on one side, Maddie pinioned him on the other, and by the pained look on his face, the Pitbull had wasted no time in taking him by the throat.

Normally, Vicky would have enjoyed watching Maddie shake him till his teeth rattled, but piled on top of her opening night jitters, the whole thing made her queasy. And now Josie, the person she counted on to talk her off the ledge, was flipping out.

Knuckles rapped the door. "Curtain in five." Vicky patted her French twist, then brushed her hands down the front of the navy blue suit she'd borrowed from Adrianna. Earlier, her mother had stuck her head backstage, and Vicky had been stunned—and touched—to discover that Adrianna was almost as nervous as she was.

Not approving, mind you. But nervous.

Josie muttered to herself as she paced. Vicky couldn't make out the words, but they were irrelevant anyway. The show must go on. She took her friend by the shoulders, gave her a shake. "Knock it off, Jo. You're on your mark in two minutes." Josie stared at her, uncomprehending. "Josephine Marie Kennedy, you're on in two minutes! Now *knock it off*!"

"Okay, okay." Josie dragged a few deep breaths, straightened her shoulders. "Break a leg, girlfriend," she said, and went out.

After a last once-over in the mirror, Vicky followed her.

She paused in the wings, heart racing, throat closing, as Josie took her place on stage. A moment later, the lights dimmed.

Then the curtain rose, and everyone, cast and audience alike, was plunged into an abandoned subway tunnel, bleak and gray, cluttered with the detritus of those who walked the bright streets above, happily ignorant of the dim and colorless world below their feet.

A long moment passed before a narrow spotlight picked out Josie's form huddled against a graffiti-covered wall, legs drawn up, head on her forearms, thin body curled like a comma around her empty belly. Everything about her, the slump of her shoulders, the curve of her spine, depicted the despair of a teenage runaway at the end of the line.

Then she lifted her face, and the harsh beam exposed the strain etched there. But it also revealed one tiny spark still flickering in her eyes. Would it be enough to keep her alive until her sister found her?

The question captured the audience at once, and it captured Vicky too. In an almost magical transition, her character settled over her. She forgot to be nervous, forgot about Ty and Adrianna and the rest of the audience. In fact, donning the preppy demeanor like a familiar coat, she felt for the first time in her life both serene and stimulated at once, her heart galloping, yet her nerves steady.

If she'd stopped to consider it, she might have decided that after all her searching, she'd finally found nirvana. But when she crossed out of the wings and into the dark underbelly of the city, she was too caught up in the story's spell to think about anything else.

For ninety minutes that spell held her fast, until the curtain fell on her abject misery as she knelt, suit filthy, stockings torn, head bowed over Josie's broken form. Then the thunder of applause from the other side of the curtain brought her back to reality. Josie leaped to her feet, fist pumping, and the rest of the cast and crew tumbled onto the stage, sweeping both of them up in jubilation.

Catapulting from sorrow to joy in a heartbeat, Vicky let herself be shoved into line with the rest of the cast. Holding hands as the curtain rose, they bowed in unison. The audience was on their feet. Cheering. Weeping. Flowers landed on the stage, single roses, bunches of carnations. Ty stepped into the footlights to toss a huge bouquet at her feet, another at Josie's. And Vicky's heart, already bursting, positively overflowed.

Nothing could ever, ever top this perfect, once-in-a-lifetime moment.

TY COULDN'T TAKE his eyes off Vicky. She looked like a quarterback who'd just won his first Super Bowl, dazzled and disbelieving at once. And why shouldn't she? She'd done something every bit as amazing. No longer could anyone deny that she was born to act; even Cruella had tears in her eyes.

He wanted to congratulate Vicky himself, but Matt's arm was locked around her. Spoiling her big night with a fistfight wouldn't win her back, so he waited until everyone adjourned to the Italian place across the street. While they milled around in the lobby waiting for a table, he managed to get close to her.

She'd changed into those skinny jeans again, with a silvery, shimmery tank that clung to her curves. Coming up behind her, he put his lips to her ear. "Honey, your friend was right. You killed that part."

She looked over her shoulder at him, chin tilted up, blue eyes wide and startled. He wanted to gobble her up.

He decided to go in for a kiss instead. No tongue, not in the lobby, but a full-on, soft-lipped, serious kiss that should go halfway toward the apology he owed her and get her thinking about how bad she wanted to go back to his place and hit the sheets.

But he never got to her lips, because someone elbowed him in the side. He let out an "oof" and swung around.

Madeline glowered up at him, pixie face tied in a furious knot.

"Leave her alone, asshole. She doesn't need you ruining her night."

He glowered back. The little squirt had harangued him for twenty minutes before the curtain went up, and he'd reached his limit with her. "Listen pipsqueak, I'm not gonna ruin her night. For your information, I'm in love with her."

Oops, it popped out before he knew it. He whipped his head around to see if Vicky heard it, but thank God, she was busy introducing Josie to Jack, with all the squealing that entailed. Ty used the uproar to step around to Vicky's other side, away from Madeline. The little runt could just try to move him and see how far she got.

Josie finally calmed down enough to catch his eye. She gave him a big smile. "Hey, cowboy." Then she noticed how close he stood to Vicky. She put two and two together, pointed a finger at Vicky. "You said he's a hokey cowboy."

Vicky looked bland. "He is. He's also an idiot, an egomaniac and a son of a bitch."

Josie let out a snort. "In other words, you're crazy about him. I can't believe you didn't tell me."

Maddie muscled in. "She's not crazy about him. She thinks he's an asshole and wishes he'd drown in the East River. Which might happen tonight if he doesn't leave her alone."

All eyes swiveled toward him. Maddie snarled like she might bite him.

Then the waiter showed up and herded them through the busy dining room to a long table set back in a corner, close to the wall and out of the fray. Ty finagled the seat next to Vicky, who ignored him like he wasn't there. The pipsqueak grabbed the seat on his other side, too close for comfort. He kept his arm pressed to his side so she couldn't elbow him again.

The food came in courses, and voices rose steadily as the wine made the rounds. Lil took out her camera, snapping candids, and everyone shouted to everyone else. Everyone except him. He was an island surrounded by a sea of hostility.

For a man used to being at the center of fawning females, it was a new and unpleasant experience. Maddie ignored him, except to snarl occasionally. Cruella, seated across from him, froze him out. From the head of the table, Isabelle, his dear, sweet Isabelle, telegraphed a warning that couldn't have been clearer if she shouted it in his ear: *Ruin this night, and die.*

And Vicky dropped every conversational gambit he threw at her. In fact, she was so indifferent that he actually started to question whether he'd get her into bed that night. And he absolutely had to get her into bed. He had to make her see that Josie was right; even though he was an idiot, an egomaniac, and a son of a bitch, she was crazy about him.

That would be a hell of a lot easier to do if she was underneath him.

Throwing back his last swallow of Chianti, he clunked the glass on the table and decided not to refill it, for the simple reason that if he drank any more he'd have to take a leak, which he couldn't do without losing his seat to the pipsqueak. And he'd be damned if that happened. As long as he was sitting next to Vicky, there was still a chance he'd come up with something.

The problem, he realized as the night went on, was that she'd gotten the upper hand. He'd let down his guard, forgotten the importance of keeping her off balance.

Waiting until she reached for her wineglass again, he

leaned in and spoke quietly into her ear. "Vicky, honey, you sure you want to keep hitting the wine? You know how you get."

That got her attention. She turned her head to stare him down. "Exactly how do I get?"

He kept his voice down as if not to embarrass her. "Horny."

"*Horny? I get horny?*" Her outraged tone drew every eye.

He turned his palms up. "I tried to keep it quiet, sugar."

Her pink cheeks flushed red. She hissed under her breath. "Isn't it enough you humiliated me in Amboise *and* Texas? Do you have to ruin this night for me too?"

Finally, he was getting somewhere. "Honey." He met her furious gaze. "I never meant to hurt you, either time. I'm sorry from the bottom of my heart."

VICKY GROUND HER teeth. How could he *do* this to her? Did he *enjoy* hurting her? Was he that much of a rat bastard?

She wanted to ignore him, to pretend he wasn't sitting there smelling so good, like fresh air and warm man. But that was hard to do when his magnetic field sucked every cell in her body toward him, forcing her to put up a physical fight just to keep from crawling into his lap.

She'd gotten the lowdown from Isabelle, knew he was teaching at NYU, living practically around the corner from her. What she didn't know was why, after making it crystal clear *twice* that he didn't care about her *at all*, he was still trying to get to her.

It couldn't be that he needed to get laid. NYU—hell, all of New York City—was a banquet laid out with a man like Ty in mind. Yet all night long he'd been vying for her attention. And now he'd gotten it with his soulful apology. She wanted him to take it back so she could keep ignoring him in peace.

Staring him down, she refused to be distracted by his golden eyes or his windblown hair. And she absolutely would not be affected by his sinful smile. The Sundance Kid. Phooey!

Her voice was steady. "Why are you here, Tyrell? What do you want?"

He smiled, slow and sexy, and damn it, he *did* look like Sundance. She could kill Josie for putting that in her head.

"Honey, I want to take you home with me." His voice was low and warm and so, so tempting.

She firmed her jaw, kept her voice down too. "Why me? You must have girls crawling all over you on campus."

"I'm not interested in girls. I want a woman. I want you."

His lips were smiling, but his eyes were serious. She didn't know what to make of him. She started to lose her footing.

"Why are you saying these things? Why can't you leave me alone?" Her plaintive tone made her cringe.

"Is that what you want, to be left alone?" He held her eyes, shook his head slowly. "I think you've been alone long enough."

"I have not," she sputtered. "I like being alone. And anyway, I'm not alone. I have friends. And my family. And now I have this." She waved a hand to indicate their celebration, and the cause for it. "I don't want a man. I don't want you."

That would have shut most men up, but this was Tyrell; his ego knew no bounds. He shook his head again, slowly. "Sweetheart, nobody likes to be alone. I'm sick of it myself."

He sounded sincere and her heart almost went out to him. But then he shrugged like he was making the best of things. "I admit you're a handful, sugar. Prickly as a porcupine, and you love to pick a fight—"

"I do *not* love to pick fights! That's *you*. You needle me and needle me, trying to get a reaction, just like you're doing now!"

He gave her a pitying look. "Nice try, honey, but your reverse psychology won't work on me. Now, like I was saying, you're prickly—"

"You're a *jackass*!" she hissed. "Why did I ever—"

She stopped at his smug smile. His cockiness was unbelievable! If she didn't get out of there, she'd be the one starting a brawl.

Standing abruptly, she shot a smile around the table. "Thanks for coming, everybody. I can't tell you how much I appreciate it. But I have to be at work in a few hours, so I'm heading out."

She'd caught them by surprise. "Hang on, Vic," Matt said, "I'll call you a cab."

But Vicky wasn't sticking around, not even to wait for Maddie, who'd picked the wrong time to go to the bathroom. "Don't bother, Matt, I'll hail one outside. Good night, everyone!"

And she beelined for the door.

"GOD*DAMN* IT!" Ty swore. If she bolted in a cab he'd be back to square one.

Deaf to Matt's threats and Isabelle's pleas, he sprang up from his seat to give chase. But Cruella was quicker. Slinging her body halfway over the table, she caught a handful of his shirt, holding him back.

For a surreal moment his legs churned the air like a cartoon character's, while his body stayed where it was.

Then his snaps unsnapped, Adrianna lost her grip. And he shot through the restaurant without a backward glance, shirt flapping open over his chest.

Hitting the sidewalk at a run, he spotted Vicky stepping into a cab at the curb. He caught the door before she pulled it closed, shoved her over with his butt, and landed on the seat beside her.

"*What the hell?*"

He grinned at her outrage. "Where we going?" he asked as the cab swung away from the curb.

"*I'm* going home. *You're* getting out."

Shooting a glance over his shoulder, he saw Matt spill out onto the sidewalk, head swiveling. His gaze skipped over the cab as it turned right onto Ninth Avenue, and Ty relaxed, stretched an arm across the back of the seat.

"Why not share the fare," he said reasonably, "since we're practically neighbors?"

"Because I can't stand you, that's why." She scrunched against the opposite door.

"Come on, honey, I said I was sorry."

"Sorry doesn't cut it. You broke my heart."

She didn't sound heartbroken anymore. She sounded pissed. In fact, her defiant head toss reminded him of Brescia, just before she took a chomp out of him.

"Sweetheart," he said in the same gentle voice he used on his fractious mare, "the truth of it is, I broke my own heart too."

For a long moment she stared at him, blue eyes dark and unreadable in the streetlight. Then the cab stopped at a light. She shoved open the door and bolted out into traffic.

It caught him completely off guard. Blistering a curse, he dug out a twenty, jammed it in the slot, and shot out into the street—directly in the path of a black Hummer limo that was gunning it through the red light.

His reflexes saved him. Pivoting on one foot, he plastered himself to the cab as the Hummer blew past, its draft dragging at his open shirt. Drunk bachelorettes bobbed up through the sunroof, waving champagne and siren-calling him to join them. He tossed them a wave, grateful to be alive, then yelped when a taxi shot out from the curb, missing him by an inch.

"God*damn* it!" he ripped out. Only in New York would traffic be as thick as fleas at midnight! Stabbing his middle finger at the pokerfaced cabbie, he dropped an F-bomb on the whole damn city.

Gaining the sidewalk in one piece, he gulped a breath, spotted Vicky legging it down Forty-second Street, heading for Times Square. God*damn* it, he'd lose her there for sure in the post-theater throngs. He broke into a run.

Zigzagging between tourists, around light poles and trash cans, he cursed a blue streak under his breath. Never in his life had he chased after a woman. Now here he was, running through Manhattan *in cowboy boots*. Cowboy boots that were built—like he was—for swaggering, not sprinting.

Why the hell was she making this so hard?

She turned left on Seventh, making tracks. He barreled around the corner, closing the distance.

But now the crowd was thicker, moving like a herd of grazing sheep. It slowed him down. He wanted to scream.

Up ahead, Times Square opened out in a blaze of neon, as bright as daylight and teeming, as usual, with people of all ages and nationalities, gaping up at the huge billboards, trying to spot themselves on the screens that showed the street-level crowds.

Through the sea of heads, Vicky's sheaf of blond flashed in and out of view. For a moment he lost her altogether, then spotted her again just a few yards ahead.

He was closing in when he got trapped at the light on Forty-fifth. She made it across, leaving him in the dust.

Gnashing his teeth, he craned his neck, glimpsed her dart into the Marriott Marquis. He bit out another curse. That place was enormous, which he happened to know because the grad school girls had taken him to its famous revolving rooftop restaurant. The hotel housed other restaurants and bars, too. Vicky could disappear into one of them, or cut through to another exit and out onto a side street. He'd never find her then.

The light changed at last and he bolted into the intersection, carving a path through pedestrians, throwing "sorry" over his shoulder as he jostled and wove.

Charging through the front door, he skidded to a halt, looking around wildly. To the right was a security desk; in the center, a circular bank of elevators. This wasn't the hotel's lobby—that was on the eighth floor, as he'd learned when the grad students tried to persuade him to get a room with them—but even so, guests and new arrivals crisscrossed the space, going in and out of the building and the ground-level shops.

Glimpsing blond hair disappearing into an elevator, Ty took a gamble. Darting through the crowd, leaping over a trailing suitcase, he hurled his body through the closing doors.

CHAPTER TWENTY-SEVEN

VICKY FLATTENED AGAINST the wall as a body hurtled into her elevator, crashing against the back wall. The other woman in the car shrieked. Her husband yanked her behind him, legs braced to defend her against the half-dressed barbarian invading their civilized hotel.

Gaping at the invader, Vicky wanted to scream. How had he found her? Why wouldn't he *leave her alone*?

Recovering herself, she lunged for the doors. Too late; they closed, and her palms slapped cold brass.

Frustrated and furious, humiliated and hurt, she spun around to confront, once and for all, the exasperating ego-maniac, the insensitive jackass, the maddening *pain in her ass* who drove her to bail out on her own celebration and flee him through the streets of New York.

Then she got a look at his face. Her jaw snapped shut. Her neck hair stood up. And her fight-or-flight instinct turned on a dime, screaming in her head to *get the hell out of there*!

Simmering like a pot left too long on the stove, Tyrell scraped his hair back with his fingers and trapped her gaze. Sweat gleamed at his temples, his breath hissed through his teeth. Straightening to his full, impressive height and breadth, he seemed to fill the car. Vicky gulped. The couple wedged in the corner inched along the wall toward the door. With luck, they'd escape and call security before he could strangle her.

Then the elevator dinged, the doors opened, and all four of them tumbled out. The couple turned left and hoofed it down the hall. Vicky bolted right, but Ty caught her in two strides. Spinning her like a dancer, he pulled her against him, chest to chest, and strapped both arms around her.

"We can do this easy," he growled, "or we can do it hard."

"Or I can scream bloody murder," she snarled back.

"Try it. I'll stuff you down that laundry chute."

"At least I'll be away from *you*."

"I'll be right behind you. We'll finish this in the basement, where no one can hear you scream." His tiger eyes burned bright.

Damn it, she did *not* feel like sliding down the laundry chute.

"Get it off your chest, then," she threw at him, bravely. "Tell me about your *aha moment*."

His jaw went tighter. "You see? It's that smart mouth of yours that gets me so hard I can't think straight."

Clamping her arm in an unbreakable grip, he marched her to the stairwell door, threw it open, and propelled her through. It fell closed with a sinister thunk.

Backing her against the dingy wall, he slapped his palms on the concrete, caging her in. The bare ceiling bulb glared down on his sun streaks, turning them to brass. His eyes were slits.

"I almost got creamed by a Hummer chasing after you."

"Too bad. About the *almost* part."

His lip curled menacingly. "I can turn you over my knee, tan that pretty fanny of yours."

"Wouldn't you just love to?" She curled her lip back at him. "I'm wearing the leopard spots. With the matching bra. Not that you'll ever see them again."

His eyes went dark. "You'll show 'em to me," he promised, and his voice rasped her skin. "Before the night's over, I'll peel 'em off you with my teeth."

Her mouth went dry. Butterflies swooped in her stomach. How could she want him so badly after everything he'd done? After she'd come so far?

She tried to shove him away, but she might as well push against a barn. His chest was hard under her hands, hard and warm, rising and falling with his ragged breath.

Oh God. She should get her hands off him *right away*.

But his shirt was open, his chest hair tickled her palms. And his abs were *right there*. Like big squares of chocolate, only even more tempting. How could she not touch them?

She flicked a glance at his face, and wished she hadn't. His eyes burned. She'd forgotten that he could read her mind.

"Go ahead." His drawl was barely a whisper, hot and sensual.

She licked her lips. Dropped her eyes to his waist. Dragged her fingertips down, down, till her thumbs hit the first ridge, then the second. Then the third. His stomach quivered under her touch. Sweat filmed his skin.

She let a noise slip out, a wanting noise born in the wet heat between her thighs. It swirled up through her quivering stomach, curling around her thrumming heart until it spilled out in a moan that galvanized him like electricity.

His mouth came down on hers, hard and wet, kissing her like he was starving for it. He shoved her shirt up to her neck and pulled her bra down, popping her breasts out into his hands.

She went back at him the same way, slanting her lips,

sucking his tongue. Sliding her hands under his shirt, raking her nails down his back. Lost in the heat, she forgot about heartache, about tomorrow, next week, next year. All that mattered was this minute, all she wanted was him.

The noises they made, the groans, the whimpers, were a language all their own, speaking need and saying *now*. She fumbled with his jeans while he opened hers, pushed his hand down the front. Slid his fingers inside her soaking panties, inside her. Drew the moisture out and rubbed it around.

Her fingers went nerveless, his button-fly beyond her. Pushing her hand aside, he freed himself, then wrapped her palm around him, so hard, so hot, and stroked himself with her fist.

"Oh God, please." That was her own voice, begging. "Please, please, please . . ."

His lips dragged across her cheek, down her jaw, to her throat. "Tell me what you want, honey. Tell me, and I'll give it to you."

"You," she gasped out. "Inside me. Now."

He let go of her hand. She kept stroking his cock as he pulled her off the wall and walked her to the railing. He pulled his hand out of her pants, and she tried to stop him.

"Trust me," he said. Then he turned her around, bent her over the rail. Pulled her jeans over her rump, let them drop to her ankles.

"Mmm," he hummed. Cool air fanned her buttocks. He palmed her cheeks. "Honey, your ass is beautiful. I could eat it up." He took a bite.

"*Seriously? Now?*" Her whole body quivered. Behind her, he laughed, a hot, throaty sound. And peeled her leopard-spot panties off with his teeth.

He'd won that round but she didn't care; the rip of foil riveted her. His knee spread her thighs. He must have felt her

tense up, because he stroked a hand over her back. "Don't
worry, honey, you're so wet I'm gonna slide right in."

"Promises, promises," she ground out through her
teeth. Then, "Yes. Yes," she moaned out, as he gripped
her hips and thrust. "Yes," as he buried himself, "yes, yes,
yes," as he pumped hard and fast.

She gripped the railing till it scored her palms. Her
breasts bounced, her breath rasped. Turning her head, she
watched him over her shoulder. His hair flopped over his
forehead. His chest glistened with sweat.

He locked his gleaming eyes on hers. "I got you, honey,"
he panted out. "Now touch yourself. Come with me."

She could do this. She could come with him in the
stairwell of a Times Square hotel. "Okay, yes." She found
the sweet spot. "Oh. My. *God!*"

His fingers dug into her hips. The cords in his neck
stood out in ropes.

And then she squeezed her eyes shut, body quaking,
heart pounding. Her knees folded and she let herself go.

They flew over the edge together.

A DOOR OPENED a few floors up.

Ty muttered a curse. This was no time for company.
He was practically helpless, with one arm hooked under
Vicky's hips holding most of her weight, the other propped
on the railing holding his own.

Then boots drummed the stairs, bringing Vicky to life.
"You okay?" he asked, afraid to release her.

"Yeah, I'm good." Her voice quavered, but she stepped
away from his arm, had her jeans hoisted and zipped and
her tits tucked in before he got his own fly buttoned.

It was a false alarm, though. The guy stopped at the
floor above them, another door opened and closed, and
silence reigned again.

Still, Vicky looked skittish; head down, hands clasped.

He recognized the symptoms, a textbook case of quickie remorse. In a minute she'd try to bolt again just on principle.

He could *not* let that happen.

Draping an arm over her shoulders, he went for big-strong-man-reluctantly-asking-the-little-woman-for-help. "Honey, I'm afraid I need a hand. I must've pulled something in my back."

Her eyes came up, guilt-stricken. "Oh God, it's my fault! I practically collapsed after . . ." She let it trail off, blushing so red that he almost felt bad for faking it. Almost.

He grimaced, bravely facing the pain. "If you wrap your arm around me, I'm pretty sure I can make it to the elevator."

"Sure, okay. Um, let me close your shirt first. People will think we . . ."

She was so damn cute when she was embarrassed. He held off teasing her—there'd be time for that later—and let her snap his snaps without bothering to point out that his fingers weren't injured. It gave him a minute to admire her pink cheeks and long lashes without getting his nose bitten off.

"You can tuck it in if you want to," he said when she finished.

She narrowed her eyes, but he must have managed to look innocent because all she said was "It's fine like it is." Then she stepped under his arm, looped hers around his waist, and helped him hobble to the elevators.

When they got in, he pushed the button for eight. "What's on eight?" she asked.

"The lobby, honey. I'm checking in."

"You are? Why?"

"No way I can get home with this back." He wagged his head dolefully. "Last time this happened I was in bed for a week."

"Seriously? Maybe we should go to the emergency room."

"Been there, done that. They'll just tell me to stretch out on a nice, firm bed." The elevator stopped and he made a pitiful stab at hobbling toward the doors. She ducked quickly under his arm again.

"This is ridiculous," she said as he headed for the check-in sign. "You can't stay here for a week."

"Where better? At least they'll bring me room service."

"I suppose. But . . ." She looked so confounded that he bit his cheek to keep from grinning.

"I need a room," he said to the young woman at the desk, "with a king-sized bed." Vicky stepped back as if to signal to the woman that she wouldn't be sharing it with him. He bit down harder on his cheek. She'd be in his bed, all right. She just didn't know it yet.

He signed the receipt, then they hobbled back to the elevator. When the doors closed behind them, he hit the button for twenty-six, then flicked a quick glance at Vicky. She looked skittish again, like guilt might not carry her as far as his room. So he tried a different tack.

"In case I didn't mention it, you were amazing up on that stage tonight. You pretty much tore my heart out at the end. Even Cruella teared up."

She turned a pretty shade of pink. The doors opened, and her arm looped around his waist again. "I was lucky to have such a great first role," she said as he steered her to his room.

He swiped the card through the slot. "You're too modest. I don't know much about the acting business, but I can recognize talent as well as anyone." He kept his arm over her shoulders as he limped inside. "And honey, you've got talent in spades."

She smiled at him, shy and sweet. She hadn't aimed that smile at him in weeks, and it hit him hard in the solar plexus. His heart skipped a couple of beats, then took off at a sprint. And his cock, that foolproof barometer of sexual attraction, stiffened again, not ten minutes after he'd come so hard he almost went down on his knees.

No question about it. Vicky got to him, inside and out. He locked the door behind them.

The bed looked huge in the tiny room, covered by a fluffy white comforter and eight giant pillows. He hobbled toward it and she went along willingly, supporting him when he leaned on her. This would be so damn easy.

Too easy. She'd think he flattered her just to get her in bed. And while that was true as far as the timing went, he actually meant every word he'd said.

He'd never convince her of that, though, so it was probably best if he made her good and mad one more time before he got inside her again.

Pausing at the bedside, he scratched his jaw thoughtfully. "Of course, I have to take most of the credit. If not for me, you wouldn't be on your way to stardom."

She reacted automatically. "*Seriously?* You want the credit for my success, assuming it ever happens?"

He tightened his grip on her shoulders. "You bet I do. Hell, the whole fake flirtation was my idea. And it was me that wrecked the reception and landed us in the news." He turned his free hand palm up, like it was obvious. "You have to admit it, honey. If not for me, you'd still be slaving away at Marchand, Riley, and White, wondering when Winnie was gonna bang your new secretary. You definitely owe me."

Her brows slammed down. "The only thing I *owe you*, Tyrell Brown, is a kick in the nuts. I got fired because of you! I was investigated by the Committee on Professional Standards! I could've been disbarred!"

"But you weren't, were you?"

"No, but—"

"So what's the problem?" He ticked it off on his fingers. "You're out from under Cruella's thumb, away from a job you hated anyway, you get free coffee every day, and you're finally doing what you always wanted to do."

He could hear her teeth grind. She couldn't deny it, so she went on the attack.

"Why are you in New York, anyway?"

"I got offered this teaching job. Thought I'd see how it fits."

"And?"

"And I like it. More than I expected to. They offered me another year and I'm thinking about it."

"Another year in New York?" She blanched. "What about your ranch? Don't they need you there, doing ranch stuff?"

"Joe doesn't need me day to day. And I can fly back whenever I miss it too much." He cocked his head. "Make you nervous having me around the corner?"

"Pfft. I couldn't care less."

"Good. 'Cause I'll be dropping into Starbucks every morning so you can whip me up a latte."

Her jaw tightened. "Do you have any idea how many calories are in a latte? You can kiss your corrugated abs good-bye."

"Honey," he said, with a pause for effect, "I think we both know which one of us likes to kiss my abs."

VICKY LOST IT. She didn't care if his back hurt. She slapped both palms on his chest and shoved.

And the sneaky bastard pulled her down on top of him, laughing his fool head off! His back didn't hurt! He'd suckered her in—*again*—but this time she'd make him pay for it.

He held her around the waist, but her hands were free. Shoving one down between them, she went for his balls.

They were easy to find, since his cock was hard as a nail—*again*—pointing the way.

But he read her mind—*again*—and flipped her like a pancake, flattening her with his chest, pinning her to the bed, laughing so damn hard he could hardly speak.

Not suffering the same affliction herself, she rained F-bombs all over him, for all the good it did. She tried bucking him off. His weight held her down.

He framed her face with his hands, grinned his infuriating grin. "Say uncle, honey."

She drummed her heels on the mattress.

"I can lie here all night," he drawled out, "squashing your bladder."

Suddenly she had to pee. He was devious beyond belief.

"Uncle," she bit out. "And I need to use the bathroom."

"Promise you'll come back to bed?"

She set her jaw. Met his glittering gaze. "For five minutes. That's my final offer."

With a grin that reminded her she was in no position to make final offers, he rolled off.

In the bathroom, she dawdled, finger-combing her hair, splashing cool water on her overheated face, dragging her feet because she knew what would happen when she got on the bed with him. And she wanted it. She wanted him. He stirred her up, woke her up, made her laugh, at him, at herself, at life in general.

Josie was right, she was crazy about him.

Setting her palms on the sink, she met her own eyes, remembered the last time she'd stared into a mirror deciding whether to have sex with Tyrell Brown. He'd bruised her heart on that airplane, then broken it in Amboise, and stomped on the pieces in Texas. If he hurt her once more tonight, she'd have only herself to blame.

But she'd survive. It would be awful, but she was more resilient than she'd known, and she'd survive. Much worse would be feeling like a coward and living with regret, wondering what might have been if only she'd given it a try.

Ty lay on his side, head propped in his hand, unfairly gorgeous with his jumbled hair and stubbly jaw. His tiger eyes squinted against the bedside light, his lips curved invitingly. He patted the bed in front of him and she climbed on like an obedient cat, stretching out, mirroring his position. Less than a foot of bedspread divided them.

"Did your back hurt at all?"

"Not even a little." He stroked a hand down her bare arm, all the way to her fingertips. His drawl flowed like honey. "I had to improvise, 'cause none of this is going the way I planned."

"You figured I'd just fall into bed with you?"

"I figured if you wanted me even a tiny little fraction of how much I want you, you'd fuck me anywhere, anytime."

She shrugged one shoulder. "Well, I guess you were right, since we just did it in the stairwell."

His fingers trailed up her arm again, slipped under her bra strap. His knuckle skimmed the swell of her breast, the lightest touch, but it set her skin on fire. She wanted him again. Wanted him still. The desire never really went away.

"Sweetheart, before we go any further—and I aim to go *a lot* further—I have to admit that a few minutes ago I told you a little white lie."

Her chest tightened, but she kept her tone light. "You mean, besides the whole I-hurt-my-back white lie?"

"Yeah, this is a different one." His thumb stroked her nipple to a peak. "You shouldn't hold it against me, though, because the thing is, I told it to myself first. And for a long time, I believed it. I only figured out the truth yesterday, when I saw you." He caught her eyes and held them. "I didn't come to New York to teach. I came for you."

Her heart thump-thumped. "For me?"

He nodded slowly. "When I got home from France, I couldn't sleep. I couldn't fuck. I couldn't think about anything but you. And believe you me, I tried."

His hand drifted up. One fingertip traced her collarbone. "That's why I started hanging out with Molly. Not for sex, you understand. That didn't happen. But to try and forget about you. Because, honey, you made me feel all kinds of things I didn't want to feel."

His knuckles brushed the curve of her neck, so softly she barely felt it. "Then you came out to the ranch, and everything fell into place. All I could think of was that I wanted to keep you there with me. And when you left"—he paused—"honey, when you left, I realized I don't want to be there without you anymore."

He heaved a sigh. "I'd rather not be in love with you. But I am."

She cocked her head, not sure she'd heard right. "You're . . . in love with me?"

"Mmm-hmm."

Her lips curved. "Really?"

"Mmm-hmm."

"You don't seem very happy about it."

"Well, honey, like I told you before, you're trouble with a capital T."

Her hackles went up. "*I'm* trouble? Tyrell Brown—"

He knocked her onto her back and his lips came down on hers, tongue pushing past her teeth. His hand dove under her top, under her bra. She lifted into his palm, clawed his shirt up with her fingers.

"See what I mean?" His lips dragged over her jaw. "We have a little disagreement, and right away you distract me with sex." He unzipped her jeans.

"You shouldn't let me get away with it," she gasped out, wriggling them off, then digging into his, pushing them down, reaching for his hard-on.

"I know. But you're a good lay." He lifted her hips, buried himself in her.

She arched her back, taking him deep. Her legs locked around him. "And you love me," she gasped out.

"And I love you." He rocked in and out, in and out. "I fucking love you, Victoria Westin."

Warmth spread through her like a shot of whiskey. She locked her eyes on his, raked her nails down his arms. And said the words that sang in her heart.

"I love you too, Tyrell Brown."

CHAPTER TWENTY-EIGHT

JOSIE SCOWLED ACROSS the counter at Ty. "What in the name of the sweet baby Jesus did you do to Vicky?"

Before he could answer, she held up a hand. "No details, please. The real question is, how is she supposed to give another brilliant performance tonight when she's so tired she can't tell a grande from a venti?"

His smile was smug. "Trust me, honey, she knows a venti when she sees one."

Josie laughed. "Good one, cowboy. Perverted Starbucks humor. I like it." She called into the back. "Hey Vicky, Sundance is here, and he looks fresh as a daisy."

The same couldn't be said for Vicky. She brightened when she saw him, though, which lifted his heart even higher than it already flew. He needed to get his hands on her *right away*.

"Sweetheart, you need to untie that apron and come with me this minute."

She glanced at the clock. "I've got another half hour."

"I'll cover for you," Josie said, "as long as you *promise*

you'll take a nap before tonight." She cut a speaking look at Ty.

He raised his right hand. "I swear I'll put her straight to bed."

She rolled her eyes.

Out on the street, Vicky squinted against the midday sun. Ty wrapped an arm around her, steered her toward his place. "Josie's right, honey, you're peaked. We'll get those clothes off and I'll tuck you straight into bed." He gave her a squeeze. "I could use a nap myself, so I'll slide on in there with you."

She smirked. "You'll slide on in, huh?"

He looked offended. "Only a dirty mind would twist such an innocent comment into something X-rated."

That made her laugh. She snuggled against his side, and the butterflies—yes, butterflies—in his stomach fluttered drunkenly.

"Don't you have to teach this afternoon?"

"Not till three. I canceled my office hours this afternoon, so I'm all yours till then."

She looked up at him. "I really do need sleep."

"I know you do, honey, and I promise to keep my hands to myself. You, on the other hand, can do whatever you want with yours."

How was a woman supposed to keep her hands off Tyrell Brown when everything from his long, lean legs to his sun-kissed mop of hair cried out to be stroked and squeezed and made love to?

It couldn't be done.

In the end, it was Ty who drew the line. "Sugar, I never thought I'd hear these words come out of my mouth, but you need to quit fucking me and go to sleep."

He was right, but she pouted anyway.

Laughing at her mulish expression, he tucked her in close to his side. "Don't worry, honey, we can do it all night. In fact, my place is closer to Starbucks. You should probably just move in."

Her head shot up. "Move in? I just stopped hating you a few hours ago!"

"And look how far we've come already. Why, by this time tomorrow, you'll want to get married."

"Married?"

"It seems sudden to me too. But if you play your cards right, and by that I mean you keep wearing these"—he dangled tiger-striped panties from his pinky—"I'm open to discussing it."

"Discussing it?" She sputtered. The man was impossible!

"I know you're nervous about bringing it up, but you don't need to repeat everything I say. I can already see how it makes sense from your point of view."

"My point of view?" She repeated him again, but honestly, he'd rattled her down to her DNA.

"Sure. You're crazy in love with me." He said it like it was obvious. "It probably started when I strolled into court in my suit and tie. I noticed how you couldn't keep your eyes off me. Then that sexathon in Amboise really fanned the flames. Hell, if I hadn't been such a dick at the end, we'd probably be married already. So I get it. You figure we've wasted too much time, and you're ready to jump right in."

She'd recovered enough to arch a brow. "I am, am I?"

He shrugged one shoulder. "Stands to reason, what with your biological clock ticking like a time bomb." He rolled right over her snort of disbelief. "I have to warn you, though, I'm looking for a houseful of kids. Four or five at a minimum." He patted her flank. "You're a little skinny through the hips, but you'll widen out after the first two or three."

She sat up straight. "I'm in bed with Cro-Magnon Cowboy! What's wrong with me?"

"Don't blame yourself. I'm hard to resist."

She flopped back on the pillow. "You really are. I don't know why, but you really are."

He rolled on top of her, laughing easily, and caged her head with his arms. His hair flopped forward, his tiger eyes crinkled. But as he looked down into her face, his huge grin faded until he looked so solemn that her breath caught in her throat. "Ty, what's wrong?"

"Not a single thing." His drawl wrapped her like velvet. "For the first time in forever, everything's good."

He stroked her cheeks with his thumbs. "I'm real glad you're finally doing what makes you happy. And I'm okay with living here in the city, just as long as we go back to the ranch every now and then."

Her heart melted. "But the ranch is your home."

"It'll be your home too—after all, every movie star needs a ranch out West. But when you're working, we'll live wherever you need to live."

Her hands stroked lightly over his strong back. "You really want to get married? To me?"

"Call me crazy."

She laughed. It *was* crazy. But it was exactly right. Nobody made her laugh like Ty did. Nobody drove her as nuts. Nobody sent her body into orbit or her heart into overdrive like he did.

But what did he see in her?

"I don't know anything about cows."

"Steers, honey. I'll teach you all about them. We'll go out on a roundup, make love under the stars."

"But I'm not much of a rider."

"I disagree. You ride like a pro."

She pinched him. "I meant horses."

"Oh, horses. That's okay, I'll teach you."

It sounded too good to be true.

"You don't hate city living?"

"It's got its moments, but mostly I like it. And I'll like it a hell of a lot better when you're sleeping in my bed every night."

That sounded good too.

She chewed her lip. "Before you commit, I have a confession to make. It's about the whole cowboy thing."

His brow creased.

"You know I tease you about it a lot."

"Yeah, I noticed."

"The boots and the shirts and the drawl and everything?"

He looked worried. "Uh-huh."

"The thing is." She cupped his stubbly cheeks in her palms. "I hate to say this because it makes me feel like an idiot. But all that cowboy stuff really turns me on."

His eyes rolled back in relief. "You had me going, honey. I tried picturing myself in a black turtleneck and it just about choked me."

That made her grin. But they weren't in the clear yet. There was still the elephant waiting at the foot of the bed, poised to crush out their happiness.

Lifting her chin, she met it head on. "What about Lissa?"

"What about her?"

"I know how much you loved her."

"I still love her. I always will."

Her eyes fell. Her heart too.

Then Ty slid a finger under her jaw, lifted her head to meet his gaze. "Nice try, sweetheart, but you're not getting out of it that easy." His eyes were unshadowed. A small smile quirked his lips. "I'm not gonna run out of the room this time. You're stuck with me. And if I know Lissa, she's laughing her ass off right now, thinking about all the trouble you're gonna give me for the rest of my life."

He dropped his head, kissed the corner of her mouth. "I love you, honey. Now you need to get some sleep, so quit rubbing your tits on me, I'm not falling for it again."

Rolling onto his back, he snugged her down onto his shoulder. His heart thump-thumped a steady rhythm in her ear. She drew a deep breath, sighed it out. Her leg draped over his thigh, her palm rested on the cobble-stones.

The elephant had left the room. She closed her eyes and slept.

Now, *two* sneak peeks!
More weddings and more fun from

CARA CONNELLY

Avon's rising contemporary romance star.
First, take a quick look at Cara Connelly's
delicious Avon Impulse novella

The Wedding Date

It's on sale NOW from Avon Impulse and
available at your favorite e-retailer.
Then, don't miss an early look at
the next in Cara's series,

The Wedding Vow

On sale fall 2014 and available in mass market
and e-book from Avon Romance.

An Excerpt from
The Wedding Date

"BLIND DATES ARE for losers." Julie Marone pinched the phone with her shoulder and used both hands to scrape the papers on her desk into a tidy pile. "You really think I'm a loser?"

"Not a *loser*, exactly." Amelia's inflection kept her options open.

Julie snorted a laugh. "Gee, thanks, sis. Tell me how you *really* feel."

"You know what I mean. You've been out of circulation for three years. You have to start *somewhere*."

"Sure, but did it have to be at the bottom of the barrel?"

"Peter's a nice guy!" Amelia protested.

"Absolutely," Julie said agreeably. "So devoted to dear old Mom that he *still lives in her basement*."

Amelia let out a here-we-go-again groan. "He's an optometrist, for crying out loud. I assumed he'd have his own place."

Julie started on the old saying about what happens when you *assume*, but Amelia cut her off. "Yeah, yeah. Ass. You. Me. Got it. Anyway, Leo"—tonight's date—"is a definite step up. I checked with his sister"—Amelia's hairstylist—"and she said he's got a house in Natick. His practice is thriving."

"So why's he going on a blind date?"

"His divorce just came through."

Recently divorced men fell into two categories. "Shopping for a replacement or still simmering with resentment?"

"Come on, Jules, give him a chance."

Julie sighed. Slid the stack of papers into a folder marked "Westin/Anderson" and added it to her briefcase for tomorrow's closing. "Just tell me where to meet him."

"On Hanover Street at seven. He made reservations at a place on Prince."

"Well, in that case." Dinner in Boston's North End almost made it worthwhile. Julie was always up for good Italian. "How will I recognize him? Tall, dark, and handsome?" A girl could hope.

"Dark . . . but . . . not tall. Wearing a red scarf."

"Handsome?"

Amelia cleared her throat. "I caught one of his commercials the other night. He's got a nice smile."

"Whoa, wait. Commercials? What kind of lawyer is he?"

"Personal injury." Amelia dropped it like a turd. Then said, "Oh look, Ray's here. Gotta go," and hung up.

Putting two and two together, Julie groaned. Leo could only be the ubiquitous Leo "I feel your" Payne, whose commercials saturated late-night television, promising Boston's sleepless that he *would not quit* until they got every penny they deserved—minus his one third, of course.

"How did I get into this?" she murmured.

For three years, since David died, she'd tried explaining to her sister that her career, her rigorous training schedule—she really *would* do the marathon this year—

and their sprawling Italian-American family kept her too busy for a man. And Amelia, even though she didn't buy it, had respected Julie's wishes.

Until now.

The catalyst, Julie knew, was Amelia's own upcoming Christmas Eve wedding. She wanted Julie—her maid of honor—to bring a date. A real date, not her gay friend Dan. Amelia loved Dan like a brother, but he was single too, always up for hanging out, and he made it too easy for Julie to duck the dating game.

So Amelia had lined up three eligible men and informed Julie that if she didn't give them a chance, then their mother—a confirmed cougar with not-great taste in men—would bring a wedding date for her.

Recognizing a train wreck when she saw one coming, Julie had given in and agreed to date all three. So far they were shaping up even worse than expected.

Jan appeared in the doorway. "J-Julie?" Her usually pale cheeks were pink. Her tiny bosom heaved. "Oh Julie. You'll never believe . . . the most . . . I mean . . ."

"Take a breath, Jan." Julie did that thing where she pointed two fingers at Jan's eyes, then back at her own. "Focus."

Jan sucked air through her nose, let it out with a wheeze. "Okay, we just had a walk-in. From Austin." She wheezed again. "He's *gorgeous*. And that drawl . . ." Wheeze.

Julie nodded encouragingly. It never helped to rush Jan.

"He said . . ." Jan fanned herself, for real. She was actually perspiring. "He said someone in the ER told him about you."

That sounded ominous.

Julie glanced at her watch. Five forty-five, too late to deal with mysterious strangers. If she left now, she'd just have time to get home and change into something more casual for her date.

"Ask him to come back tomorrow," she said. "I don't have time—"

"He just wants a minute." Jan wiped her palms on her gray pleated skirt. At twenty-five, she dressed like Julie's gram, but inside she was stuck at sixteen, helpless in the face of a handsome man. "I-I'm sorry. I couldn't say no."

Julie blew out a sigh, wondered—again—why she'd hired her silly cousin in the first place. Because family was family, that's why.

"Fine. Send him in."

Ten seconds later, six-foot-two of Texan filled her door. Tawny hair, caramel eyes, tanned cheekbones.

Whoa.

Her own sixteen-year-old heart went pitty-pat.

He crossed the room, swallowed up her hand in his big palm, and said in a ridiculous drawl, "Cody Brown. I appreciate you seeing me, Miz Marone."

"Call me Julie," she managed to reply. Her hand felt naked when he released it, like she'd pulled off a warm glove on a cold winter day.

No wonder Jan had gone to pieces. He was tall, the way an oak tree's tall. Lean, the way a cougar's lean.

She gestured, and he took a seat, his beat-up leather jacket falling open over an indigo shirt with pearl snaps and a belt buckle the size of Texas. When he crossed one cowboy-booted ankle over the other snug-jeaned knee, spurs jangled in her head.

Her mouth went dry.

She picked up her pen, clicked it off and on, off and on. "So, you're new to Boston?"

Cody Brown unfurled a slow, eye-crinkling smile. "What gave me away?"

She huffed out a laugh. "Okay, that was dumb."

God, she was as bad as Jan.

He waved a hand. "Not at all," he drawled, "you were

just being polite." The December wind had stirred up his hair. The fingers he raked through it did nothing to tame it. "You're right, I'm brand-new to Boston. Just got here last week, and been working every day since I touched down."

"I see," she said, staring at his stubble, the way it shadowed his jaw. She made herself look down at the yellow pad on her desk. "Are you looking for a house? A condo?"

"I'm thinking condo."

She made a note. "Your wife agrees?"

"I'm not married."

She glanced up. "Engaged?"

He shook his head. "No girlfriend either. Or boyfriend, for that matter." He broke into that smile again.

She set her pen on the desk. "Who referred you to me?"

"Marianne Wells. Said you found her dream house."

Julie remembered her, a nurse at Mass General. "Yes, I found a house for her. For her and her *husband*." She put an apology in her smile. "That's what I do. I match couples with houses."

Cody tilted his head. "Just couples? How come?"

"It's my specialty."

He nodded agreeably. "Okay. But how come?"

She shifted impatiently. "Because it is." *And that's all the explanation you're getting.* "Now, Mr. Brown—"

"It's Cody to my friends." He smiled. "Most of my enemies too."

She wished he'd holster that smile. It lit up the room, exposing how drab her office was. Tasteful, of course—ecru walls, framed prints, gold upholstery. But bland. She hadn't noticed just how bland until he walked in and started smiling all over it.

She clicked her pen.

His smile widened and a dimple appeared, for God's sake.

Then he spread his hands. His big, warm hands. "Julie," he said in that slow, Texas drawl. "Can't you make an exception for me?"

She tried to say no, to resist his pull. But he held her gaze, tugging her irresistibly toward blue skies and sunshine.

Her breath gave a hitch, her stomach a dip.

And her heart, her frozen heart, thumped *at last.*

CODY'D THOUGHT HE was too damn tired for sex, but from his first glimpse of Julie Marone—moss green eyes, chestnut hair, slim runner's body—he'd been picturing her out of that business suit and spread across his bed, wearing a lacy pushup bra and not another damn thing.

Then her breath caught, a sexy little hiccup, and he was halfway hard before he knew what hit him.

Damn it. He didn't need to get laid half as much as he needed a place to live. After seven straight overnights in the Mass General ER—and an eighth that would begin in just a few hours—he was finally due to get some time off. Four days, to be exact, which gave him exactly that long to find a condo, sign the papers, and write the damn check.

But Julie wasn't cooperating. Not only did she have his cock in an uproar, she wasn't inclined to hunt up a condo for him. She kept feeding him a line about *couples*, like she was some kind of karmic matchmaker or something.

Seriously, what kind of realtor gave a shit who she sold to? A house was a house; a condo was a condo. Money was money. Right?

Whatever. She was hot for him too, and even if he wasn't in a position to do anything about it right at the moment, he wasn't above using it to get what he wanted.

Deliberately, in a move that had yet to fail him, he put his palm to his chest, rubbed it back and forth slowly.

Her eyes dropped to follow the movement.

He let her think about it.

She swallowed.

Then, shamelessly, he worked his drawl. "I'd sure be grateful if you'd help me out. I been staying next door at the Plaza—and don't get me wrong, it's swanky, for sure—but I need my own place so I can bring Betsy on East with me."

Her eyes snapped up. "I thought you didn't have a girl-friend."

"Betsy's my dog. Part coon hound, part Chihuahua." He did the smile again. "She'll like you. You both got that feisty thing going on."

Her brow knitted, and he bit his cheek to hold back a laugh. She probably wasn't sure how to feel about being compared to his dog. He could tell her it was a compliment—Betsy was the only woman who'd never disappointed him—but he didn't want her to get cocky.

What he wanted was for her to forget her cockamamie rule about couples and find him a condo in the next four days. That meant keeping her interested in him. So he played his strongest card, the one that worked with all the ladies. Worked too well, in fact. But he wasn't going to argue with that now.

"The problem's my schedule," he went on, spreading his palms. "Me being a doctor and all."

He waited for her to rip her clothes off.

She didn't.

For five long seconds, she stared straight into his eyes. Then she opened a drawer and took out a business card, set it on the desk in front of him.

He dropped his eyes. *Brian Murphy—Century 21.*

What the fuck?

"Murph's a friend of mine," she said, her voice cool and flat. "I'm sure he can help you." She snapped her briefcase shut.

Cody couldn't believe it. The doctor thing *always* made women go crazy. So crazy that they stopped seeing Cody Brown the man and saw only Cody Brown, MD, their ticket to a McMansion in the burbs and vacations in Cabo.

But this chick was the opposite of attracted. She'd gone downright frosty.

He was in uncharted territory.

Desperate, he went into full seduction mode, hit her with the eye-lock sexy-smile combo, playing it out in super slow-mo.

First he caught her eyes. Held them. Let a long, silent moment slide by like a river of molasses.

Then slowly, leisurely, as if he had all night to get it done, he curved his lips. First one side. Then the other.

She paused.

He deepened his drawl. "I want *you*, Julie."

She clicked her pen.

"Give me one day," he crooned. "Just tomorrow, that's all."

Click click. "Are you sure you wouldn't rather rent first? Check out the neighborhoods?"

He shook his head. "I'm not picky. Someplace close to Mass General will do me fine, where I can take Betsy for a run."

She hesitated, obviously wrestling with some inner demon.

He put his money on the horny realtor.

"Beacon Hill could work," she said at last.

Not a smidgen of smugness seeped into his voice. "That where the Old North Church is? One if by land, two if by sea?"

She smiled, finally, a pretty sight. "No, that's in the North End. You could look there too, especially if you're a fan of Italian food. The restaurants are amazing."

He stood up. So did she. She was taller than he expected, which meant she had long legs.

He liked long legs.

"Let's go try one out," he said like it was only natural. "I'm sick of room service."

She looked startled. "Oh. Um. Thanks, but I have a date." She gave a nervous laugh. "A blind date, actually. And a closing in the morning."

"Seriously?" he blurted.

Her eyebrows shot up.

He did damage control. "A closing in the morning? I shouldn't be surprised. You must have lots of those." He nodded, sagely. Wondered why in the hell a looker like her had a *blind date*.

One of her brows came down, but she arched the other like she was assessing his intellect, wondering if he was actually smart enough to be a doctor. Then she lifted her briefcase and came around the desk, herding him through the door. "I can give you tomorrow afternoon. I'll line up a few places and we'll get started around one."

"Sure. Let me give you my number." Maybe she'd get lonely, give him a booty call.

"Give it to Jan," she said, sticking a fork in his fantasy.

In the outer office, Jan looked like a Munchkin behind her oversized desk. "Take Dr. Brown's number," said Julie, on a march to the door. "Then go home. I'll check in after the closing." And she was gone.

"Well hell," Cody muttered. She'd blown him off. What about the eye-lock sexy-smile combo? He was *sure* that'd put her in heat.

Huh.

He turned to Jan. A new sparkle lit her eyes.

"You're a *doctor*?" she said.

He let out a sigh.

An Excerpt from
The Wedding Vow

SIX THOUSAND, EIGHT hundred dollars, and ninety-eight cents.

Maddie let the bill flutter to her desk, where it settled like a leaf between her elbows. She dropped her head into her hands.

Lucille, her lovable, irresponsible, artistic sister, wanted to do a semester in Italy, studying the great masters.

Well, hell, who wouldn't? The problem was, Lucy's private college tuition was already stretching Maddie to the max. The extra expense of a semester abroad meant dipping into—no, wiping out—her meager emergency fund.

Still, considering all they'd been through, Lucy's carefree spirit was nothing short of a miracle. If keeping that miracle alive meant slaving more hours at her desk, Maddie would make it work somehow.

Knuckles rapped sharply on her office door—Adrianna Marchand's signature staccato. Maddie slid a file on top of the bill as Adrianna strode in.

"Madeline. South conference room. Now." Adrianna scraped an eye over Maddie's hair and makeup, her sleeveless blouse. "Full armor."

Maddie shook her head. "Take Randall. I'm due in court in two hours and I'm still not up to speed on this case." Insurance defense might be the most boring legal work in the world, but it was also complex, and she was buried. She waved an arm at the boxes stacked on her cherry coffee table, the hundred case files that marched the length of her leather sofa. "Remember how you dumped all of Vicky's cases on me after you *fired her for no reason*?"

Adrianna iced over. "*No one's* job is guaranteed at this firm."

Maddie glared, unwilling to show fear. But she was outclassed and she knew it. Adrianna's stare could freeze the fires of hell, and as one of Marchand, Riley, and White's founding partners, she could, and would, fire Maddie's ass if she pushed back too hard.

"Fine, whatever." Kicking off her fuzzy slippers and shoving her feet into the red Jimmy Choos she kept under her desk, Maddie whipped the jacket of her black silk Armani suit off the back of her chair and punched her fists through the sleeves. Then she spread her arms. "Full armor. Satisfied?"

"Touch up your makeup."

Rolling her eyes, Maddie dug a compact out of her purse, brushed some color onto her pale cheeks, hit her lips with some gloss. Then she poked her fingers into her caramel hair to give it some lift. She wore it spiked, like her heels, to make herself look taller, but at a petite five feet she was still a shrimp.

Adrianna nodded once, then charged out the door, setting a brisk pace down the carpeted hallway. "Step on it. We've kept your new client waiting too long."

Maddie had to trot to keep up. "*My* new client? Because I don't have enough work?"

"He requested you specifically. He says you're acquainted."

"Well, who is he?"

"He wants to surprise you." Adrianna's dry tone made it clear she wasn't kidding.

Before Maddie could respond to that ridiculous statement, Adrianna tapped politely on the conference room door, then gently pushed it open.

Meant for large meetings with important clients, the room was designed to impress, with Oriental carpets covering the hardwoods, and original landscapes by notable artists gracing the walls. But it was the long cherry table that really set the tone. Polished to a gleam and surrounded by posh leather chairs, it spelled confidence, professionalism, and prosperity.

Bring us your problem, that table said, *and we will solve it without breaking a sweat.*

And if the room and the table weren't enough to convince a prospective client that Marchand, Riley, and White were all that, then the million-dollar view of the Manhattan skyline through the forty-foot-wide glass wall would drive the point home. Who could argue with that kind of success?

Now Maddie's new client stood gazing out at that view, his back to the door, one hand in the pocket of his expensively cut trousers, the other holding a sleek cell phone to his ear.

Through that phone, Maddie heard a woman's tinkling laughter. He responded in rapid Italian. Not that Maddie understood a word of it. Her Italian began and ended with ordering risotto in Little Italy. But she'd had a short fling with a gorgeous Italian waiter, and she recognized the rhythm of the language. It was the sound of sweaty sex.

Clearing her throat to announce their presence earned

her a wintry glance from Adrianna. But the man ignored them utterly. Maddie crossed her arms and looked him up and down with an affronted eye.

He was tall, over six feet, and she put his weight at a lean one-ninety. Broad through the shoulders, narrow at the hips, he bore himself like an athlete, graceful and relaxed—as if he wasn't standing six scant inches from thin air, sixty stories above Fifth Avenue.

Though he claimed to know her, she couldn't place him by the sliver of his face reflected in the glass, or by the sleek, black hair curling over his collar, too long for Wall Street, not long enough for the Italian soccer team.

Everything about him—his clothes, his bearing, his flagrant arrogance—screamed rich, confident, and entitled.

He must be mistaken about her, she decided, because she honestly didn't know anyone like him. And given his casual assumption that his time was more important than theirs, she didn't want to.

She held it together for as long as she could, tapping her foot, biting her tongue, but as the grandfather clock in the corner ticked into the fifth long minute of silent subservience, her patience ran out. She uncrossed her arms and reached for the doorknob. "I don't have time for this shit."

Adrianna's hand shot out and clamped her arm. "Suck it up, Madeline," she gritted through her teeth.

"Why should I? Why should *you*?" Under normal circumstances, Adrianna had zero tolerance for disrespect, so why was she putting up with this guy's bullshit?

Flinging a resentful look at the mystery man, she didn't bother to lower her voice. "This guy doesn't know me. Because seriously, if he did, he'd know I won't stand here burning daylight while he talks dirty to his girlfriend."

"Oh yes you will," Adrianna hissed. She released Maddie's arm, but caught her eyes. "You'll stand on your head if he says so. He could mean *millions* for this firm."

The man in question chose that moment to end his call. Casually, unhurriedly, he slipped the phone in his pocket. Then he turned to face them.

Maddie's heart stopped. Her lips went icy.

Adrianna started to speak but he cut her off, his vaguely European accent smoothing the edge from his words. "Thank you, Adrianna. Now give us the room."

Without a word, Adrianna nodded once and left them alone, closing the door softly behind her.

His complete attention came to rest on Maddie, a laser beam disguised as cool condescension. Her blood, which had gone cold, now boiled up in response, pounding her temples, hammering out a beat called Unresolved Fury, Frustrated Objectives, Justice Denied.

"You son of a bitch," she snarled. "How dare you claim an acquaintance with me?"

He smiled, a deceptively charming curve of the lips meant to distract the unwary from eyes so intensely blue and so penetratingly sharp that they might otherwise reveal him as the diabolical felon he was.

"Ms. St. Clair." Her name sounded faintly exotic on his tongue. "Surely you don't deny that we know each other."

"Oh, I know you, Adam LeCroix. I know you should be doing ten to fifteen in Leavenworth."

His lips curved another half inch, past charming, to amused. "And I know you. I know that if you'd taken me to trial, you'd have done an excellent job of it. But"—he shrugged slightly—"both of us know that no jury would have convicted me."

"Still so cocky," she simmered. "And so fucking guilty."

ADAM HELD BACK a laugh. Madeline St. Clair might be tiny enough to fit in his pocket, but she had the grit of a two-hundred-pound cage fighter.

When he'd last seen her five years ago, she was a bloodthirsty young prosecutor, spitting nails as her then-boss, the U.S. Attorney for the Eastern District of New York—who had his eyes on higher office—shook Adam's hand and apologized for letting the case against him go as far as it had.

Playing magnanimous, Adam had nodded gravely, said all the right things about public servants simply doing their jobs, and with a wave for the news cameras, disappeared into his limousine.

Where he'd cracked a six-thousand-dollar bottle of Dom Perignon and made a solitary toast to a narrow escape from the law.

It had been his own damn fault that he'd come so close to being caught, because he *had* gotten cocky. He'd made a rare mistake, a minute one, but Madeline had used it like a crowbar to pry into his life until she'd damn near nailed him for stealing the *Lady in Red*.

The newly discovered Renoir masterpiece had been sold at Sotheby's to a Russian arms dealer, a glorified mobster who cynically expected a splashy show of good taste to purge the bloodstains from his billions. Adam couldn't stomach it, so he'd lifted the painting. Not for gain; he had his own billions. But because great art was sacred, and using it as a dishrag to wipe blood off the hands of a man who sold death was sacrilege.

Adam had simply saved the masterpiece from its unholy purpose.

It wasn't the first time, or the last, that he'd liberated great art from unclean hands. He told himself that it was his calling, but he couldn't deny that it was also a hell of a lot of fun. Outsmarting the best security systems money could buy taxed his brain in ways that managing his companies simply couldn't. Training for the physical demands kept him in Navy SEAL condition. And the adrenaline rush, well, that couldn't be duplicated. Not even by sex.

No woman had ever thrilled him that intensely or challenged him so completely on every level.

But now the shoe was on the other foot. One of his own paintings—his favorite Monet—had been heisted clean off the wall of his Portofino villa.

Just the thought made his teeth grind.

Oh, he'd find it eventually; he had no doubt of that. He had the resources, both money and manpower. He was patient. He was relentless. And when he got his hands on the bastard who'd infiltrated his home—his sanctuary—he'd make him pay for his hubris.

But in the meantime, he had a more immediate concern. The insurance company, Hawthorne Mutual, was dragging its feet, balking at paying him the forty-four million dollars the Monet was insured for.

Forty-four million was a lot of money, even to a man like him. But it was the company's excuse for holding it up that really pissed him off. They needed to investigate the theft, they claimed, because Adam had once been a "person of interest" in the theft of the Renoir.

In short, Hawthorne's foot-dragging could be laid at Madeline's door. She'd damaged Adam's reputation, impugned his integrity. Cast a shadow of doubt over one of the richest men in the world.

Never mind that she'd been right about him.

Because she was visibly chomping at the bit, he moved as if he had all day, strolling to the far end of the room, where a leather sofa and club chairs clustered around a coordinating coffee table. This would be where clients chummied up with the partners after meetings, rubbing elbows over scotch and cigars while the lowly associates—like Madeline—scuttled back to their offices to do the actual work.

He poured himself an inch of scotch from the Waterford decanter on the table, then relaxed into the sofa, stretching one arm along the back, letting the other drape carelessly over the side, whiskey glass dangling from his fingers.

Her steel gray eyes narrowed to slits. "What do you want, LeCroix? Why are you here?"

Lazily, he sipped his scotch, enjoying the angry flush that burned her cheeks. In the prosecutor's office, they'd called her the Pitbull. He was glad to see she'd lost none of her fire.

Watching her simmer, he remembered how her intensity had appealed to him. How much *she'd* appealed to him. Which was surprising, really. As a rule, he liked a solid armful of woman, and Madeline was barely there.

At the time, he'd told himself it was because she'd damn near taken him down. Naturally, he had to admire that.

But now he felt it again, that tug of attraction. Something about those suspicious eyes, that spring-loaded body, went straight to his groin. An image of her astride him, nails gouging his chest, eyes blazing with passion, flashed through his mind. Was she as hot-blooded in bed as she was in the courtroom?

Regrettably, he'd never find out. Because he was about to piss her off for life.

He crossed his legs with studied nonchalance while all five-foot nothing of her bristled with temper.

"Hawthorne Mutual is holding up payment on the Monet," he said. He didn't bother to describe the painting; she'd remember it. Five years ago she'd subpoenaed an inventory of his art collection. He'd complied—at least as to his *legal* collection.

"Someone stole the Monet?" For the first time, she smiled, a wicked grin.

He flicked imaginary lint from his knee. "Apparently, even *my* security isn't unbreachable." And wasn't that a sore spot?

She barked out a laugh. "What goes around, comes around, LeCroix. With your history, Hawthorne will never pay—what was the insured value? Forty-four million?" She sneered, clearly enjoying the irony. "They'll keep you in court for years."

He let her savor her last taste of victory. Then he hit her where it hurt.

"Not me," he said, succinctly. "Us. They'll keep *us* in court. Because you're representing me. For as long as it takes, whatever it takes."

Her chin actually jerked as she took the blow. Then he finished her off with a short jab to the kisser.

"From now on, Madeline, you work for me."

MADDIE SLAMMED HER door so hard that her diploma jumped off the wall, glass splintering as it hit the floor.

She didn't spare it a glance, just threw herself into her desk chair and glared at the door, waiting.

Five seconds later, Adrianna barged in, loaded for bear. Planting her fists on the desk, she fired both barrels. "Get your ass back in that conference room and unmake whatever mess you just made. Adam LeCroix is the most important client who's ever walked into this office."

"He's a criminal," Maddie lashed back. "He should be in an eight-foot cell, not strutting around Manhattan thinking he can buy anybody he wants. Thinking he can buy me!" She jabbed a finger in his general direction. "He can go fuck himself. I'd rather starve than work for him."

"Then you'll starve," Adrianna shot back. She drew herself up, breathed in, breathed out. "You're fired."

"Good!" Maddie snapped open her briefcase and dumped out the legal pads. In went her personal things. A photo of Lucy in her cap and gown, smile brightening the cloudy day. Another of Lucy on her first day at college, waving from her dorm window. Lucy again, at her small gallery showing, face alight with wonder and promise.

Maddie stilled. Her eyes dropped to the bill poking out from under *Johnson v. Jones*. No job meant no semester in Italy for Lucy. Hell, it meant no semester of any kind for Lucy, unless the poor kid took on the same crippling school loans that still hamstrung Maddie. That kind of debt took away your choices, killed your dreams. Left you at the mercy of people like Adrianna Marchand . . . and Adam LeCroix.

She had no choice but to give in. Cornered like a rabbit, she lifted her eyes to Adrianna. Who smiled her evil she-wolf smile.

"I knew you'd see reason," said the she-wolf. Then she reached across Maddie's desk, hit the intercom button. "Randall, get in here."

"Yes, ma'am!" He snapped out a verbal salute, sped into the office in record time. Cursed with red hair and freckles, he blushed like a virgin when Adrianna turned her carnivorous gaze upon him.

"Take this." She scraped *Johnson v. Jones* into a pile and thrust it into his arms. "Judge Bernam's expecting you in his chambers in two hours for a settlement conference. Don't disappoint me."

Randall went pale. "But—"

Adrianna stared him silent.

"Don't worry," Maddie cut in, mercifully, "it's *pro forma*. The plaintiff's not ready to settle."

Randall's momentary relief died as Adrianna pointed at the boxes on the coffee table, the files on the couch. "Those are yours too. Get them out of here."

As a brand new hire, Randall had the lightest caseload of any associate. Naively, he still believed that evenings and weekends were his own. His dawning horror would have evoked Maddie's pity if she hadn't had her own horror to reckon with: Adam LeCroix, billionaire businessman, international playboy. Art thief extraordinaire.

She swallowed hard, tasting her bitterest defeat.

Five years ago she'd almost nailed him. A circumstantial case, but if only she'd been allowed to take it to trial, she could've made it stick. She could've convinced the jury that LeCroix was not only the mastermind who outwitted Sotheby's state-of-the-art computerized security, but also the Spider-Man who scaled walls, ghosted past armed guards and, in under four minutes, poofed with the *Lady in Red* rolled up in a three-foot tube.

But her boss was too chicken to take LeCroix on. With his eyes on a senatorial bid, he wasn't willing to risk having a high-profile defeat splashed across the front page of the *New York Times*. So Maddie had watched LeCroix waltz out of her office, wave to the media whores who worshipped him like a celebrity, and cruise away in his black stretch limo.

That had been bad. But this . . . this was a nightmare. She was at the man's mercy. There was no way she could walk away from her job at Marchand, Riley, and White and into another that paid as well. Not in this economy.

She suppressed a shiver. Not since she'd left her father's house had she felt so vulnerable to a man. She'd sworn never to let one control her again, but now LeCroix had her by the proverbial balls. And he was diabolical. If he learned about her childhood, he'd use her personal demons to turn the screws tighter still.

She couldn't—and wouldn't—hide her revulsion at working for him, but she could never let him know how much it cost her.

ADAM ENDED ANOTHER phone call, checked his watch. Six minutes. By now, Madeline would have capitulated and she'd be processing her defeat. Girding her loins—

that image made him smile—for the short walk to this conference room and the crow-eating apology the Marchand vixen would expect her to deliver.

His smile grew to a grin. That would be the day. He might have Madeline's back to the wall, but he knew better than to expect an apology out of her. And he didn't want one.

What he wanted was his forty-four million dollars, and to see Hawthorne's high-and-mighty CEO—Jonathan Edward Kennedy Hawthorne IV—blanch when Adam showed up with his former prosecutor in his corner.

Hawthorne mistakenly believed that because his great-whatever-grandfather came over on the *Mayflower* and started what was now the oldest, most hide-bound, hoity-toity insurance company in America, he could jam Adam up. That he'd quail at veiled threats to dredge up old rumors about the *Lady in Red.*

Not likely. If Hawthorne's smarmy lawyers had done their homework, they'd know Adam didn't give a damn about bad publicity. He didn't give a damn about the press or the public or the next story about him on Page Six of the *Post.*

What he cared about was not getting screwed over by *anybody.* Most assuredly not by some blueblood who thought his money was better than Adam's simply because it had more age on it.

Well, Hawthorne had a big surprise coming. Never in a million years would he expect Madeline to join forces with Adam, when the whole world knew she'd done everything in her power to convict him. Why, the press had made hay with it across the globe, sensationalizing the story of the upstart prosecutor's tenacious pursuit of the self-made billionaire, dubbing it the Pitbull versus the Piranha.

For that reason alone, her mere presence on his payroll would neutralize any once-a-thief, always-a-thief argument Hawthorne could make about the Monet. And if he cooked up some other reason to deny Adam his money, then he'd turn her loose on him. Hawthorne wouldn't have a chance against the Pitbull.

His grin widened. The icing on the cake was that Madeline would hate every minute of it. He couldn't have dreamed up a sweeter revenge if he'd tried.

When the idea had first come to him a week ago, he'd wondered how he could rope her in. The woman had more integrity than anyone he'd ever met. But a quick and dirty investigation into her finances turned up her Achilles' heel—her sister Lucille. Sixty percent of Madeline's income went to cover the girl's expenses. Room, board, clothes, travel, and the killer—tuition at the Rhode Island School of Design. The kid got some meager financial aid, but she took no loans at all. Madeline covered every penny of it.

She literally couldn't afford to lose her job.

After that, all it took were some vague promises of future business to her shrew of a boss, hinging, of course, on Madeline's cooperation, and he had her right where he wanted her.

The door to the conference room opened and the Pitbull herself strode in. She snarled over her shoulder at whoever remained in the hallway, then slapped the door shut and stalked the length of the room, a short stick of dynamite, ready to explode.

He couldn't suppress another smile. He'd always loved to blow things up.

She pulled up in front of him, close enough that even from her unimpressive height she was looking down at him. She snapped out one word.

"Why?"

He let his brows rise a centimeter. Gave her not one inch of ground.

"Why what?"

"Why me? It's stupid to expect me to help you with the Monet. One thing you're not is stupid." She crossed her arms. "That means you're dragging me into this for revenge. Since it's been five years, and the only price you ever paid for stealing the *Lady in Red* was to get more attention from your fans in the press, why risk a forty-four-million-dollar recovery by putting me in the middle of it? Why not find someone who might *actually believe* you didn't steal your own Monet, and leave me the fuck alone?"

Adam swirled his scotch. When he'd envisioned this inevitable moment, he'd imagined responding to her attack with a swift accounting of her precarious financial condition, followed by a hard boot in the ass to bring her into line. Now that the time had come, he didn't want to do either of those things. He liked her this way, with fire in her eyes.

The truth was—and this surprised him—he wasn't quite comfortable using her sister as a sword to force her to her knees. Maybe he had a soft spot for sibling affection—he wouldn't have guessed it, having none of his own. But more likely it was his business sense kicking in. After all, her feistiness would be an asset in his battle with Hawthorne. It wouldn't behoove him to break her spirit.

But he did have to show her who was boss.

"Do sit down," he said in an even tone that neither challenged nor gave ground. Then he dropped his gaze to the chair, a clear signal that if she wanted to meet his eyes, she'd have to park herself in it.

After five deliberate seconds plainly meant to show

that she was sitting because she *wanted* to, not because he commanded it, she let one cheek touch leather. It hardly made a dent; she couldn't weigh more than ninety pounds soaking wet.

She'd left her jacket in her office, and her sleeveless top stretched over breasts that fit her proportions exactly. Not that he was looking; he kept his eyes on her face, but his peripheral vision caught the action as they swelled up and out with each annoyed breath.

"Listen, LeCroix—"

"Adam," he cut in. "My top advisors go by given names. I find they speak more freely that way." He smiled slightly. "Although you don't seem to have a problem speaking your mind to the boss."

"You're not my boss. I work for Marchand, Riley, and White. You're my client. I'm "—here she choked on her words—"your attorney. You don't pay me. The firm does. I don't report to you. I represent you. That's all."

He tilted his head, did a sympathetic smile this time. "Perhaps Adrianna wasn't clear. It's true that you aren't *directly* on my payroll. But make no mistake. You work *for me*. You report *to me*. I am your *only* client, and my whim is your command."

She shot out of her chair and he almost laughed. He *had* gone a bit far with that last part. But really, she was asking for it.

"You can take your *whim*—" she snarled, but he cut her off again.

"I'm sure you have many fascinating and original ideas about what I can do with my whim," he said, "but that's not what I'm paying for. I'm paying for your time, your efforts, and your undivided attention. And by undivided I mean twenty-four seven."

Her eyes bugged. "I have a *life*, you know."

"Do you?" Insulting.

Her cheeks went up in flames.

He could have told her what he knew right then and there, that not only were her finances in the crapper, her love life was circling the bowl along with them. But why let her know that his private investigators had turned her life inside out? He'd save that bombshell for another day.

Still, her lack of romantic involvements—past and present—surprised him. His investigators had checked as far back as her undergraduate days at Boston University and found no relationships lasting longer than a three-day weekend. Granted, it would take a brave man to bare his junk to her—he'd find himself short a nut if he looked at her crosswise—but even so, there'd been no shortage of interest through the years. It was Madeline who refused to get serious.

Her flushed face told Adam that there was a story there. In time, he'd find out what it was. For the moment, though, he had all the leverage he needed.

"Get your things," he said, "I'll take you home."

She bristled. "I can get home on my own, when I'm good and ready to go."

Ignoring her, he set his glass on the table, pulled out his phone. "Fredo, bring the car around. We'll be down in five."

"I'm not riding with you!"

He dropped the phone in his pocket. Rose to his full six-foot-two, and watched her head tip back to hold him in her furious glare.

He curved his lips, part smile, all menace. "Five minutes, Madeline. With your things, or without them. That much is up to you."

And he walked past her and out the door.

At Avon Books, we know your passion for romance—once you finish one of our novels, you find yourself wanting more.

May we tempt you with . . .

- **Excerpts** from our upcoming releases.

- Entertaining **extras**, including authors' personal photo albums and book lists.

- Behind-the-scenes **scoop** on your favorite characters and series.

- **Sweepstakes** for the chance to win free books, romantic getaways, and other fun prizes.

- Writing **tips** from our authors and editors.

- **Blog** with our authors and find out why they love to write romance.

- **Exclusive content** that's not contained within the pages of our novels.

Join us at
www.avonbooks.com

AVON   *An Imprint of* HarperCollins*Publishers*
www.avonromance.com

Give in to your Impulses!

These unforgettable stories only take a second to buy and give you hours of reading pleasure!

Go to *www.AvonImpulse.com* and see what we have to offer.

Available wherever e-books are sold.

AVONIMPULSE